The Gnostic Keepers

By

Marietta Rodgers

Deep Indigo Books
Published by Indigo Sea Press
Winston-Salem

Deep Indigo Books
Indigo Sea Press
PO Box 67201
Winston-Salem, NC 27114

First Deep Indigo Books edition published
July, 2018
Deep Indigo Books, Moon Sailor and all production design are trademarks of Indigo Sea Press, used under license.

For information regarding bulk purchases of this book, digital purchase and special discounts, please contact the publisher at indigoseapress@gmail.com

Cover concept & design by Aaron A. Alvarez
Manufactured in the United States of America
ISBN 978-1-63066-481-7

A special thanks to the amazingly talented artist, Aaron A. Alvarez, for designing the cover.

To Jim Beuerle, my love, my best friend and my favorite person to do nothing with. Thank you for bringing so much joy to my life and a perpetual smile to my face. You are my, "sweet unrest."

Bishops Go Sunbathing and Angels Make a Plan

It was 397 and the bishops were getting restless in what was now the third Council of Carthage. They were inside the Cathedral Church of Carthage, and it had been a long afternoon; the African heat was becoming intolerable. The doors were shut, so they didn't even have the benefit of the sea air.

"May I just remind everyone that we are not having a vote today. This is simply an acknowledgement of the decree of Damascus and what our former Pope Athanasius wrote in his Easter letter to the Bishop of Alexandria," Bishop Augustine of Hippo said as he wiped the sweat away from his forehead with his hand. There was some mild murmuring and a few coughs that came from the other bishops present. Bishop Augustine knew that they were not all in agreement as to what should be in the canon of scripture. Everyone secretly had their favorites that they wished would be included.

Bishop Augustine read the canonical list aloud: "The Old Testament: Genesis, Exodus, Leviticus, Numbers, Deuteronomy, Joshua, Judges, Ruth, four books of Kings, two books of Paraleipomena, Job, the Psalter of David, five books of Solomon, the books of the twelve prophets, Isaiah, Jeremiah, Ezechiel, Daniel, Tobit, Judith, Esther, two books of Esdras and two books of the Maccabees. In the New Testament: four books of the Gospels, one book of the Acts of the Apostles, thirteen Epistles of the Apostle Paul, one epistle of the Apostle Paul to the Hebrews, two Epistles of the Apostle Peter, three of John, one of James, one of Jude and the book of the Apocalypse of John."

Bishop Augustine said "The Apocalypse of John" with a sneer and wrinkled his nose.

"I prefer the Apocalypse of Thomas myself," the Bishop of Tripoli said.

"I don't know why there should be an apocalypse at all; it ruins a perfectly nice story if you ask me," the Bishop of Byzacena said.

"How else are you going to scare the wits out of the ignorant and bind them to the Church forever? It doesn't matter; no one reads from it anyway," the Bishop of Tripoli said.

"I've never actually read it all the way through," the Bishop of Byzacena admitted.

"Bishop Augustine of Hippo has read the list of the Holy Scriptures, and henceforth these are the only works deemed inspired by Christ. All other books are outlawed and to be gathered and burned. Anyone caught reading from these forbidden books will be deemed a heretic and subject to persecution. Their property will be confiscated and will belong to the Church, and they will be excommunicated, etc. etc.," the Bishop of Carthage said. He couldn't be bothered to go through all the formalities; it was too hot for that.

In truth, no one knows for sure what writing Christ did or did not inspire, but that wasn't going to stop them from making a judgment on it anyway.

"This is a way to root out our best and brightest. We must embrace a new era of Biblical literalism," the Bishop of Numidia said.

"I didn't think there were that many Gnostics left to be rounded up," the Bishop of Nicaea said.

"There are still some on the fringes and don't forget the Donatists. I know a man who still teaches from the Apocrypha, and I've heard rumors of others as well," the Bishop of Numidia said.

"Well, they must stop at once or they will find their books, along with their possessions, belonging to the Church," the Bishop of Nicaea said.

The Bishop of Carthage got up to speak again. The Bishop of Nicaea sighed, and the Bishop of Byzacena was trying to fan himself with a prayer booklet.

"I say this meeting is adjourned; if everyone can just sign at the bottom of this official document as witness to these proceedings, we can go outside and enjoy a bit of sunbathing."

It took less than five minutes for all the bishops present to sign; they had definitely set a new record.

The cathedral door burst open, and bishops could be seen running out of the cathedral as if it were on fire. Some of them stripped down to their undergarments, frolicking and carrying on down by the sea, as if they had not just decided the history of Christianity. One Carthaginian who was witness to the spectacle joked, "It was a true holy see."

***

"Well, they've finally gone and done it; it's official," Uriel said.

"They've had it worked out already for quite some time," Michael said.

"No mention of you in the new book, eh?" Gabriel asked as he and Michael laughed heartily. The three were standing by Arariel's River. It was named after the Archangel Arariel because he was in charge of lakes, oceans, bodies of water and marine life. It was a crystal-clear river filled with swans.

"I told you they wouldn't like the Book of Enoch," Michael said.

They watched as an ophan rolled by, which meant a cherub was also nearby. Ophanim always followed around cherubim, as if they were their pets. No one knew why; it was just one of many inexplicable things in heaven.

A moment later Zophiel, a cherub, walked passed them. Cherubim had four faces, that of a man, an ox, a lion and an eagle, the body of a lion and the feet of an ox. They had four wings covered with eyes, which Uriel thought was a bit much since the ophan who always traveled with them had a hundred eyes which covered their wheel-shaped bodies. How many pairs of eyes does one angel need? Whenever you had the feeling you were being watched, you usually were by an ophan. All the angels are asexual, but they are always referred to with the pronoun *he*.

Zophiel stopped in front of them, and all his faces stared blankly at the trio. The lion face spoke first, "What tidings?"

Uriel was always unnerved by the cherubim, especially when one of their animal faces spoke; and when they did speak, it was always so prim and proper. He wasn't sure why God made them

3

like that unless He had a sense of humor. God, in fact, did have a wonderful sense of humor, but Uriel had no way of knowing that; he had never spoken to God directly, only the Angel of Presence who is God's voice.

"The people officially decided on a book," Uriel said, trying to not let his voice quiver.

The ophan rolled right up to Uriel's feet; and all his eyes, which were every color imaginable, stared at him. This unnerved him even further.

This time it was the eagle that spoke, "What people?"

"You know, the people of Earth. They have decided on one official book."

"What book?" the eagle asked.

Uriel wanted to roll his eyes. It was just another example of how the upper echelon didn't have a clue, nor did they care about what was going on with humans. There were some exceptions, of course, but most were too consumed with themselves.

"The book of scriptures . . . you know, the story of God."

Uriel couldn't believe it; the faces of Zophiel still looked blank, so he added, "The Bible."

Finally there was some recognition on the faces of Zophiel.

"Oh, that one," the eagle said.

The other faces were already bored with the conversation and looking elsewhere. They were trying to get the attention of the eagle. The lion roared, the ox was snorting and the man wasn't even trying to be subtle; he kept clearing his throat.

"Well, we must be going now; we are running very late."

Uriel didn't bother asking what he was running late for; the cherubim did things in their own time. In the past when they've tried to explain it, Uriel had no idea what they were talking about.

Zophiel walked away with his ox feet, and the ophan rolled along beside him.

Michael and Gabriel, who were both 6'5", were standing so close to one another that they looked like one person. They were more than unnerved by the cherubim; they were terrified of them. They both had their backs against the wall, which was made out of white marble. Everything in heaven was made out of white marble, except for all the paths which were paved with gold and the heavenly gate which was made out of pearls but were still white.

4

Look at them; they are terrified of one cherub, and these two are supposed to be warriors, Uriel thought.

Uriel swatted away a wisp of cloud that was hovering around his face. There were always wisps of clouds for some reason. It was as if it were some poor angel's job to constantly crank a machine, so that they would have perpetual clouds.

"It isn't right and I don't just mean the book I'm mentioned in. What about the Book of Phillip or the Book of Mary? What about the Book of Judas?"

"The Book of Judas is a lost cause. The people hate Judas, and you can't convince them otherwise. The betrayal of Jesus is kind of a hard thing to forgive," Michael said.

"Didn't he betray Jesus for thirty goats?"

"Thirty goats? Don't be ridiculous; it was ten goats. Do you think anyone could afford to give away thirty goats?" Michael asked.

Uriel ignored them. "They put that awful Apocalypse of John in there; after we carefully worked out the story of a benevolent God, mankind had to ruin it like they ruin everything else. We give them the inspiration to build cities, and they get burnt to the ground by their perpetual wars. Where is John anyway?"

"He is assisting an Angel of Dominion, Zadkiel, I believe."

"I want to speak to him this instant."

Uriel tried to snap his fingers, but they barely made a sound.

"How have you not learned to snap your fingers?" Gabriel asked.

"Well, it's only been eons; give an angel time." Uriel tried again and managed to make a small snapping sound. An Angel of Power appeared, looking none too pleased.

"I'm terribly sorry to have disturbed you; it won't happen again."

Uriel snapped his fingers again quickly before the Angel of Power could even respond. It made a small *snap*, but it was good enough for the angel to disappear. He hoped he sent him back to the right place. Uriel had never quite gotten the hang of snapping his fingers; and to make matters worse, he could never focus on the face of who he wanted to appear in his mind or the place he wanted to go to. It usually took him a couple of tries to get it right.

"I'll summon John for you," Gabriel said and snapped his fingers.

5

John appeared and, like the Angel of Power, he didn't seem too pleased. Uriel didn't care because John was a man, a very important man, but still just a man. Men were one of the few people he could boss around. Uriel, Michael and Gabriel were all archangels, just one level above the lowest level in the angel hierarchy. The lowest level were just regular angels, and there were tons of those. They usually had to do all the errands of the upper levels, and they were typically the ones who delivered messages to men on Earth in the form of burning bushes, etc. The hierarchy of angels was Seraphim, Cherubim, Ophanim, Thrones, Dominions, Powers, Principalities, Archangels and Angels. There is the Angel of Presence, who goes by many other names, who is above the hierarchy. The Angel of Presence is second in command next to God, but the Angel of Presence is God in a form that can be seen. So The Angel of Presence, who is God, is second in command to himself. It was all very confusing and better just to not think about it or you'd get a headache.

"I want to talk to you about that stupid book you wrote."

"Not that again. We've been over and over that," John said.

"Well, we will go over it again and you'd better mind your manners, or I'll have you sent back to Earth until the end of time; and won't you be embarrassed when it doesn't end the way you wrote it."

Uriel did not actually have the power to send John back to Earth until the end of time; that had to be approved by an angel higher up, but John didn't know that. His bluff worked because John quickly changed his demeanor.

"I wrote down everything I could recall from my vision."

"What? Wait, you never used the word 'vision' before."

"Yes, well, that is what it was—a holy vision."

So this holy vision came from an angel?" Uriel asked.

"Yes, it looked like an angel."

"Which angel was it?"

John looked down at his feet in distress. Gabriel and Michael were remaining quiet; they were thoroughly enjoying the spectacle.

"Well, it was more of a dream really."

"What? You never mentioned it was a dream before either. It's no wonder it sounds completely mad, all that business about 'whores of Babylon' and 'the mark of the beast.'"

"I was in prison, you know, on the island of Patmos. What else was I supposed to be doing but dreaming and writing?" John asked defensively.

"Yes, yes, I remember. You realize it is your version of the apocalypse that is going to be the one that mankind reads and believes from now until the end of time. Why did you have to make it so scary? Couldn't you have toned it down a little bit or left some of it out?"

"I may have embellished a bit . . . ." John's voice trailed off and once again, he looked down at his feet.

"What do you mean by 'a bit'?"

"I wasn't the one who embellished it. You see, I'm not a very good writer; and I thought the whole thing kind of sounded rather boring really, so I got Virgil to spice it up."

Gabriel and Michael could not contain themselves any longer, and they both doubled over with laughter.

"Virgil? You mean the poet, the one who wrote the *Aeneid*?" Uriel asked.

Gabriel stopped laughing long enough to say, "I love that epic poem."

"I love that poem too," Michael said.

"It's an epic poem, which is a bit different from a regular poem," Gabriel said.

"Who cares about the blasted poem? I can't believe the book about the end of time was plagiarized."

The word "blasted" was about as strong a word as angels were allowed to use. They never cursed unless it was an emergency; and, even then, you had to get prior approval.

"Your book—make that Virgil's book—is now canonical scripture. Men are going to destroy all the other books and excommunicate the people who still want to read them. We have to do something about this."

John just stood there with a sheepish expression, as if to say, *I'm sorry I fouled up the end of time.* He didn't know what he could do about it. Michael and Gabriel both drew their swords and pointed them at John. That was always their first reaction when something needed to be done. They didn't have the patience to use their wit, which was just as well since they didn't have any wit to use.

7

"I'll show you what an apocalypse looks like. Get out of my sight, you wretch."

Uriel just barely snapped his fingers and John disappeared. This time he didn't care if he got back to the right place. In fact, he hoped he hadn't sent him back to the right place. He hoped he had accidentally sent him to hell. It would be a good two days before they figured out he wasn't supposed to be there and send him back. Things didn't run as smoothly and efficiently there as they did in heaven. Two days in a fire pit would do him some good and make him think twice about making the biggest blunder in history.

"I wouldn't mind having a word with Virgil too," Uriel said.

"I believe he's in hell right now," Michael said.

"I don't see why he should be allowed to roam wherever he wants."

"We needed a liaison between heaven and hell, and Virgil dwells in purgatory," Gabriel said.

"A lot of angels are fond of him," Michael said.

Gabriel and Michael still had their swords out.

"Put your blasted swords away," Uriel stated.

"You know, if you say that word one more time today, you'll have to face an inquiry by the Angels of Virtue and have to explain why you had to use such strong language," Gabriel said.

Uriel knew he was right; and the minute they knew what he was planning on doing, whatever that something was—because at the moment he had no idea—they would put an end to it.

The angels were supposed to interfere with mankind as little as possible because of that whole business about mankind having free will. Uriel didn't see why they had to have free will, especially since they always messed things up.

"Something must be done."

"We are going to need some help and someone with a little more authority on our side," Michael said.

Uriel liked how this was becoming a *we* project instead of a *me* project. He needed all the help he could get.

"Vehuaiah, the Seraph who oversees rules, time and history might be able to help us."

"Do you think he would help? Like you said, he's in charge of the rules and I hear he's a stickler for them," Gabriel said.

8

"He is a stickler, but fortunately I know his weakness."

"Is it fire?" Michael asked.

"I bet it's scorpions," Gabriel said.

"Don't be absurd. I'm not going to threaten him. The day I threaten a seraph is the same day I become a permanent resident in hell. No, I was thinking more along the lines of a bribe."

"What kind of bribe?" Michael asked.

"Chocolate."

"He's not going to help you with something of this magnitude for chocolate. Besides, he already has a lot of it," Gabriel said.

"It's worth a try; he has quite a sweet tooth."

Angels weren't infallible; they could make mistakes and had vices like a sweet tooth, just like anybody else. You didn't have to look any further than Lucifer and his rebels, who were once angels, to prove that point. Lucifer's weaknesses were pride and vanity; he thought he could rule heaven better than God.

Uriel smacked away a whiff of cloud that was hanging just below his chin and giving him a venerable beard.

"Okay, let's say the chocolate works and let's say further that Vehuaiah agrees to help you—then what? Even Vehuaiah doesn't have the power to completely rewrite history. He can only bend or stretch it like taffy," Michael said.

The word "taffy" made Gabriel rub his belly. He wished he had some right now. He couldn't snap his fingers to make taffy appear because that was something from Earth, and they weren't allowed to have any earthly possessions in heaven. Heaven had clearly-defined rules but if you thought hard enough, you could circumvent some of them. Heaven, though, could make some earthly foods; they had many fields. They grew all their own food and that included sugarcane. They also had vineyards because if there were one thing they loved most, it was wine.

"Don't worry; I have a plan. I don't think any rewriting of history will be necessary."

"The last time you said you had a plan, I ended up in front of the Seraph Jeliel and he had to repair my wing," Gabriel said.

"That plan wasn't well-thought-out. I had gotten tigers and cats mixed up; I forgot that tigers were the ones with the sharp claws that could tear your flesh apart. This plan has been thoroughly thought through."

That was stretching the truth a bit; he had not thought it all the way through yet, but he had every intention of thinking it all the way through after he went to his room in the Mal'ak Heykal, commonly called the Palace of the Angels, and took a nap.

Fools and Flatulence

It was 397 and the reach of the Roman Empire extended far and wide across the lands. It hardly mattered in the lives of the little village of Hadria, Italy. Philip and Thomas of Hadria were brothers, but looked absolutely nothing alike. Thomas was older at twenty-two, but only by a year, and had red hair and hazel eyes, while Philip had raven black hair with eyes to match. Philip, although a year younger, was a little taller and thinner than his older brother, who was short and squat. Their mother had died when they were very young, and their father had passed away last winter. The young men were educated; they were taught their letters by their father and could read. Philip and Thomas made their living as healers, as had their family for generations. They were both unmarried although Philip had a couple of girls interested in him, but it never amounted to anything. Thomas only had one, the buck-toothed daughter of the magistrate. It didn't matter, though; both brothers enjoyed their bachelorhood and each other's company. They couldn't imagine being separated.

Thomas was boiling water in a brazier in one of the rooms of their two-room house, and Philip was busy poking an old man named Solomon in the foot.

"Do you feel anything, Solomon?" Philip asked.

"Not a thing," Solomon said.

Philip gave Thomas a solemn look. He knew what his brother's look meant and nodded.

"Solomon, your foot is infected and I'm afraid I'm going to have to take your foot."

"Take it where?" the old man said and sniffled.

"I'm going to have to cut it off."

"You can't do that; I need that foot. How am I supposed to get around and work my field?"

"I can make you some crutches like we made for Francesco," Philip said and his brother Thomas shook his head. It was the

11

wrong thing to say; Solomon hated Francesco. They had hated each other for so long that Thomas wasn't even sure why they hated each other. Solomon and Francesco were both very old and probably couldn't remember why they hated each other either. He suspected it was the hate that kept the two of them going; both were so stubborn, they absolutely refused to die.

Solomon leapt off the table; for an old man he was surprisingly quick, or at least the mentioning of his mortal enemy made him quick.

"I don't want to hobble around like that old fool. God gave me two feet, and I'm planning on using both of them until I die."

"If I don't take your foot, you will die for sure," Philip said.

"Well, I will die with both of my feet. I'm not going to be limping around in heaven for eternity."

Thomas finished boiling the water and sat the pot aside. "You don't want to die before Francesco, do you?"

Solomon snorted. "I'm not dying before that old fool."

"If you don't allow me to take your foot, you most assuredly will," Philip said.

Solomon looked at Philip and Thomas; he was unconvinced. He didn't think these two boys had the right to tell him when he was going to die. They didn't know anything; they were just babies. Solomon thought anyone under sixty was a baby. "Just give me something for the pain; you're not getting my foot. If God wants my foot, why, he can just come down from the heavens and take it himself, which he won't because he's God and what does the almighty need with an old man's foot?"

Thomas stifled a giggle and Philip just sighed; he could see the old man was resolute.

Who knows, this old man is so stubborn, he probably will get better just to spite me, he thought.

Thomas gathered up some white willow bark. "Here, you'll need to chew on this to relieve the pain, and it will help reduce any fever."

"A man comes to babies about his foot and gets told he needs to have it removed and to chew on a tree," Solomon huffed and snatched the bark out of Thomas' hand.

"Woe to the flesh that depends on the soul; woe to the soul that depends on the flesh," Philip quoted.

12

Solomon gave Philip a wary eye and pointed a shriveled finger at him. "You boys be careful about which books you quote from; not everyone here is as nice and forgiving as I am. You're nice boys even though you don't know nothing from nothing."

It was hard to tell if Solomon were being sarcastic or not; he only had one facial expression, and that was a scowl so deep it looked like it was carved into his face. Solomon hobbled out of the brothers' home, mumbling something about the Lord not wanting his foot.

"How long do you give him before that infection takes hold?" Thomas asked.

"I give him another week and after that, it will be too late. Do you think he's right about the gospels?"

"Father raised us to respect all the gospels; they are all inspired by God's divinity. Only God will tell me what not to read."

"Maybe God will come down from heaven and tell you what to read, right after he tells Solomon he wants his foot."

***

"You need to throw him out on his ear," John of Hadria said to his father.

"I can't throw him out; he's a mute. Where would he go? What would he do?"

Adolfo had never spoken a word although he could hear perfectly well. Nobody is sure why he couldn't speak; his mother had tried to get him to talk for years, but finally gave up when he was around fourteen. Adolfo, who was now eighteen, had just showed no interest in it. He did, however, love to grunt, which drove John mad. Adolfo was tall with brown hair shorn close to his head and chestnut eyes that were wise beyond their years. Adolfo had never known his father, and his mother died three years ago.

His mother would come in a couple of times a week to cook and clean for John and his Father. Adolfo wasn't about to cook or clean, so John had taken over both those duties, as well as his duties as a scribe. John's father treated Adolfo like another son and educated both boys. John's father was bed-ridden with

13

pneumonia; and after his mother died, John's father took Adolfo in and looked after him.

Adolfo didn't cook or clean; the only thing he did do was illuminate John's manuscripts with hues of blue, gold, red and green. He excelled at it; it was the only thing he wanted to do.

You would think that given the fact he was a mute, he would be easy to get along with, but you'd be wrong. Adolfo was taciturn; he was the only one in Hadria who had a deeper scowl than Solomon, and even he gave Adolfo a wide berth. Adolfo tried to bite anyone who got too close to him. John, with his mane of curly blond hair and blue eyes, was a jovial and garrulous sort. The two were like oil and water. John would talk to him all day and get no response, other than the occasional grunt.

"Put down those paints and come eat your supper, you gargoyle," John said.

His father, who propped himself up in bed, shook his head. "You should really try to get along with him; I won't be around forever."

"You better not die on me and leave me with this tombstone. I'm taking you to see those two healers in the morning. Those brothers will cure you right up."

"I don't think I can make the journey."

"I'll carry you if I have to, right after I finish copying these manuscripts for Peter."

"I really wish the two of you would not work on those manuscripts for Peter."

John did not have to ask his father what he meant by "those manuscripts." He knew he meant the Gnostic Gospels or as some called them, the Apocrypha. They were the non-canonical books of God and were forbidden by the Church. Peter invited people into his home every Sunday and read from the Bible, including those books that were not sanctioned by the Church, which these days was a dangerous thing to do.

"All works written about God have value, Father." Adolfo grunted in agreement. He was a cantankerous young man, but also pious. His illuminations were breathtaking and could bring tears to your eyes. Peter relied on John to make copies of gospels and prayer books and Adolfo to make them come to life. They also copied secular works that Peter would sell and would give John

14

and Adolfo a share of the profits. It was how they were making their meager living.

John could read and write, but he did not have the artistic talent for illumination. They didn't know if Adolfo could read or not, but what was certain was that he had a God-given talent for illustration.

"I just want you boys to be careful. Anyone caught reading, distributing or even possessing those books will be punished."

"I am not afraid; even the Church sometimes gets things wrong, Father." Adolfo grunted twice, which either meant he agreed or he was hungry. His father made the sign of the cross at the blasphemy.

"Besides, if anyone from the Church comes around here, Adolfo will scare them off with one look," John said and winked at Adolfo who stared at him blankly. "Now, let's eat." He slapped the paint brushes out of Adolfo's hand quick as a cat. He had learned to be quick because if you weren't, you would get bitten for your efforts. Adolfo grunted reluctantly and sat down at the table. John handed his father a bowl of broth and talked all throughout dinner while the other two just listened, saying nothing, because even if you were not mute, when John was on a roll, you couldn't get a word in edgewise.

***

Peter of Hadria was reading from the Gospel of Mary to the only two people in attendance, Simon and Lorenzo. The attendance at his scriptural readings and prayer meetings had dropped off since the Church ruling at the Council of Carthage. Peter was exceptionally tall and could easily be spotted in a crowd. Although he was only middle-aged, his head and beard were completely white. His wife, Mary, had died three months ago; and since then, he'd been in a melancholy malaise.

Peter said to Mary, "Sister, we know the Savior loved you more than the rest of women. Tell us the words of the Savior which you remember, which we do not nor have we heard them."

Peter paused and looked at Lorenzo, who was clutching his stomach and looking uncomfortable. Lorenzo was old, almost as old as Solomon with the rotting foot. He had only wisps of white

15

hair on the sides of his head, and the top was completely bald. His face was clean-shaven, but his most noticeable feature was his humpback. In addition to his humpback, which sometime ached and made his gait appear as if he were intoxicated, he had irritable bowels which could erupt like an active volcano at any time. Now it looked like one of those times that it might erupt.

Simon tapped his cooking spoon against his stomach. "Is that thing going to blow? Do we need to clear the room?" Simon was a short, middle-aged bachelor with short brown hair and a scar on his right cheek. No one was quite sure how he got the scar because he told a different story about it every time, whether it was wrestling a bear or fighting off marauders. The truth was probably nowhere near as glamorous and probably just a clumsy accident from his youth.

Simon was quite the cook and always carried around a spoon with him in case he was asked to cook something on the spot. He needed to be prepared at all times, like a warrior with his weapon. As of yet, he had not been called upon to use it, but he knew it was just a matter of time.

Peter smiled his warm, friendly smile. He was much more diplomatic than Simon, who had a tendency to just blurt out whatever was on his mind. "Shall we take a break for a moment while you go to the privy?"

"No, I'll be fine; please continue."

Simon tapped Lorenzo's stomach again. "You tell us now if you're about to let one go. The last time you did it, you cleared out an entire church. Do you remember that, Peter? It was during Easter mass. The bishop was drinking the blood of Christ from the chalice and nearly choked when the smell reached him."

Peter didn't answer. Simon had the tendency to exaggerate a little. Lorenzo did break wind during Easter mass, but only a few people smelled it and it quickly dissipated. It certainly could not have reached the bishop because they were seated all the way in the back. The bishop did however cough after drinking the blood of Christ, but it probably had gone down the wrong way.

Peter continued reading, "Mary answered, 'What is hidden from you, I will proclaim to you.'" He stopped again because Lorenzo was almost doubled over. Rather than bring it up again and cause Lorenzo any more embarrassment, he said, "Let us stop there for today; it is growing dark outside."

Lorenzo and Simon both seemed relieved. Lorenzo, because he was in obvious discomfort and Simon, because he didn't want to be knocked out by a foul odor. Peter put the Book of Mary out of sight with the rest of the Gnostic Gospels. Peter had a three-room house, which had felt empty since his wife Mary had died. The room they were in was the largest and at one time had as many as fifteen people at a time in it to hear Peter's readings, but not anymore. The people did not want to risk the Church's wrath.

"It's a sad state of affairs when people can't make the short journey to hear God's word," Simon said.

"It's understandable though; most people live simple lives and consider the Church law. You can't blame them," Lorenzo said, having trouble fastening his cloak around his humpback.

Peter fastened Lorenzo's cloak for him. "If you two want to stop coming, I'd understand."

Simon wrapped Peter gently on the knuckles with his spoon. He had used the spoon more times to hit people with than he had using it cooking. "Don't talk nonsense now. I will come in rain, snow or shine to hear the word of the Lord."

Lorenzo coughed. "I will come as well. Not in rain or snow, of course—that makes my bones ache—and not when it's too hot—I start to feel faint. Also, not when my bowels are acting up, but every other time I will."

"When aren't your bowels acting up, you old fool?" Simon asked.

The two men left Peter alone in his home and had only been gone a few seconds before he smelled it. The odor was like rotting eggs that had been left out with a month-old corpse.

Lorenzo had left a parting gift, and Peter walked outside to get some fresh air.

17

Excommunication

"Do any of you recant your heresy? Heresy is a terrible crime, and may I remind you that the Apostle Paul condemns it as a damnable offense," the Bishop of Naples said. Then he read, "I am astonished that you are so quickly deserting him who called you in the grace of Christ and turning to a different gospel—"

It was at this point one of the heretics passed the loudest gas any of them had ever heard. The crowd that was gathered in the town square stared blankly at the bishop. It was so quiet you could hear a pin drop until the first brave soul began to laugh, and then more began to laugh; even the heretics themselves laughed. The only one not amused was the Bishop of Naples; he had not finished what Paul had said about heresy and was sure that he had not finished his sermon by farting. He had traveled a long way for these proceedings, and he was determined to carry it out to the letter. The bishop waited for the laughter to die down before he continued. He had lost his place, so he started with:

"Even if an angel from heaven should preach to you a gospel contrary to that which I have preached to you, let him be accursed. As it has been said before, so now I say again, if anyone is preaching to you a gospel contrary to that which you received, let him be accursed."

Another bout of gas from one of the heretics rippled and echoed throughout the village, followed by more laughter. At least he had finished reading this time. The bishop glared at the civil magistrate, who was also laughing, but one look from the bishop silenced him immediately. The crowd was a mixture of villagers who knew and respected the heretics and those who were outraged at the blasphemers and wanted to jeer and throw things at them. Most of them had come prepared with some cabbage or ripe tomatoes.

The first execution for committing heresy had been in 385, just over twelve years earlier. It had been carried out by the

Emperor Maximus. The Bishop of Avilie had been charged with witchcraft, but really it was because he agreed with Gnostic opinions. He was tried and then tortured. The bishop had confessed and been executed. The pope was upset by this execution and in the future thought it should only be used for extreme cases.

The Bishop of Naples raised his hand to silence them. He now just wanted to hurry up with the proceedings because it looked like it was about to rain. Except for a gray overcast, there was still a picturesque view of the Adriatic Sea. Just as it looked like a torrent of rain would come down, it didn't; instead it began to hail. One of the balls of hail caught the bishop right in the eye. He swore under his breath, so no one else could hear him.

I will have to do penance for that later, he thought.

It hailed for about a minute and then stopped. He decided now would be a good time to light the candle he was holding before it started to rain, hail or—the way these proceedings were going— he wouldn't be surprised if a plague of locusts swept through. The candle was just part of the ceremony. The Church deemed it as a ceremony, even though it felt nothing like one, mainly just because they loved a good ceremony.

"Philip, Simon, Lorenzo, John, Peter, Thomas and Adolfo of Hadria, the Church declares an anathema. You are hereby excommunicated and all your property and lands will be seized and go to the Church. All of your heretical books have been rounded up and will be burned."

He pointed to the pile of manuscripts that had been carelessly thrown in a pile. There was a bonfire burning, ready to devour the heretical books. Among the crowd, there were a lot of eager faces who couldn't wait to see them burst into flames. Before the bishop could give the nod, a downpour of rain put out the fire. He stomped his foot; this was all he could stand. This whole proceeding had been a mockery from start to finish.

"In the year of our Lord 397, you are hereby condemned by the magisterium of the Church, the holy pope, who is the supreme authority on matters of faith and the authentic teachings of the Church. You are to be expelled from Hadria, banished, never to return. You are to be deprived of a Catholic burial, forbidden to hold a position of authority in the Church; you may not make a will or be an accuser, a witness or a judge in a court. You may not receive the Eucharist or set foot in a church ever again. You are enemies of the state as well as the Church."

It was a harsh sentencing; Normally an excommunication included the chance of redemption through penance over a period of time, but these heretics were not being offered that chance because these weren't poor ignorant peasants; they were intelligent men who could read and write and had with good professions. They knowingly continued to preach and read the heretical gospels. They were being used to set an example to others; the Church will not be challenged.

The bishop, magistrate and the heretics were the only ones left at the forum; everyone else had taken shelter because the rain was coming down in buckets. Some of the villagers were very disappointed there would not be any throwing of vegetables at the heretics today, but they didn't want to go out in the rain and catch their death. The bishop sighed. The ceremony did not go as planned; a bell was supposed to be rung three times, and he was supposed to close his Bible and then blow out the candle. The last part signified the end, but since no one wanted to go out and ring the church bell and he had already closed his book so that the pages wouldn't get wet and the rain had already put out the candle, he just simply waved his hand.

The magistrate and the bishop ran to seek shelter in the church, leaving the heretics all alone. The rain stopped just as suddenly as the hail had, and then the sun came out. It was as if God himself had timed it all just for them. The heretics looked at one another; they could not go home because they no longer had a home or any possessions; the Church said so.

"Let us go," Peter said.

Simon began to pick up some of the vegetables that a few of the villagers left behind. Adolfo grunted and took off his tunic. It seemed that everyone just wanted to get out of the rain and had forgotten about the heretics and the heretical gospels. Adolfo placed them all in his tunic, tied it shut and with that, the heretics left Hadria for good.

***

20

"Make it rain; make it rain!" Uriel was yelling.

Michael and Gabriel were running about heaven as if they were possessed, which is impossible; angels are immune to possessions. Man, though, is easily susceptible to possessions; and indeed, the demon Belphegor loved to take over human bodies. Most of the people didn't even know they were being possessed because he never made them do anything too crazy. Oh, occasionally he would have to do something, like make a person speak in tongues, or else Lucifer would catch on that he only possessed people to stuff his face full of food and copulate.

The three angels were at the Looking Pool, watching what was taking place in Hadria. The Looking Pool was just as the name it implied; it was a giant fountain filled with crystal clear water where any angel could come and watch what was taking place on Earth at the present time. They were the only three angels there at the present. Most angels didn't even bother ever looking into it because after so many years, mortals had become very predictable and never seemed to learn from history.

Uriel, Michael and Gabriel had been granted permission from the Seraph Ramiel who was in charge of weather. Fortunately, Ramiel did not care for humans and didn't inquire as to why they wanted to let rain pour down on the unfortunate creatures.

"I'm trying to focus on the right place. There we go; that should do it," Michael said, snapping his fingers.

"You just made it rain in Egypt," Uriel said. "It might help if you actually looked down at Hadria to make it rain in Hadria . . . instead of Egypt."

The snapping was never the issue—well, it was for Uriel who could never do it very well—but it was mainly focusing on what you wanted to achieve.

"Wait. I got it," Gabriel said and snapped his fingers.

"You got it in the right place, but it's hailing now, not raining," Uriel said. Technically, Ramiel had only given his permission to make it rain; but given his disdain, they doubted if Ramiel cared if a sharp ball of hail took out a mortal's eyeball.

"Blasted," Gabriel said and covered his mouth. "Getting weather right is hard."

Gabriel made the hail turn to rain, and it began to rain down in Hadria. Michael made big fat raindrops, the kind that hurt when they hit you in the face.

"Would you just look at those poor unfortunate men, having to be excommunicated just because they wanted to protect all of God's inspired writing," Uriel said.

Michael and Gabriel began to laugh.

"Did you see the look on the Bishop of Naples' face; he looked as though he were constipated," Gabriel said.

"The fire is out now, and it looks like the whole town has dispersed. The bishop and the magistrate have taken cover as well," Michael said.

"The heretics are all alone," Gabriel said.

"Don't call them that."

"Sorry."

"Good, make it stop raining and make the sun shine bright to warm them up," Uriel said.

Gabriel snapped his fingers and made it stop raining. He snapped them again to make the sun come out.

The Seraph Jehoel appeared out of the thick clouds and sang the customary seraphim greeting.

"Holy, holy, holy is the Lord of hosts; the whole earth full of his glory."

The seraphim sang that as a greeting, as a farewell and other numerous times throughout the day. It was either some strange compulsion, or they were sucking up to God to maintain their status at the top of the sphere. It could get a little annoying after a while, and Jehoel sang off-key with a screech.

The archangels said "hullo" instead of singing it back. Uriel sang it back to a seraphim once and he looked at him with scorn so he never did it again.

"What are you doing?"

Seraphim were even more pompous than the cherubim because they saw themselves as being most favored by God. Uriel thought fast on his feet.

"We were just admiring God's creations."

It was the safest answer Uriel could think of because no one would contradict it.

"'Doubt that the stars are fire; doubt that the sun doth move; doubt truth be a liar; but never doubt I love.'"

The archangels look at Jehoel blankly.

Blasted. Is he is saying we are lying or is he just spouting rubbish poetry? Uriel thought. He also wondered if it still counted as bad language if he thought *blasted* instead of saying it.

"It's Shakespeare," Jehoel said.

So it is rubbish poetry after all.

Vehuaiah, a seraph who was in charge of time had once told Uriel about Shakespeare. He said the real writer of all that rubbish was actually Robert Wellesley and not William Shakespeare. Robert was a wanted criminal and did not want the attention, so he will let William take all the credit; and in return, William paid him a fee. Uriel did not want to correct Jehoel, though.

Jehoel looked at the three of them with pity.

How do they serve God when they don't even have one brain among the three of them?

Jehoel could stand the sight of them no longer and bid them farewell.

"Holy, holy, holy is the Lord of hosts; the whole earth full of his glory."

The seraphim had six wings but rarely used any of them because they thought it very uncouth to go about flapping their wings like a chicken.

"Hey, the men are leaving. One of them is taking the gospels with him. What a clever fellow that one, the one who grunts. There is something to be said about never speaking and that is, you can be sure that nothing stupid will come out," Gabriel said.

"You should try it sometime," Uriel said.

"Are you sure these are the men you want? There are others you could pick," Michael asked.

"Yes, I've been watching these men for a while now, and I think they will do quite nicely," Uriel said.

"It seems the other people of the town have quite forgotten the heretics," Michael said.

"That's because they have all gathered in the church to get out of the rain and because the bishop is having a banquet so there's free food."

"There's a lovely spread of fish and bread," Uriel said.

"I would have added a variety of cheeses," Gabriel said.

"The men are leaving Hadria," Michael said.

"I have plans for them. We will need to contact them somehow

23

and let them know of their mission," Uriel said.

Once again, Uriel wasn't sure what the plan was, but he would figure it out as he always did after a nice long nap.

Devil May Care

Azazel was overjoyed. "Finally, they are getting rid of the Apocrypha. The Church has said they are heretical and must be destroyed."

He pushed down the head of a soul who was sticking out of the Stagnum Ignis or, as most demons called it, the Lake of Fire.

"You know, you don't have to push everyone's head down that pops up. It must be hard to breathe down there. Poor souls. They have all eternity to suffer, no sense in making them suffer every minute of it," Rosier said.

"You're right. Er . . . hey, you there."

A soul popped his head out, but it wasn't the same one. He looked at Azazel and Rosier and quickly stuck his head back below the surface.

"Mortals will no longer know the name of Uriel and what he did to me."

"I don't think mortals care very much for such things. The only things that seem to matter to them are eating, drinking, waging war and copulating."

"Would you choose differently if you had to do it all over again?" Azazel asked.

"Do you mean would I choose the winning side? No, I don't mind hell so much. You meet some interesting people," Rosier said.

"That's true; a man came in last week who had been a tradesman in his mortal life and he didn't realize he was dead. He tried to sell me some furs. Can you imagine? I laughed so hard, I nearly cried. I told him no one would ever buy furs down here."

"I like the writer Virgil; he gives me all the latest gossip on the angels in heaven when he comes in," Rosier said.

"You mean the fellow who writes that poetry rubbish?"

"It's not all rubbish."

"I do wish I could have gained a higher rank, though. I'm still

25

the same rank I was in heaven," Rosier said.

When all the rebellious angels were cast out of heaven, Lucifer just kept the same hierarchy. Rosier had been an Angel of Dominion.

"I'm lucky I didn't get demoted," Azazel said.

"Yes, very unfortunate thing, your tripping when leading the charge on Michael and his army."

Azazel had been a seraph.

"Holy, holy, holy is the Lord of hosts; the whole earth full of his glory," he sang.

"I wouldn't sing that too loudly around here," Rosier said.

Belias flew down among them and was holding something in his hands. Unlike the seraphim, the devils didn't have problems flying. They didn't care how uncouth flapping their wings looked; it was very practical in getting from place to place. They figured they had been cast out of paradise like Adam and Eve and no longer had to obey rules or etiquette.

"Lucifer has made up some new schedules," Belias said as he handed one to Rosier and one to Azazel.

Lucifer liked to shuffle the devils around in the different circles of hell and contrive new punishments. He didn't want anyone getting bored or dissatisfied with their jobs.

"Well, it looks like I get to stay here among the angry; but instead of poking their heads down with a stick, I'm to throw stones at them. It's like he's not even trying to be creative anymore," Azazel said.

"I have to oversee the greedy, but it says instead of having them push a large stone uphill, we are to let them roll it downhill because it will be a lot more entertaining. I have noticed that the punishments seem to be a lot lighter than usual, and some of them aren't really that harsh at all. I think Lucifer no longer wants to play the role of tormenter," Rosier said.

"You look unusually happy, Azazel; I mean, considering we are demons and are supposed to be miserable and inflicting misery on to evil souls. It's the reason why God made hell in the first place. He wanted to create an atmosphere of fire, blood and the eternal wailing of anguished souls," Belias said.

"He's happy because the mortals are doing away with the Apocrypha that he's mentioned in because now no one will remember him or Uriel. Other than Uriel passing judgment on you for your part in the rebellion, Azazel, I don't think there is any other mention of you in the good book," Rosier said.

"I don't think there is any mention of you at all in the good book, Apocrypha or otherwise. Besides, what's most important is that it will anger that thick-headed Uriel because no one will know about all of his heroic deeds. Mortals don't seem to want to preserve their history for some reason. They are always throwing things away or some other group of mortals destroys them."

"Says the devil who just yesterday burnt our last copy of *Beowulf* because he didn't like the ending."

Belias and Rosier laughed.

"It's not funny. Something must be done to ensure all the books are obliterated."

"You could just collect all the books," Belias said.

"How would I do that?"

"You can send a demon to earth to collect them."

"That's a great idea, but Lucifer would never approve something like that," Azazel said.

"You could tell him you were sending a demon to earth to get mortals to sign over their souls to him," Belias said.

"If I lie to Lucifer, one of you will be poking my head down in the Lake of Fire with a stick."

"You don't need to lie. You just omit the part about the books; besides, there's no reason the demon can't accomplish both. Also, I don't see why he would mind your burning gospels; in fact, I think he'd rather like the idea," Belias said.

"It sounds risky. Who could I trust to get the job done?"

"I know; you should send Baal. He is very efficient and trustworthy," Rosier said.

"Baal . . . is he the one who likes to possess mortals so he can stuff his face and copulate?" Azazel asked.

"No, you're thinking of Belphegor," Rosier said.

"Belias, would you mind fetching Baal and bringing him here?"

"Well, I really should pass the rest of these schedules out, but I suppose I could make time."

Belias flew off; it only took a few minutes to fetch Baal because he was nearby tormenting the gluttonous.

"Baal, I need you to go down to earth and collect all the Gnostic Gospels," Azazel said.

"Don't forget about getting mortals to sign over their souls," Belias said.

"Oh yes, and get some souls while you're at it."

"I thought the mortals were getting rid of those themselves. How am I supposed to know if I've collected them all anyway?"

"They are getting rid of the books, but never trust a mortal to do anything right. You still have groups of people who read them. I don't know how you'll get them all, but you'll think of something," Azazel said.

"I think that soul in the lake is trying to say something," Baal said and pointed to a head whose mouth was making a gurgling noise.

"Yes, what is it? Say it; we don't have all day," Azazel said.

"I am not supposed to be here," the soul said.

"Yes, yes, that is what they all say," Azazel said.

"Uriel accidentally sent me here. I am the apostle John."

"Are you the mortal that wrote about the end of time?" Rosier asked.

John didn't want to say that Virgil wrote most of it because who knows what the demons did to plagiarists.

"Yes, that was me. Can I please get out of here?"

Azazel pushed his long stick out in front of him. "Grab hold of that and I'll pull you in." Azazel pulled John out of the Lake of Fire.

"So Uriel sent you here. It figures; he could never concentrate enough to get that right. Don't worry, we will get this mess straightened out and you'll be back with those saints before you can say 'eternal damnation,'" Azazel said.

"We are so honored that you are here. Would you be willing to sign my copy of the Book of Revelation?" Rosier asked.

"You have a Bible . . . here? Do you know what Lucifer would do to you if he found that? Why do you have a Bible?" Azazel asked.

Unlike in heaven, demons could have any earthly possessions they wanted. Lucifer didn't care.

"We don't get many books down here and the ones we do get, you usually burn, because you don't like the ending," Rosier said.

28

"I don't like the ending of the Bible either, come to think of it; it's too scary. There should be lots more flowers and cakes and less destruction and famine," Azazel said.

"Can you sign mine too?" Belias asked.

"I don't believe the two of you. How can we in good conscience torture heretics and send people like Virgil to limbo when every devil and devil's mother owns a Bible?"

"What's a conscience?" Rosier asked.

"Never mind. There will be no signing of Bibles today. We've got more important things to do, like sending Baal to earth."

"We also have to send John back to heaven," Belias said.

Rosier snapped his fingers and John disappeared. The only problem with that, though, was that Rosier was worse than Uriel when it came to concentrating. For all they knew, Rosier could have sent him to another circle of hell, or even back to earth for that matter.

Three Heads are Better Than One

Uriel watched Michael and Gabriel practicing with their swords. Zachariel, an Angel of Dominon, appeared before him. God must really favor the Angels of Dominion because they are divinely beautiful—they are the loveliest of angels to behold—but even on Zachariel's heavenly face, he could tell that he was none too pleased. Uriel was a patron of the arts and was supposed to be inspiring and supporting mankind in all of their artistic endeavors, namely the building of churches. He gave Zachariel a weekly report on the different works he had helped come to fruition, and he writes them all down. Uriel has done this faithfully since the evolution of man, but with his obsession with preserving gospels, he had quite forgotten about it. Zachariel was holding his scepter, on the end of which was an orb that radiated light.

"Can I hold your scepter?" Michael asked.

Zachariel sighed. Michael asked this question every time he saw him; and even though he always said "no," he kept asking anyway, so he decided to let him hold it for once and maybe he would stop asking him about it.

"All right, Michael, but just this one time."

"Hey, if he gets to hold it, then so do I," Gabriel said.

They are like two babies; they behave worse than humans sometimes, Zachariel thought.

"Michael, you can hold it for a while and then you must give it to Gabriel. I want it back when I have finished my business with Uriel."

Zachariel gave the scepter to Michael. He and Gabriel giggled and flew off it with it.

"You forgot our weekly meeting. I must say that is highly unlike you."

"I have had a lot on my mind as of late."

Zachariel rolled out his scroll to get down to business. That was one thing Uriel liked about him; he minded his own affairs.

"Let's begin then, shall we?"

Uriel had to think fast; he had not done anything this week. He said the first thing that came to his mind.

"I inspired the Roman senator Pammachius to build a basilica in Rome."

Uriel had not inspired Pammachius to do any such thing, but planned on inspiring him just as soon as Zachariel left.

"That's excellent." Zachariel wrote that down on his scroll. "Anything else?"

"No, that's it; that was my primary focus this week."

"Where in Rome will you inspire him to build this basilica?"

"Um . . . a hill."

"Which hill might that be?"

How am I supposed to know the name of every blasted hill in Rome? Uriel thought.

"The Celian Hill," Uriel said and hoped he hadn't confused it with someplace else.

"Ah, the Celian Hill. I see where you are going with this; it's really brilliant and probably your best idea in a long time."

Uriel was glad Zachariel knew where he was going with it because he had no idea.

"It was such a lovely sentiment to build it over the homes of John and Paul, who were martyred."

Who are John and Paul? Does he mean John and Paul of the Bible? Why are there so many Johns and Pauls in this blasted world. I have to stop thinking that word; it isn't proper, Uriel thought.

Michael and Gabriel flew back, but they were without the scepter. Neither one wanted to make eye contact with Zachariel.

"You tell him," Gabriel whispered.

"No, I think you should tell him; it's your fault," Michael whispered.

Zachariel rolled up his scroll and looked at the two of them.

"Where is my scepter?"

"It's been confiscated," Michael said.

"Who confiscated it and why?"

"The Presence of God," Gabriel said.

Zachariel scowled. His lovely forehead crinkled up, and for once he looked tired. Had it been anyone else who had confiscated

31

his scepter, he could have asked for it back, but you didn't ask the Presence of God for something back. That scepter was given to him at the beginning of time, and he had never lost it.

"Why did the Presence of God take my scepter?"

"We were shooting light from the orb, and the Presence of God must have noticed it because he appeared before us and asked if he could have the scepter. He must have thought it was pretty," Michael said.

"So let me get this straight. The Presence of God, the being who speaks for God and is God, made an appearance just so he can have my scepter? He is the Presence of God; he can make a thousand scepters that shoot light if he wanted to. He could make a scepter that shoots out rainbows or fire or frogs, for that matter."

"Do you want us to ask for it back?" Michael asked.

Zachariel snapped his fingers and vanished.

"I think he may have left to go get approval to say a really bad word," Gabriel said.

"Hush. I have a plan," Uriel said.

"So what is the plan and will we be using our swords?" Michael asked.

"We need to send a message to those men, and I don't think you will need your swords."

Uriel saw the look of disappointment on Michael's and Gabriel's faces. They had not used their swords since the great battle where they cast Lucifer and the other rebels out of heaven. Uriel remembered that glorious day and how Michael wouldn't give him a sword because he was not properly trained with one. He did however get a white horse, which he sat on regally, even though he couldn't get it to gallop or do anything else he instructed it to do. Things could have easily gone a different way, but Azazel tripping and falling on his own armor because it was too large for him was really the beginning of a long line of mistakes.

"Okay, you can bring them just in case."

"How shall we send them a message? Can we do a burning bush?" Gabriel asked.

"No, that's been done already. We want to be more creative," Uriel said.

"How about a burning tree?" Michael asked.

"We might start a forest fire," Uriel said.

Gabriel pondered what else they could possibly set ablaze.

"We could go as an animal. Talking animals are always impressive," Uriel said, thinking of the cherubim.

"We could go as an ass," Michael said, and he and Gabriel laughed. They could say the word "ass" as long as they were referring to a donkey. It was one of those loopholes that they childishly enjoyed.

They might be as old as time, but they are probably the most immature beings I've ever met, Uriel thought.

"How are we going to get permission to leave and visit earth?" Michael asked.

"We will get permission from Vehuaiah."

"Wait, we don't have any chocolate yet to bribe him with," Michael said.

"We will just have to go this time without it. Does anyone know where Vehuaiah is this time of day?"

"He's probably observing Japan. He's fascinated with their architecture and culture," Gabriel said.

"No, you're thinking of Samael," Michael said.

"Is that why he's always wearing a kimono?" Uriel asked.

"Is that what that is? I always thought he was wearing a dress," Michael said.

"Isn't that what we are wearing?" Gabriel asked.

"These are robes."

Michael closed his eyes and focused on Vehuaiah. Then he snapped his fingers. They looked around and there was Vehuaiah, weighing his vast supply of chocolate on a scale.

"Greetings, Vehuaiah," Michael said.

Vehuaiah, who had not heard them arrive, was startled by Michael's voice. He was annoyed at being disturbed, but greeted them anyway.

"Holy, holy, holy is the Lord of hosts; the whole earth full of his glory," he sang.

Uriel waved his hand. "Yes, yes, holy, glory and what not."

"What doth thou want?" Vehuaiah asked with as much dignity as he could muster.

"Doth wants . . . I mean, we want your permission to visit earth," Uriel said.

"What business do you have on earth?"

"Vanity," Gabriel said.

Vehuaiah raised an eyebrow and scratched one of his six wings.

"Gabriel is making a jest. We need some men to help us with a task."

"Would He approve of your task?"

Uriel had no need to ask who *He* was and had an inner monologue with himself that went something like this: *I don't want to lie to Vehuaiah, but I honestly don't know if God would approve or not. It is to preserve works inspired by Him so would he want them removed from the earth, lost to mankind forever? He does always stress the importance of free will. Maybe he would say it is their book as much as it is his, and they have a right to edit it any way they want. Is it really about preserving holy works, though, or is it just because I don't want my name and my great deeds forgotten? I was responsible for warning Noah of the Great Flood in the Book of Enoch. I condemned Azazel and passed judgment on him as one of the fallen angels. I rescued John the Baptist from the massacre of the innocents. I carried John and his mother to the holy family after their flight from Egypt. I was sent to instruct Ezra.*

"I'm still waiting for an answer."

"Wait, I'm not quite done yet."

"Done with what?"

Uriel ignored him and continued his inner monologue, *In the Apocalypse of Peter, I get to be one of the Angels of Repentance. I am listed as one of the angels who will rule at the end of time. I won't be celebrated in the feast day of the Synaxis.*

That last one did it.

"Yes, He most certainly would approve."

***

"Where are we going?" Simon asked.

Peter tugged on his white beard. He stood a head taller than the next tallest in the group, who was Adolfo. The seven men had decided to go to Perusal where Peter's sister had some land.

"At least we will be able to tend the crops and animals. It's a modest existence, though."

"I don't think the gargoyle likes farming; do you, ole stone face?" John asked Adolfo.

Adolfo grunted and bit into an apple.

"See, he hates it," John said.

"My back is killing me," Lorenzo said and rubbed his hunchback.

"Stop complaining or I will whack it with my spoon," Simon said, holding his cooking spoon and threatening Lorenzo with it.

Thomas ran a hand through his red hair and started to sing from the "Book of Psalms." "Your love is before my eyes; I walk guided by your faithfulness. I do not sit with deceivers, nor with hypocrites do I mingle."

"You skipped a few lines," Philip said.

"I'm singing the part I like; don't interrupt me."

"I hate the company of evildoers; with the wicked I do not sit. I will wash my hands in—"

Thomas broke off singing and pointed to what appeared to be a turtle with three heads. "What in the name of God is that?"

"Lucifer has sent one of his foul demons to possess this poor turtle," Simon said. "I'll take care of it."

Simon raised his cooking spoon as if he were Saint Michael himself, leading the charge against Lucifer and whacked the turtle on all three heads.

"Blasted," Uriel the turtle head said.

"You shut your filthy demon mouth," Simon said and hit him again.

All the turtle heads started to talk at once.

"Be quiet. I will do all the talking," Uriel said to the turtle heads of Michael and Gabriel.

"Let's not listen to any more of their blasphemy," Simon said. He began to walk off and the others followed.

"Wait, we must speak with you," Uriel the turtle head said.

The three-headed turtle started walking after them. They crept along so slowly that the men were almost out of earshot within a few steps.

"Can't you two move any faster?" Uriel asked.

"Maybe it wasn't a good idea to be a turtle. We should have been something that can move a little faster," Michael said.

Uriel yelled as loud as he could, "We are not demons; we are

35

the angels Uriel, Michael and Gabriel! We are like the trinity, you see, three persons in one being."

"Three turtle heads in one shell," Gabriel said.

The men kept right on walking and ignoring the turtle. Then Michael opened his mouth, and they stopped in their tracks.

"I am Saint Michael the Archangel; I lead the army of God against evil. I am the Defender of Faith and the Angel of Deliverance, and I command you to listen to me." It was said in a voice so powerful that it didn't even sound like it came from Michael. His words were delivered with a great gust of wind that chilled the men to their bones, and the earth shook beneath their feet.

"Where did you get that voice?" Gabriel asked.

"The Presence of God gave it to me in exchange for the scepter," Michael said.

"I don't remember him giving you that and I was with you," Gabriel said.

"He spoke to me in my mind. He said if I gave him the scepter, he would give me his voice for a little while," Michael said.

"Will you two be quiet," Uriel said.

The men were in awe and bowed before the three-headed turtle.

"You are in possession of some forbidden gospels, I believe," Uriel said.

Adolfo clutched the sack of books close to his chest.

"It's all right; we don't wish any harm to them. We have a divine mission for you. You must safeguard these books, as well as any other Gnostic Gospels you may encounter along your travels. They must endure until the time is right," Uriel said.

"What time would that be?" Peter asked.

"When the keepers of such books are no longer under the threat of heresy, and the books are safe for all to read," Uriel said.

"That could be forever," Philip said.

"Not forever, but it will be a long time, longer than the life of a normal mortal," Uriel said.

John had taken out some parchment and was sketching the turtle. He wasn't a bad artist, but he wasn't a great one like Adolfo.

"Be sure to make my head the most handsome," Gabriel said.

"So who will protect them after the last of us is dead?" Thomas asked.

"You let me worry about that. I don't think I can stop you from being killed, but I believe I can make sure you have long lives. You will be the next . . . what's the name of that man?"

"What man?" Gabriel asked.

"The one who lived a long time on earth," Uriel said.

"His name was Malakai," Gabriel said.

"Methuselah," Peter corrected. "Lorenzo and I feel as old as Methuselah already, and we certainly won't live as long as our younger companions."

"If the two of you should die before your companions, they can carry on concealing and protecting the gospels themselves."

"Can't we just bury them in some place where they will never be found until the time that you mentioned arrives?" Lorenzo asked.

Uriel tried to look at the other two turtle heads for guidance, but he couldn't turn his head that far. It sounded like a very logical and rational question; but since Uriel never took either of those things into consideration, he wasn't about to start now. "I don't want to take the chance because it could be a very, very long time before the Church stops condemning them. In truth, I'm not sure when that time will be and you mortals have a knack for losing everything important to mankind," Uriel said.

"Can I get a new body?" Lorenzo asked.

"No, I'm afraid you will have to make do with the old ones."

"Unless you want to be a three-headed turtle," Michael said.

"They wouldn't be able to protect anything as a three-headed turtle," Gabriel said.

Peter, who was the unspoken leader of the group because he was the wisest and most patient of the bunch, stroked his wispy beard.

"I cannot speak for my companions, only myself, but I will do as you command."

"It would be my honor to serve our Lord," Philip said.

"I share the feelings of my brother," Thomas said.

"Will there be any wine involved?" Lorenzo asked.

"Wine? I'm sure there will be loads of wine." Again, Uriel had no idea if this were true; thus far he had been making things up as he went along, and it seemed to be working well for him. He wanted to get all the men to help because the more people trying to protect the gospels, the more success they would have.

"It would be a privilege to help; I will whack anyone who tries to interfere with my spoon. What about you, John?" Simon asked.

John, who was still sketching the turtle, looked up. He accidentally made Uriel's head much bigger than the other two.

"Huh? Oh yes, I think it will be quite an adventure."

"What about the mute one?" Uriel asked.

Adolfo looked at the three-headed turtle and grunted.

"How are we to carry out this task? We were on my way to my sister's home, and we had planned to tend crops and raise cattle. I don't want to put my sister and her family in jeopardy if someone were to discover the books," Peter said.

"Where do we go?" Philip asked.

"You will journey to the Paromeos Monastery in Scetis. There you will become monks and live a spiritual life."

"Don't forget to protect the gospels, though," Michael added.

"Are their gospels in Scetis?" Philip asked.

"How should I know?" Uriel asked.

"Scetis is in Egypt in the desert," Thomas said.

"This plan seems difficult and full of missteps. I have so many questions. Why did you choose us? How long do we remain in Egypt? What happens if we die or the gospels are discovered?"

"Those are all good questions and I will answer them in good time," Uriel said.

Uriel made a note to himself to figure out the answers. His list of things to do and figure out was starting to grow long.

"What if the monks of Paromeos won't allow us to live among them?" John asked.

"Don't worry; they are good monks. They will take you in. We must leave you now and return to the heavens. We will watch over you and meet again from time to time when necessary."

"Can we receive a blessing before you leave?" Lorenzo asked.

"May the blessing of almighty God, the Father, the Son and the Holy Spirit descend upon you and remain with you forever," Uriel said.

Each man made the sign of the cross and then headed north to start their long journey toward Egypt.

"That went rather well," Michael boomed, using the Presence of God's voice, which shook the ground again and made a squirrel topple out of a tree, along with all its nuts.

Gabriel giggled. "Did you see the look on their faces when you spoke? I thought the one with the irritable bowels was going to have an accident."

"Enough of that; that voice is only used in case of emergencies and not for jest," Uriel said.

"Let's get out of here; this turtle shell is becoming uncomfortable," Gabriel said.

Michael was about to snap his fingers, but remembered they didn't have any hands.

"We might have a problem."

Blue Men and Cold Soup

Paromeos Monastery in Scetis, Egypt was surrounded by desert in the Nitrian Valley. It was founded by Marcarius the Great, and the monastery's name meant *that of the Romans*. The mighty Romans had conquered lands far and wide, and their great empire seemed it would last an eternity.

It was 402 AD, almost five years since the heretic monks had left Italy. They had settled into monastic life with a quiet ease. The archangels had been right; the monks took them in with no questions asked. They weren't allowed to bring in any possessions so they had to bury the bag filled with the forbidden gospels in a limestone cave, a couple of kilometers outside the monastery, where they checked on it from time to time. They had been excommunicated and weren't allowed to receive the Eucharist or to even set foot in a church, let alone be monks in a monastery; but they were in Egypt over 2,000 kilometers away and out of the watchful eye of Rome.

The monks at Paromeos were hermits and lived such a reclusive existence that no one ever took notice of them. They also spoke rarely, which suited the silent Adolfo, but proved difficult for the garrulous John. They had not heard from the archangels since that fateful day so it almost seemed like a dream. They figured it was best to stay put until they received further words from the angels. They didn't know if there were now any other Gnostic Gospels in existence, or where they might be, but at least the ones they'd brought with them were safe and sound.

A plague had swept through the year before, drastically reducing the number of monks so that allowed for the survivors to assume a higher rank. Brother Peter, whom everyone looked up to for his great wisdom, was appointed to Claustral Prior, which was second in command to the Abbot; and Simon, who was known for his piety and for his willingness to bang a brother on the head with a spoon when required, was made a Dean. As Dean, he was the head of the cathedral chapter.

Adolfo, John, Philip, Thomas and Lorenzo were content to just be monks. Lorenzo had learned a great deal about wine from a monk who looked even older than he and could often be seen in the small vineyard tending to the grapes. His bowels had only grown worse over the years and he could often be seen running to the privy.

Philip and Thomas proved to be great healers and were invaluable during the time of the plague so they primarily worked in the hospital. Since John was a Scribe and becoming a halfway decent artist, he was put in the Scriptorium. Besides Adolfo's skill at being irascible, he had a great talent for drawing and painting so he was also put in the Scriptorium to make beautiful illustrations on prayer booklets. There he could frown and grunt as much as he liked.

All the monks were content with their lives at the monastery and almost wished their encounter with the angels had been a dream.

The monks lived austere lives with few possessions or luxuries; the only affectation could be found in the church dedicated to the Virgin Mary where Peter was currently praying the rosary. The candlesticks, as well as the chalice, were gold and the altar was made of marble, gold and silver with various gems. Hanging above the altar was a large gold crucifix. There were numerous silver lamps gilded with copper. The most valued possession, though, at least to the monks, were the relics of St. Moses the Black under the altar.

Moses the Black was a slave of a government official in Egypt who had dismissed him for theft. After that, he had become the leader of a gang of robbers and thieves. Following one robbery, he had hidden from the authorities by taking shelter with the monks of Paromeos. He then gave up his old way of life and became a great spiritual leader. He was later ordained a priest. A group of outlaws attacked the monastery and Moses choose to be martyred, rather than fight or run away. He had become a great apostle for non-violence.

"Hail, Mary, full of grace, the lord is with thee; blessed art thou among—"

John burst open the church doors. He stopped in front of Peter;

41

he was out of breath from running.

"We are under attack," John managed to say in between gasps of air.

Peter calmly put his rosary down, stood up and cleared his throat because he had not spoken in a while.

"Who is attacking us?"

"The Berbers are upon us, and there was not even an alarm raised as to their coming so I can only assume they are killing everyone in their path. We must leave now and head for the cave before it's too late."

"It's probably the Blue Men, the Tuareg warriors. Where are the others?"

"I don't know, hopefully some place safe," John said.

"We must save the relics of St. Moses," Peter said.

John was going to protest, but the older man was already walking towards the altar.

They were just about to leave when a man entered the church. He was wearing a blue robe with an indigo veil. He shouted something in an Amazight or a Berber dialect that the monks didn't understand, although they didn't really need to understand what he was saying because in his right hand he was carrying a club.

"Get out the side door quick. We will make our way through the keep and outside," John said.

John headed toward the door to the keep, Peter following close behind still stubbornly clutching the relics. The Blue Man was swift and he was gaining on them. Another Blue Man entered the church from the keep door. They were trapped. John stepped in front of Peter with his arms out in an attempt to shield him from the blows which were about to rain down upon them.

***

Just outside the Church of the Virgin mother, Adolfo, Philip, Thomas and Lorenzo were running for their lives. There were six Blue Men carrying spears hot on their heels.

"One of us has to get to the cave. We need to split off; Philip and Thomas, come with me to the Church of St. Michael and we will lose them in the crypts. Adolfo, you're the quickest; you try and get to the cave. When we split, hopefully all the Tuaregs will follow us," Lorenzo said breathlessly.

Adolfo, the mute monk, broke off from the group, running as hard as he could, his face hardened, determined to make it to the cave. The rest of the monks stayed on course towards the church. The Blue Men paused but only for a second and decided to split the group in half, so three followed Adolfo and three followed the others. The odds were now even for Lorenzo, Philip and Thomas, but three-to-one against Adolfo.

"That didn't go as I had hoped," Lorenzo said. He was in a lot of pain, and his humpback was really slowing him down because he was more sidestepping than running. He knew it was slowing down Philip and Thomas, so he made a quick decision. If he turned around and faced the men, he could give Philip and Thomas a chance at getting away. He remembered the strange archangels and hoped somehow they could protect him and the others from death.

"Keep running, don't you dare stop."

Philip and Thomas were starting to lose steam; they weren't used to running and didn't have the stamina. The Blue Men showed no sign of fatigue; they stopped and looked at the hunchback. It appeared as if they were debating about whether or not they should even bother killing an old man with a hunchback. They did not have the same dilemma about Philip and Thomas, so they launched their spears. The spears hurdled through the air on a straight trajectory towards Philip and Thomas.

***

In the refractory Simon was sitting down to have his communion meal.

"Humble our hearts, oh Lord and make us thankful for these and all of our blessings. In Christ's name. Amen," Simon prayed. He was alone; the other monks had already had their communion meal, but Simon had stayed behind to pray. The soup was cold, but he didn't mind. As the cook, he usually was the first to sample his own labors and would be making a fresh pot tomorrow. He heard shouting going on outside. Some of the voices were those of other monks, but there were also some very strange and unfamiliar ones. He stood up and instinctively grabbed his spoon. He would face whatever this was head-on. He didn't have long to wait, as a man dressed in a blue robe and indigo veil burst in the room. He was carrying a large club, which would certainly do much more damage than Simon's spoon. Still, he didn't have any other weapons, and there was no other way out of the refractory. He stood his ground; he wasn't afraid of death.

Saint Peter the Gatekeeper

"This is disastrous," Uriel said as he leaned on one of the twelve white gates of St. Peter. The archangels were lucky that Vehuaiah had been watching them in the Looking Pool and brought them back. Otherwise, they would have remained on earth as a three-headed turtle until death; and, given the lifespan of a turtle, that could have been for another eighty years. Uriel could not resist the sweet smell of the chocolate; when Vehuaiah wasn't looking, he grabbed fistfuls of bars and shoved them inside his robe.

Uriel listened to the harp-playing with a frown. A harp was always playing. They rotated seraphim in shifts to play the harp since they were the ones with all the musical talent. They continually played and were supposed to be entertainment for the souls waiting to get into heaven. Most of the souls didn't give a fig about the harp-playing; they were too concerned about getting sent to hell. The archangels normally enjoyed the melodies played on the harp, but unfortunately a seraph named Raziel was playing, and he was one of a few seraphs whose playing left much to be desired.

"They will be here soon and it will all work out," Gabriel said.

"I thought I told you to put them some place safe. Didn't Vehuaiah tell you the Berbers were going to attack the monastery and kill the majority of the monks and make off with all its treasures?" Uriel asked.

"I forgot to ask him. I picked the place because it was in Egypt far away from Rome and because they had a church named after me," Michael said.

"Well, good job. They are all dead and I'll have to convince Vehuaiah to send them back, which won't be easy since they're now dead."

St. Peter was busy telling some poor soul about all of his sins. There are books kept on each living mortal; and when one dies, an

45

angel is sent to fetch that book and bring it to St. Peter so he could pass judgment. Peter controlled all the keys to the kingdom of heaven.

He's very smug for someone who thrice denied Jesus; I never denied him once, let alone thrice and I don't get to have the keys, Uriel thought.

It wasn't long before they began to hear a commotion. It seemed that someone in the line of souls was creating a ruckus.

"What's going on back there? Do you know where you are? You are at the gates of heaven, so show some respect and conduct yourself accordingly," St. Peter said.

Whoever was causing the disturbance paid no heed because the shouting only got louder.

Uriel, Michael and Gabriel went down the line to investigate. Uriel looked at all the faces as he passed; some were forlorn, others happy, but most were frightened. He felt sorry for them, living a mortal life, trying to please God and then dying and having to wait in anticipation to see if they could walk through the gates or be cast down in an eternal pit of fire. Uriel had never visited hell, but heard it described in great detail by Virgil, the true author of "Revelation."

We will have to rename it the Apocalypse of Virgil, Uriel thought.

They reached the epicenter of all the turmoil. A man was shouting and pointing at another man and yelling, "He bit me!" Then he pointed at another man and said, "And he hit me with a spoon."

"No need to wonder any further about the whereabouts of the monks," Gabriel said.

"This isn't good, behaving like this in front of St. Peter and the gates of heaven while awaiting judgment. They are not helping their cause by biting and hitting. Where in blazes did Simon get a spoon anyway? You can't take possessions with you to heaven. I'm fairly sure that is written in the Bible somewhere, as well as being a firm rule in heaven," Uriel said.

"I think it's in the book of Matthew. Sell your possessions while you're on earth so you will get treasure in heaven," Michael said.

"What treasure? I've been here since the beginning of time

and have never gotten a treasure," Uriel said.

Gabriel bent down to pick something up. It was a pearl; it must have fallen off the heavenly gate.

"Here you go, your first treasure."

Uriel smiled and ran his fingers over the luminescent pearl.

"What was all that business about a rich man and camels getting into heaven?" Gabriel asked.

"I didn't think we allowed camels into heaven," Uriel said.

"We really need to brush up on our Bible; it's unseemly for archangels not to know the Bible front to back," Michael said.

"Yes, but which Bible—the shortened canonical version that humans pulled out of the air or all the gospels that include all of God's inspired works?"

"Well, either really," Michael said.

"You seven need to follow us," Uriel said, pointing to the monks.

"Who are you and what business do you have with us?" Simon asked.

"We are the archangels Uriel, Gabriel and Michael . . . you know, the three-headed turtle," Uriel said.

"Well, you certainly have a lot of explaining to do. You said we would live long lives.

Why did you let us get our heads bashed in by a bunch of men in blue dresses?" John asked.

"I didn't know that any of this was going to happen, and I can't shield you from bodily harm. As for the head-bashing-in thing, you can blame this one for that," Uriel said, pointing to Michael.

"Why is it so cloudy and foggy here? I can barely see a hand in front of my face," Lorenzo said.

"God likes clouds, that's why," Michael said.

"Now come along, we have to go see the Seraph Vehuaiah. We need to send you back at once," Uriel said.

"Why do we have to go back? I want to stay here; I don't want to go back down there. It's hard down there; you never know when someone is going to attack you with clubs and spears," Philip said.

"You have to go back; you haven't completed your task. The books are still down there in the cave, and they could fall into the wrong hands," Uriel said.

"We never found out any other Gnostic Gospels," Simon said.

"We never really looked," Thomas said under his breath.

"Never mind that now. Our first priority is protecting the books we do have," Uriel said.

The monks followed Uriel and the other archangels. They heard someone yell from behind them, "Hey, why are they getting to move ahead in line?"

Michael drew out his sword and puffed out his chest.

"If you must know, they are on a special holy mission; and if I were you, I'd be much more worried about your mortal soul. We know all about the time you copulated with another man's wife." Michael had no idea who the man was or if he had copulated with another man's wife; but from his experience, it turned out to be true more times than not, and from the look of terror on the man's face, he had judged right.

It would not be so easy with St. Peter, though. They reached the gate and tried to pass through unnoticed.

"What is going on? You can't take them back there. I haven't even gone over their list of sins yet." St. Peter might not be an angel, but as an apostle and the very first pope, he had special favor with God and wasn't to be brushed aside so easily.

His beard could use a good trim, Uriel thought.

"It is important that we take these men to see Vehuaiah right away. They are on a special holy mission," Gabriel said.

"No one gets beyond those gates without my reviewing their sins."

"They are monks, for seraphim' sake, holy men; surely they automatically qualify," Uriel said.

"Hey listen, I've had enough monks pass this way to know that they are just as capable of sin as anyone, and I've even had to send some to *you-know-where*."

Uriel almost chuckled at St. Peter's squeamishness to say the word *hell*. He was afraid to say it, as if Lucifer himself might appear and drag him down there in the deepest, darkest, most desolate part of hell.

"All right, fine, get their books, but make it quick or I'll have to tell Vehuaiah that you detained us."

The angel Cassiel sighed. He was the one in charge of retrieving all the books. He looked as though he could go to sleep and sleep for 1,000 years.

48

"What are your names?"

Peter the monk spoke for the group. "We are Peter, John, Philip, Adolfo, Thomas, Lorenzo and Simon of Hadria."

"I'll need you to be more specific with John, Thomas and Simon," Cassiel said.

"John, son of David of Hadria, monk of Paromeos; Thomas, son of Cladius of Hadria, monk of Paromeos; and Simon, son of Alfonso of Hadria, monk of Paromeos," Peter said.

"That should do it." Cassiel flew off to what the angels called the Sin Den. It contained every book on every human being, all the way back to Adam himself. When Cassiel returned, you couldn't even see his face; the books were stacked so high, he was straining underneath the burden. He sat them down and gave St. Peter the one that was on top, which belonged to Thomas.

St. Peter licked his finger and turned the page. He read out loud to himself, but he was mumbling and the group could only catch snatches of phrases like "dancing naked in the moonlight and lied to parents . . . missed a mass." St. Peter flipped through some other pages and looked up. "This one may pass."

A very relieved Thomas opened the gate and went through.

St. Peter did the same for the rest of them, occasionally mumbling transgressions. He was down to Adolfo and hardly even looked down before he declared, "This one most certainly may not pass." He closed the book to indicate that was the definitive word on the matter.

"What did he do?" Uriel asked.

"What didn't he do? There's murder, adultery, blasphemy, theft and one I don't even think we have a name for."

"Blasphemy? He doesn't even talk; how can he commit blasphemy?"

Adolfo grunted as if to back up the claim.

"The book is never wrong."

Uriel snatched the book right out of St. Peter's hand. He opened the front page titled "Alfonso of Hadria, son of Daniel." He slammed the book closed.

"You've got the wrong book. This is *Adolfo* of Hadria, not *Alfonso*."

St. Peter looked at the book, then looked at John and then at the archangels suspiciously.

"Very well, Cassiel, go get the book," St. Peter said without even acknowledging the mistake.

I wonder how often that happens and how many poor souls he has mistakenly sent to hell? How many souls are in heaven that should be in hell for that matter? There could be murderers and fornicators among us and we'd never know it, Uriel thought.

St. Peter, as if he could read Uriel's thoughts, said, "I do not make mistakes."

I certainly wouldn't trust my immortal soul to him. I'd demand a second opinion from someone who is not so senile.

Cassiel brought St. Peter the book, presumably the right one this time. Peter looked down at the book and up at John a couple of times, sometimes raising an eyebrow.

"What a strange boy."

"Can he pass or not? The last time I checked, being strange wasn't a sin; and if it were, we'd have to cast out half the lot of angels in heaven."

"He may pass," St. Peter said with a wave of his hand.

John and Uriel passed through the gate where the others were waiting on the other side.

"Now we must go see Vehuaiah and convince him to send them back," Uriel said.

"We just got here. I'd like to see my father and drink in all the beauty of heaven. I'd like to talk to God," Lorenzo said. "We don't have time for any of you to find family members; we have to act quickly. You must retrieve the gospels and safeguard them until the time is right, and no, you may not speak to God. No one speaks directly to God; you must speak to the Angel of Presence who is the voice of God. When he says something, it's the same as God saying it. He is the Angel of Presence, Voice of God, Presence of God, the Metatron, the Face of God . . . he is known by many names. An angel named Sandalphon demanded to speak directly to God once and would not take no for an answer. The Presence of God finally relented and let him speak to God, or himself rather, however you want to look at it and Sandalphon was never seen or heard from again, and that was 10,000 years ago."

"I remember Sandalphon; he was a good angel, just extremely curious and always craving answers," Michael said.

"What do you think happen to him?" John asked.

"There is a lot of speculation, but presumably the moment he looked upon God, his face melted off and he turned to ash," Gabriel said.

"That's terrible," Philip said.

"I heard God sent him to limbo," Michael said.

"I don't think so or Virgil would have told us about it. We are wasting time with all this talk," Uriel said.

"You know, Vehuaiah is really tough and unyielding. Don't you think you might have better luck with the Seraph Azrael or even Samael?" Gabriel asked.

"You know, you might be on to something. Azrael is master of death and keeps a record of all the dead. We could try him first and, if he refuses, go to Samael. You are not so bad at thinking; you should try it more often."

Gabriel beamed as if Uriel were praising him and not insulting his intelligence.

The group went to find Azrael. Uriel could have snapped his fingers, but decided to walk so that the men could at least see a little bit of heaven. He thought the walk over would satisfy some of their curiosity.

"I can't believe we are walking on clouds," Thomas said.

"Look closer," Michal said.

Thomas did look closer and he could see they were walking on a path. The path was paved in gold.

"Is this real gold?"

"Of course it is, do you think God would make roads out of fool's gold?" Uriel said; but now that he thought about it, he didn't know for sure it was real gold because he had never examined it too closely but had just assumed God only made things of the highest quality.

The monks marveled as they passed the Palace of the Angels, made of white marble, of course, and saw the pillars with specks of gold and silver in them. Up ahead, a cherub was directly in their path. Their four heads were arguing with each other; it seemed there was a disagreement about where they wanted to go. The ophan that accompanied it kept rolling into the cherub, trying to get it to move. The face of the man looked down at the ophan, who kept bumping him.

"Stop that, or you'll find yourself short an eye."

The ophan blinked its eyes and ceased the bumping.

"I want to go to the St. Bede's Library," the head of the lion said as it was trying to make the body move in that direction.

"I want to go to the Looking Pool," the head of the ox said.

Cherubim had the body of a lion and the feet of the ox, so it took both of them in order to make them move. If neither were willing to cooperate, it could stand there forever.

"I want to have an ox head for supper. I've never had ox, but I bet it's tasty," the lion said.

"We'd better go around them; they could be there a while," Michael said.

The men had not said a peep; they were too busy gaping at the Cherub and the wheel with a hundred eyes. The closest thing to a cherub they had seen was the three-headed turtle of Uriel, Michael and Gabriel.

"Hullo," Gabriel shouted at the cherub and grinned just like it were any other day in the life of an angel.

The ophan and the cherub did not return the hullo; they just looked at the group and then the two heads began to argue again.

They found Azrael; he was busy jotting names down in the *Liber Mortuorum* or *Book of the Dead*. St. Peter kept a record of the sins of everyone who had ever existed, living or dead, but Azrael wrote down just the names of the deceased. It was a large book that floated in midair and always remained open. It would remain open until the end of time. It also could not be moved; you couldn't borrow it for a little light reading. The problem with the *Liber Mortuorum* was that once the names had been written, they couldn't be unwritten. Uriel hoped he had reached Azrael in time before he had a chance to write down the names of the monks.

"Hullo, Azrael," Uriel said.

"Hullo ah . . . oh my, who have we got here?" Azrael asked. He was the only seraph they knew of who didn't sing, "Holy, holy, holy is the lord of hosts; the whole earth full of his glory." He also spoke plainly which Uriel liked.

Azrael looked highly amused. He loved it when there was a bending of the rules. He was a renegade in that regard, not the Lucifer kind of renegade mind you, but he liked to stir the pot. Azrael was the complete opposite of Vehuaiah, who was a stickler for the rules. Uriel was now convinced they had come to the right angel.

"These men are recently deceased and I wanted to see if you had already written down their names."

"When did they die?"

"They died today."

"No, I'm a week behind; we've had so many names of late because of the plague so I can say with certainty that I have not."

Uriel clapped his hands together, very pleased. Gabriel and Michael also clapped their hands, but they were unsure of why they were doing so, other than Uriel looked happy for once.

"I would like for you not to write down their names," Uriel said.

"Well, as I said, I'm a week behind so if you need some extra time, you'd have a few days."

"No, you don't understand. I don't want you to write down their names at all."

"You mean ever?"

"Not ever, just a couple of centuries until people become more reasonable about things and more enlightened."

"Reasonable and enlightened about what things? Do you mean that—what's that phenomenon called—oh, electricity is discovered?"

"What's electricity?"

"Never mind, you've probably never been told about it."

"Just wait in writing down the names until the mortals let people read the *Apocryphal,*" Michael said.

Uriel was annoyed at Michael for butting in because he was going to phrase it better. He didn't like the word "Apocryphal" because it meant the books were of dubious origins . . . and they certainly weren't. The monks were listening to the exchange and not fully comprehending it, and the same could be said for Michael and Gabriel too.

Azrael snickered. "You mean. the books that are all about your heroic exploits: Uriel the brave, Uriel the wise, Uriel who plays a prominent role in the end of time. You wouldn't be trying to preserve those books for that reason, would you? You know how God hates vanity and believes in free will."

"Well, it might be one reason," Uriel admitted. "I think it would be really sad and a great loss for mankind if they were to disappear entirely, never to be seen again."

"I agree with you."

"You do?" Uriel asked incredulously; he was used to getting more resistance.

"I will misplace their names for a few centuries, but when the time is right, I will have to write their names in the *Liber Mortuorum*."

"That's all I ask," Uriel said.

Azrael grinned. He would "misplace" the names for a few centuries and when the time was right, record them and just say it was an oversight. Oversights happened all the time; they called them oversights, but in reality some of them were pretty big foul-ups.

"Have you guys thought about the possibility that you are not the only ones with a desire for those books?"

"What do you mean?" Uriel asked.

"I mean whenever there is *good,* there is usually also *evil.* Have you checked to make sure there are no demons who may have a grudge against you? Anyone who may want to impede your quest or just cause trouble in general?"

"Why did you make those rabbit ears when you said 'good' and 'evil'?" Michael asked.

"They are called quotes and good and evil are subjective terms, open for interpretation. I'm simply referring to what others may call *good* and *evil*."

"I have no idea what you just said," Michael said.

"I haven't thought about it at all. You might be right; they did find themselves in a spot of trouble, what with being killed by Berbers and all. Maybe it was the work of a mischievous devil. I wouldn't put it past Azazel to want to destroy the books. After all, they don't reflect well on him, making him see more of a buffoon rather than a menacing devil."

"Don't forget that little matter of your passing the judgment on him that cast him out of heaven and into hell," Gabriel said.

"You're right; he may still be holding a grudge over that one," Uriel said.

"The Berber attack wasn't Azazel; it is a well-documented fact that the Berbers attacked many Christian monasteries and Paromeos was definitely one of them.

The monks had remained quiet throughout the exchange,

trusting the angels knew what they were talking about and how to proceed. If they had any inkling that Uriel was making it up as he went along, they may have felt differently and demanded their names be written down, in which case Uriel would have had to comply.

"If Azazel is trying to cause trouble, he wouldn't do it himself; he would send someone in his stead. He rarely goes down to earth," Uriel said.

"Probably because he so hideous-looking," Michael said, getting a laugh out of Gabriel, but no one else.

"None of them look attractive; they lost that privilege when they double-crossed God," Uriel said.

"If it is the case that Azazel has sent someone to earth, you had better send someone of your own. You will want to send a trustworthy and reliable angel," Azrael said.

"I don't think we know any trustworthy angels," Uriel said.

"I think Netzach is a good choice. I believe you have used him some before in the past, and he's always been completely reliable," Azrael said.

"Is he the one with the odd-looking wing?" Gabriel asked.

"Yes, but I wouldn't bring that up; he's very sensitive about it."

"All right, we shall use Netzach. Now we have to settle the business of where to put these monks where they will be safe and not recognized," Uriel said.

"They might be recognized if they returned to their home in Hadria, but surely no one in other parts of Italy would recognize them; it's been five years," Michael said.

"I'll let you take care of it then, but this time see to it that it is a place that won't be attacked by marauders."

"Also, they need to try and save more books. So far, we still only have the originals," Uriel said.

"I know just the place," Gabriel said.

Leper Island

The island of Lerina in Gaul was a Roman-controlled island surrounded by the *Mare Nostrum* which meant "Our Sea." The Romans were not shy in letting the rest of the world know what belonged to them. The sea was made up of different tints of azure, and the island was filled with pine and eucalyptus trees. The Cistercian Monastery of Lerins was well on its way in construction. It already had a cloister, refectory, scriptorium and chapter hall. The construction was led by a local hermit named Caprasius of Lerina and his followers, who were from all over the area but mainly Gaul, Rome and Brittany. With this diverse group, it was easy for the seven monks of Hadria to blend in and not stick out.

The monks retrieved the Gnostic Gospels from the limestone cave before the archangels sent them to the exotic paradise. The Berbers had not ventured into the cave; if they even noticed it at all, they were only interested in the treasures of Paromeos. Just like Paromeos, the monks were accepted there without any questions. They suspected it had something to do with the archangels and their powers of suggestion. This time the monks were not alone; Uriel had sent the angel Netzach to help safeguard the books and keep them out of trouble. He was disguised as a human using the name Tiberius. Peter doubted they would find any other Gnostic Gospels here on the small island of Lerina. Books were a rarity and the Gnostic Gospels were rarer still, since the Church had gathered all they could find and burned them. Peter was beginning to think that they may possess the only copies left.

The Cistercians were all about self-sufficiency and hard work so the monks were always busy. It was a very austere way of living, but they were never bored. They wore long white flowing robes that had to be washed regularly because they got dirty so easily.

Lorenzo had already created a vineyard; his first few batches of wine proved to be undrinkable, but he was determined to create the perfect wine. His study of viticulture was without rival on the island. His hunchback & his stomach continued to bother him. The other Cistercian monks got use to his flatulence during prayer, meals and at various other inopportune times. Lorenzo designed and built a wine storage room and smokehouse, which was necessary to help speed along the aging process. The clever Gaul monks built barrels in which to store the wine. Lorenzo spent hours working in his vineyard, and the sun had aged his face another ten years so some of the other younger monks took to calling him Methuselah. His white hair was reduced to two thin wisps on the side of his head.

John and Adolfo worked mainly in the scriptorium, but each monk was expected to do their fair share of manual labor so they couldn't spend as much time as they wanted there. John, the flamboyant and outspoken young monk, went through each day as happy as a lark, determined not to let the taciturn, bitter and gloomy Adolfo drag his spirits down. The other monks took to John like a moth to a flame and gave Adolfo a wide berth. Adolfo's illustrations were so exquisite that everyone talked about them, but no one talked directly to the vexed, brooding young man. John scribbled away, copying texts. His penmanship was also talked about because it was so aesthetically pleasing. He continued to draw and paint in his spare time.

Peter and Tiberius worked in the various gardens. They had a whole field where they just grew spelt, which was used to make bread. They grew artichokes, beets, radishes, cucumbers, cabbage and asparagus, as well as a variety of herbs. There was even an olive orchard. The monks had utilized a lot of what was already provided naturally by the island, but they had to plant apricot, plum, peach and fig trees. There was an abundance of eucalyptus trees so they could make plenty of eucalyptus oil. The smell of eucalyptus permeated the air with its sweet perfume. The sun aged Peter as well; his face and hands were rough and coarse like leather, but Tiberius remained ageless. He was untouched by the sun or any of the other elements; his skin remained as smooth as a baby's, and he had a rosy complexion. Peter loved working in the garden; he loved the feel of dirt in his hands. Tiberius hated working in the gardens; he hated his name and he hated work in general. He missed the daily gossip of his fellow angels, the pearly white gates of heaven and even the clouds. He would even put up with Uriel if it meant he didn't have to be a mortal on Earth anymore. He was there though because he was assigned a task, to try and keep the monks out of trouble.

All this trouble just to protect some silly books, he thought.

Simon was put in the kitchen; the fact that he always had his cooking spoon with him probably persuaded the abbot to assign him there. He was making beet soup and adding various spices to it that Peter had given him from the garden. He had to work outside sometimes milking the cows and helping to make repairs as they all did, but he spent most of his time in the kitchen where you could hear him singing.

"Thoroughly wash away my guilt, and from my sin cleanse me. For I know my transgressions; my sin is always before me. Against you, you alone I have sinned; I have done what is evil in your eyes so you are just in your word and without reproach in your judgment."

He liked to sing the Psalms; those were his favorite. He didn't know any secular songs, which is just as well, because the abbot would probably not like that. He had a nice singing voice, a low baritone.

Philip and Thomas were on St. Marguerite Island, the next island over. There was a leper colony established there, and Philip and Thomas helped treat the lepers and tried to ease their pain. They were the only ones willing to volunteer. It was a full-time job because more and more lepers were being sent there each month, some in worse shape than others. There was one particular leper named Marcel, who was from Lugdunum in Gaul, who they enjoyed talking to the most. He had been a gladiator before being struck down with leprosy. With the loss of his sensation and muscle weakness, he could no longer hold a weapon. Then the lesions appeared, along with labored breathing, the precursor to leprosy; and he was dismissed from the gladiators before he could make his fortune or be killed—they tended to have short life spans. It was just as well because the gladiator games no longer existed after Rome officially adopted Christianity, plus they were far too expensive. The Romans had lavish appetites when it came to everything, especially entertainment.

"What was it like fighting in the Colosseum?" Philip asked.

"He's told you that 1,000 times; stop making the poor man recount his battles just because your life is so boring," Thomas said.

"My life isn't boring and besides, you like hearing about it just as much as I do so don't pretend otherwise."

Thomas liked to give his brother a hard time. It was true he did very much enjoy the stories; they were a bright spot in their mostly mundane days at the Lazar house.

"I don't mind retelling the stories; it passes the time," Marcel said.

Thomas and Philip sat down by his bedside. Marcel was covered in bandages from head to toe, and all that could be seen were his milky white eyes.

"It stood in the very heart of Rome and it was so loud; the cheering was like the rumbling of thunder. When I close my eyes, I can still hear thousands of people yelling and clapping. I've never seen so many people in my life in one arena or anywhere for that matter. It was as if all the people in the world were there. Sometimes if they didn't like you, they would throw things at you. I went by the Roman name Retiarius because the name Marcel of Gaul would not go over well. We were entertainers first and foremost; we had to put on a good show. As electrifying as the crowds were, though, the violence that took place there was unspeakable."

Thomas and Philip looked disappointed; they wanted to hear about the unspeakable violence that took place in the arena. Marcel, sensing their disappointment, added, "I will tell you about it though, of course."

The monks brightened and leaned in closer to hear the story because Marcel's shortness of breath made him whisper sometimes.

"We were typically broken off in pairs and had to battle each other. The winner of the first fight would go on to fight the winner of the next fight and so forth until there was only one gladiator left, and he was deemed the winner. I won one such battle; it was down to me and a Roman called Servius. I had him pinned down; Servius called for mercy, but the crowd would have none of that. They turned their thumbs sideways, indicating that I should slash his throat. I had no choice but to do so."

Marcel went quiet and looked past the monks as if he were looking back in time, back to the arena. It was several minutes before he spoke again.

"Sometimes we put on an entire show reenacting famous battles from the Punic Wars or Macedonian Wars. Other times they brought in animals, mostly lions that had not eaten for several days. I saw one gladiator get eaten alive. They were—"

Marcel was interrupted by a leper who was calling for assistance.

"Brother Philip and I have to be getting back to our duties. I'd like to hear more about your adventures later, though."

"I'd like to hear about your adventures for a change," Marcel said.

"Oh, you would not believe the adventures we have had. One time—"

Philip interrupted Thomas with an elbow. "I'm afraid we haven't had many adventures."

Philip and Thomas rose and walked away from the bandaged leper.

"What was that elbow for?" Thomas asked.

"You were about to say something about our past. In case you have forgotten, we are on a divine mission to protect the Gnostic Gospels. This is supposed to be a secret; if it got out that we had the gospels, they would be removed and burned—not to mention the fact that we've died once already. What do you think people would think if they knew that fact? Surely, they would think it was an evil act of Lucifer; and we'd find ourselves on trial, a trial that could only end with one possible outcome, and that is our deaths. Besides, the archangels have taken great care to place us somewhere safe."

"I don't know how much care they've really put into it; remember what happened to us last time? I was beaten with a club and gored by a spear," Thomas said, lifting up his robe to show his wound.

"Put your robe down before someone sees you. I think they made a wise choice this time. This is a fairly remote island, hardly worth invading. We are just poor monks living off the land," Philip said, trying to run a hand through his raven black hair; only it was tangled and his fingers kept getting stuck.

"I don't see what harm it could do to reveal a little bit to Marcel when he's bared his soul to us. Besides, what can he do? He's dying. Everyone here is dying. We don't need to worry about clubs or spears here."

Philip helped one of the lepers into a chair, and Thomas changed the bandages on another. They didn't mind so much; the hard part was watching them die. There were men, women and children who came from all over. They were plucked from their homes and placed on this island to ensure quarantine. The expenses to maintain the Lazar house and its inhabitants were paid for by the monks of the Cistercian Monastery; and, in exchange, the lepers had to be converted to Christianity. Most were already Christians and some converted happily, grateful for the care; but a few, like Marcel, refused to be converted. He was an unapologetic pagan, which presented a problem for Philip and Thomas because any practice of paganism was forbidden. Not that he was practicing paganism or anything else—the man could barely get around—but this was a matter of the soul. Philip and Thomas liked Marcel very much and did not want to see him removed from the island so they kept his paganism a secret. It seemed like a harmless lie, and he would probably die soon anyway. Besides, where else would he go? The thing Thomas and Philip felt bad about more than the lie was the fact they knew for sure there was a heaven and were afraid that Marcel might not get to go there.

"What do you think God's rule is on paganism?" Thomas asked.

"He probably doesn't care for them much; they worship false gods," Philip said.

"Yes, but he loves all of his creations, including pagans."

"That's true, but he loves the people he sends to hell; and yet he still sends them there anyway," Philip said.

"Really, he doesn't send them there, though; Saint Peter does and he's a cranky old man."

"God trusts him to handle it so we should too," Philip said.

"Marcel is good; God can't possibly send him to hell. Maybe at the very least, he could send him to limbo and Virgil can keep him company," Thomas said.

"Yes, but he's murdered many people. They don't allow murderers into heaven."

"It wasn't his fault; he would have been killed if he had not. Besides, he was a slave; it wasn't his choice to fight."

"Maybe we should try one last time to get him to convert," Philip said.

Philip and Thomas walked over to the mummy who was propped up in bed.

"Marcel, we feel we must implore you one last time to convert. We are worried about your immortal soul," Thomas said.

Marcel closed his eyes and for a minute the monks thought he had drifted off to sleep, but then he laughed. It was a wheezy laugh, and he started coughing afterwards. Thomas gave him some water. When he finally stopped coughing, he said, "I tell you what; I'll convert on one condition."

Thomas and Philip got excited; they had achieved their goal.

"What's the condition?" Philip asked.

"I did go to a Christian mass once. I'll never forget the priest said, 'But you will exceed all of them, for you will sacrifice the man that clothes me. Already your horn has been raised . . .' I left before he finished. I would very much like to read the rest of the passages from that gospel."

Philip opened his mouth as if to say something and then shut it again. Thomas shuffled his feet, unsure of what to say. They both knew the passage very well and where it came from. It was from the Apocrypha from the Book of Judas.

***

"How are things going with your monk friends?" Azrael asked while writing the names of the dead in the *Liber Mortuorum*.

You would think he would grow weary of writing names down in that book eon after eon, Uriel thought.

"They seem to be doing well; they lead very dull lives if you want to know the truth."

"Did they find any more of the other gospels?"

"No, unfortunately not. I've had Michael and Gabriel looking for others who possess any of the other books, but they've had no luck." He looked over at Michael and Gabriel who were busy practicing with their swords. "Probably because they are too busy waiting on another uprising."

"They do indeed seem ready for another great battle," Azrael said.

"It's ironic that two simpletons like them are the most well-known and respected of the angels by mankind."

"I think someone is jealous."

"Certainly not. Okay, maybe a little, but only because I've done some great deeds too."

"Yes, and we know all about them. I've read the Gnostic Gospels many times. We have lots of copies of them in St. Bede's Library. You know, you can go there and read them as much as you want, anytime you want. You don't have to mess about with these mortals. You don't really care what they think, do you?" Azrael said, plucking a rogue feather from one of his six wings.

"I do care what they think because they are the only ones who appreciate it. No one here cares about such things."

Michael snuck up behind Uriel and said, "Someone is a sourpuss." It startled Uriel and made him jump because he used God's voice. Gabriel laughed at his sidekick's joke. The ground shook, and Azrael nearly knocked over his bottle of ink.

"He hasn't asked for his voice back yet?" Uriel asked.

"No, I guess he is still having fun with Zachariel's scepter."

Just as Michael said his name, Zachariel himself appeared as if he had been summoned. He pointed at Michael and said, "You damn fool," then snapped his fingers and vanished.

"I told you he was getting permission to call you something bad. He must have been standing in line a long time to get approval," Gabriel said.

There had in fact been a long line, and Zachariel had not been the only one waiting there to get permission to use strong language against Michael. Others were in line to get permission to use strong language against Gabriel and Uriel as well.

"You know, we haven't had a meeting about what kind of artistic endeavors I was inspiring in mankind since that day. It's probably because he was standing in line that whole time."

"You know, I saw Virgil yesterday and he told me a bit of news that might interest you," Azrael said.

"What did that plagiarist say? Did he reveal that he also wrote the entire New Testament as well as the Apocalypse of John?"

"He said that Baal has been sent to Earth."

"Baal the Wicked, Baal the Malevolent, Baal the Corrupt . . . that Baal?" Uriel asked.

"You forgot Baal the Cruel and Baal Who Dances," Michael said.

"Baal Who Dances? I didn't know he liked to dance," Gabriel said.

"He doesn't; I have no idea why they call him that. Demons have a funny sense of humor."

"Who sent him and why?" Uriel asked.

"He wasn't sure; they don't have time to gossip there as much as they do here. I guess they have their hands full with torturing souls day in and day out. He did say that Baal left shortly after talking to Azazel."

At the mention of Azazel's name, Uriel grimaced and wrinkled his forehead. He was the one who passed judgment on Azazel that condemned him to hell for eternity. Azazel would not rest until he'd taken revenge on Uriel. He knew this for a fact because after he passed sentence on Azazel, he actually said, "I will not rest until I have my revenge on you." He was slightly afraid of Azazel because he was a seraph before being cast out and he still wielded a lot of power."

That's been eons ago; surely he's not still mad about that little minor incident. Besides, he had condemned himself by taking part in the rebellion against God, Uriel thought.

"We don't know if it were Azazel who sent him or even if he did, what the reason was," Uriel said.

"He could have just sent him down to fetch some chocolates," Michael said.

"They aren't allowed to have chocolate in hell," Gabriel said.

"We can make it here; we are just not allowed to indulge in it. There's a big difference; moderation is fine, but gluttony is a sin," Azrael said.

"Tell that to Vehuiah," Gabriel said. "He has more chocolate than any other angel in heaven."

"We are always walking a fine line here in heaven between good and evil. It's enough to make an angel worry himself sick over it," Michael said.

"My point is, you don't know why he is there or who sent him, but it would be prudent to keep an eye on your monks and tell them—"

Azrael was interrupted by three seraphim who were singing "Holy, holy, holy is the lord of hosts; the whole earth full of his glory."

Azrael was the only one who didn't bother singing it. One of them sang it two more times before passing them by.

"I don't know why all the seraphim don't get together and form a chorus. As I was saying, you need to tell your monks to be vigilant. Baal is cunning and if he is after the books, he will try everything he can to get them."

"Well, that is exactly why I sent Netzach to watch over them. Don't worry; everything will turn out well," Uriel said.

"That's what you said about the dinosaurs," Michael said.

"Well, how was I supposed to know that the Angel of Dominion Hayyel had messed up their design. They weren't supposed to be that big. There was no way that they could exist with man, so God had to wipe them out."

"It's too bad because they were fun to watch. I especially liked the really ferocious one with tiny hands," Gabriel said.

Azrael listened to this exchange and shook his head. "Netzach will have to be careful; angels aren't as devious as demons, and Baal has one of the most devious minds around."

That's what he thinks; I can be as devious as any demon when I have to be. I should be called Uriel the Devious. Uriel the Defender of Faith. Uriel the Gnostic Keeper.

Save My Soul

"He heard a priest reading from the Book of Judas? That's a bit odd, don't you think?" Philip asked.

"I don't think it's unusual; we weren't the only ones who accepted those teachings. There was Marcionism, Valentinianism, Docetism, Arianism, Ebionites, Montanism and other views that have been deemed heterodox by the Church. I'm sure there are other surviving gospels; we can't have the only copies that have not been burnt by the Church. I don't know why the angels selected us as the Gnostic keepers," Thomas said.

"It was probably the only way they could be sure that at least some of them would endure, or perhaps they didn't think it through at all. They didn't strike me as the thinking type."

"Their plans do seem a little reckless," Thomas agreed.

"We have to go get the Book of Judas so Marcel can read from it and gain some peace from its wisdom. It would just be for one night, and just think, we'd be saving his immortal soul.

Surely it's worth the risk."

"I don't know; maybe we should consult the others."

"The books are here on this island. We'd have to take a boat over to Lerina and back. I don't want to wait. He doesn't sound good, and I don't think we have much time. If he died while we were gone, his soul would go to hell for all eternity and it would be our fault," Philip said.

"All right, we will go retrieve the book and let him have it for one night and then return it to the hiding spot in the morning," Thomas said.

The monks grabbed some shovels and stepped outside into the evening air. The smell of eucalyptus and salt water filled their nostrils. They had buried the gospels in a sack underneath a eucalyptus tree about a mile north of the Lazar. They didn't bother being too elaborate about it because there was no risk of discovery on the island. Most of the lepers they received were dying or near

66

death. When they got to one particularly tall tree, they stopped.

"I think this is the one." Philip checked the bark and saw the "X" carved on it. "This is the one."

They began digging and did so until the sun went down. Finally, Thomas said excitedly, "I found it!" He searched through the sack and found the Book of Judas. Thomas closed the sack and put the bag back in its hole. The monks reburied the gospels and headed back. Philip hid the gospel under his robe, just in case anyone were watching.

When they arrived back at the Lazar, they found Marcel sound asleep. His breathing was wheezy and labored. Thomas gently nudged the Gaul awake.

"We've brought you the Book of Judas," Philip whispered.

"Oh, my friends, this means so much to me. I will read it straight away so I may satisfy my curiosity. Tomorrow you may have it back and tell your order that I have agreed to be baptized."

Philip and Thomas were overjoyed. They had done a good deed; they had saved a man's soul.

"Are you able to read the words?" Thomas asked.

"Yes, my eyesight is not completely gone yet."

"Well, we will leave you to it then."

"May your God bless you," Marcel said.

"After tomorrow, he will be your God too."

***

Azazel rubbed his temples; the ceaseless agonizing screams were giving him a headache. He was overseeing the circle of impalement, which was nothing more than a circle of long sharpened sticks plunged in the ground with people impaled on them. It was Lucifer's latest punishment for wrathful souls. It was cruel, but not very inventive.

He pushed down someone who was trying to work his way off the stick. The soul let out an ear-shattering scream. "There was no need to push so hard."

"I'm terribly sorry; I'm just in a foul mood. I shouldn't take it out on you."

"You nearly pushed me all the way to the bottom."

"I said I was sorry."

"Well you should be. I hope you are never assigned here again."

"Oh, hush up."

Rosier walked down the path towards Azazel. He had to weave in and out of the impaled souls, barely noticing the stench of putrid flesh. Putrid flesh, burnt flesh, sweaty flesh . . . it was overwhelming if you weren't used to it. Rosier accidentally bumped one of the souls. It was a woman who was quite beautiful, aside from the fact that she had a giant hole in her belly from a sharp stick.

"Watch where you are going," she said.

"I'm sorry; I didn't see you there," Rosier said.

"Are you new at this or something?"

"I'll have you know, I've been doing this kind of thing for eons. I used to have a respectable position in heaven too."

The woman was not at all impressed. "I can see why they threw you out of heaven."

Rosier said nothing. He knew it was better to keep silent than engage the wrathful. They seemed to remain angry even after their deaths, and punishing them for it only made their tempers worse.

"Baal is back and he has something with him," Rosier said.

"Where is he? I want to see him at once."

"He's talking with Virgil and then he will be here straightaway."

"Do you think he has at least one of the books?" Azazel asked.

"He had it covered up in cloth, but I would think so."

"I hope it's more than one. I'd love to see the look on Uriel's face when he finds out I have his precious Apocrypha."

"I say, I should like to read that," a soul nearest to Azazel said.

"Certainly not. Don't you know it's rude to listen to other people's conversations?"

"How can I not hear your conversation? I'm almost on top of you. Besides, it gets boring being impaled all day long."

"Maybe you should have thought about that before you died," Azazel said and pushed her down the pole. The woman screamed and then called him several foul names.

"Just ignore them or they will go on all day," Rosier said.

Someone covered in head-to-toe bandages came walking toward them.

"It's a mummy," Rosier said. Azazel pulled the woman off the stick and grabbed it. He didn't even have the sharp end pointing towards the mummy.

"Calm yourselves; it's only me," Baal said and started to unwind his bandages.

"Did you disguise yourself as a mummy?" Rosier asked.

"I was disguised as a leper at a Lazar. I gained two of the monks' trust and convinced them to let me read from the Book of Judas," Baal said as he removed the cloth from the book.

"The Book of Judas—it's been so long since I've read that one," Rosier said and started to reach for it. Azazel smacked his hand away.

"I'm going to burn it."

"You know Judas might not like it if he finds out you burnt his book. Can't I at least read it before you burn it? I get so bored sometimes," Rosier said.

"I tried to tell him that, but it's like talking to a rock," said the lady who was now standing beside the devils.

"What are you doing off your stick?"

"Do you see how thick he is? You pushed me off, you fool."

Azazel realized he was still holding it in his hand. He thrust the stick back in the ground. "Sorry about that."

The woman only scoffed and then slowly with a blood-curdling scream lowered herself back on the stick.

"I don't think Judas will hear about it. Besides, when is the last time anyone has seen or heard from Judas or Lucifer for that matter? It's great that you got one of the books, Baal; maybe next time you can capture all of them," Azazel said.

"I'm sure I can outwit those monks and retrieve the other books, but I don't think I can steal all the copies that exist in the world if there are any others."

"I'll be satisfied just thwarting Uriel in this one thing."

"What do you want me to do now?" Baal asked.

"Just stay here for a while until we think of a plan about how to get the remaining books."

"I almost forgot how foul the air is here."

"You'll get used to that again in no time," Rosier said.

"Why don't you fools be quiet? A person can't even hear themselves think around here with your incessant blathering," the

69

woman said as she kicked her leg out and hit Azazel in the kneecap.

Azazel scooped out some fire with his hand. Devils could not be burned by hellfire because it would make performing one's duty a bit hard if you were burnt to ashes. He hurled a bluish-red fireball at the woman. The fireball missed and hit the man next to her, catching his hair on fire. The man screamed in agony. Azazel rushed over to try and put the fire out, turning his back to the woman, who reached her head out and bit him on the rump.

"There's just no decency left in the world," Azazel said.

"What can you expect from the wrathful but wrath?" Rosier said.

"It's too hot in here," the woman complained.

Azazel sighed. "Do you ever stop complaining?"

Rosier wiped the sweat from his forehead. "She's got a point; it is rather hot in here."

Thief in the Night

Thomas looked at the empty bed. He placed his hand on it; it wasn't warm so he had not been there for some hours now. The table by his bedside had nothing on it. They had questioned every leper and no one had seen him leave. He and Philip scoured the entire Lazar and the island. Marcel and the Book of Judas were nowhere to be found.

"Where is he? He couldn't have just vanished. We are on an island," Philip said. He had worked himself up to near hysterics.

"Do you think he died during the night?" Thomas asked.

"Don't be stupid; if he'd died during the night, his body would be here and so would the book, but both are missing."

"Pardon me, but could I get a glass of water and a fresh change of clothes?" asked a leper named Arnaud, who was just one bed over.

"In a minute. How could he have even gotten off the island? The boat is still here. I don't understand this at all. He was nearly dead when we left him last night. He sounded like he had a hundred stones sitting on his chest," Thomas said.

"Thomas, I have a terrible feeling in the pit of my stomach. I think we have been fooled. Don't you remember the archangels warning of us demon mischief? It's why they sent Netzach to watch over us."

"Well, he wasn't here with us; he was with the others. It's not our fault. I wouldn't think even a devil would stoop low enough to disguise himself as a leper."

"Who's going to tell the others that we lost the Book of Judas?" Philip asked.

"It's not the others I'm worried about, it's that Archangel Uriel. He's the one that charged us with the task of preserving the books; he's the one who will be angry," Thomas said.

"Those books have caused us nothing but trouble. I say we give up and demand to be let in to heaven."

"Please, I'm terribly thirsty," Arnaud said again.

"In just a minute. I agree; let's go see Netzach and demand he take us back to heaven," Thomas said.

"Do you think the others will go with us?"

"I don't know and I don't care anymore; I'm done with this impossible task. The world doesn't seem to want these books to exist."

Arnaud had finally grown impatient. He got up and walked over to Thomas. He put a deformed hand upon his shoulder, and it looked as though he had sausages for fingers.

"What did I say—" Thomas started to say when Arnaud stuck his face that resembled a rock because it was covered with lesions right in front of his face. He recoiled from the sight and the stench of him.

"Now, listen here. I know you have leprosy, and I know you want water and a fresh change of clothes. Philip and I want to go to heaven; we all want something, but we are going to have to wait a moment." He grabbed Arnaud by the shoulders and escorted him back to bed.

"If we stay, some demon will probably just come and steal the rest of the books anyway," Philip said.

"I have to go to the privy," a leper named Gaston shouted.

"What is with these lepers today? You would think they were dying or something," Thomas said and parted his red hair with his hand to keep it out of his face. He and Philip were both in desperate need of a haircut.

"I can't help but feel like we are letting Uriel and the other archangels down. They are holy books, regardless of what the Church thinks," Philip said.

"Where is our breakfast? I'm hungrier than a bear that has just woken up from his winter slumber," a leper named Devereux said.

"Is that so? Well, then you can go hunt your own breakfast like a bear then," Thomas said.

"I can't believe we were so trusting; he really had us convinced he was a dying leper. His name probably wasn't even Marcel," Philip said.

"Well, of course, it wasn't Marcel. Have you ever heard of a demon named Marcel? His name was probably Raum or Seere or something like that."

"You don't think it was Beelzebub or Lucifer himself, do you?"

"Don't be ridiculous; I'm sure they would send some lowly demon to do their dirty work," Thomas said.

"I'll bet he was never a gladiator either."

"Well, if he is a demon, he could hardly be a gladiator, now could he?"

"Why not? He was a leper," Philip said.

"That was just to deceive us," Thomas sighed. "Why don't I attend the lepers and you go fetch the boat and take it to Lerina? Let the others know what happened and bring them here."

"Maybe Netzach can figure out how we can get it back."

"Unless he can appear in hell and snatch it from the jaws of Lucifer, I don't see how."

"Do you think Lucifer has jaws?" Philip asked.

"Just go to the boat, please."

Thomas walked over to Devereux's bed first because his request of going to the privy seemed the most urgent out of the other leper requests. Devereux was not in his bed.

He probably made it to the privy by himself, he thought.

He fetched a pitcher and went outside to the well to pump some water for Arnaud and nearly bumped into Philip. "I thought I told you to take the boat to Lerina."

"That's just it; I can't find the boat."

"What do you mean? It was just here this morning; remember how you commented that Marcel didn't take the boat because it was still here," Thomas said.

"I know it was here a little while ago, but now it's not."

Thomas marched over to where they usually kept the boat. "It's not here."

"I told you that already." The tide rolled in and splashed Thomas' bare feet. He jumped back because the water was cold.

"Do you think Marcel came back and took the boat?" Philip asked.

"Don't be ridiculous; why would he come back to steal our boat? What use would he have for it in hell?"

"I imagine a boat would come in very handy when having to travel over a lake of fire."

"I don't think they need a boat to travel over a lake of fire;

they have wings. I think . . .."

Thomas walked back toward the Lazar without finishing his thought and Philip followed him. He checked Gaston's bed and then Arnaud's; both beds were empty.

"What are you doing?" Philip asked.

"I think I know who took the boat."

"Do you think it might have been a different demon?"

"No, it was no demon. I think it was three impatient lepers who took it, and they are now on their way to Lerina to file a grievance against us."

***

Honoratus just wanted to live a simple life as a hermit on the island of Lerina; but word spread, and he was soon joined by disciples so he founded a monastery. Years after his death, he would be canonized as a saint and the island renamed Saint-Honorat. For now, though, he was just Honoratus, the well-educated monk from Gaul, staring at three lepers who just came ashore. The lepers approached the hooded monk and fell at his feet.

"What dire circumstance has compelled you to come to our island?"

"I assure you, sir, we would not be here if those two good-for-nothing monks attending to us were doing their jobs," Arnaud said.

"What good-for-nothing monks? We don't have any good-for-nothing monks. All monks are good for something, just as all people are good for something."

"Well, then let me be more specific, sir. I mean Brother Philip and Brother Thomas; they would not get me any water."

"He's right, sir; I had to go to the privy, and neither one of them would help me," Gaston said.

"Yes, sir, and I was hungry and they wouldn't fetch me anything to break my fast," Devereux said.

"I see, and is it still the case that all three of you are still suffering from your needs?"

"Yes sir, I'm as parched as a damned soul in the eternal flames of hell," Arnaud said.

"I'm so hungry, I could eat dung from the privy," Devereux said.

"I had to go to the privy really badly," Gaston said.

"You 'had' to go to the privy? Did you already go?"

Gaston blushed. "I went over the side of the boat. I couldn't hold it an instant longer. The boat ride was so long that I have to go to the privy again but this time for a different reason.

"So all three of you are quite capable of laboring for hours to get to this island, but you can't fetch your own food and water or go to the privy unassisted? And am I now to understand that the very urgencies that compelled you here in the first place have now become monumental urgencies? I'm afraid you three suffer from what I like to call a logical fallacy."

"It's the principle of the matter, sir; we wanted to let you know how we were being treated," Arnaud said.

"And how are you being treated?"

"As we have said, our basic needs are not being attended to."

"You say your basic needs are not being met, but here you stand alive and well, apart from your current disagreeable pains which I have already proven through reason that you made substantially worse all on your own."

The lepers just stared at the monk in wonderment. They weren't sure what reason had to do with their current dilemma.

Tiberius, known as Netzach to all the angels of heaven, walked up the beach towards them.

"You . . . I didn't catch your name."

"I am Arnaud and this is Gaston and Deveraux," Arnaud said, pointing to the other two lepers, who were still puzzling over what to do.

"Well, Arnaud and Deveraux, I want you to walk to that building, which is the refectory, straightaway," Honoraus said, pointing to a small building. "The monk in there is named Brother Simon. Tell him that Brother Honoraus said for him to make you something to eat and to fetch you some water."

"I'm rather hungry too now," Deveraux said.

"He will get you both food and water." Honoraus looked at the monk who was clutching his stomach. "Gaston, is it?"

"Yes, your holiness."

"Brother Honoraus will do just fine. Tiberius here will take you to the privy, and then you may go with your friends to the refectory to get some food and water as well."

Honoraus bowed and walked away. Tiberius watched him until he was out of sight.

I used to be a respected angel, and now it seems it's my job to take men to the privy, he thought.

Tiberius held out his hand to the poor creature in front of him. The gesture made Gaston tear up a little bit.

"No one has offered me their hand in many years. I thank you, sir; I can't walk very well. God bless you."

As they walked towards the privy, Tiberius said, "You must not think ill of Brother Philip and Brother Thomas. I'm sure they were just preoccupied."

"Indeed they were; they were going on about some book missing and Marcel who up and vanished."

"Who is Marcel and what book were they discussing?"

"Marcel is a leper who came from Lugdunum. He was always bragging because he used to be a gladiator, as if that were something to be proud of. He was a slave most likely. "

"You said he vanished; do you think he drowned?" Tiberius asked, tripping over a rock and nearly falling.

"It's possible he drowned. Brother Philip and Brother Thomas were all in a panic because they looked all over the island for him and the book and couldn't find one trace of either."

"What book were they looking for?"

Gaston scratched his leathery face that looked like stone. "Maybe I shouldn't say anymore. I don't want to get into trouble. I was eavesdropping and wasn't supposed to hear what they were saying. Sometimes I act like I'm asleep so I can learn things because no one ever tells me anything."

"I assure you, you will not get into any trouble, but I need to know what book you're talking about."

They were standing in front of the privies now. Gaston was really clutching his stomach tightly. He would not be able to hold it in much longer.

"You'll have to forgive me; I'm not religious and never have been. My parents weren't too keen on religion and never took me to church. I only agreed to baptism so I can stay on the island because they send lepers away who don't agree. I didn't have

76

much of a choice in the matter. Marcel was one of the few lepers who did not want to be baptized and accepted into the Church. The brothers were vexed about his immortal soul. I don't know why they even troubled themselves, his being a gladiator and all; it's unlikely his soul will be going to heaven."

"Never underestimate God's forgiveness," Tiberius said, although he wondered if even he would be allowed back in heaven after this was all over.

"As you say, sir; I'm sure you would know."

"What did Marcel look like?"

Arnaud didn't understand the question. "He looked like a leper, sir."

"I mean, did he have red eyes or anything like that?"

"I don't know, but he was covered in bandages so he was probably worse off than most. The monks didn't think he had much longer to live, which is why they complied with his wishes. You know one time when Marcel was sleeping, I heard him speaking in some language; and at the time, it made the hairs on the back of my neck stand up. It sounded strange . . . but I think it was some kind of evil tongue. It was like Lucifer himself had come up from hell and possessed him. I never trusted him. You know, one time he wanted me to sign something and when I asked what I was signing, he said, 'Never you mind.' I told him I don't sign anything without reading it first so he snatched back the paper and said, 'Never mind, we wouldn't want you there anyway.' I don't know where he was talking about, but I'm sure it wasn't any place good."

Arnaud went inside the privy before Tiberius could ask him any more questions. Tiberius heard a very loud sound of relief, followed by flatulence, followed by a foul odor.

It was more than Tiberius/Netzach could take. *I am the angel of beauty and love, and I'm standing here listening to a leper use the privy. I've had quite enough; I'm going home,* he thought and snapped his fingers.

When Gaston was finally done, he opened the door to an empty beach.

"Everyone is disappearing off these islands; if I'm not careful, I'll be next," Gaston said, watching a crab amble by. "I'm hungry; I wonder if that monk makes crab stew."

You Can't Go Home Again

Netzach appeared right in front of the gates of Heaven. He was just about to walk through when he heard an old grumpy voice, "Where do you think you're going?"

Netzach knew that voice; it was the voice of St. Peter. "This is where I live."

Saint Peter scratched his beard, "And who are you?"

"I am the angel Netzach. Don't you remember? I assist the Archangels Uriel, Michael and Gabriel."

St. Peter snorted. "Those simple-minded cuttlefish, they tried to usher in seven monks without being judged, can you imagine? I told them I was having none of that and got the book out on each and every one of them."

"Yes, I know all about it. May I pass through the gates now?"

"Who did you say you were again?"

"I'm Netzach."

"How do you spell that?"

"N-E-T-Z-A-C-H," he spelled out slowly.

"And where did you say you are from?"

"I'm from Heaven."

"Cassiel," St. Peter yelled out, "go get the book on Netzach of Heaven!"

"What book? There is no book on me; I'm an angel."

Cassiel looked at Netzach and then at St. Peter. "He is an angel; he's the one who has to run all the senseless errands for Uriel."

"Who says they're senseless?"

"Um . . . no one," Cassiel said.

"Ah . . . I know you very well. You are the one who's always going hither, thither and yon for the cuddlefish. Why didn't you say so in the beginning?"

One of the seraphs played a false note on the harp because he was too busy watching Netzach and St. Peter.

Netzach was angry. "I did say so." He stormed through the gates without looking back. He passed by the seraph playing the harp.

"Holy, holy—"

"Stop singing those blasted words all the time."

The seraph stared at him in disbelief. "Holy, holy, holy is the lord of hosts; the whole earth full of his glory," he sang very quickly before Netzach could cut him off again.

Netzach closed his eyes and tried to focus on Uriel and tried not to think about pulling out all of his feathers. He snapped his fingers and disappeared, leaving behind a seraph who was mumbling something about sending him to the bowels of hell. When he reappeared, he was standing in front of Uriel; and, as always, right near him were Michael and Gabriel engaging in sword play. If there were ever two archangels who needed another war, it was these two.

"What in St. Peter's name are you doing here?" Uriel asked.

"I had enough of that foolishness so I left."

"You have to return right away. What if something happens to the gospels?"

"Something already happened to them. Well, at least to one of them."

"What do you mean?"

Michael and Gabriel had stopped swinging their swords long enough to listen to the conversation.

"Did you know everyone thinks I just run senseless errands for you and that I am your puppet?"

"What? Who thinks that?" Uriel asked innocently.

Michael and Gabriel burst out laughing. "We may have actually started that rumor," Michael said.

"Well, maybe a few people say it—but, never mind that, what happened to my books?"

"Your books? I thought they were for all mankind. I wasn't aware that the holy gospels belonged to any angel," Netzach said.

"Yes, of course, that's what I meant."

"I don't know which book, but I'm fairly certain one was stolen by one of Azazel's disciples."

Gabriel patted Uriel on the head like a small child. "Maybe it was just The Gospel of Truth."

"That's actually my favorite one; it's very poetic," Michael said.

"I didn't even know you liked poetry . . . or reading, for that matter," Gabriel said.

"Just because you have spent an eternity with someone doesn't mean you know everything about them."

"Netzach, you must return to Lerina before the other books get stolen. Are you disobeying an archangel's orders?" Uriel asked, standing up really straight and trying to sound forceful.

"I am disobeying this order, and I don't care who you take the matter up with. I'll just tell them what it is you had me doing, and that will put an abrupt end to your interference."

"You will return to Lerina and carry out your duty," Michael boomed, using the voice of God, which shook the ground beneath them.

Netzach quickly kneeled. "My lord, forgive me. I did not know this was your wish; I thought it was just a fancy of the archangels. I will return at once, and please forgive me for questioning your wisdom."

"I will forgive you on one condition. When you next return, you must bring back some of that excellent French wine."

"I thought we weren't allowed to bring mortal objects into heaven."

"All things are possible if I will it."

As you wish, my lord." Netzach snapped his fingers and disappeared.

"That's how it's done," Michael said in his normal voice.

"Michael, I could kiss you if you weren't such a fool," Uriel said.

"Why should that stop you?" Michael asked.

"This is no time for merriment; we have to figure out what was stolen and how to get it back."

"You know what we need?" Gabriel asked.

Uriel was afraid to ask; usually Gabriel's ideas were silly at best.

"We need a spy."

"Gabriel, that is ridicu—" Uriel interrupted himself because for once, Gabriel had a good idea. "Gabriel, that is brilliant."

"I was the one who got Netzach to return to Lerina," Michael said, feeling a little jealous.

"You both have done well; and, as a reward, I'm giving you each a piece of Vehuaiah's chocolate," Uriel said and reached into his robe, producing two pieces of chocolate.

"I can't believe Vehuaiah let you have some of his precious chocolate," Michael said with his hand extended like a child. "Wait, I thought we were supposed to be giving him the chocolate as a bribe, not asking him for chocolate."

"I didn't exactly ask him for it; I stole some from his hoard."

"Shouldn't you give this back to him?" Gabriel asked.

"No, you can go ahead and eat it; I'll just have to replace them later. Now, who can we get as a spy?"

Michael didn't even wait until Uriel had completed his sentence before shoving the chocolate in his mouth.

"I just couldn't resist the temptation. They looked so delectable," Uriel said, eating a chocolate.

"We need someone who is smart and has access to hell," Michael said.

"That's too bad; we don't know anyone like that," said Gabriel, who was taking small bites of his chocolate because he wanted to savor it.

"Yes, we do; we could get Virgil to spy for us," Uriel said.

"I doubt he would spy for you after you called all his work rubbish and you called him a plagiarizer," Michael said.

"I didn't say any of that to his face, though."

"That doesn't matter; you can't say anything around here without it getting around the whole kingdom of heaven. There are ophanim who are always watching with their many eyes and listening," Michael said.

"Blast those ophanim," Uriel said. Michael jumped and Gabriel put a finger to his lips. They looked around underneath clouds.

"Don't say things like that. You never know when ophanim are about; and, if they heard you use that kind of language, you'd be in deep trouble," Gabriel said.

"Michael, why don't you summon Virgil and I'll get out of sight? You can tell him that you need him to spy on Azazel."

"All right." Michael snapped his fingers and Virgil appeared.

"I said, 'Wait until I was out of sight,'" he whispered.

"What did you say? Why are you whispering?" Michael asked.

"He said, 'I said, wait until I was out of sight.' I have excellent hearing," Virgil said.

"Oh, yes, I did forget that part, didn't I?"

Virgil was growing impatient. "What is it that you want? I was right in the middle of telling a story about the time I met Marc Antony."

You pompous, disrespectful writer of drivel, Uriel thought. Virgil looked at him through narrowed eyes as if he could read his thoughts.

"We want you to spy on Azazel for us," Michael said.

"Who is *we*?"

"I mean, I would like for you to spy on Azazel and his disciples," Michael said.

Gabriel was shuffling uncomfortably.

"I see, and why should I do that?"

"Because I ordered you to," Michael thundered in the voice of God.

Unlike Netzach, Virgil didn't even flinch. "Come now, I know all about the Presence of God giving you his voice. I can't imagine why, though. I want to know what I get out of this deal."

"I will make you the official author of Revelation. It will henceforth be known as the Apocalypse of Virgil," Uriel said. An audible gasp was heard from Michael and Gabriel.

"We both know you don't have the authority to do that."

"No, but Azrael does and I believe I can convince him to approve it."

"Very well, what kind of information am I trying to obtain?"

"I need to know every move he makes, in regards to trying to thwart my efforts to safeguard the Gnostic Gospels."

Virgil raised an eyebrow. "The Apocrypha?"

Uriel winced at the word *Apocrypha*. "Yes, and I need to know what demon he has working on his behalf. I need to stay a step ahead of him. Also, I believe he already has one of the books. I need you to retrieve it and bring it back."

"All right, we have an accord. I will head back there now; it was Eligos I was telling my story to. I will find out what I can and come back here when I have something useful."

"Agreed."

"Well then, off you go. What are you waiting for?" Uriel asked.

"I need one of you to send me to hell; I am just a man, after all."

Uriel started to snap his fingers, but Virgil stopped him. "No, Michael, you send me back." Uriel's reputation for sending people to the strangest places was known far and wide.

Michael snapped his fingers and Virgil disappeared. "You shouldn't have made that bargain with him."

"Nonsense, Azrael will approve, don't you worry," Uriel said.

"Worry about what?" Michael asked.

"Never mind."

"Do you have any more chocolate?"

Bird Brain

"I don't understand. The Church wants me to go where?" The Bishop of Naples asked. Severus, the Bishop of Naples, was a portly, red-faced, rather lazy man. He could not figure out for the life of him why he was being sent to some remote island in Gaul.

The messenger from the Church repeated it again, "His holiness would like for you to go to the island of Lerina."

"Have I offended someone?"

The messenger sighed; he was eager to get back home. "How should I know that? Do you think the pope goes around telling me what his reasons are for doing things? He's the pope; he doesn't need a reason."

"Do I have to go?"

"No, of course, you don't have to go. You can be defrocked."

"I just can't believe this. I'm being sent to a barren island in the middle of nowhere."

"It's not barren; there are plenty of trees, plants, food and monks who live on the island. There is also a Lazar."

The messenger thought the bishop was going to faint. "A Lazar?"

"You are to administer the Eucharist to the lepers there."

"I can't administer the Eucharist to a bunch of lepers. I might get leprosy."

"God calls us each in our own time."

"What in blazes does that mean? Be gone, you naïve, you whore of Babylon."

"I'll need you to sign this," he said and stuck a piece of parchment and quill in the fat man's face.

The Bishop snatched them from his hands. He scrawled his name across the parchment and gave it back to the messenger, who turned on his heels and walked away. Baal snickered as he walked away from the bishop. Had he thought to inquire any further about the matter, he would have found out that no one from the Church

84

had authorized anything. Baal had disguised himself as a monk and made up the story. Not only did the pope not authorize it; he could never even remember the Bishop of Naples' name and often referred to him as "what's his name."

The Bishop started throwing things in his trunk. He had been Bishop of Naples for ten years, and he could not believe he was being sent to a leper island in Gaul. It was a slap in the face. *I am held in such high regard here; being Bishop of Naples is a prestigious position. I must have angered the pope somehow. I don't know how I could have offended him. When he visited, I offered him all the best wine and food and let him have my own room, while I took a small, dank room that had a draft,* he thought as he gathered his belongings. It would be a long journey, and he wouldn't be able to take too much with him in the way of comforts. He would mostly have to take just the provisions he needed to get through the journey. His servant, Gilberto, was readying his horse as well as his own. He was going to accompany his master to some wild, untamed Gaulish island.

There are just a bunch of hermits and recluses on that island. They work all day under a hot sun and eat and drink sparingly. They might as well have just sent me to hell. The bishop quickly made the sign of the cross. *Forgive me, Father.*

"We are ready, my lord," Gilberto said.

The bishop looked around his very comfortable house one last time and sighed. "I don't know if we will ever return, Gilberto. I fear we are off to some savage island and our days of wine-drinking and merriment are over."

Gilberto only nodded because he'd never gotten to take part in any of that wine-drinking and merriment.

They got up on their horses, and the bishop's horse buckled for a moment under the weight.

"We will be lucky if we aren't robbed and killed before we get out of Naples."

"Yes, my lord," Gilberto said and wondered if he were going to have to hear the bishop complain the whole journey. "I believe we can make Hadria by nightfall, my lord."

"That name sounds awfully familiar."

"Yes, my lord; it's a small village by the Adriatic Sea."

"Yes, but have I been there?"

"My lord was sent there on official Church business to excommunicate some heretics."

"Oh yes, I remember now; that was the oddest day of my life—well, next to this one. Do you know that one of those heretics broke wind right during my sermon about Paul. It was the loudest and most disgraceful thing ever. It smelled as if the man had moved his bowels. What a strange day; and if that weren't enough, one minute it was a calm, clear day with no sign of a storm and the next thing you know, it was hailing balls this big." The bishop put his index finger and thumb together to make a wide circle to indicate the size. "The hail came crashing down; then, just as pretty as you please, it ceased and then it began to rain. Hard and heavy rain came pelting down, and we had to seek shelter."

Gilberto was trying to maintain his composure. The idea of someone passing gas during the pompous bishop's sermon amused him.

I bet his eyes nearly bugged out of his head, he thought.

"Yes, it was a very strange day. Whoever heard of seven heretics in one small village? It ended very well, though; they had such a feast prepared for us. The wine was so sweet with a hint of honey."

Once again Gilberto only nodded; he wouldn't know anything about having sweet wine that had a hint of honey.

"Well, they won't have a feast prepared this time because they may not know we are even coming; and, even if they did, I doubt those savages would know how to properly receive a man of my stature. I hope that backwards place has some suitable accommodations available."

The bishop sighed, and Gilberto thought he might actually enjoy a moment of quiet, but the bishop was not yet remotely finished.

"They had several delectable cheeses and the grapes, Gilberto, you would have been amazed at the taste of the grapes."

Gilberto was sure he would be amazed since he had never tasted a grape in his life.

"The magistrate was a bore; he told the most boring stories. It's not his fault though, poor soul, never having traveled or experienced life. I had to regale those simple folk with tales of Naples and Rome. I also told him about the council in Carthage. You should have seen them; their unsophisticated eyes were filled with wonderment. I told them all about all the animals in Africa, and they couldn't believe such things existed." He closed his eyes as if trying to recall it all. It would be the last thing that the Bishop would recall for a while because, just as he opened his eyes again, his head hit a tree branch and knocked him off his horse. The fat bishop landed with an audible *thud* in what smelled like horse manure.

"My lord, are you all right? Can you hear me?" There was no response from the bishop. Gilberto had to hold his nose from the stench of the manure. Just to be sure he was completely unconscious, Gilberto slapped one of his chubby cheeks, and it left a red handprint. Gilberto could contain it no longer; he laughed harder than he ever had before in his life and would ever again probably. He replayed the image of the fat man getting knocked off his horse over and over in his mind; and finally, when his side hurt from laughing so much, he sighed because he now had something else to consider.

How am I going to get this fat, pompous, poor excuse of a holy man back on his horse?

***

Peter, Philip, John, Adolfo, Thomas, Lorenzo and Simon were standing together in a secluded area on the beach. Several tall eucalyptus trees obscured them from any eyes that might be watching.

"You lost the Book of Judas to a demon?" Peter asked angrily. "You didn't think it a bit odd that a uneducated gladiator could read?" Peter asked.

"Keep your voice down. Yes, at least we think so; and not that it did not occur to us, but we were too preoccupied with saving his soul," Philip said.

"What do you mean you think so? Either you lost the book or not."

"No, the book is lost for sure; I meant the part about Marcel's being a demon."

"I should have sent Netzach on the island to watch over you two. Where is Netzach, by the way?"

Right on cue, Netzach appeared, startling the group.

"Where did you go?" Simon asked.

"I had to report back to heaven and update Uriel on the fact that one of the books has gone missing." He left out the part how he'd told Uriel that he didn't want to come back, but was forced to by the voice of God.

"How did you know the Book of Judas had gone missing?" Lorenzo asked.

"I didn't know it was the Book of Judas; I just knew it was one of the books. One of the lepers told me that he'd overheard Philip and Thomas talking about a book missing and about Marcel."

"Someone overheard your conversation? You two need to be more careful about where you speak about such things," John said. Adolfo grunted in acquiescence.

Simon hit Philip and Thomas on the head with his spoon. "That hurt! Hey, you still have food on that spoon," Thomas said as he and Philip wiped the food out of their hair.

"Stop it. This is no time for silly games. What did Uriel say about the book? Was he mad?"

"He was more concerned than angry."

"What is his plan then? How do we recover the book?" Simon asked.

"He didn't mention a plan. There might not even be a plan."

"We can't just give up that easily," Peter said.

"Well, what do you want from me? He didn't tell me what his plan is; he is an archangel and I just do what I'm told."

"We have to be more careful in the future, all of us. It's obvious some demon wants these books really bad, and I'm sure it's not to preserve them for mankind." Peter said.

"I'll bet they've already burned the book," John said, and once again Adolfo grunted in agreement with his young friend.

"If he has, there is nothing we can do about it now. The best thing we can do is make sure we safeguard the other books," Peter said and pointed to Philip and Thomas. "You two be more careful who you trust next time."

"Well, if you can't trust a dying leper, then who in this blessed world can you trust?" Philip asked.

"No one. You trust no one from now on. Do you understand?" Netzach asked.

I guess I will have to go back to being called Tiberius again.

I hate that disgusting Roman name, he thought. He did take comfort in the fact that he knew exactly when and how the Romans would fall. Vehuaiah, who was responsible for history and time, loved to brag about his knowledge. He could not tell these things to the men, though; the angels weren't supposed to reveal such knowledge to mortals, although he wasn't sure if technically these monks were mortals or not—after all, they had died once already.

The group returned to their rooms, all except Philip and Thomas, who returned to Leper Island, as it was known. They took turns rowing the boat.

"I thought we were doing such a noble deed. We were going to save a man's soul," Philip said.

"How are we supposed to know that his soul was damned already?"

"I guess next time, even if a man's soul is at risk and wants to read from one of the Gnostic Gospels, we will have to refuse."

"Indeed we must, although it would be hard for me to refuse a dying man," Thomas said.

"Even if he is dying, we must refuse."

A parrot flew in and perched right on the bow of their boat; it had beautiful red, green and yellow plumage. These exotic types of birds were commonplace throughout the island, and Philip and Thomas didn't even give it a second glance. The first few weeks they were there, though, they'd stared and gawked at the birds as if God thought the other birds he created were too plain and decided to paint their wings all the colors of the rainbow.

"I guess we should have suspected something. It was a bit strange that he asked to read that particular gospel."

"How were we supposed to know he was a foul demon sent from hell to steal books away from us?" Philip asked.

"Because Netzach said there might be a foul demon sent from hell who wanted to steal the book away from us."

"Oh, right. Well, I didn't know he would be so cleverly disguised. I mean, you must admit, it was very clever."

"Yes, what do you think would have happened to him if we had actually poured holy water on him?" Thomas asked.

"I imagine his grotesque face would have melted off into a rather distasteful-looking puddle."

"Do you think they are really grotesque?" Philip asked.

The parrot was still perched on the bow of their boat and looking at Thomas, as if waiting for him to answer.

Thomas shrugged. "The Bible says they are."

"Netzach says we must safeguard the remaining Gnostic Gospels and trust no one from now on."

"Yes, and in the future we must be careful about discussing these things in earshot of other people."

They heard a small screech. "Gnostic Gospels," the parrot said.

"Oh no, it's one of those parrots that can repeat words," Philip said.

Thomas swatted at the parrot with one of the oars and missed. "Get out of here, you!"

The parrot paid no heed to the warning and remained on the bow of the boat.

"I think we should dig up the—" Thomas paused and looked at the parrot "—you-know-what and find a safer place to put them," Philip said.

"I agree; besides, I always forget where we hid them."

"It's not that difficult; they are buried a mile northwest from the Lazar under the largest eucalyptus tree marked with a big X."

"Eucalyptus tree. Gnostic Gospels," the parrot said.

"You be quiet, you stupid bird." Thomas went to swat the parrot again, but this time he lost his balance and fell over the side. Thomas struggled to get back into the boat. He was not a very good swimmer. Philip helped his brother back in by extending his arm. He had to be careful that he didn't fall in too. When Thomas got back into the boat, he was dripping wet and shivering from the cool breeze. He shook his fist at the bird and scowled. "I'll strangle your lousy neck, and Simon will have a nice bird for his stew!" The parrot blinked; it had not moved an inch the entire time.

"Just leave the witless bird alone, Thomas."

The parrot took flight as if it were offended at being called *witless*.

"It's about time that stupid bird took a hint," Thomas said.

Philip took over rowing while Thomas dried out.

"You know, Philip, I know we messed up with the Book of Judas, but I think we will be much wiser in the future."

"I agree, Thomas; we've learned our lesson. We won't let any more books escape our grasp."

Drunk Hellhound

Virgil liked the freedom he had to roam throughout heaven and hell. He picked up a lot of valuable information along the way, information that sometimes proved to be very useful. The fact that the Book of Judas was now somewhere in hell was useful information. Virgil pondered his current situation. Uriel had agreed to name him official author of the Book of Revelation.

The Apocalypse of Virgil has a nice ring to it, he thought.

He decided he would do everything within reason he could to retrieve the book. He took the ferry across the Lake of Fire. He was the only soul who'd ever stepped on the ferry that didn't belong there. The ferryman, a demon named Phenex, hated the fact he had to take this man who was neither devil nor a damned soul around anywhere he wanted.

What makes him so special that he can go hither and thither without so much as a by-your-leave? One of these days this arrogant man is going to get what he deserves, and I hope I'm around to see it.

Virgil knew that Phenex resented him, so sometimes, to irk the ferryman, he asked to be taken somewhere out of the way; and then he would tell him he just remembered he had to stop off elsewhere. The demon would have to turn the ferry around. He did not have time this visit to play tricks on the lowly demon; he had urgent business to attend to. Phenex took him past the people who committed the sins of lust, gluttony and greed. He watched as the greedy souls were running some kind of race. Several of the devils were poking them in the behind with sharpened sticks and laughing. One man won the race and jumped up and down in gleeful delight. Apparently, the winner got to chase behind the other greedy souls and poke them in the back side. Phenex stopped at the souls of the wrathful. Virgil got off the ferry and, before he could say anything to the demon, he was already pushing the ferry down the lake.

Virgil took the path down into the valley of the wrathful. He knew the path well; he had come to know all the paths in hell well and even knew some secret passages that not every demon knew about. It was just another example of useful information he was able to glean from unsuspecting demons. He had to be careful, though; some demons were smarter than others. There was no danger with Azazel and Rosier, though. He stopped when he got to the Circle of Souls who were all impaled on sharp sticks.

Impalement is so very unoriginal, he thought.

Virgil saw Azazel and Rosier and walked over to them. Rosier stood a head taller than Azazel and was a dark, reddish-brown color. Azazel had lighter pigmentation than Rosier; not all devils looked alike just as not all angels looked alike. They had a lot in common with one another; after all, the devils used to be angels. Virgil pinched his nose; he didn't know how they ever got used to the stench or the moaning.

One of the women impaled yelled at him, "And who is this high and mighty person who just thinks he can walk wherever he pleases without having to be punished?"

"Be quiet, wench. Don't pay any attention to that cantankerous old crone, Virgil. She won't ever be quiet," Rosier said.

"Be quiet, you good-for-nothing devil."

Rosier just ignored her because she wanted him to say something so she could argue back. The souls had different ways of passing the time, and this woman did it by annoying whoever was around.

"I was just here visiting Elisos and thought I would come by and see if there were any interesting news."

"Haagenti got demoted to the equivalent of angel. Apparently, he wasn't watching over the souls in Lust like he was supposed to, and most of them got all the way to the threshold between hell and limbo before they were caught. Some of them didn't even try and run; they were busy copulating—such is their lusty nature and all," Rosier said. The devils, like the angels, were androgynous creatures; but Virgil was a man, and he really missed lovemaking.

Virgil nodded; he hoped he wouldn't have to listen to too much more of that kind of thing. He wanted to know about the book.

"Hey, tell him about the book," Rosier said.

Azazel paused; he seemed a little unsure. "How well do you know Uriel?"

"Oh that old sop, I can't stand the sight of him. He doesn't like me; he thinks my writing is drivel, and he's jealous that I get free range of both dominions. He's no friend of mine."

Azazel seemed relieved. "Then you will be glad to hear that I pulled one over on that—what was the word you called him?"

"I called him a 'sop'."

"Yes, I pulled one over on that sop."

"He sent Baal to Earth to steal the Gnostic Gospels that some men were hiding for Uriel," Rosier said.

Azazel was a little annoyed that Rosier rushed to tell him because he wanted to be the one to say it; after all, it was his victory.

"Did Baal succeed?"

"Not exactly; he was only able to steal one, the Book of Judas. Baal just needs a way to figure out how to get the others, "Azazel said.

"Hey, maybe Virgil can help us," Rosier said.

Virgil bowed. "How may I be of service?" He asked that, but in his head he thought, *how can you be of service to me?*

"You're in heaven a lot; you can spy for us. Find out Uriel's plans so we can stay a step ahead of him."

"What a great idea! And if the information you find proves valuable, I'll reward you by arranging an audience with Lucifer," Azazel said.

Virgil was intrigued. He had been coming to hell for hundreds of years, knew every secret passageway, every demon and had talked to everyone of interest in hell; the only thing he had never done was speak to Satan. The supreme devil was rather reclusive and only came out of his lair when absolutely necessary. He conveyed his will through messengers, one of whom was Belias, a good friend of Azazel. He was the devil who passed out torture assignments. Virgil had never even laid eyes on Lucifer and only had a vague idea what he looked like, through various demons' descriptions of him.

I could write the best book of all time, maybe title it "Lucifer, a Life Story." That's a drab title; I'll have to work on that.

"I'll do it. Where is the book right now?"

"It's being guarded by the hellhound Barghest until we finish up our duties here, and then we are going to burn it and have a little celebration afterwards," Rosier said. "Would you like to come to the celebration?"

"I'm afraid I can't; I must really be on my way. I am so delighted to hear that you tricked that fool, though."

The impaled woman saw Virgil starting to leave. "Hey, where do you think you're going, Mr. Hubris?"

Without saying anything, Virgil walked over to her and kissed her full on the lips. Azazel and Rosier thought it was hysterical. The woman only stared at him in open-mouthed disbelief.

"That should quiet her down for a while," he said and winked. The woman did, in fact, remain quiet for the rest of the day.

Virgil looked around for the Qeren, the special horn that called Phenex. It had been placed in a groove carved in the mountainside. There were other horns spread throughout hell that you could use, but some say the Qeren is the very same horn that Michael blew before the battle in heaven. He doubted if that were true because if it belonged to Michael, it would be in heaven and that fool would be blowing on it constantly.

Virgil blew the Qeren. It made a loud, but pleasing hum; it sounded like the humming of someone with a deep baritone voice. He blew it again for good measure and waited for the ferryman to appear. While Virgil sometimes took Phenex out of the way, Phenex would get him back by taking his sweet time whenever he called. Virgil began to pace and stroked his long white beard. When Phenex finally arrived, Virgil had been waiting for half an hour.

"I'm terribly sorry; I was on the other side of hell," Phenex said, smiling and revealing a set of black teeth. He had, in fact, been just around the corner waiting and giggling. Virgil smiled in return; he wasn't going to give Phenex any satisfaction.

"Where to, my lord?" Phenex asked in a sneer.

Virgil thought about that; he didn't want to tell him to take him to Barghest because that might arouse suspicion. He wouldn't have any business with a hellhound.

"Take me to the lustful."

I'll take you there, chain you to a rock and have you drag it around for all eternity, Phenex thought.

When they finally arrived to where the lustful souls were being persecuted, Virgil had worked out how he was going to get the book. The area was completely empty.

"Where is everyone? Where are all the lustful souls?"

"You'll have to walk down to the treacherous; that's where they have been moved," Phenex called out as he departed. Another horn was sounding, which meant he needed to ferry the recently-departed to their final destination. He was smiling wickedly because he thought he had pulled another one over on Virgil, knowing ahead of time that no one was there and making him walk. He did not know that Virgil had come to see Barghest.

Why are the treacherous souls being grouped with the lustful? Lucifer is never satisfied. I can't wait to meet him and take his measure, he thought.

Virgil could see the glowing red eyes of Barghest, the hellhound. He had black fur as black as midnight and was as big as a wild boar. Virgil approached and Barghest growled at him, revealing razor-sharp fangs. On the ground, nearly obscured by fur was the Book of Judas. Virgil reached into his robe and pulled out a decanter of spirits. He always carried a decanter of spirits with him, which he sipped on only medicinally, of course. He convinced himself every day that he was getting a fever and took a sip . . . even though dead people couldn't get a fever. Barghest was curious and stopped growling to inspect the strange item. Virgil poured the contents into his bowl. Barghest sniffed the dish first and then took a lick with his long-forked tongue. The beast must have decided that he too had a fever because he greedily lapped up the rest.

All I have to do now is wait, he thought.

Immediately, the spirits took effect; his fangs receded back into his foul-smelling mouth and his jaw relaxed. The hound was large for sure and could probably absorb a lot of alcohol unaffected, but not even something his size could withstand the amount of pure alcohol that Virgil had given him. He laid his massive body down, spread his giant paws out and closed his eyes.

Virgil waited a while longer until the hound was in a deep sleep. He had succeeded in getting a hound of hell drunk, which he guessed was probably the first time in recorded history. What he didn't know was, it actually was not the first time; the first time had been in 1037 BC, when Belphegor had come back from one of his eating, drinking and copulating expeditions. He had brought back a jug full of spirits and hidden it behind a rock for later. A hound of hell caught its scent and found the jug. When Belphegor went to retrieve it, he'd found an empty jug and a passed-out hellhound.

Barghest was still lying on the book, so Virgil slowly lowered his hand under the great beast's rump. The hellhound stirred, but did not wake; after some pulling, Virgil managed to pull the book out and tuck it safely in his robe. He took a last look at Barghes that had begun to snore.

He decided to walk down to where the lustful and the treacherous souls were being tortured so that he could establish an alibi. Like most of the torturing, the punishment didn't always fit the crime . . . if indeed, there were a crime. Virgil had been around long enough to know that some people in hell should really be in heaven. It all seemed very subjective; different sins were looked upon more harshly than others. Virgil kept this opinion to himself, though; he didn't dare share it openly. Even though Virgil was already dead, he was in limbo, the in-between place. He wanted to eventually be sent to heaven or, at the very least, not sent to hell. He was on good terms with most in heaven and hell so he wanted to keep it that way.

He had continued to write novels and stories long after his death. They would unfortunately never be seen by mortals, but both angels and demons alike loved them. He was a living legend, if you will. Although like any great man, he knew he had some who resented him and would like nothing more than to see him falter. He was putting his much-cherished position in danger by helping Uriel. Azazel had the power to bar his access from hell, putting an end to his meanderings and wealth of material for good stories. He was also in danger of not being allowed back into heaven by helping Azazel. Uriel did not have the authority to bar his access into heaven, but some of his seraph allies could and it would take little persuading, once they learned he'd helped *evil*. He had to admit the danger both electrified and thrilled him. He felt more alive and mortal now than he ever had when he was alive, at least that he could remember—it had been a very long time since his death. He had to be extremely careful and give both sides just enough of what they wanted without either catching on that he was working them both.

Virgil had brooded for years over the so-called Apocalypse of John. John was a simpleton who couldn't think of an elegant phrase if one fell off a tree and hit him in the head. He recalled his meeting John when he was imprisoned on the island Patmos. Alive or dead, his charm and wit seemed to allow him access to just about anywhere he wanted.

"Why do you look so dejected?" Virgil had asked.

"I want to write down this dream I had about the end of the world. It was given to me by an angel, but I can't seem to capture it properly," John had said.

"Tell the dream to me and I shall help weave a story, a kind that has never been heard before." And so John told him the story, and Virgil did weave a story that had never been heard before. Virgil excluded some of John's more banal details and embellished more on the exciting parts, and that was the book to be forever known as Revelation or the Apocalypse of John. He hoped that would change soon, though.

When Virgil had arrived where they kept the treacherous souls, it was extremely crowded. None of the souls were enduring any kind of painful torture or shaming, such as being poked in the behind with a stick. They were all just sitting around talking to one another like they were at a social gathering and not enduring any of the pain and monotony an eternity in hell was supposed to provide. He looked around to see if he could find the demon or demons in charge. His eye caught a demon named Amon, who looked really frantic.

"Virgil, thank God you're here," Amon said and covered his mouth after saying it. Even though it was just a saying, Lucifer would not be pleased to hear one of his demons saying the phrase "thank God." Lucifer thought the only being you should be thanking is he himself, even though he'd led a failed rebellion that resulted in him and anyone allied with him being cast out of paradise and into a cesspool of misery.

"What's going on here, Amon?"

"I have to watch the lustful while Haagenti is being punished for letting them escape. You may have heard about that."

"Yes, I did hear about that. Why are they just all sitting around?"

"There isn't even enough room in here to move so I just let them all sit. It's quite nice for a change actually. One does grow weary of eternal torture. I really need a break, though; I've been down here all day by myself with no help. I don't want to leave them because I'm afraid they might escape and the same thing that is happening to Haagenti will happen to me. Can you watch them a little while for me?"

Virgil hesitated; he was really anxious to get out of there. The longer he stayed down there, the greater the risk that someone could discover he had the book.

"All right, but I only have a few minutes. I have an appointment in heaven I need to keep."

Virgil looked around; if he weren't feeling so anxious to leave, he could have better appreciated the fact that everyone was smiling. They were clearly enjoying themselves. He was not enjoying himself, however; he was growing more impatient and anxious by the minute. As always, when he was anxious and growing impatient, he started pacing back and forth but stopped when a voice called out to him, "Hey, you there. Aren't you Virgil?"

Virgil sometimes ran into souls he had known from *above*, but it wasn't too often because hell was a big place packed with a lot of sinners.

"Who wants to know?"

"It's me, Titus Gallus. I was a servant for the emperor Augustus."

"Ah yes, I remember you; you had a very pronounced limp as I recall."

"Yes indeed; it's the very same limp that landed me here. I was never very sure-footed and one day I tripped, carrying a hot plate of soup, which landed right in the Caesar's lap. Augustus had me crucified; it took two days for me to die."

"Ah yes, the Romans do love a good crucifixion. What a painful way to die; I'm so sorry, Titus."

"It's okay; it's nothing compared to what I normally endure here day after day."

Titus continued to talk, but Virgil wasn't listening; he needed to get out of there. He didn't want to be caught in hell with the book still on him.

"Uh, say there, Titus. Can you tell Amon—he's the devil in charge of torturing you—that I had to be on my way. I'm already late for an appointment."

"It would be my pleasure, my lord. I always liked your stories. I can't read, but my son was able to learn and he would read them aloud to me. I think your work is much better than a boil on a frog's butt."

"I beg your pardon."

"Caesar used to say that your work was worse than a boil on a frog's butt. I disagree; I think it's better. I'm sure he's down here somewhere, and I will be sure and tell him that if I ever see him. He may have been important up there; but since we are both dead and in hell now, I figure we are equals, and I can say whatever I want."

Virgil had never heard his work described in such a way. "Indeed, don't forget to tell Amon." He picked up the nearest horn and called for Phenex. To Virgil's surprise, Phenex came right away and didn't keep him waiting.

Virgil felt uneasy; it wasn't like Phenex to hasten to his call. *Don't be paranoid; if he knew the book were missing and had any idea that I had taken it, he would have already sounded the alarm.*

The rest of the ride went by in silence, for which Virgil was grateful because it gave him a chance to think about his next move. In the distance he could see the entrance, and standing right in front of it was Baal.

What is he doing there? Surely, he hasn't already deduced that I stole the book.

Baal had not seen Virgil and Phenex yet because they were obscured by a cliff that jutted out of the rock above; soon, though, they would pass it and it would be too late.

"I'll just get off right here," Virgil said and jumped onto dry land, losing his footing and almost plunging backward into the Lake of Fire.

"But we're almost there."

"I'll walk the rest of the way; I could use the exercise."

"Suit yourself." Phenex didn't ask any more questions; he was glad to be rid of the pest. He turned the boat around at the cliff

99

while it was still eclipsing Baal's view, and then he was out of sight.

Virgil waited until he was gone and looked around for the secret passage. He knew it was there somewhere, but he had not used it in years. He rubbed his hand over the rock face and felt an indenture in the smooth surface. He pushed the stone; it moved, revealing a path. The air inside smelt rather stale like the door had not been open for some time. It was pitch black inside, and Virgil could not see a hand in front of his face.

He went back outside and saw a sharpened stick lying on the ground. It looked like the same kind that the devils were using earlier. He wasn't sure how it got all the way up here, but he felt very fortunate that it was. He tore off a piece of his robe and wound it around the stick. He bent down and was just able to get the tip of it in the Lake of Fire. It lit and now he had a torch. If there were one thing there was abundance of in hell, it was fire.

He started down the path and looked at all the strange pictures carved into the rock face. It was the devil's tongue, and it had probably been there for eons. He wondered what Baal was doing there. Was it just a coincidence or was he actually waiting for him?

He could finally see a bit of light. The secret passage went all the way into limbo, his home. *I have to tread carefully; that Baal is a clever one.*

Baal was a clever one; in fact, among his other titles, he was known as Baal the Clever. He was just coming back from his trip to Earth when Virgil saw him. He had no idea that the Book of Judas he had just stolen had gone missing. Baal was patting himself on the back because he had just pulled off a coup. Not only had he gotten Philip and Thomas to give him the Book of Judas, he had overheard their conversation on the boat as to where the other books were buried. He had transformed himself into a parrot, the very same parrot that was on the bow of their boat and found their distress really amusing. The gospels were in the exact location that the monks had said they were, under the large eucalyptus tree with the X. Baal now had in his hands the sack containing the rest of the Gnostic Gospels

A Bishop Washed Ashore

"How could they be gone?" Peter asked.

"We went to check on them and the entire sack was gone," Philip said.

"Do you think one of the lepers took it?" Tiberius, otherwise known as Netzach, asked.

Philip looked down at his feet and let the sand squish between his toes. A crab which was walking along sideways stopped to look at his foot for a moment, but then continued on its way. It must have found the dirty foot with an in-grown toenail unappealing.

His brother Thomas spoke up, "No, we checked everywhere and there was no trace."

Tiberius shook his head. He knew mortals were careless, often weak-minded and negligent, but these two were even more so than usual. They were above even the Roman who he had met once who'd drowned trying to save a badger that had fallen down a well. "Uriel will be grieved to hear this. I must tell him right away so he can come up with a plan."

"I guess you must, Tiberius," Peter agreed reluctantly. The monks had gotten used to calling him that name, but Netzach found it to be too mortal and too Roman for his taste. He wished they could have picked a nice Egyptian name, but he didn't look at all Egyptian.

The angel was just about to snap his fingers and return to heaven when a commotion was heard not too far down the beach. A boat had arrived and with it two men. The commotion seemed to be that one of the men was really fat and was having trouble getting out of the boat, while the other, who was a slight fellow, was trying his best to pull him out.

"I say, Gilberto. What's wrong with you? Pull, boy!" The bishop called him "boy" when he was vexed with him; and even though Gilberto was not exactly sure of his age, he guessed it was around thirty so he was hardly a boy. Indeed, he felt like he had one foot in the grave and with everything he had to endure from the bishop, he was sure the other foot would be there soon as well.

Netzach was the first to reach the pair, followed right behind by Peter, Philip and Thomas.

"I say, you there," the Bishop of Naples said, pointing directly to Netzach. "Can you give us a hand?"

Netzach rolled his eyes, but neither man noticed because of their preoccupation with getting the fat man out of the boat.

Yes, I was once a respected angel, but not anymore. Now I'm just a mortal who helps lepers to the privy and fat men out of boats, he thought. Netzach grabbed one arm while the slender servant grabbed the other, and they both tugged with all of their might. They finally succeeded in getting the bishop out of the boat, but he lost his footing, no doubt because he had been at sea a while, and fell into the sand. Once again, Netzach and the smaller man each grabbed an arm and managed to pull the bishop upright. The bishop was completely red-faced and his bald head was sweaty, as if he were the one who had done all the exertion. Thomas, Philip and Peter were standing behind Netzach, quietly observing the scene.

"Let us help you with your trunks," Thomas offered.

"Thank you, young sir. I dare say, I expected more of a welcoming than this," the bishop said.

"Welcoming? Were we to be expecting you?" Thomas asked.

Peter and Philip grabbed a trunk and had just barely managed to clear the boat when it landed in the sand with a soft *thud*. Netzach stood there and watched, not offering to help. He had already pulled a fat man out of a boat and pulled him out of the sand; he was not going to lift any of the fat man's trunks.

"No one even told you I was to be expected?" the Bishop of Naples asked incredulously. He puffed his chest out and dusted the sand off his robe with his hands. "I am the Bishop of Naples." The Bishop clearly thought the monks were supposed to be impressed, but they just looked at one another. "This is my manservant Gilberto," the bishop said, waving his hand in Gilberto's general direction.

"Well, your holiness, I'm sure you've had a long journey and would like to see your quarters," Peter said.

"I should say so," the bishop scoffed.

"How is it that you've come across the sea with just you and your manservant in this tiny vessel?"

"Oh, there was a man who was leading us here. What was his name again, Gilberto?"

"It was something Gaulish, sir."

"Yes, there was a Gaul guiding us."

Peter asked the obvious question. "Where is your guide?"

"Oh, he fell overboard."

"He drowned?" Philip asked.

"Drowned? I dare say not. Have you ever met a Gaul who couldn't swim?"

There were a lot of Gauls on the island, and some could swim and some couldn't; but Philip wasn't sure why just the fact that if you were a Gaul, it meant you could swim.

"I'm sorry, your holiness; I don't understand. If he didn't drown, than why isn't he with you?" Philip asked.

"Are you deaf, boy? I just told you, the man fell overboard. I thought you monks were supposed to be learned."

"You didn't help him back in the boat?" Thomas asked.

"How could I possibly do that? It would have taken far too much effort to swing the boat around to pick him up; and besides, he is floating on Gilberto's trunks which he threw overboard, so he's perfectly safe." He didn't mention that Gilberto had to throw his own trunk overboard because the bishop was unwilling to throw any of his.

"There's a Gaul floating somewhere out in the *Mare Nostrum* on your manservant's trunk?"

"You are slow to catch on; I confess I had hoped to find someone of wit on this god forsaken island with whom I could converse about the grander things of the world: philosophy, art, rhetoric, wine—"

Philip interrupted him, "Oh, we have a monk who knows a lot about wine. Brother Lorenzo has cultivated a very fine vineyard."

"Well, I'm glad to hear it. Come along with my trunks, Gilberto."

Thomas and Philip helped Gilberto with the bishop's trunks.

The bishop started to say something, but sneezed instead; then another sneeze immediately followed.

103

"Is that eucalyptus I smell? Eucalyptus bothers my nose something awful. Dear God, Gilberto, I shall never be able to speak again because I'll be too busy sneezing."

One can only hope, Gilberto thought.

"We are happy that you are here, of course, but why is it that we are graced with your presence?" Peter asked.

"I should like to know the answer to that as well. Clearly I have upset someone in the church hierarchy—although I can't imagine who—to be sent to such a place. I was simply told by a messenger that I was to go to the island of Lerina for an indefinite period of time to administer the Eucharist. I was told this by a mere messenger and not from the pope or, at the very least, another bishop. He also said—and I can't believe this is true—that you have an adjacent island with a Lazar and I am to administer the Eucharist to the lepers there. You don't have an island of lepers, do you?"

"Yes, my brother Thomas and I look after them and tend to their medical needs," Philip said and reacted just in time to catch the bishop as he nearly fainted.

"Eucalyptus, lepers, Gauls—we have been sent to the very bowels of hell, Gilberto."

Anywhere you are is the very bowels of hell, he thought.

"You've had a long journey, and I'm sure you will feel better after you've settled in to your room," Peter said.

The monks escorted the bishop through the door to his room. The dimensions of the room felt like they were that of a packing crate. It had a small bed, a chamber pot and a chair.

"Is this a broom closet?" the bishop asked.

"This is your room," Peter said.

"This is the smallest room I've ever seen in my life; it doesn't even have a writing desk. My servants had bigger rooms than this."

Gilberto nodded. It was true; this was a rather small room compared to the rooms in the bishop's grand house.

"This is our best room; we are but humble monks here. We don't have many luxuries; we live simply as our lord Jesus Christ did," Peter said.

"It doesn't say anything in the Bible about our lord living in a broom closet."

"You have the only room that has a view of the sea," Thomas said and pulled back the tapestry. Philip quickly got behind the bishop because he thought he might faint again, but he didn't; he just sat down in the chair.

The bishop caught Peter's eye. It was the first time he was really seeing the monk. The bishop didn't normally make eye contact with whom he thought of as his inferiors, which was just about everyone . . . except for God and the pope. He looked at the others who were watching him earnestly, all except Gilberto, who was anxious to get to his own room and away from the bishop.

"You look familiar. Have we met before?"

***

Once again Netzach was standing in front of Uriel, Michael and Gabriel.

"This is terrible; now all of the books are gone," Uriel said.

"Maybe it's time to give up on this," Netzach said.

"Just let them be lost forever and the words never to drip from the lips of mankind again?"

"You're being overly dramatic," Michael said.

"Stop pouting, Uriel, angels aren't supposed to pout," Gabriel said.

"Oh, hang the both of you," Uriel said and then disappeared.

"He disappeared and he didn't even snap his fingers," Michael said.

"Someone must have summoned him."

"I knew it; I told him that repeated bad language was going to get him into trouble."

"Now he will have to face an inquiry from the Angels of Virtue," Gabriel said.

"What kind of punishment do you think he will get?" Netzach asked.

"It depends; he might have to fetch books for St. Peter."

"I better get back down below before those monks cause any more trouble." Netzach snapped his fingers and disappeared.

Virgil was walking towards them, and he was carrying something.

"Hullo, Virgil," Michael said.

"Where is Uriel? I have something for him that I think he might want."

"He said one too many bad words; he will probably be with the Angels of Virtue for the rest of the day."

"What are virtues anyway?" Michael asked.

"Oh, you know, patience, courage, good temper, charisma . . . things like that," Gabriel said.

"Well, I hope Uriel has other virtues because he doesn't have any of those."

Virgil coughed.

"Are you ill, Virgil?"

He handed Michael the Book of Judas. "Give this to Uriel."

"The Book of Juda," Michael read.

"That's *Judas*."

"Oh, right. I'll keep it safe until he returns."

"You know, some of these have smudges and the words have been blotted out. I could correct those for you."

"Immortals cannot tamper with the written word of mortals. If you did, it would undo time," Michael said.

"Do you remember when you almost undid time? You were trying to correct a recipe for bread pudding," Gabriel said.

"I remember Uriel smacked the quill from my hand before I could write anything. Have you ever had bread pudding? It is almost worth undoing time for just a bite."

Virgil coughed again.

"For the love of the Holy Ghost, Virgil. You need to stop going to hell so much; the foul air doesn't seem to be agreeing with you," Michael said.

"It never troubles the wolf how many the sheep may be."

"What sheep?" Gabriel asked.

"Nothing. If I can't fix the gospels, what about those monks who are aiding you?"

"They are immortal too; they've already died once, even though their names have not been written down in the *Liber Mortuorum* yet."

"When you see Virgil, tell him I have retrieved his lost book."

"That's great, but now the others have been stolen."

"What? Do you know how hard it was to smuggle that book out of hell. I had to get a hellhound drunk to get this. I don't see how I'm going to be able to get all those books back without being noticed. Was it Baal who stole the books?"

"Yes, Netzach seems to think so," Michael said.

"No, Netzach said it was stolen by a parrot."

"How could a parrot steal a sack full of gospels?"

"Wait, maybe he said Baal was disguised as a parrot," Gabriel said.

"I still don't see how a parrot stole an entire sack of gospels, whether he was disguised as Baal, St. Peter or the Presence of God."

"The Presence of God wouldn't need to steal the gospels. He has everything that was and ever will be already memorized."

"It was clever of Baal to disguise himself as a parrot," Michael said.

"Baal the Clever, Baal the Deceiver and now Baal the Parrot."

"Don't forget he was also a leper."

"Will you two just focus for a second," Virgil said.

"I think you need to see the Angels of Virtue too and learn some patience," Michael said.

"I have no idea how to get the others back. Azazel had plans to have a celebration and burn the Book of Judas. He most assuredly will want to do the same to the others."

"They were having a celebration? I'd like to go to a celebration."

"They might be having bread pudding," Michael said.

Virgil walked away and left Michael and Gabriel to discuss desserts. He would have to return to hell to steal the gospels back. He just didn't know how he was going to do it.

I hope they don't have any more hellhounds guarding them; I'm out of spirits, he thought.

The Two Faces of Virgil

"How could we have possibly lost the Book of Judas? Barghest was guarding it," Azazel shouted.

"Barghest was passed out drunk, and the book was gone when he woke up," Rosier said.

The demons watched as the souls who had committed the sin of sloth ran over hot coals with their bare feet. One poor soul fell and burnt her hands and knees, as well as her feet. Lucifer thought it was the perfect punishment for the lazy slobs. The demons thought it was good fun and gave out a prize to the soul who got across it the fastest. The prize was an entire day free from torture. It didn't sound like much, but when you have to endure torture day after day for eternity, you will eagerly take even one day.

So far, the best time had been seven seconds by the Greek athlete Orsippus who was from Megara. He had won many of Greece's Olympic games in running, and he liked to run all of them naked. He shed the burden of clothes to overcome the wind resistance that he believed was slowing him down. He'd even remained naked during his crowning, much to the crowd's delight. After Orsippus, everyone started taking their clothes off and running naked; it had become a Hellenic tradition.

It was ironic that this man was in hell for the sin of sloth but when asked about it once, he'd simply shrugged. This was not uncommon; a lot of souls not only had no idea why they were in a particular level of hell, but also some didn't even know why they were in hell at all. It was all left to the discretion of St. Peter, who Azazel knew for a fact had sent many souls to hell who had no business here. He was sure Orsippus was one of them. It was a raw deal to have your soul sent to eternal damnation due to the oversight of an old man. Far be it for Azazel to say anything because nothing would be done about it. Lucifer didn't care, and St. Peter always insisted he didn't make mistakes.

"How did he get drunk?"

"It's most likely that Belphegor brought back some spirits from his drinking, eating and copulating expeditions," Rosier said. Belphegor really loved all of those things, which was probably why he was called Belphegor the Drunk, Belphegor the Hungry and Belphegor who Copulates.

"It doesn't really matter how he got drunk. What matters now is the whereabouts of the book," Rosier pointed out.

"I had planned such a lovely party around throwing that book in the Lake of Fire. I had some very fine cheeses set aside. Well, the cheese has all melted because of the heat, but still it would have been nice."

"Should we try to look for it?" Rosier asked.

"Oh, what's the point? Barghest was probably so drunk he chewed it all up."

"The point is that it is destroyed and that's what you wanted, after all."

"I suppose," Azazel said and watched as one soul tried to leap over the hot coals. Belias was flying in at the same time, and the two collided. Belias landed on top of the man, "Get off me!" he screeched.

"I'm terribly sorry," Belias said and tried to help pull up the man, who only smacked his hand away. "How rude." Belias walked away from the man who was widely gesticulating with his hands and insisting he should get to do it over because the clumsy demon had interfered.

"I'm sorry, but you will have to wait until it's your turn again."

The man looked at the line; it snaked around for miles. He spat at Belias.

Belias had to collect himself; he was a little out of breath from flying so fast.

"I have good news and bad news," Belias said.

"What's the good news?" Rosier asked.

"Baal has stolen the rest of the Gnostic Gospels."

"That's great. We can continue then with the original celebration I planned. Wait. What's the bad news?"

"A rock fell on Baal and hit him in the head and—"

"I asked, what's the bad news?"

"I wasn't finished. He had the sack containing the gospels, but then a rock fell on his head and knocked him unconscious. When he woke up, the sack was gone. He fell near the edge of the high cliff, so he assumes the bag fell in the Lake of Fire and was incinerated."

"This is unbelievable; I mean how much bad luck can a demon have in one day?" Azazel asked.

"I wouldn't be so upset. I mean, you wanted all the books gone and they are. It doesn't matter how they were destroyed; it just matters that Uriel can't get his paws on them again," Rosier said and patted his friend on the shoulder.

"You know you can still have a celebration. I mean, since when do demons need a reason to celebrate? We are known far and wide for our celebrations, festivities and jubilees," Belias said.

"I don't think word has gotten out about our penchant for grand parties. Mortals just think we are all about torture and fire," Rosier said.

"We are much more than just that, aren't we, Orsippus? Come to the celebration with us and have some cheese." Orsippus, who was not wearing any clothes, nodded and said something in Greek.

"What did he say?" Azazel asked.

"I don't know. Greek is not one of the languages I speak," Rosier said. There were about 6,000 different languages spoken in hell, so it was definitely a barrier in communication since the devils had no idea what was being said half the time.

"Maybe we can get a hold of some Greek food. I bet Orsippus would enjoy that. What do Greeks eat again?" Belias asked.

"They eat olives, I think."

"That's it? Well, maybe we can find some olives to dip in the melted cheese," Azazel said.

One soul was about to take off running over the coals; but before he could take a step, the soul behind him, a man, pushed him down on the coals. The man howled in pain, and the man who pushed him howled with laughter.

"Damn you! It's bad enough I had to put up with you during life, but why do I have to put up with you in death? I don't know what's worse, you or hell."

"Quit your bellyaching and get on with it; it's not like we have an eternity," he said with a smile. He was clearly enjoying antagonizing the man.

"If you hadn't been so lazy, you wouldn't be down here."

"You're down here too, you old fool, so don't try to put on airs."

"I'd say we've got some brothers here who don't get along," Rosier said.

"That happens from time to time. I've seen entire families cast in the same circle," Belias said.

"Hey, let's invite them to the celebration too. Hey, you there, excuse me," Azazel said and waved his hands. The men stopped arguing long enough to look at the demon with a quizzical expression.

"How would you both like to come to a celebration I'm having?" The man looked at Azazel and then his brother.

"I'm not going anywhere if he's going to be there," one brother said, flinging a hot coal at the other while running over the hot coals before he could take revenge.

***

What Azazel thought was bad luck was really the cunning of Virgil. He had taken the secret passage from Heresy that led all the way to Greed. When he came out, who should be standing there with his back turned to him but Baal, and he was carrying the sack. He panicked; he didn't know what to do. If that sack got back to Azazel, he would never be able get it back; but if he were caught, he would lose all the freedoms he enjoyed. Virgil thought fast, looked around and saw a good-sized rock. He picked up the rock and hit Baal on the head with it. The demon fell to the ground; he was out cold. He moved Baal near the great cliff that hung over the Lake of Fire. He sat down on the rock beside him.

Hopefully he will think a rock fell on him, and the bag of gospels fell in the Lake of Fire. If not, I may want to lay low for a while, he thought. Rocks fell all the time; after all, what was hell but a huge cavern miles and miles beneath the Earth right next to the Earth's core, which was why it was extremely hot.

Virgil picked up the sack and took the passage from Greed all the way into limbo. He didn't dare take the ferry; Phenex would immediately demand to know what was in the sack. Even if he didn't, he could tell someone later that he had seen him with it, and even Azazel was not that dense; he would figure out what had happened. He had more than fulfilled his bargain with the angels; he had recovered all of the stolen gospels. Uriel would have to keep his word and put his name on it. He had also fulfilled his pledge to Azazel by supplying him with information about Uriel; at least he hoped so. He really wanted to meet Satan; not too many people could boast about that. Demons were not known to be honest or keep their word. It was Virgil who had given Azazel the idea of getting the Bishop of Naples over to the island where he would surely recognize the monks and have them arrested, thereby getting the monks out of the way.

Virgil twirled his beard around his finger. *With my name on Revelation and a meeting with Satan, that will surely reap all kinds of story ideas. I'm on my way to being the most famous dead person ever*, he thought.

The Innocent Pope

Philip, Thomas, Simon, Lorenzo, Peter, John and Adolfo had their hands shackled together. The monks were entering Vatican City in Rome, escorted by the magistrate and several soldiers of the papal army, which were mainly hired mercenaries. The Bishop of Naples and his servant Gilberto returned home; in addition to discovering the heretical monks, he also learned that no one had summoned him to the island, least of all the pope. The faces of Peter, Philip and Thomas had looked familiar to him, but it wasn't until he saw Lorenzo that he remembered who they were. Not even the bishop could forget a hunchback with a flatulence problem. The charges were serious, and the penalties would no doubt be equally as serious. They were not supposed to be receiving the Eucharist or even setting foot in a church, let alone posing as monks. Their trial this time would take place in St. Peter's Basilica, named after Peter, the first pope, whose bones were directly below the high altar. This was the same St. Peter the monks had met at the pearly gates in heaven, who insisted on going through all of their sins and tried to send Adolfo to hell. It was strange to think of his bones existing in one place and his soul in another. Peter, also known as Simon, was crucified on a cross with his head downwards. Many people believed he had requested it because he didn't think himself worthy to die in the same manner as Jesus; but, in reality, it was because the Romans who had put up the cross, accidentally put it upside down and couldn't be bothered to fix it. In fact, his last recorded words were, "You idiots; fix this cross. I hope your empire crumbles."

The monks passed some people who were making a pilgrimage to the holy city. They stared at the fearsome-looking mercenaries and the shackled monks who were their captives. Peter heard one of them say, "Those must be the monks." It turns out they weren't just making a normal pilgrimage to Rome; they had come for the express purpose of witnessing the trial of the heretical monks. When the monks were shoved into the Basilica doors rather roughly by the papal army, the monks were surprised at the crowd that had gathered. The pews were jammed packed, and many people were standing along the walls. There must have been over 4,000 people there. The walls were high and supported by many Solomonic columns that had a spiraling twisting shaft. The story was that they had come directly from the Temple of Solomon. The mercenaries finally shoved the crowd aside and took the monks all the way up to the front until they were standing in front of the chair of St. Peter. Sitting in that chair was Pope Innocent I.

Pope Innocent was well on his way to making a name for himself for preserving the purity of the Catholic Church and Church discipline. He was wearing a pallium, the traditional ecclesiastical vestment of the pope, and scowling at the monks from underneath his heavy papal crown.

"Deacon Martino, read aloud the list of charges."

A short man, almost dwarf-size, wearing the traditional diaconal vestment of a deacon, stood up and held up a parchment.

"The Holy Roman Papacy charges Peter, Simon, John, Lorenzo, Adolfo, Philip and Thomas of Hadria of violating the Anathema that was issued against them by the Church and double heresy."

The Pope frowned and motioned the deacon to come forward.

"What is double heresy?" the pope asked the deacon in a whisper.

"Well, they'd already committed heresy once, which they were excommunicated for, so this makes the second time."

"It doesn't sound very official; please strike it from the record."

The deacon dipped his quill in some ink and drew a line through "double heresy."

"You may precede, Deacon Martino."

"These men standing before you were issued an Anathema by the Church during the year of our lord 397, as witnessed by the Magistrate of Hadria and Bishop Severus of Naples."

The pope laughed at the mentioning of the bishop. He thought it rather amusing that the fat man thought he had been called to serve on an island full of hermit monks and lepers in Gaul.

The Deacon handed Pope Innocent the document where the magistrate and the bishop had signed.

"They were excommunicated from the village of Hadria as well as the Church, forbidden to receive the Eucharist or hold any position of authority in the Church," the deacon said.

The pope looked at the seven monks who were still shackled. They did not have anyone representing them. "Well, what do you have to say for yourselves?"

Lorenzo, whose stomach was acting up due to his nerves, could not hold it in any longer. He broke wind and the more he tried to suppress it, the louder it got. It reverberated throughout the entire courtroom. The courtroom erupted with laughter; even the dwarf-like deacon snickered . . . everyone, that is, except for the pope who felt a sense of déjà vu. His face turned purple; he exploded with anger and said in his most caustic tone of voice, "You dare make a mockery of this court."

"Pardon me, sir; I have a rotten gut. It's forever giving me trouble," Lorenzo said.

"Silence. It's bad enough that you all were posing as holy men, taking part in church worship and administering the body and blood of our Lord, but I will not have the papal court made into a perversion. I've heard enough, Deacon Martino." The pope rose from the chair of St. Peter and approached the monks. Adolfo grunted and the pope shoved a holy finger into his chest.

"Your holiness, please, I wouldn't do that—" John started to say, but it was too late. The Pope let out an ear-shattering scream and retracted his finger. Adolfo smiled; he had bitten a lot of fingers during his short life, but never one that was infallible.

***

The seven monks found themselves at the gate of St. Peter once again, but this time they were so charred from fire they were unrecognizable. Philip was in front and approached the wizened old man with the gnarly beard. Saint Peter raised an eyebrow.

"Well, caught fire, did we?"

"I was set on fire," Philip replied.

"Terrible way to die; I've seen worse, though."

"Yes, it was extremely painful. We'd like to talk to Uriel."

"Who is *we?*"

Philip motioned behind him at the six other blackened figures.

"Looks like we had ourselves a little human sacrifice. Remember those, Cassiel; those were the good old days. There were the Carthaginians; they had human sacrifices, and what was that other group?"

"The Mesopotamians and Etruscans also did them," Cassiel said.

"The Etruscans? Oh, yes, I remember. They were a strange sort."

"I need to speak to Uriel; it is an emergency," Philip said.

"Listen to this one, Cassiel. He's making demands. The only person you will be speaking with is me. Now, tell Cassiel here your name, so he can get your book."

"Cassiel, we've met before. We are the monks who were helping Uriel."

Cassiel squinted. He couldn't make out any of their features. "I do seem to recall some monks who were here years ago."

"Please, just summon Uriel. He will tell you who we are and explain everything."

"The only thing Cassiel is going to do is get your book. Now, tell me your name."

"Uriel. Uriiiiiiieeeeeel," Philip shouted.

"You don't have to shout; I'm not stone-deaf. Cassiel, go and get the book on this burnt creature who says his name is Uriel."

Uriel heard his name and appeared before the burnt monks. Michael and Gabriel also appeared, because they too had heard the commotion and didn't want to be left out.

"What is going on here? I won't tolerate this disorderly behavior. There is the right way of doing things and there is the wrong way. I do things the right way here at the gates of heaven," St. Peter said.

Uriel looked at the monks' faces. He couldn't make out any features except for the humpback of Lorenzo. His eyes grew wide in surprise. "What happened to you?"

"What do you mean, what happened to us? Weren't you watching? We were burnt alive by the Church," Thomas said.

"I can't always be watching; I do have other things to do. I mean, I am the patron of the arts, after all. I can't believe it; I leave you alone for an instant and look what happens. You let yourselves get burnt alive."

Michael reached out to touch Simon, who was still smoldering.

"We didn't let anything happen. We were caught in Lerina by the Bishop of Naples and summoned back to Rome to stand trial. We were found guilty of violating the Anathema and then sentenced to die," Thomas said.

"You left out the best part," John said.

"Oh, yes, and Adolfo bit the finger of the pope."

"What? You can't do that. You can't go around biting the fingers of popes. That is a mortal sin," St. Peter said.

"Actually, it's never happened before so I'm not really sure what kind of sin it is," Gabriel said.

"I am the first pope there ever was, and I say that if a man bit my finger, it would be a mortal sin."

"Never mind him. Let's go see Azrael; he will send you all back," Uriel said.

"No one is going anywhere until I read their sins; then I will decide who is going where."

Uriel did not want to wait while St. Peter sifted through the monks' sins.

"Use the voice of God to tell this old fool to let them pass," Uriel whispered to Michael.

"Let them pass now," Michael thundered, using the voice of God. The ground beneath their feet shook, and a few pearls fell off the gate. Gabriel smiled and went over to pick them up.

"Forgive me, Lord. I did not mean to anger you," St. Peter said and bowed as low as his old frame would allow him.

Michael, Gabriel, Uriel and the seven charred monks passed through the gate.

"The voice of God has really come in handy. I wonder when He is going to ask for it back."

"I wonder what He sounds like without his voice," Michael said and poked Simon again, who still had not ceased smoking.

"Stop that," Simon responded irritably and hit Michael with his cooking spoon. Not only had the spoon—an earthly possession that was not supposed to make its way into heaven—made it once into heaven, but this was the second time. Miraculously, it had not burnt up in the fire even though it was made out of wood. "This is it; I am not going back to Earth, and I don't care what happens to the other gospels."

"Me too; I'm tired of getting murdered," John said and Adolfo grunted in agreement.

"Calm down, everyone. First of all, let me say that Virgil has managed to retrieve all of the gospels that Baal had stolen. They are currently in my possession," Uriel said.

"That's great; now you don't need us anymore," Peter said.

"That's not true; I still need you. These books have to get sent back to Earth; they do not belong here in heaven. It is one of our laws that you cannot keep earthly goods in heaven. These books are mortal and must remain among mortals." Uriel stopped and looked at Simon. "I haven't the faintest idea, though, how you keep managing to get that spoon up here."

"I'm not going back," Simon repeated.

"I will need you to go back eventually; but don't worry, we can wait a while. We will at least wait until everyone from the Church and your village who could recognize you are dead, so we can prevent any more unfortunate accidents."

"Accident? The pope had us tied to a stake and set on fire," Lorenzo said, clutching his stomach. Even after having the majority of his body singed, his stomach still managed to give him problems.

Uriel waved away this minor detail with his hand. "We have time; as I said, we will wait until everyone who could recognize you has died and then take you back at a less volatile time in history. You seven seem to keep getting yourselves into trouble."

"You'll be waiting until hell freezes over because I'm never returning," John said.

Michael looked puzzled. "I thought hell was supposed to be hot."

An ophan rolled their way and stopped in front of Adolfo. All one hundred of its eyes widened and looked at the smoldering men. Thankfully, the ophan had quick reflexes because it rolled away before Adolfo could bite it. Uriel waited to see if the ophan returned or the cherub who must have been with it because there was never one without the other, but nothing else showed up.

When they got to Azrael, he had his face pressed almost in the

Liber Mortuorum, which was floating transfixed in midair and would remain so until the end of time. After millennia of having to stare at a book, his eyes were strained. He raised his head when he saw Uriel, Michael and Gabriel and whatever it was that was with them.

"I need those things. You know, I forget what they are called; but they help, you see," he said.

"Well, you only have to wait about 900 years for glasses to be invented on Earth. It will be here before you know it."

As a general rule, they weren't supposed to have things in heaven that had not been invented on Earth yet because God did not like to fool around with history's timeline, but there were special circumstances in which you could get something if you really needed it.

"I copied a name wrong from St. Peter's list. Instead of writing the name *"Alberto* of Cales," I wrote *"Alberta* of Cales" and some poor woman was struck down accidentally. It took a while to straighten it all out and send her back. It was hard because she didn't want to go back. She said she didn't have anything to do anyway, and she was bored. Can you imagine that, wanting to die because you're bored? Anyway, I think I am going to ask Vehuaiah for a pair of glasses." Vehuaiah was the seraph in charge of the rules of time and history, the same one Uriel was bypassing because he was such a stickler for the rules.

"Who do you have here with you?"

"These are the monks who are helping me preserve the Gnostic Gospels on Earth. They've gone and got themselves killed again if you can believe it."

"Were you able to save all the gospels then?"

"Well, there might be some still floating around down there on Earth; I just haven't been able to detect them. I did get back the ones that Baal stole. I wish I could see Azazel's face; I'm sure he is beside himself."

"Great, well, I can finally enter these monks' names in the *Liber Mortuorum.*"

"Well, that's why I'm here. I need you to hold off on doing that."

"Why? You said you retrieved the books."

"Virgil retrieved them," Michael corrected.

"Virgil? I would keep a wary eye on that one; he is not to be trusted."

"You can trust him when you have something to offer him," Gabriel said, and Uriel glanced sideways at him.

"What did you offer him, Uriel?" Azrael asked.

"I may have told him that I would remove John's name from the Book of Revelation and add his."

"You did what? You'll never get anyone to approve that. I mean, God likes Virgil—don't get me wrong—but he is not going to remove John's name. He is an apostle, after all."

"I thought you would be able to approve it. Oh well, a minor detail that I am sure will work itself out. Anyway, I want you to hold off on writing their names down. I do have the books; but, as you are aware, I can't keep them in heaven indefinitely. They will eventually have to go back and when they do, I will send the monks along with them."

"We are not going back," Philip said.

"If the monks don't want to go back, Uriel, you can't send them against their will."

"They will change their minds. I'm going to send them back during a time when they will be safe."

"Vehuaiah told me there wasn't a time in Earth's history that wasn't volatile. There is always some war or massacre going on."

"You know what I mean, a time when there is relative peace and prosperity."

"So what do you plan to do with them until then? I mean, you can't let them roam around heaven looking like that. Eventually someone is going to tell on you."

"I will let them stay here and reunite with their loved ones and then retrieve them when the time is right. I'll at least wait until the fall of Rome."

"What do you mean 'the fall of Rome'?" Thomas asked.

"Um . . . never mind; forget you heard it."

The monks didn't want to argue further; they knew there would be plenty of time for that. Until then, they wanted to enjoy being in Paradise.

Monks in Paradise

The monks loved living in heaven; it really was a paradise, mainly because they were reunited with their loved ones. Peter and his wife Mary could be seen strolling through heaven hand-in-hand. He had not been the same since she had died; and now that he was reunited with her, he vowed never to leave her side.

John found his mother and father, and Adolfo reunited with his mother as well. He still did not talk, but there was a noticeable difference in him. He smiled more and grunted a lot less. His father, whom he had never met, was in hell and his mother would not speak about him.

Lorenzo, whose stomach had still not quieted down, could often be seen moping about. He found his childhood sweetheart; but, between his unbearable flatulence and his hunchback, she did not wish to reunite with him. He stopped moping, though, after finding his paternal grandfather whom he had adored as a boy.

Thomas and Philip met their father; their mother was in hell. They discovered that their mom had had an affair and that Philip had a different father, who was also in hell. They were forever damned in the circle of Lust.

Simon found his twin brother, Antonio, who had died of fever in childhood. They were identical in every detail, right down to their love of cooking. The only way to tell them apart was that Simon always carried the cooking spoon.

Everything in heaven was beautiful and aesthetically pleasing to the eye. God had a knack for symmetry and design. Although some would vehemently disagree and say that heaven was too white; everything was white, from the clouds, to the robes everyone wore, to the gate of heaven, which was made out of pearls.

Adolfo was in his element, reunited with his mother, painting and grunting to his heart's content. He never had to substitute colors; every color was always readily available. John would sit around eating and regaling the women with stories, which he

121

embellished for dramatic effect. You could hear giggles reverberating throughout heaven. If it were possible to get fat in heaven, John would have been as large as an ox because he did nothing but sit around and eat.

Peter passed the days with his wife reading. Saint Bede's Library in heaven had copies of every book ever written. He was currently reading the *Aeneid* by Publius Vergilius Maro . . . Virgil, as he was known to the world. Ironically, Saint Bede's Library had copies of the Gnostic Gospels, and people in heaven did read them from time to time; but that wasn't enough people to satisfy Uriel's desire for recognition.

Simon spent most of his time cooking and experimenting with different dishes, adding a spice here and there.

Lorenzo was drunk on wine most of the time and could be found passed out in heaven's vineyard. He had to be helped up because his hump made it difficult for him to get up by himself. There was no vineyard on Earth that could compare to the vineyard in heaven; the grapes were the sweetest Lorenzo had ever tasted. The grapes were made by God and unavailable on Earth; they made the most delicious wine, better than anything mortals could make. Heaven also had a nice stock of aged wine, and it was Lorenzo's goal to drink every last bit of it. He particularly loved the Retsina, the white wine made by the Greeks.

Thomas and Philip spent their time trading medical knowledge with the other healers in heaven. Azrael had fixed the monks' bodies; they no longer looked as though they had been roasted on a spit. It would have been unsightly for them to roam around heaven in such a state. He didn't go as far as to fix Lorenzo's hump or bowels, though, the latter much to the chagrin of everyone in heaven.

Virgil strolled into Saint Bede's Library on his way to meet Uriel; he stopped in to visit Peter. He saw him sitting and reading a book that looked all too familiar. Virgil enjoyed talking to Peter; he admired his intellect. They were about the same age and similar in appearance, especially with their white beards. They were even sometimes mistaken for one another. Virgil was pleasant and charming to everyone, but he didn't really have any friends and that's the way he preferred it. So Peter was as close to a friend as Virgil would allow.

"Another fine day in God's paradise."

Peter looked up from Virgil's epic poem. "To which paradise are you referring, the Garden of Eden or heaven?"

Virgil smiled; he loved Peter's wit. The Garden of Eden and the story of Adam and Eve was not quite the way it was depicted in Genesis. For one thing, Lucifer was not a serpent. He was made into a serpent by Moses, the author, because he was supposed to be evil and hideous and what better form to take than a serpent. In actuality, Lucifer was at first a fish, but he realized he could hardly entice anyone to do anything in that form so he was changed into a skunk. He got Adam and Eve to eat from the tree of life, not so much by coaxing as by threatening to spray a terrible odor on them with his tail. Eve was not made from Adam's rib. Eve was actually made first and Adam second, and they were both made from mud piles that formed after it rained. Also the tree of life was not an apple tree; it was a peach tree. Moses changed the peach tree to an apple tree because he simply abhorred the taste of peaches. He didn't like their pits or how messy they were to eat. The other thing was that Adam and Eve were not embarrassed to be naked; they were used to it and much preferred it because they found clothing restrictive. In fact, just like Orsippus, the Greek athlete in hell, Adam and Eve remained naked after they died. You could see them in heaven from time to time, walking around without any clothes, arguing about whose fault it was that they got kicked out of the Garden of Eden. The Bible was full of these little inaccuracies, but God didn't mind because the point was still the same. God was all about the broader message, something that mankind always seemed to miss.

"Are you enjoying the book?" Virgil asked.

"I'm enjoying it immensely; it's too bad the author is a no-good braggart."

Virgil laughed. "You wouldn't be the first to say so." Out of his peripheral vision, he could see Uriel, Michael and Gabriel. "Don't look now, but the unholy trinity is coming this way, and I have a feeling they are looking for you and your friends."

Michael and Gabriel had their swords drawn, just in case; you never knew when the mortals might want to rise up and overthrow heaven. They were ready for anything. Uriel rushed over and shoved a sack into Peter's arms; it was a sack that Peter was all too familiar with. He slammed Virgil's book closed.

"No, I'm not doing it."

"I'm afraid you all have no choice. If you don't and the gospels are destroyed forever, I will let everyone know that you had a chance to protect them, but you chose not to because you are selfish."

"You'll be like Judas the Betrayer. Only your name is not Judas; it's Peter," Gabriel added lamely.

"This whole thing sounds like your problem, not ours."

Uriel ignore Peter's protests and spoke to Virgil, "I'm going to need you to continue to get information from Azazel. If he finds out that the monks are back on Earth with the Gnostic gospels, he will either figure out the books were never burned or that we found some new ones, and he will send his cohort Baal to steal them."

"I'm done with the spying business. You still haven't given me what you promised the first time I agreed to spy. My name still is not on the Book of Revelation."

"I'm working on it; these things take time."

Uriel had been working on no such thing; he had forgotten all about his promise to Virgil.

"It's been nearly fifty years."

"What, fifty years? What year is it?" Peter asked.

"It's the year of our Lord 450. Well, you know how fast time flies in heaven. One day you look out and man is scratching shelter out of a rock, and the next time you look, he has invented electricity."

"What's electricity?" Peter asked.

"Never mind; it's no affair of yours."

"I'm not leaving. I'm dead and so are Lorenzo, Philip, Thomas, John, Adolfo and Simon. We don't belong on Earth anymore. I want to stay with my wife."

"If you don't, I'll turn you all back into charred meat."

"You can't do that," Peter said.

"Oh, couldn't I?" Uriel had no idea if he could do that . . . probably not.

"This isn't fair. We are comfortable here."

"Well, speaking of 'we,' where are the rest of your friends?"

"I'm not really sure but, more than likely, Lorenzo is passed out in the vineyard. He drinks too much wine."

"What? There are rules. This is heaven, not some—" Uriel paused because he couldn't remember what Vehuaiah called a place where you drink. "This isn't some drinking house." Just in case his meaning was unclear, he added, "you know, a house where you drink."

"Rules. What rules? I'm beginning to think there are no rules here and that everyone just does as they please," Peter said.

"Please, I'll give you whatever you want if you'll return to Earth. Do you want to be farmers or tradesmen instead of monks? Take all the wine you want with you."

"I don't drink."

Uriel noticed the *Aeneid* on the ground and rolled his eyes, which didn't go unnoticed by Virgil.

"Take as many books with you as you want."

"So you can take books *from* heaven, but you can't bring books *into* heaven?"

"Like I said, there are rules. They may have been written a long time ago, but some of us still try to abide by them."

Virgil made a noise that was either a laugh or a cry for help. "I don't want to go, and I doubt you can convince the others either."

"Don't worry about that, "Uriel said with a haughty snort. "Just leave that to me."

A Soul Doesn't Fall Far from the Tree

The city of Aquileia in Italy, located at the head of the Adriatic Sea, was one of the world's largest cities in 452; it was a colony of Romans. It was no small feat on Uriel's part to get the monks to go back to Earth to continue their "divine" mission. Uriel was unable to convince Peter; but in the end, it had been his wife, Mary, who convinced him to go. She did see it as a divine mission, but unlike Uriel, her reasons were more noble. Uriel had to bribe, cajole and beg the men before they relented. He regaled them with descriptions of the city. He told them how well merchants lived there and how Lorenzo could sell wine, Simon could be a baker and sell his wares, John and Adolfo could sell books and Peter could bind them. He convinced Philip and Thomas that a city as large as Aquileia was always in need of skilled physicians. The picture he painted was that of a utopia, almost heavenly. He gave all of them money to get set up, which he said there was no rule against it. The rules seemed to be against anything coming into heaven, but God didn't seem to mind things going out. God hated clutter. For once, Uriel was right about something; it was almost a utopia, and the former monks were doing quite well for themselves.

The Romans had built roads that connected Aquileia to Bologna, and these roads were the ones people traveled to buy and sell their goods and services. They once again had the Gnostic Gospels with them, but this time they decided to divide them up and hide them so they would be harder to find and steal.

Philip and Thomas were treating people in their sanctuary, something they picked up from the Greeks who called them *Asclepius*. People came flooding into their sanctuary from all across the country. The holistic approach of the treatment of the whole, rather than an analysis of just parts, was in fashion again. The brothers had their bookshelves lined with the *Hippocratic Corpus*, the collection of the work of Hippocrates. They had learned from talking to others in heaven that diseases were indeed caused naturally, just as Hippocrates said, and not by God. God had better things to do than to mess about with mortals' bodies. It was within one of these works that the Gospel of Thomas was inserted.

"You want me to start running and jumping and hurling large stones?" the man from Milan asked.

"Yes, it's called exercise," Thomas said.

"But how is that going to help? It's my heart that's giving me trouble."

Thomas poked him in the belly. "It will help you stay trim and not put so much pressure on your heart."

"If I'm running and jumping about, that will make my heart worse."

"Trust me on this; exercise is always important, no matter what troubles you."

"I traveled hundreds of miles to have my heart fixed, and you tell me to run around like a fool."

"That's not all. I also want you to take this sack of garlic with you," Thomas said and handed the man the sack.

"What's this for?"

"Garlic is good for the heart. I want you to chop it up, grind it, put it into a broth and add it to your meals."

This seemed to mollify the man from Milan a little. He obviously didn't want to return to his home and tell his family that he had missed months of working, just to be told he needed to lift rocks. He wanted something to show for it.

"I'm serious, though, about the exercise. Hippocrates said it is good to stay fit."

"I don't care what a hippopotamus told you; I'm not jumping around like an idiot."

Thomas sighed. "Fine, don't jump, but at least do some running. Just pretend you are running in Olympia or the Colosseum in front of hundreds of people cheering you on."

The man's face brightened. "I can do that. In fact, I don't see why with enough practice that I could do that for real."

Sure, if it weren't for the fact that you are as fat as a sow and older than Methuselah. I'm sure you could compete against Rome's finest, Thomas thought.

127

Philip looked at his brother and smiled. He was truly happy; they both were. It was not as good as being in heaven—nothing was—but it was the next best thing. He just hoped there was no trouble brewing.

***

Rosier and Azazel were standing under the Quiet Tree, which is not at all serene as the name sounds. It is a 500-foot tree wreathed in flames. It got nicknamed the Quiet Tree because within its thousands of branches, blasphemers were hung by their tongues.

"The Quiet Tree is boring; there's nothing to be done here," Rosier said as he cast a rock into a pit of sulphur and watched the smoke rise in the air.

Azazel coughed. "Don't do that; it stinks."

"I spoke with Belphegor the other day, and he had just come back from a possession. He had possessed this mortal man in Aquileia. That's in Italy," Rosier said.

"Why that place?"

"The man's wife was known far and wide for her beauty, and Belphegor wanted to copulate with her."

"Belphegor the Copulator."

Rosier laughed. "That almost rhymes if you annunciate it."

"Anyway, he stopped at this sanctuary to use one of their baths, and he thinks he saw two of Uriel's monks."

"He must be mistaken. I thought Uriel had given up on that quest to find and safeguard the Apocrypha. Besides, the copies he had were burnt."

"Well, he thought it was probably a coincidence and hardly worth mentioning, but the sanctuary was ran by two brothers, one with raven black hair and one with hair redder than the flames here."

Azazel scratched his chin and some skin flaked off. Every demon in hell was in need of a good moisturizing. "Is that so?"

"It might be worth sending Baal to check it out."

"I suppose it couldn't hurt."

The demons jumped in alarm as a woman came crashing to the ground. She must have fallen a hundred feet. Occasionally some of the branches broke from the weight, and souls would come tumbling down, unable to scream because their tongues were still wrapped around the branch.

"Poor woman, such a harsh punishment for so small a thing," Rosier said.

"Let's untie her tongue and let her rest for a while," Azazel said and carefully removed the branch; as soon as he did, the woman said, "You stupid demon, who told you I wanted that untied?"

"Oh, I'm terribly sorry. Here, I'll put it back."

The woman smacked his hand away. "Don't bother; you'll probably just mess it up with your clumsy demon hands. Besides, the branch is broken so I can hardly use it again, now can I?"

"Well, there's no need to take that tone," Azazel said. He looked at her closely. "Hey, aren't you that woman who was impaled on a stick? You are one of the wrathful. How did you get here?"

"Wouldn't you like to know? Where did they get you, crawling out from under a rock with the other worms?"

Rosier patted the shoulder of his friend, who looked hurt. "Don't listen to her, Azazel. I know you didn't crawl out from under a rock."

"Oh, look who else decided to open his mouth and let his wisdom tumble out."

"Well, that was uncalled for. You know, eternity might go better here for you if you weren't so taciturn," Rosier said.

Azazel had enough of the woman's lip. He grabbed her around the waist and flew all the way to the top of the tree, 200 feet in the air, and wrapped her tongue around the highest branch.

"I hope you fall out of this one and break every bone in your body."

The woman couldn't reply, but she gave Azazel such an icy stare that even in hell, it made him a shiver.

Some of the people here are scarier than the demons. I hope they never decide to mutiny, he thought. He looked down and saw that Baal had joined them. Azazel did a 360 in the air; he liked to show off sometimes and landed beside Baal in perfect form.

"Nice landing," Baal said.

"I was just telling Baal about what Belphegor had told me."

"You know, I always thought something wasn't right about those gospels coincidentally disappearing without anyone actually seeing them get burnt up. I'll bet Uriel got them back somehow," Baal said.

"We accounted for them. Don't you remember? Barghest got drunk and lost the Book of Judas, and your sack fell into the Lake of Fire after a rock hit you on the head," Azazel said.

"Yes, but we think that's what *might* have happened; we never really had definitive proof. I think maybe I should check out this city of Aquileia. "

"All right, it couldn't hurt. You could become a merchant or maybe disguise yourself as someone sick again," Rosier said.

"No, I think—" Baal started to say something when a man fell from the tree right on top of him. Fortunately for Baal, he wasn't on a very high branch so the impact wasn't as bad as it could have been.

"We seem to have a lot of souls falling from the tree today," Rosier said.

"Maybe they were ripe." Azazel laughed at his own joke, but none of the other demons laughed. Baal untied his tongue.

"I'm terribly sorry," the man said.

"How come you always get the nice people, and I always get the mean ones?" Azazel asked.

"You look familiar," Rosier said to the man.

"I'm the Apostle John. Remember, you were supposed to get me back into heaven, but somehow I ended up in that tree."

"I am so sorry; this is terrible. Please don't think badly of us; normally we are more organized than this," Azazel said.

"Well, not really," Baal said.

"Someone will escort you back," Azazel said.

"You are most kind. Could I trouble you for some water? Hanging by your tongue in an inferno does make one a little parched."

Water was a rare commodity in hell, but they did keep some on hand for special circumstances. Rosier felt bad about John. "Of course, follow me and we will get some from Belphegor's special hoard of Earth treasures." Rosier and John walked away and in the distance, Baal and Azazel could hear Rosier say, "Do you mind if we just stop off so I can retrieve Revelations? I would be honored if you would sign it."

Azazel shook his head in disgust. "I want you to go to Aquileia and see what you can find out. Also, see if you can get some people to sign over their souls. How many souls did you get on your last journey?"

"On my last journey, I got two souls. I got a fat bishop and his manservant."

"A bishop? That's excellent; see if you can get more on your next visit. We want to make it look like we're doing this for Lucifer's sake, in case there are ever any inquiries."

"Do you think there might be any inquiries?"

"I doubt it; no one seems to know their tails from their horns in this place."

Lucy

Virgil could hardly believe it, but Azazel had kept his word about setting up a meeting for him with Lucifer for his role in the Gnostic caper. He was on his way there now and he was so excited, he could hardly contain himself. Even the sight of Phenex, the ferryman, couldn't dampen his spirits. There was a deep scowl on the demon's face; and behind it, Virgil knew, was a seething hatred. Everyone knew that Virgil was going to get to talk to Lucifer, something not even many demons could boast about, including Phenex.

I don't see why this mortal piece of refuse should get to meet with his worship and I don't. I'm the one that's got to ferry around these pathetic souls all day, he thought.

Virgil wisely kept quiet and didn't look at him, lest he *accidently* fall into the Lake of Fire. He didn't need to say where he was going; Phenex already knew. Phenex stopped the boat at the deepest and darkest part of hell called Lucifer's Lair. Virgil's excitement was waning a little bit, and fear started to creep in as he stared into the black cavern. Phenex saw the look of fear on Virgil's face and smiled.

"You know, no soul who has gone into Lucifer's Lair has ever returned. Inside of Lucifer's Lair, there are the worse sinners of mankind. They are chained to rocks which they have to carry around for all eternity. Worms feast on their eyes, and there are deadly serpents all around. It's so cold in there that your saliva and tears immediately freeze. Lucifer is terrifying to behold. He is ten feet tall with pitch black eyes and when you look into them, you can see 1,000 dead souls. When he speaks, a two-headed snake comes out, and his voice is so terrifying that you have to cover your ears." Phenex did his best not to snicker; seeing the look on Virgil's face was priceless.

Virgil hopped off the ferry and took timid steps inside the dank cavern. As he got further inside, he began to see a light; and the further he walked, the brighter it got. He got to an iron door, and there was something written above it in the demon tongue. Virgil had spent so much time down here that he had picked up a few words. He thought he must be mistaken in the interpretation, but he swore it said *Welcome One and All*. Virgil gave a timid knock on the door and waited. Eventually a demon he had never seen opened it.

"You must be Virgil; I am so happy to make your acquaintance. I've read all your work and I greatly admire you," the demon said.

"I'm sorry, who are you?"

"I am Lucifer."

Virgil was astounded. Standing in front of him was the lord of all evil; but, not only was he not ten feet tall, he wasn't even five feet tall. In fact, he was almost dwarfish. He was wearing a large crown; and the circumference of it was too big for his head, so instead of sitting nicely on top, it came down to the middle of his forehead. He had unusually long horns and tail, which looked comical on his small stature. Lucifer looked more like a horned lizard than a demon. Lucifer took his hand and escorted him into a lovely sitting room. To Virgil's surprise, it wasn't the least bit cold, nor was there a smoldering heat like the rest of hell. It was a very comfortable temperature. Also, he noticed that there were no foul smells of sweat, pus and sulphur. The room actually smelt like lavender, and he didn't hear any shrieks of pain or wailing. Virgil looked around and didn't see anyone chained to a rock; he didn't see anyone else at all.

"You are the king of all evil?"

Lucifer laughed. "Well, yes, but we don't use such fancy titles here. You can just call me Lucifer or Dark One if you prefer."

"Where are all the great sinners?"

Lucifer looked puzzled. "What great sinners?"

"Where's Judas?"

"Oh, would you like to meet Judas? I'll call him." Satan picked up a bell and rang it. A man came out from the next room carrying a tray with tea and desserts.

"Judy, this is Virgil, the great poet."

Virgil was sure he didn't hear Lucifer correctly because it sounded like he'd just called him Judy instead of Judas.

"How nice to finally meet you. Lucy has told me so much about you."

Virgil looked at the face of Judas Iscariot and then at the dwarfish Lucifer to make sure they weren't mocking him, but they both looked at him pleasantly.

Did he just call the dark lord "Lucy?"

"It's very nice to meet you too, Judas."

"Sit down and make yourself comfortable; I'm sure you have a lot to ask me."

Virgil originally had a lot to ask him; but now, sitting here in the comfortable room with all the pleasantries of home, his mind was a complete blank. He opened his mouth to say something, but could think of nothing and shut it again. Neither Judy nor Lucy noticed his discomfort.

"I understand that you are writing a new book," Judas said.

"Yes, I thought I could add the tales and exploits of Lucifer," Virgil said and then added, "and you too, of course, Judas."

"Won't that be nice, Judy?"

Judy shook his head in agreement.

"So is it just the two of you here?"

"Marcus and Gaius are normally here, but they are currently on sabbatical," Judas said.

"I'm sorry, who are Marcus and Gaius?"

"You know them as—"

Judas interrupted Lucifer. "You know them better as Brutus and Cassius."

"Ah, yes, I wondered about them. Wait, did you say they were on sabbatical?"

"Yes, they are in Milan."

"What part of hell is Milan?"

Judy laughed. "Milan, Italy."

"They're on Earth?" Virgil asked incredulously.

"Sure, why not? They had not left hell in a hundred years; it was way overdue."

Satan started to interject something, "We don't—"

Judas once again interrupted his master. "We don't get many visitors. Belias sometimes comes in here to give and receive messages. He hands out all the schedules to the demons so they know what tasks they are in charge of and where to be." Virgil looked at Lucifer who was sipping his tea and didn't seem to mind in the least being interrupted.

How did he know that was what Lucifer was going to say? They must know each other so well after so many years together that they finish each other's thoughts. Judas makes out the demons' schedules? Who is really running hell here?

"You make out the schedules?"

"Yes, I make out the schedules. Lucy makes minor changes from time to time. I like to think that everything is a joint effort. We are all in this together, after all."

He obviously doesn't get out much. Has he met the demon Belphegor, whose soul purpose is to possess as many people as he can in order to eat drink and copulate?

"Very true," Lucy agreed. He managed to get those two words out before Judas was able to interrupt him.

Lucifer isn't in here torturing anyone. It's just the opposite; he relies heavily on a few to speak and convey messages for him. The demons would be infuriated if they knew Judas, a mortal, made up their work schedule, Virgil thought.

"I'd like to ask you about your rebellion in heaven, if you don't mind. Why did you want to take over heaven?"

"I couldn't stand—"

"He couldn't stand the design any longer."

Lucifer nodded his head delightedly and sipped more tea. He made an indelicate *slurp* which provoked a disapproving look from Judas.

"My apologies," Lucifer said, looking like a scolded child.

"I'm sorry; I don't understand. You didn't like the design?" The question was for Lucifer, but he directed it towards Judas since he was the one who seemed to be the mouthpiece.

"God refused to change anything. He wanted everything white from top to bottom, and he wouldn't take Lucifer up on any of his suggestions. They had irreconcilable artistic differences."

"So the rebellion was over aesthetics?"

"Yes."

Virgil wasn't sure if he should laugh or not because this had to be a joke. The look on both of their faces, though, said it wasn't.

"So you, along with hundreds of other angels, got cast out of heaven for eternity because you weren't allowed to change any of the architecture?"

"Well, the other demons don't know that," Judas said.

"What do you mean?"

"They think it was about taking control for power and changing the system."

Virgil sipped his tea to hide his smile. This was not a version of the rebellion that he had ever heard and obviously only a few people knew about.

"Weren't you concerned about other angels getting hurt?"

"Well, you have to stand up for what you believe in and besides, no one was actually hurt. I don't know if you are familiar with the story, but the charge was led by Azazel who tripped and fell over his own armor, causing the other angels to trip over him and thus pretty much ending the war before it started." Virgil did know that part of the story very well.

"How do you feel about being cast into hell for all eternity?"

"Good," Lucifer said. Virgil waited for him to continue, but apparently "good" was his only thought on the matter; either that or he thought that's the only word he could get in edgewise.

Judas was happy to elaborate for him, though. "He's fine with it because he can decorate however he wants; he did this room himself."

Virgil had to admit it was a nice room.

"So your only interest is in design. What about all this business of torturing souls?"

"Not his idea; that was God's idea. He thought it set up a good balance that way. So Lucifer plays the part of the villain."

I can't write about any of this; it's ludicrous and no one would believe it. I hope Judas has a better story.

"What about you, Judas? Why did you betray Jesus and how do you feel about being in hell?"

"He was a good friend and I do regret betraying him, but I really needed the money. I had debts to pay. As for being here, I don't mind so much. I find that I am very useful."

"You say you had debts, but you ended up giving the silver back."

"Well, I gave it to the chief priests; they were the ones I owed the money to."

"You obviously felt really bad about it, though, because you hung yourself."

"That was an accident. I was climbing up a tree, and my

fishing rope managed to get tangled up around my neck. The branch broke, the rope caught on another branch on the way down and that was that."

"So wait. Why are you here then? As the betrayer of Christ, you are the worse person in human history." He looked at Judas, who looked hurt by that so he tried to soften his words. "Sorry, I mean, how is it that you are here if your death was an accident?"

"Peter was always jealous of me because I was one of His favorites. He said that I belonged in the deepest, darkest place of hell, and I would be forever known as Judas the Betrayer. As you know, Peter has full discretion when it comes to sending people to hell."

Both Judas and Lucifer seemed totally oblivious to the look of disbelief on the confounded Virgil's face.

"Do you like the cakes? I made them myself."

Virgil stared at him. He almost didn't hear the last question; he was too busy trying to absorb the revelation he'd just heard. When the question finally registered, he said, "They're nice; thank you."

"Well, I should think you have a lot of material to make a grand story."

Virgil nodded politely. He didn't know what he had; all he knew was that he could not write about it. It would upset the order of things and cause a lot of chaos.

"I should probably be going; I have a lot to process."

"I'll call Phenex for you." Judas picked up a horn and stepped out the door. Like all the horns in hell, it produced a low, deep sound like a baritone that made your ears vibrate. Judas walked back into the room.

"It's rather stuffy out there."

"It was nice meeting you, Judy, and you as well, Lucy."

"Mhhhhm . . .. "

"We were both very glad to meet you. You're welcome to come back when Brutus and Cassius are here, and they can tell you all about Julius Caesar," Judas said.

Yes, and they would probably tell me they killed Caesar because they didn't like having to wear togas, he thought.

Virgil left the odd pair and made his way back to the ferry. He saw Phenex approaching with a smug look on his face. He had fooled the great Virgil.

"I'll bet you saw so many unspeakable terrors that you will never be able to sleep again."

Virgil considered for a moment at what he just witnessed. "You have no idea."

The Stranger

"Is there anything I can help you with?" Lorenzo asked the man. The man was young, probably in his early twenties, a far contrast to Lorenzo, who was seventy-five. The man was also a perfect physical specimen; he looked as though he were chiseled from stone, also a far contrast from Lorenzo who looked like he was hammered from stone with the stonecutter using wild swings, taking no great care in the outcome. The stranger was wearing a simple black cloak, and his boots were worn as though he had traveled a great distance in them. He was holding a bottle of very expensive wine; it was so expensive because it was made in heaven, and no wine on Earth could rival its heavenly body and fragrance.

The man pulled the cork off and smelled the wine. "I believe I have smelled this wine before."

"I assure you, sir, that you have not. It comes from a faraway land."

The man in the black cloak looked almost amused. "Perhaps I'm mistaken then. I believe this is too expensive for me. Do you have a nice local Italian wine?"

"As a matter of fact, I do. We have a very fine vineyard right in here in Aquileia." Lorenzo tried to open a barrel of wine; and, after a little prying and some loud flatulence from the effort, he got it open.

The stranger seemed not to take notice of the gaseous odor.

Lorenzo dipped a ladle in the barrel. "Try a sip and tell me what you think."

He dipped his head down and sipped from the ladle Lorenzo was holding. "Oh my, that is delicious. It's not too sweet or bitter."

Simon walked in carrying his cooking spoon. "Lorenzo, I need some wine to use in my bakery."

"You're using wine to make bread?"

He whacked Lorenzo on the head with his spoon. "Don't

question my methods; I'm trying something new." He grabbed the ladle out of the stranger's hand and dipped it into the barrel. Then he turned around and walked out with it.

"I'm so sorry; please forgive his rudeness. He's taken one too many blows to the head," Lorenzo said.

The stranger seemed not to take offense and bowed.

"Would you like to buy the Italian wine?"

"You know, I don't think I'm thirsty anymore. I'm suddenly feeling famished."

The man was gone before Lorenzo could even begin to protest.

"Blasted Simon. He's always coming in and scaring off my customers," he said aloud. He put the lid back on the barrel and pouted.

Business has been slow today, and Simon scared away my only customer. I might as well call it a day, he thought. Lorenzo made sure all the chains on the barrels were secured and that the locks were fastened. He decided he would head over to see Peter, John and Adolfo. Simon walked down the street, past some of the merchants. The street was nearly deserted because it was harvest time and people were busy tending their crops. Lorenzo waved to Regulus, who was also a wine merchant. Regulus scowled at him and did not wave back. Lorenzo had to smile because Regulus did not sell even half the amount of wine that Lorenzo did. The man simply could not figure out how he was able to do so well. He recalled the first time that Regulus had confronted had him about it.

"I don't understand how you do it. Where does your wine come from?"

"The same place as yours."

"You lie; your wine is different. I've never tasted anything like it, and I've been all over God's land."

"I'm telling you the truth; it's not my problem if you don't believe me."

He obviously couldn't tell him that the wine came from heaven. Regulus resented the fact that Lorenzo would not tell him his sources. Unbeknownst to Lorenzo, Regulus had paid someone to spy on him so he could find out his secret.

Lorenzo walked into the small shop where his friends sold

their books. Standing there talking to John was the stranger in the cloak.

"I thought you were hungry," he said to the man.

"I am hungry; I'm hungry for knowledge," he said with a grin. John was grinning like a fool. He would do anything to make a sale and that meant pretending that whatever came out of a customer's mouth was the most witty and charming thing he had ever heard. John was extremely happy as a merchant. He was often humming some tune or other, mostly ones he just made up on the spot. Nothing ever seemed to get to him. Before the stranger walked in, John was working on a copy of *De Civitate Dei,* or *The City of God* by Augustine of Hippo. He had just written the line, "God is always trying to give good things to us, but our hands are too full to receive him," which had not quite dried yet. He loved Hippo's words.

Adolfo was also overjoyed to be a merchant. Of course, being mute, he had no way to express that love. Also it was difficult for others to discern since he was always scowling and grunting, but he was also in his element.

John, the Christian philosopher, spoke so passionately about God. He had committed certain passages to memory. His favorite was, "The bodies of irrational animals are bent toward the ground, whereas man was made to walk erect with his eyes on heaven, as though to remind him to keep his thoughts on things above."

While John was busy trying to woo a customer, Adolfo was the epitome of concentration. He looked as though he were trying to wield his quill with his mind, so focused was he on what he was doing. Adolfo had been working on the same commission as John was before the stranger walked in; it was the illustration of a man caught between vice and virtue for *The City of God.* The picture depicted a man in a red cloak sitting down, and all around him were angels praying and blowing trumpets. The angels represent the virtue. Beneath the man were many naked women with arms outstretched, trying to tempt the man into the carnal knowledge of the flesh. Adolfo was grunting and blushing while drawing the naked women. He had never been with a woman or seen one without clothes or even ever been around women, except his mother. He was trying to copy the work of another, where no doubt that illuminator knew the curve of a woman.

141

The stranger was taking in the parchments one by one with his eyes. He ran a finger over one of them. Adolfo, John and Peter did not make too many book sales because only the wealthy could afford books, plus it took a long time to make just one. The first stage in creating a codex was to prepare the animal skin. The skin had to be washed with water and lime and then soaked for a couple of days. Then the hair had to be removed and the skin dried by attaching it to a herse with a cord in order to prevent tearing. After that, the area of skin was attached to the cord and wrapped around a pippin. Then a lunarium, which is a crescent-shaped knife, was used to scrape away the remaining hairs. Once the skin was completely dry, you gave it a deep clean and processed it into sheets. You could get about three sheets per calf skin so the process took a long time. When they did sell one, however, they made quite a bit of money.

John had the perfect disposition for selling. He was charming, persuasive and he simply didn't take no for an answer. No one who ever came in to look, ever got away without buying; that's how good John was . . . and sometimes he even persuaded them to buy more than one book.

John surveyed the young stranger. He had on a simple cloak, his boots were worn and he didn't have a manservant with him. Indeed, he wasn't even carrying anything to keep the sun off his fair skin. He gave no appearance of being wealthy, but John knew that looks could be deceiving. He could just be a scholar who had saved some money to purchase a book in his field of study. Maybe he was a philosopher. If that were the case, he had plenty of philosophy books.

"How may I help you today, sir?"

"I just wanted to look at your selection."

"Indeed and tell me, sir, what is it that interests you?"

"Religious texts."

John winked at Adolfo, who only scowled at him. "You know, I was just saying to myself that this looks like a very religious young man and I was right. You're in luck; we have Lucian of Antioch, Anthanasius, Augustine, Tertullian . . . and a few others."

"I was thinking maybe something by Valentinus, Marcion or Ptolemy."

Adolfo had been concentrating so hard on the fruits of the

fairer sex up until that point. Upon hearing the stranger's request, his quill went flying out of his hand and he knocked over the ink. Lorenzo farted audibly, as he did in times of stress and surprise. Peter, who was holding a calf skin, dropped it back in the lime with a splash.

Peter, unlike John, was not very happy. He missed his wife, reading at his leisure and having conversations with other intellectuals. Heaven had no shortage of intellectuals. It had its fair share of imbeciles too. He preferred reading books to making them.

"I'm so sorry, sir; the teachings you mentioned are declared heretical by the Church, as you must know," John said.

The stranger looked at all four men in the room, taking in their reactions. "Oh, nonsense. No book should be off-limits to men of education."

"Indeed we are men of learning, sir, but we must obey canonical law."

"I can pay any amount."

John looked for a moment as if he might be entertaining the offer, but only for a moment. "I'm sure you can, but again we don't have such things here."

"Have you ever read the Apocrypha?"

"No, I have never read those gospels. They are forbidden and have all been rounded up by the Church and burned. I doubt there are any left in existence."

"Oh, I've heard rumors and whispers to the contrary." The roles had been reversed. The stranger was smiling and had John eating out of the palm of his hand.

John was unsure how to respond to this and, for once, was at a loss for words. He tried to take the conversation in a different direction. "Can I interest you in Augustine of Hippo?"

The stranger ignored John's question and seemed oblivious to his consternation. "I find the Apocalypse of Peter especially fascinating."

John wiped his brow; he was sweating, even though it was not a hot day. He was eager to get the stranger out of the store. What if another customer came in while the stranger was talking about heretical gospels? The stranger, who decided he had toyed with John enough, said, "Well, I guess I'll have to take my money elsewhere. Good day to you, fine gentlemen." All eyes were on the stranger as he walked out of the room, into the streets and seemed to disappear in a puff of smoke.

John started to pace back and forth. "Do you believe that man? Honestly, I'm just a poor book maker. What right did he have asking me about the Apocrypha? Do we look like people who have the Apocrypha lying around?"

"We do have Apocrypha lying around," Peter said and picked up a codex that had the Gospel of Mary tucked inside it.

Adolfo had already forgotten the stranger and was back to frowning over the naked woman he'd just painted.

"You know, I think that might have been that demon what's-his-name," Lorenzo said.

"Don't be so suspicious all the time," John said.

"Lorenzo is right; stay alert and keep an eye out for anything unusual."

John peered over Adolfo's shoulder and snickered. He grabbed the parchment before Adolfo had a chance to bite him. "Look at this. Look at this!" he was shouting. Peter and Lorenzo looked at the parchment and the naked woman, then smiled, barely able to contain their laughter. Adolfo had drawn the naked woman with breasts at least three times the size of her head.

Judge Not Lest Ye Be Judged

"You are looking well today. Have you been bathing in the Eternal Springs?" Uriel was stalling for time; he had not been working on inspiring anyone to do artistic endeavors on behalf of God. He had managed to inspire Senator Pammachius to build a Basilica on the Celian Hill in Rome. He named the church Titulus Pammachii. *Inspire* wasn't the right word. He, Michael and Gabriel had taken on the shape of a three-headed turtle again, but this time told Azrael about it so he could bring them back. Michael threatened the Senator to build a church using the voice of God. That was a long time ago though, and Uriel had not been working on anything new.

The Angel of Dominion, Zachariel, stared at Uriel and raised an eyebrow. "You know I don't bathe in the Eternal Springs, not since what happened 5,000 years ago."

Uriel made a blank expression. He knew Zachariel didn't bathe in the Eternal Springs; everyone knew it. "I don't recall; you'll have to tell me that story."

"I'm terrible pressed for time, maybe another time."

"You're pressed for time?"

"Yes, I'm pressed for time and I really need to go over your progress."

"Yes of course, well—" Uriel was interrupted by yelling.

"Oh, what now?" Zachariel asked.

"Perhaps we better go see what the trouble is. You never know when there might be another rebellion."

"Don't be silly; all the rebels have been cast out."

"Yes, but it only takes one dissatisfied angel to start a rebellion."

"Dissatisfied angels?"

"Well, I noticed that Cassiel is terribly dissatisfied. Why, just last week, he told me he'd like to strangle St. Peter with his own beard."

Zachariel rolled his eyes and looked at the Clock of Ages. The Clock of Ages was over thirty feet high and could be seen from any place in heaven. Heaven's time was not the same as Earth time. It was always correct and always running. The only time it would ever stop running would be at the end of time.

"Do you know how much time has passed on Earth since I've been talking to you and we haven't accomplished anything."

The yelling started again.

"I'm telling you, we might need to arm ourselves."

Zachariel was out of patience. He rolled up his scroll and put it back in his robe. "I will be here at the same time tomorrow, and I want to hear what you've been working on," he said, snapping his fingers and disappearing.

Michael and Gabriel were flying as fast as they could, flapping their wings like a couple of birds who looked like they had not yet mastered the art of flying. They collided with one another and fell down at Uriel's feet.

"Why are you flying when you could just snap your fingers? You really shouldn't flap about like that; it's unbecoming of an archangel."

"We wanted the practice; it's been an age since we've flown anywhere," Michael said, unsheathing his sword.

"It's started," Gabriel said.

"What's started?"

"The rebellion," Michael said out of breath.

"What rebellion?"

"It's Cassiel; he tried to strangle St. Peter with his own beard."

"Are you jesting?"

"Why would I be jesting?" Michael asked puzzled.

"Because I just stood here less than a minute ago and told Zachariel that there was probably a rebellion starting and that Cassiel was disgruntled and would probably try to strangle St. Peter with his own beard."

"Well, if you knew he was going to do that, you should have said something. I could have been practicing my parries and trapping," Gabriel said.

"I have no idea what that means, but I didn't know; I made it up to get rid of Zachariel because I haven't been working on inspiring mortals with any divine inspiration."

"Well, it's begun, I tell you. It started when St. Peter called Cassiel a fat bird with no brain. Cassiel snapped and leaped on him, seizing his beard; and Hayyel and Vehuaiah had to pull Cassiel off of St. Peter, who was trying to beat Cassiel with that large crucifix he wears around his neck," Michael said.

"Where are Cassiel and St. Peter now?"

"They've been separated. St. Peter is with Hayyel, and Cassiel is with Vehuaiah," Michael said.

"So the fight has been broken up, and the two have been separated. Then there is no more rebellion; it's been stopped in its tracks."

"You don't know that. It's the perfect time for someone else to strike, while everyone is distracted. Ophanim could launch themselves down a hill and trample you to death," Gabriel said.

Michael held up his sword. "I'll poke out every one of their one hundred eyes."

"Put your blasted swords away. There is no rebellion; but if Cassiel and St. Peter are not at the gate, then that means there are people waiting to hear their fates," Uriel said.

Michael and Gabriel were crestfallen; it had been so long since they had been in a battle, and there didn't seem like there would ever be another one.

"Well, come on, we have some fates to judge," Uriel said.

The idea of being able to judge the fate of mortals perked them up, though. St. Peter had been hogging that job for many years now. It was time someone else got a crack at it; and what better someone else than Uriel, Michael and Gabriel, the trinity of incompetence.

When they arrived at the gate, the line was backed up; they couldn't even see the end of it. There were some souls who were starting to get restless.

A seraph playing the harp looked nervous. "Thank goodness you are here. They were growing so impatient, I thought they were about to strangle me with my own harp strings."

"Hey, what kind of place is this? This is no way to run Heaven!" a man shouted.

The three archangels went over to where Peter normally stood. Gabriel picked up a fallen pearl. This was the third one that had fallen off the gate. "I don't think God is a very good carpenter. He

147

should just stick to being omnipotent."

"Who is next?" Uriel asked.

"Finally, I was about to ask if you could just go ahead and send me to hell!" the same man shouted.

A young man stepped forward; he had only one arm.

"There's something amiss about this one. I think they're supposed to have two arms," Michael said.

"Not always, sometimes these mortals get into accidents. Did you have an accident, young man?" Uriel asked.

"Yes, your worship."

Uriel smiled and nudged Gabriel and Michael. "He called me 'your worship.' I like the sound of that. Go on and tell us what happened; don't be frightened."

"I had to cut off my arm with my own sword."

"I see and why is that?" Gabriel and Michael were content with Uriel doing most of the questioning since he was the brains of the brainless group.

"Earlier in the year, I was attacked by a pack of wolves. I was able to fend them off, but not before one bit me in the arm."

"Yes, yes, I see. Wolf bit arm. Please continue, dear boy."

"Months went by and the arm began to ooze pus and started to turn green where the wolf bite was, so I took my sword and chopped it off. I died later from a fever resulting from the injury."

"Wait. How did you fend off the wolves? Did you bite the wolf back that bit you?" Gabriel asked.

"Well, I always have my sword with me, and I used it to drive the wolves away. It didn't occur to me to bite one of them."

"You know I bit one of the rebels during the great battle," Gabriel said to Michael.

"You never told me that."

"I was in close-range combat with Orabus. He knocked me down and jumped on top of me so I bit him because he said he was going to pluck every one of my feathers out."

"Be quiet! What is your name, young man?"

"My name is Ernesto of Lisbon."

"Why don't the two of you run and fetch this young man's book."

Gabriel and Michael scurried off, nearly knocking each other over again in their eagerness. Uriel smiled at the young man. "So you said you're from Lisbon; that's in Portugal, correct?"

The young man smiled in return. "Yes, your worship."

I could get used to this job, he thought.

When Gabriel and Michael finally returned, neither was carrying a book, but Michael had a parchment.

"Where's the book I asked you to go get?"

"There wasn't a book; this was the only thing there," Michael said.

Uriel snatched the parchment out of Michael's hand and read it.

"I, Ernesto of Lisbon, son of Amancio, do hereby forfeit my soul upon my death to Baal the Malevolent."

"It says here that you forfeited your soul to Baal," Uriel said.

"I can't say I know a Baal."

"Baal is a demon."

"I don't know any demons."

"He was probably in disguise. Why did you forfeit your soul?"

"I don't recall ever doing that."

Uriel showed him the parchment and the "X" by his name.

"I can't read, your worship."

Uriel looked it over and sighed. The official seal of Lucifer was stamped on it, and it was all perfectly legitimate, except for the way Baal obtained it.

"I'm sorry, young man, but we can't let you in," Uriel said and began trying to snap his fingers. Finally he made a small *snap*.

"Where did you send him?" Gabriel asked.

"To the gates of hell where he will await Phenex, the ferryman. At least that's where I hope I sent him."

Uriel looked at the long line. "All right, who's next?'

***

Baal was waiting patiently for Azazel to finish. He was lowering a man into a boiling cauldron of blood face-first with a rope. Such was the punishment in the Circle of Pride, well, at least it was today. Lucifer could easily change it into something different tomorrow; you could never be sure. They were in one of the darkest parts of hell; not much light was able to penetrate beyond the Tsur Nur, which was what they called the largest mountain in hell.

"No, please. What did I ever do to anyone?" the man asked.

"How should I know what you've done or haven't done?" Azazel answered rather testily.

"It's your job to know."

"It's not my job to know; it's only my job to lower your face into this boiling cauldron."

"Why? I'm innocent."

"I don't know what you did, but I suspect it's because you were too proud for your own good," Azazel said and lowered the man into the cauldron.

Baal noticed that the man didn't scream, which was unusual. When the man emerged, he was covered in blood and coughing, but his flesh was still intact. "That was quite unpleasant," he said.

Azazel untied him; and the next soul, a woman with crystal blue eyes, stepped up.

"Wait there a second, dear; I've got business to attend to," Azazel said as he walked over to where an impatient Baal stood.

"Why wasn't that man's face melted off?" Baal asked.

"Oh, it's not boiling; it's just room temperature. And it's not filled with blood; it's actually tomato juice. I guess Lucifer grows weary of human agony."

"I visited the city of Aquileia and I'm sure it's them."

"You found the monks. How can you be sure it's them?"

"They are not monks; they are merchants, but I'm sure it's them. A hunchback, a mute and two brothers who are healers, one with red hair and one with black hair. It's not a coincidence."

"Do they have the Apocrypha?"

"I'm certain it's there, probably at the book merchant's."

"Uriel is a proud fool. He should be lowered into this cauldron. He can't stand to have his name obliterated from history."

"Torture day in and day out, weeping, lamenting, smoke and ashes," Baal said.

"And the occasional drunk hellhound," Azazel added.

"The wicked never get a rest and neither do we."

"They're not all that bad. Hey, you there, fellow I lowered in the cauldron, come here."

The man eyed Azazel and Baal wearily, wondering what type of new humiliation the two had in store for him. With an air of

150

resignation, he approached the two demons. His face was still covered in room-temperature tomato juice.

"You said earlier that you didn't do anything. I bet you made a few mistakes, maybe the occasional copulation with your neighbor's wife; but on the whole, you're not a bad sort, are you?"

"I didn't cop—or whatever you said with any neighbor's wife. I didn't do anything, I tell you. That old man at the heavenly gate barely glanced at my book and said, 'I don't like the look of him' and the next thing you know, I'm riding a ferry. The ferryman asked me where I was going and I told him that I had no idea; the man in heaven didn't say what I'd done wrong. So he just brought me here."

"It sounds like St. Peter has let all that power go to his head. He could also use a dip into the cauldron. I knew that eventually it would come to this; when you have the power to decide where a soul is going to spend eternity, it can make you mad with power. I think someone else should take over that job for a while," Azazel said. He patted the man on the shoulder. "There, there, off you go now."

"Can I go back to heaven now?"

"Certainly not."

"I just stood here and told you I was sent here for no reason."

"I know, but what can I do about it? That's just how things work. I am sorry about the whole burn-in-hell-for-eternity thing, but what can I say? We are all in it together," Azazel said and pushed him along. He nudged Baal. "Sometimes you have to boost morale with kind words."

Phenex was pulling up with a soul who looked absolutely wretched.

"Look at this one; he looks like he's already been to hell. Hey, you there, wretched fellow. Come here," Azazel said.

The poor soul walked over to Azazel and Baal with his head down, clutching a piece of paper.

"What's that you have in your hand there?" Azazel asked.

The wretched man gave Azazel the paper.

"I, Ernesto of Lisbon, son of Amancio, do hereby forfeit my soul upon my death to Baal the Malevolent."

"Baal! You should be ashamed of yourself. Why did you deceive this already-wretched creature? Don't you have any pity in that demon heart of yours?

"Am I supposed to?" Baal asked.

Azazel was taken aback as if he weren't sure himself. "Well, you're supposed to have something in your heart. It's not supposed to be stuffed with sod and sheep wool. This man has got only one arm."

"You told me to keep obtaining souls while I was down there on Earth."

"Look at me, poor creature." The man with one arm looked at Azazel as he pointed to Baal. "Now, look at that foul creature standing over there. He is the one who did this to you. Go on now; take a good look. Don't look away, Baal; you have to look him in the eye and admit what you've done. What do you have to say for yourself, Baal?"

Baal was flabbergasted. He had done what he was told, and now he was getting scolded for it. He didn't know what he was supposed to say or feel. It had been eternity and all his emotions were all jumbled up and felt the same.

"I'm sorry that I deceived you."

"You certainly are sorry." The man with one arm was just watching the exchange wide-eyed. He had been to both heaven and hell in one day, and it was almost too much for him. In fact, he looked as if he might keel over and die if it weren't for the fact he was dead already.

"Now take this man to get some water and let him rest; he's had a terrible shock."

Baal frowned. "So he's not to be tortured?"

"Well, of course, we're going to torture him, but not today when he's had such a shock; we're not a bunch of savages, Baal. We are civilized demons and don't you forget it."

Glass Menagerie

In 492, Aquileia was the center of commerce in Italy, especially in agriculture. The city had brick fields, an imperial residence where important nobles stayed when passing through and even a mint. Heavily fortified with its high thick walls and heavy gates, it was almost impossible to breach, and inside was a well-trained garrison. Aquileia had withstood the war with the Marcomanni and two Visigoth attacks. There was not a sturdier or more strategically-placed city anywhere else in the world. It was most likely the reason the archangels decided to send them there. . . because it was impenetrable.

Lorenzo held the glass rose up to the light. He rotated it in his hand and watched it sparkle, catching his reflection in the glass. The hunchbacked figure staring back at him made him quickly put the rose down. He need not bother with such trinkets.

I'll never have anyone to give it to anyway, he thought. He could feel a bout of gas coming on, so he tried to stifle it by squeezing his legs together; but instead of a quiet and brief fart, it was a long and deafening fart that continued at a steady pace like a drum beat. Eli, the Jewish artisan who blew the glass, avoided looking at Lorenzo and pretended not to hear the offensive noise because he was ever the model of decorum and modesty. It was a little harder pretending he didn't smell it because he involuntarily wrinkled his nose, but bore it bravely for the sake of etiquette.

"See anything you like?" Eli asked.

"Oh, just about everything. You know me; I never buy anything, though. I just enjoy looking. A man like me doesn't need such finery."

Eli poured a glob of molten glass in the mold he was using to make a cross. "Why can't you buy anything? You are a successful tradesman. I should think you could afford that rose and a lot more."

"It isn't the cost; it's just that I have never been one for affection."

Except when I was in heaven, although that didn't feel like affection; it felt like home.

A flash across Lorenzo's peripheral vision caught his attention outside. Someone had run past him so quickly that he didn't see who it was. He went outside, but the person was already out of sight.

I guess someone was in a hurry, he thought.

Ding, Ding, Ding . . .

Lorenzo walked back inside. He had been in Aquileia for two years now and had heard the church bell ring many times, but this one was quicker and louder.

"Who is ringing that bell?"

Eli didn't answer and an expression came across his jovial face that was cause for concern.

"Eli, what's wrong? What's going on?"

More people were rushing past now, and this time Lorenzo did see who they were . . . they were soldiers. The city's garrison was being deployed.

Lorenzo went over to Eli and grabbed him by the shoulders. "What is wrong?"

Eli's placed a trembling hand on top of one of Lorenzo's. "We are under attack."

"That's impossible, the angels assured us this time . . ." Lorenzo stopped because he realized what he was saying. Eli would think he was mad and even if he didn't, the archangels had sworn him to secrecy. Besides, for all he knew, Eli could be Baal or some other demon in disguise. It wouldn't be the first time they had been fooled. It didn't matter; Eli had not heard a word he said. He just stood there staring out into space. Lorenzo grabbed the Jewish glass-blower by the arm. "Come on, let's go." Lorenzo dragged a dazed Eli out of the shop and into the streets where a crowd was beginning to form. Lorenzo looked around the crowd and saw Peter. He waved, but couldn't catch his eye. The Consular of Aquileia addressed the crowd.

"We knew this day would come again, as it has in the past; and just like in the past, we will withstand the siege. Aquileia is a fortress; we have heavily-fortified walls around the city and enough food and water to withstand a long siege. We will outlast any army that tries to attack us."

A man with a dirty face and tunic that was too small for his fat belly yelled out, "What about fleeing to the lagoons as we did the last time?"

"The city gates will be locked. No one goes in or out," the consular said.

Raised voices sounded all at once, and it was impossible to hear what they were saying. One voice rose above the others; it was the same fat man. "I have trading to do in Bologna."

"No one goes in or out," he repeated, "unless you'd like to get an arrow in your gut."

That silenced everyone. They needed to make a living, but an arrow in the gut sounded very distressing. It was hard to make a living if you were dead. Lorenzo didn't know how an arrow to the gut felt, but he did know what it felt like to be clubbed and burned to death. He knew he didn't like dying; it was very painful.

"Who are they?" a woman holding a baby asked.

"They are Huns, nomads, nothing to worry about."

The baby in the mother's arms began to wail, as if it disagreed with the consular's statement and was indeed something they should be worried about. The mother discreetly lifted her garment and placed a breast in the baby's mouth for him to suckle. The baby was once again content. Lorenzo, who did not have a breast to suckle, was not content. He was not feeling content at all.

***

The Hunnic Empire—or Huns as they were known—was something to worry about. They were a nomadic people who mainly lived east of the Volga River and in the Caucasus. Outside the city wall of Aquileia was a sea of broad brown faces, waiting patiently on their horses for orders to be given. They were a group to be feared, but the one to fear most was their leader, Attila.

Attila the Hun, despite being a squat little man, sat regally on his horse, gazing at the city in front of him. The sacking of Aquileia would be a great victory in his campaign to dominate Italy. It was by far the wealthiest city, and the reward would be great. The *Little Father*, which is what the name Attila meant, wore a green tunic with a jewel-incrusted belt; and draped around his shoulders was a fur. On top of his head was a gold crown which was covered in jewels, and dangling from it were golden tassels. His horse was equally adorned with a golden saddle and armor.

The Huns were more than nomads; they were a warrior band comprised of different groups: Huns, Ostrogoths and Alans. They were excellent mounted archers. One of his generals rode up beside him. She too was elaborately dressed, although not wearing a fur. Her tunic was adorned with intricate bead work. In the Hunnic tribe, women fought alongside men in battles and were valued just as much, if not more in some cases.

"This won't be easy. Are you sure we need this city? It is indeed wealthy with considerable coins, jewels, metals and brickfields; but those walls look impenetrable. We could ride around it and go for Rome, the main prize," the general said.

Attila's horse snorted and shifted uneasily. "I think the risk is worth it. This city is a great prize. We have 400,000 archers and enough food and provisions for a prolonged siege."

A soldier from the top of the wall of Aquileia shouted something. What he said was, "Go away, you pointy-hat people!" He was referring to the shape of the hats with pointed ends that some of the poorer soldiers were wearing. Attila didn't know what he was saying because he didn't speak Italian. He shouted back at the soldier, "Get your goat face away from there, or I'll shoot it off!" They each took turns yelling at each other, neither knowing what the other was saying. Finally, Attila aimed his bow and arrow at the goat-faced soldier and let his arrow fly. The soldier got his goat face away just in time. He shook his fist at Attila. "You'll regret that." His cavalry took their leader's shot as a signal to charge, which they did. Suddenly, thousands of men appeared up on the wall with bows. Arrows started flying from both directions. The Aquileian soldiers were trained well with bows and crossbows, and they had the higher ground. However, the Hun had the numbers, and they were more than well-trained; they were the best archers in the world. They were also moving targets, which made them harder to hit. Men started falling from the walls.

Attila sat back and watched one of his archers shoot an arrow, circle the horse around and fire backwards while riding. It was a very impressive sight. The arrows continued flying well into the evening. The sun started to go down, and within minutes hundreds of men were lying on the ground with arrows sticking out of them; most of them were Aquileians. Attila called his archers away because there was little light left. The battle would have to rage on again in the morning.

A Stone's Throw Away

"I'm sure everything will be all right. This city has been well-prepared for an attack; it's fortified, and we have the military and the provisions to withstand a long siege," Peter said.

"The archangels didn't mention anything about an attack upon the city," Simon said, raising his cooking spoon in the air as if he were challenging God to a cooking duel.

"Grrrrrr!" Adolfo said. He had taken to making a growling noise instead of grunting; it was kind of refreshing.

"I agree with Adolfo. Something feels wrong, and those angels are certainly not infallible; in fact, with their record thus far, I think they are highly fallible," John said.

Lorenzo with his hunchback sidestepped outside because he was feeling flatulent, and they were all huddled in Peter's one-room house. Lorenzo was known for clearing a room.

"They probably didn't mention it because it will come to nothing and they didn't want to alarm us," Philip said.

"I've heard about these Huns; they're supposed to be a bunch of savages," his brother Thomas said.

"I brought the Book of Peter. I'll read some passages and maybe it will give us some comfort," Peter said.

"That's an odd choice for such a time," Thomas said.

"Sorry, I meant to get the Book of Mary, but I grabbed the wrong one so we will have to make do with this one. I'll try to find some of the more positive passages." Peter opened the codex of his name's sake and began to read.

"And then God will come unto my faithful ones, who hunger and thirst and are afflicted. He will purify their souls in this life and he will judge the sons of lawlessness."

"Is that what you call positive? It sounds ominous," John said.

Lorenzo was still outside, and a stray cat happened by as he relieved himself of some gas. The cat stopped and hissed at him as if it were highly offended.

"I'm sorry, little fellow." He bent down to pet the cat on the head, and the cat scratched him with its sharp claws; it was having none of that. Now it was Lorenzo's turn to be offended.

"Well, there was no need to do that," he said and walked back inside before the cat could challenge him any further. Peter was still reading.

"This is the place of your leaders, the righteous men and—"

Voices outside were growing louder and angrier and distracting Peter from his reading.

"Was your gas that bad, Lorenzo, as to offend someone?"

"It wasn't me, I assure you," Lorenzo said, leaving out the part about the cat.

One by one the men went outside to find out what the commotion was all about. The commotion seemed to be one-sided with a woman throwing stones at a man and the man busy trying to dodge them. It was obvious they were husband and wife.

"You good-for-nothing weasel," she yelled and picked up a rather large, sharp-looking stone and hurled it at the weasel's face. In her wrath, her aim was off and the stone completely missed the husband and hit Thomas square in the shoulder, prompting a yell of pain from him.

"Hey, you hit me. There is no need for such aggression."

"Good, you're a weasel too. You're all weasels and good-for-nothings." This time she grabbed multiple stones and hurled them at each of the good-for-nothings in rapid fire succession. The men moved right and left, running into one another, trying not to get hit. Some of the stones hit their targets and some didn't, but her husband was enjoying a short reprieve, thanks to the newcomers. He stood back smiling with his arms crossed because now someone else was the target of his wife's blood lust. Peter put his hands up and waved them vigorously.

"Good lady, please stop. We are not your enemies."

This seemed to only make her angrier because she scanned the ground for the biggest stone she could find to throw. While she was busy searching, the men saw their chance. John grabbed the husband, and the eight of them ran back to Peter's house to safety. Peter slammed the door shut.

"Oh my god in heaven, what a vile beast," Philip said out of breath.

They could still hear her yelling even through the door. "You're all good-for-nothing and deserve to be thrown into the Lake of Fire. This declaration was followed by loud *thuds* caused by the stones she had thrown at Peter's door.

"That she-devil is your wife?" Simon asked.

"Yes, sir, we've been married ten years now."

"Those must have been ten of the longest years ever," Thomas said.

The husband smiled. "Oh, she doesn't mean anything by it; deep down she has a good heart."

"You mean stone heart," John chuckled at his joke, but no one else laughed. "You see because she was throwing stones at us and I said 'stone heart.' Never mind."

"Yes, we get the jest, John," Philip said. John looked hurt; it was quiet outside, so he went to the door and opened it a crack.

"I see you; you little rat. I'll take your eye out." John quickly closed the door and the door rattled with another *thump*.

"No, she's a good soul. She takes good care of me; she just has a temper. I like to call her my lioness. She's got fire, that one," the husband said.

"What did you do to incur the wrath of this lioness?" Peter asked.

"She wants to leave Aquileia because she feels it's not safe with those nomads running about outside the gates. I told her we weren't allowed to leave; and even if we could, it was too dangerous. Well, that got her madder than a hornet's nest. She said I wasn't a man if I couldn't take care of my family and that if I were a real man, I'd find a way to get us out of the city. She's just scared is all."

Peter realized he had the book in his hand the entire time and tucked it inside his tunic.

"Why does she feel she's not safe here in the city? It's been attacked several times, but no one has ever breached its walls," Lorenzo said.

"She saw a bad omen. When she walked outside this morning, there was a dead raven by our door. My wife is very superstitious and believes deeply in such things. She said we are all going to die, every last one of us."

Peter looked at the group. The woman had finally stopped

160

yelling and pelting his door with stones. He patted the husband on the back. "I'm sure the dead raven didn't mean anything; it probably got killed by a dog or cat."

"You try telling that woman that; she's as stubborn as a mule."

"I will tell her that." Peter opened the door and the wife was ready and waiting. She hurled the stone in her hand as if she were a Greek Olympian. Peter tried to dodge it, but he wasn't quick enough and it him square in the chest, sending him staggering back inside.

"Why don't I wait until she's calmed down?" he said, rubbing his chest and trying to catch his breath.

"You'll be waiting a long time," the husband laughed. "You'll be waiting until the Archangel Gabriel blows his trumpet, signifying the end of time."

***

"Holy, holy, holy is the lord of hosts, the whole earth full of his glory," the Seraph Jehoel sang.

Vehuaiah, the seraph who oversees time and history wasn't in the mood for pleasantries; he was too cross to sing the customary greeting of their rank. Angels by definition were supposed to be angelic and not cross, but every 1,000 years or so an angel gets cross. There had been a rash of cross angels, though, recently. Cassiel trying to choke St. Peter with his own beard, and Zachariel had gotten special permission to call Michael a bad word for losing his scepter.

"How did this happen?" He licked his thumb to turn the page in the Book of Knowledge, the same one that Adam and Eve read from to get kicked out of the Garden of Eden. It had in its pages everything that had ever happened and everything that will happen until the end of time.

Vehuaiah knew everything that would happen before it was supposed to happen, but today something happened that he knew was not supposed to occur.

"This is all wrong. I know this didn't occur. I want to file a formal complaint, and I want there to be a full investigation into my inquiry."

"Try and calm yourself, Vehuaiah; it's really unbecoming of

a seraph. Anger is a demonic trait," Jehoel pointed out.

"I wish I had the meanest, foulest demon here right now to beat it out of the angel or angels responsible for this breach."

"How do you know it's a breach? Perhaps you are mistaken."

"You think I don't know when an army of 400,000 Huns are going to march on a city. That army was supposed to bypass Aquileia and move on to Rome."

"You have to be mistaken. Who has the authority to change history?"

"There are some who can like Samael, and just the other day he got mad because I said I didn't like his kimono. He has a stupid obsession with that Japanese culture."

"I'm sure it's not Samael; he wouldn't do that just because you didn't like his kimono."

"Wouldn't he? Someone has been stealing from my chocolate supply. I can tell because I weigh them periodically; and you know he has a—what is the phrase mortals use—a tooth for sweets."

"I didn't know he liked chocolate. You actually weigh the chocolate?" Jehoel was stifling a laugh; he was picturing Vehuaiah meticulously weighing his bars of chocolate.

"Yes, I do weigh the chocolate; and it's a good thing I do, or else I wouldn't know that I've been stolen from. If Samael is brazen enough to change history, he would certainly not be above stealing chocolate." Vehuaiah spotted Uriel, Michael and Gabriel and summoned them over.

Michael and Gabriel were comparing swords and arguing over who had the better one.

"My sword is gold and glimmers in the sun, and yours is a heap of rusty metal," Gabriel said laughing.

"Be quiet; we've been summoned by a seraph so act like you have some dignity for once. Also, he's probably onto the fact that someone has been stealing his chocolate so pretend like you don't know anything, which shouldn't be too hard."

"I won't do an . . ." The last of Gabriel's words were garbled, due to the fact that he shoved a big piece of chocolate in his mouth.

"What did I just say?" Uriel slapped Gabriel so hard on the back of the head, the chocolate came flying out.

"Where did it go?" Michael asked, looking around to see where it fell.

"Who cares? Let's go."

They strolled over to where Vehuaiah and Jehoel were standing. Vehuaiah had gotten onto the subject of all the different kinds of chocolate.

"Holy, holy, holy is the lord of hosts; the whole earth full of his glory," Vehuaiah sang.

Uriel and Michael smiled. Gabriel did not because he still had some chocolate in his mouth that Uriel didn't knock out.

"I have a job for you three. I want you to find out some information for me, make inquiries, spy if you have to, because we have a thief and a scoundrel among us."

"Oh, you mean Virgil; well, I'm trying to get his name on the Book of Revelation and take John's off. I've filed a petition, but haven't heard anything back," Uriel said.

"What are you talking about? Someone has rewritten history; I'm on today's page and something major is happening that is not supposed to happen, and it will alter history."

"Really, what is it?" Uriel asked.

"An army of 400,000 Huns are attacking the city of Aquileia."

"Aquileia? Hey, that's the city where—" Michael was interrupted by Uriel.

"He means, that's the city in Italy." Uriel gave Michael a hard stare that would have turned Medusa into stone. Michael knew that meant to keep quiet. Something caught his eye; there was something brown on the bottom of Uriel's robe. It was the big wad of chocolate that Uriel had smacked out of Gabriel's mouth.

"The city is under attack and if it is destroyed, it will alter the future. It already has, to some degree, because people are dead today who were not supposed to be dead yet. *The Liber Mortuorum* has now been altered because names are appearing in there that shouldn't be in there today."

Michael was trying to get Uriel's attention by blowing on his ear. Uriel slapped at his ear like a fly was buzzing around it.

"I want the three of you to find out who the culprit or culprits are that did this. Keep an eye out. Also, see who has been stealing my chocolate."

"I can't imagine who would do such a terrible thing," Uriel said.

"I can and I have a strong suspicion it's Samael so I would start with him first."

163

Michael tugged on Uriel's robe. Uriel looked at Michael and followed his gaze to the bottom of his robe where the chocolate was stuck. Uriel quickly grabbed the chocolate and closed his fist around it.

"If it's not Samael, it has to be someone vile and without any scruples. We have a snake in the Garden of Eden."

"We are all angels; there is no one here who is vile and without scruples," Jehoel said.

Vehuaiah looked hard at Jehoel. "You're living in a fool's paradise, Jehoel."

"Fool's paradise," Gabriel repeated. The words were still slightly garbled because of some of the chocolate stuck in his mouth.

Uriel coughed. "We will be happy to catch the scoundrels who did this," he said.

After Vehuaiah and Jehoel left, Uriel breathed a sigh of relief. He opened up his hand; it was sticky and covered with chocolate. "I've got to go to the Eternal Springs and wash my hands."

"We'll go with you," Michael said.

"I don't know how, but I think somehow we might have changed history by placing those men there. They might somehow be altering events just by their mere presence on Earth."

"Maybe we should call this whole thing off and get them back to heaven where they belong," Michael said.

"Don't be silly; I'm not calling the whole thing off just because a little history got changed and people died who weren't supposed to die. Mortals will always die at some point; it's the only thing you can count on with them so what difference does it make when they die. We will wait and see how this whole thing plays out."

As they were walking, Gabriel casually popped another piece of chocolate in his mouth. "I wonder who the scoundrels are."

Omens

It had been weeks since Attila and his Hun army started the battle with Aquileia's garrison, and they weren't making any inroads. Aquileia still stood like a bastion of Italy. They had the numbers, but numbers didn't matter in this case because the city was a bulwark and it was not going to be breached. Not only had they shot arrows at them, they had hurled large stones at them; and for those Huns who got too close to the wall, the garrison had set fire to a mixture of sulphur, bitumen, pitch and oil and dropped it on their heads, burning those unfortunates alive. They couldn't afford to lose any more provisions, especially if they wanted to take Rome. They were starting to run out of food. Some Huns had even started eating their dead horses. Morale was low; it left a bitter taste in his mouth, but Attila knew they must accept their losses and withdraw. He called a council of all his captains, and they all convened inside his tent. He looked at each one in the eye. They were tired and looked defeated. He knew none of them would suggest surrendering to him; they were well-disciplined and loyal so he was the first to speak.

"I knew this attack would be risky, but I thought the reward was worth it. What lies in that city is riches unlike any you've ever seen. However, it seems futile to keep attacking an impenetrable city. We are running low on food, and some of the soldiers are starting to become sick. We simply won't have enough strength left to complete our objective of sacking Rome, if we keep concentrating our forces here. I believe—" Attila was interrupted by a voice coming from the wall.

"Do you pointy hats give up because we can keep going all year?" It sounded like the same voice that had taunted them in the beginning of the battle.

The Huns did not understand Italian, but got the gist of what the man was saying. The captains looked at their leader, and each of them bowed their heads. The captains left the tent and blew their horns, which was the retreat signal. The look on the faces of the men and women was one of relief as they began to pack everything up for their departure.

The garrison began to cheer as they watched the Huns depart. One of the consuls went to make the announcement to the citizens of Aquileia, who had gotten used to the fighting outside the city walls which was just becoming part of the usual noise of the hustle and bustle of the city. The merchants were anxious to get back to selling and making their living.

Attila looked back at the city regrettably; he wished he could have taken it. He was resolved to return, though, after he defeated Rome. Just as he was about to turn back around, a stork flew out into the cloudless sky, driving its small brood. It was an omen, a good omen and he knew he could not leave, not without one more final push to take the city. He had been too hasty and impatient, coming from winning swift victories prior to arriving at Aquileia, but this required more patience and calculation.

Storks are a good omen in battle, he thought; and no more than a second after thinking the Gods were going to grant him a great victory, did an arrow go flying out, skewering the stork and it fell out of the sky.

Attila was furious. "Who did that? That was a good omen given to me by the gods. Which one of you defiled the gift from the gods?"

A terrified Hun raised his hand. "I didn't realize it was an omen; I thought it was food."

Attila shook a finger at him. "You omen killer. You defiler of the Gods, You . . ." Before he could come up with another slander, he thought about it. The soldier had only killed one of he storks, after all. So it was still a good omen, and he would need to boost morale to rally his army for one last grand attack.

"Yes, you are right. It is food and a good omen. The gods are on our side; they want us to have the city. Attack! You are invincible!" he yelled. His army, seeing Attila's renewed vigor, mustered everything they had for one last final blow. They charged back to the wall, all except the Hun who shot the stork; he picked it up and placed it in a sack tied to his horse. Just because it was an omen, he didn't see the need to go hungry. The Huns caught the garrison off-guard because they had already disbanded and dispersed from the wall. The Huns had only a small window of opportunity so they put their long ladders against the wall and began to ascend before they could be crushed with stones or burned with sulphur. Another group of soldiers began to push the battering ram so they could ram the gate a few times before arrows rained down upon them. The Huns were like lightning; before the army of Aquileia could regroup, Huns were coming over the wall and the gate was smashed. Huns poured down from the walls like locusts, and more Huns rode through the city on their horses. The only thing the people of Aquileia had time to do was to run for their lives.

***

Rosier stopped in front of where Azazel stood and caught his breath. He had been running to tell Azazel the news he just heard from Baal.

"You're not . . . going . . . ," Rosier was panting so hard, the words weren't coming out.

"You really should exercise more. You know you should run with Orsippus, the Greek Olympian, in the evenings to build up your stamina."

Rosier finally regained his breath. "You're not going to believe this, but I just spoke with Baal. He's just come from the city of Aquileia; that's where the men are who are hiding the Apocrypha. He said the city was attacked by . . . "

"Attacked by whom?"

"They were attacked by . . . ," Rosier paused again and strained to remember who it was that Baal said attacked the city. "They were attacked by hens."

Azazel laughed. "Surely you misunderstood."

"I heard him plain as day. He said Aquileia was razed to the ground by hens."

"Do you realize how absurd that sounds? I know it's been a long time since you visited Earth, but hens are animals. They are only about this high," Azazel said and put his hand low to the ground to indicate the hens' stature.

"I'm only telling you what he told me. He said the hens destroyed the walls and rode into the city on horseback, shooting

167

arrows at anything that moved. They burned, pillaged and stole every treasure they could carry. They completely emptied the mint of its coins."

Azazel laughed again, but this time harder because he was trying to picture a hen on horseback shooting arrows. He stopped laughing and looked at Rosier, who was offended.

"Well, see if I go out of my way to bring you news again."

Azazel stifled a laugh. "I'm sorry, old friend. So what became of the seven men and the Apocrypha after the he . . ." He was going to say "hens," but that would get him in a fit of laughter again so he said "enemy" instead.

"Baal didn't know because he had to escape before the hens descended on him."

It took every bit of strength Azazel had not to laugh. "Well, I'm glad he didn't incur the wrath of those terrible hens."

"He didn't escape unscathed. Baal took on the form of a stork to flee the city; and as he was flying, a hen shot him right out of the sky. That's not all; the hen put Baal the Stork in his bag so that he could eat him later. He managed to escape during the confusion of the battle."

Rosier was so serious that Azazel didn't know what to make of the strange story.

"We will talk to Baal when he's feeling better and see if he can find out what became of the Apocrypha. I doubt the hens took it because I don't think they can read."

Rosier looked down at all the souls who were in a massive pit that Azazel was presiding over. "What's going on here?"

"Huh? Oh, they're murderers," he said, still thinking about the hens.

"Yes, but what are they doing?"

"The great Lucifer in all his wisdom devised a new punishment for them. He had this giant pit dug, and the pit was supposed to be filled with creepy crawly things like snakes to bite and attack them over and over."

"Those don't look like snakes."

"They aren't; they're hares." Rosier and Azazel watched as hares hopped all around the pit, trying to avoid the people who were trying to catch them. One man caught one and was petting its fur.

168

"They are positively adorable," Rosier said.

"Belphegor was in charge of rounding up the snakes, but he's terrified of snakes so he went to Earth to see if he could get other animals that creep around; but it turns out he's terrified of those too, so in the end he just gathered up as many hares as he could. He had to make about ten trips above just to get all he needed."

Rosier jumped down in the pit with the murderers, so he could catch one of the hares. He wanted to keep one for a pet. Baal came limping along down the path.

"Did the hens injure you?" he asked Baal with a chuckle.

"What? Did you say something about hens?"

"I said, I see you made it out alive and managed to escape those deadly hens."

"Hens? Where?" He looked down into the pit of murders. "Those are hares, Azazel."

"You know the vicious hens, those flightless birds that *peck* and *cluck* and *squawk*."

Baal was in no mood for jokes. "I was pierced through my side with an arrow, you know."

"Yes, I heard. Tell me how a hen holds a bow and arrow. Does it hold it in its beak or underneath its wing?"

"What HENS are you talking about? Aquileia was descended upon by thousands of Huns . . . you know, nomads, Mongols, Visigoths, etc., those bronze-skinned, almond-eyed people from the Caucasus Mountains."

Azazel stopped giggling as the seriousness of what Baal was saying started to sink in.

"Where is the Apocrypha?"

"Well, I'm alive, thanks for your concern."

"Of course, you're alive. You're a demon; you can't die from a human-inflicted wound."

Baal already had one scar on his side from where Michael had cut him with his sword long ago. It hadn't even been during the uprising; it had been just an accident. Michael was swinging his sword around, as he was prone to do and didn't see Baal behind him. It was a nasty gash and after it healed, it left an angry scar.

"I don't know whether those monks turned merchants are alive or not—probably not—because the Huns were shooting everything that moved and there wasn't a lot of time to flee the city. If they didn't bury them somewhere, they've probably been turned to dust."

"Good. I hope the books have been obliterated, and Uriel's name has been wiped off the lips of men forever."

"I don't know that Uriel's name was ever on the lips of men to begin with," Baal mumbled under his breath.

"What's that?"

"I said, even if the books are still out there, I'm done with this task. I can't do it anymore."

"Oh, come on, Baal, don't be that way. I know what you need. Hey, Rosier, hand me one of those hares."

Rosier handed Azazel the one he was holding and tried to catch himself another one. The hare squirmed in the demon's arms. "Here, this hare will cheer you up." He tried to hand the hare to Baal, who refused to take it.

"I don't want any hares. This is hell, and hares don't belong in hell. Besides, how am I supposed to take care of it when you have me running all over the Earth?"

"Don't be that way, Baal the Miserable, Baal the Hare Hater." This time Azazel forced the hare into Baal's arms. Baal released the hare and let it bound away.

"Hey, it took Belphegor a long time to catch those."

"Belphegor can go hang himself. He copulates about as much as these hares do; and if you want someone to spy on your enemies and foil their schemes, you'll have to look elsewhere."

Belphegor came stumbling down the path towards the group. He must have been nearby and heard his name. He had just returned from one of his expeditions on Earth where he had possessed a mortal's body for the sole purpose of eating, drinking and copulating. They didn't know if he had done any eating or copulating, but the way he was staggering, it was clear that he had done plenty of drinking.

"Rosier . . . Baal . . . my friends!" Belphegor yelled. He was just about to embrace the two demons in a big bear hug, when he lost his footing and took a header right into the pit of hares and murderers. Azazel looked down into the pit, and Belphegor was sprawled out lying motionless.

"Dear Lucifer's horn, Belphegor is dead," he said.

Rosier peered over Belphegor and recoiled. The smell of

170

spirits was overwhelming. He had a serene smile on his face, and then he began to snore.

"No, he's just passed out drunk is all."

A hare approached Belphegor. Its ears shot up at attention and its nose began to twitch, unsure if it should come any closer to the creature lying before it, the very same one that had taken it away from its home. It thought better of coming any closer and bounded around him instead.

"What should we do? Belphegor eats way too much and he's too heavy to lift."

Azazel, comforted in the fact that Belphegor was just in a drunken stupor and not dead, ignored the debauched demon.

"Just let him sleep it off," he said, wanting to change the subject. He could see it wasn't a good time to try and persuade Baal to do anything.

"Did you get any more people to sign over their souls?"

"Oh yes, I got two more people. A round belligerent woman from Aquileia and her docile husband."

Azazel sighed. "As if we don't have enough of those."

***

"They're here . . . they're here," Uriel shouted, jumping up and down full of nervous energy. An ophan rolled by his path, its hundred eyes all focused on the silly archangel jumping up and down like a child anticipating a sweet. Right behind the ophan, as usual, was a cherub whose four animal heads were also turned toward Uriel.

"Have you ever seen such a thing from an archangel?" the head of the eagle asked the head of the lion.

The head of the lion only roared in response as the two angels moved on through the clouds and disappeared.

"I'll go and get them and bring them back here," Michael said.

"If St. Peter gives you any trouble, just yank on his beard," Uriel said.

"Oh, you didn't hear? St. Peter has been removed from the gates for no less than a hundred years, and Saul has taken his place."

"Who is Saul?"

"I meant Paul; I keep forgetting he changed his name," Michael said.

171

"Not very clever, changing one letter in your name," Uriel said. "Why do they keep giving this important task to apostles? It should be an angel's job."

"I know, apostles taking away perfectly good angel jobs."

"You know how St. Peter was strict about letting people through the gates, well, Paul has been letting them all through. He just can't say no to anyone. He has put a sign out in front of the gate that says *All Are Welcome*," Gabriel said.

"Oh my, it might start to get very crowded in here."

Michael left to go and get the Gnostic Keepers—that was their private name for them—who had died . . . again. He returned with the men, and they were a peculiar-looking sight.

"What are those things sticking out of you?" Uriel asked.

"They're called arrows, and an army of Huns shot us full of them," Peter said.

"Did he just say an army of nuns shot them full of arrows?" Uriel asked Gabriel.

"I believe he did."

"That's strange. Why did you let them do that?"

"We didn't exactly have a choice in the matter. They pillaged the city, shooting and burning as they went," Thomas said.

"I didn't think nuns were that mean," Uriel said to Gabriel.

"Some of them are; one time I bumped into a nun, and she called me an ostrich and plucked a feather from my wing."

"I didn't know they could be so ruthless; I will give them a wide berth from now on," Uriel said.

It just hit Uriel that if they were here, then who was looking out for the gospels. "Where are my Gnostic Gospels?"

"John had just enough time to put them all in a sack and bury them near the mint or what's left of it," Philip said.

"Well, you're here now. Take those things out. You look ridiculous; you can't go walking around heaven with arrows coming out of you. It looks like some sort of torture they would devise in hell."

"They poke people with sticks in hell; at least that's what Virgil told me," Uriel said.

"Where is Virgil?" Michael asked. "I haven't seen him in a while."

"He's secluded himself in limbo; he's working on a new story about Lucifer.

Apparently, he got to speak with him," Gabriel said.

"I can barely remember what Lucifer looks like. I think I remember him being really tall," Uriel said.

Lorenzo coughed to get Uriel's attention. They really wanted the arrows removed.

"Right, well, off we go to see Azrael to make sure he doesn't write your names down in the *Liber Mortuorum*. Then you need to retrieve the gospels that John buried, and we can work on where we are going to send you next." Uriel snapped his fingers, which made a *snap*, barely above a whisper. "This is really starting to get exciting."

"What do you mean, 'send us next?' We've died three times already, and all three were really painful," Simon said.

"Why can't we just leave them buried?" John asked. "No one will dig them up; they will be safe there until they are allowed to be read again. When is that going to be, by the way?"

"I have no idea, but that's not important. We can't take a chance on that. These are the last of the Gnostic Gospels; and if something happens to them, they will be wiped out of man's existence forever. All those brave and heroic stories of me—I mean of men and angels—will be scattered to the winds and forgotten."

"They are the last Gnostic Gospels that we know about, at least," Michael added.

Adolfo grunted three times.

"Look what you've done. You've gone and upset poor Adolfo. What do you mean 'that you know about?' Didn't you bother to look and see if there were any others?" John asked.

"Well, of course, I did; that would be very careless of me, not to see if there were others," Uriel said.

I didn't really check thoroughly; I'll have to make it a point to look into that. All the others have probably been burned, though.

"Come, Michael and Gabriel, help me pull these arrows out of these poor souls."

The archangels began to pull all the arrows, shot from the bows of those ruthless nuns. Adolfo tried to bite Gabriel as he pulled an arrow out of his bottom.

"Hey, try that again and you'll earn yourself a one-way trip to hell."

"All trips to hell are one way," Michael pointed out.

"Why don't you rest now? You must be tired, what with dying and all. We will discuss the matter of where you are to go next after you're rejuvenated," Uriel said.

There was an outpouring of objections by the men and grunts by Adolfo. The noise was starting to attract other angels.

"I demand to see God!" Thomas yelled.

"You can't see God," Uriel said.

"Why?"

"Tell him why not, Gabriel."

Gabriel looked at Thomas and then at Uriel and then at Michael. "Yes, tell him why not, Michael."

Michael nervously looked at the group and the angels who were starting to gather around, and an idea struck him like one of God's lightning bolts. He decided he would let the voice of God tell them why not.

"BECAUSE I SAID SO!"

Heaven shook; Michael lost his balance and nearly fell on his own sword. The ophan from earlier was rolling backward past them, unable to slow down, its hundred eyes looking all around for someone to stop it. No one in the crowd did, though. The ground split beneath their feet. The men were terrified; they had not heard God's voice since their first meeting from the three-headed turtle. The men dropped to one knee. The other angels just snickered under their breath; word had gotten around that Michael had the voice of God.

Uriel winked at Michael.

"What do we do now?" Michael asked.

"I don't know; I'll think of something. I always think of something."

John's Apocalypse

Netzach the angel was sent to Earth to fetch the Gnostic Gospels that John had buried in a sack by the mint, which was completely gone. In fact, everything was completely gone, and there was almost no trace that the great city had ever been there. When he arrived back in heaven with the books, he found Uriel and Azrael engaged in a lively discussion. Uriel was gesticulating madly and flapping his wings in a frenzy.

"Stop doing that, Uriel; you're getting feathers everywhere," Azrael said and spotted Netzach. "And those cannot be here. No earthly possessions are allowed in heaven." Azrael had the *Liber Mortuorum* opened up, which was hovering in midair and opened to today's page.

"They won't be here for long; it's just until I find a safe place to send the men."

"Clearly there is no safe place to send the men," Azrael said.

"There is; we just have to be more careful."

"I suspect it was your meddling that altered the fabric of time; that Hun attack was not supposed to occur. You wiped out an entire city, and a lot of souls whose time had not yet come are now here. You've created a lot more work for me."

"I'm sorry, Azrael; I really am, but what could I do? You understand how important this is to me . . . I mean mankind, don't you?"

Azrael frowned. "I suppose, but this time they have to be sent back as monks or doing some other holy work down there. I'm not sending them back as merchants to make a profit and live a decadent lifestyle; it's wrong."

"All right, fine. So when and where can we send them?"

"Well, there is a time of enlightenment and learning that Vehuaiah told me about; it's a great time to be a monk. There's an abbey on the holy island of Lindisfarne; it's off the coast of Northumberland. I think they would really thrive there, and they

175

will definitely be safe."

"*Lindisfarne, Northumberland*? Did you just make those words up?"

"No, this will all be in the late eighth century."

"Eighth century!" Uriel yelled and began to flap his wings again. One of his feathers fell on *The Liber Mortuorum,* which Azrael picked up and put aside for later. He needed a new quill. "That's a long time. That's almost 300 years. We can't keep the Gnostic Gospels in heaven for that long."

"I'll put them in the restricted section of the St. Bede's Library right next to the Necronomicon. I can't keep it there forever, or it will be found. They should be safe until that time." He paused and added, "I hope." That image of the gospels next to the Necronomicon made Azrael chuckle.

"I'm glad you think this is funny."

"Do you want my help or not? It's either this, or I write their seven names down now and put an end to this business. I've already broken several rules for you, Uriel, and I'm breaking another major one by keeping those Earthly possessions here, which I won't any longer than necessary."

"All right, agreed. If it is such an age of wisdom, how come they still aren't allowed to read or possess the Gnostic Gospels?"

"I really don't know when or if that is going to happen, but for now this is the plan we are going with."

"You could find out from Vehuaiah."

"I don't know what's going to happen anymore, Uriel, and neither does Vehuaiah because of your meddling. You're creating ripples. Do you understand? Ripples in time."

"I have no idea what you mean."

Azrael only sighed. He didn't feel like explaining time and space to Uriel again. "By the way, the Angels of Dominion want to have a word with you."

"Me? Why? Do they know about this? Oh, Azrael, if they find out, they will put an end to it."

"No, no, it has nothing to do with that. They've been making inquiries about the Apostle John, and apparently you and your friends Michael and Gabriel were the last ones to see him."

"What do you mean? Where is John?"

"That's just it; no one knows where he is and he has been

missing for some time now."

Uriel tried to think back to the last time he saw John. He was upset with him about plagiarizing the end of the world. *That was a long time ago though; that was in . . .* Uriel gasped. "How long has he been missing?"

Azrael looked up at the Clock of Ages and calculated. "About one hundred earth years."

***

John the Baptist was found in hell by Virgil. He was strapped to a table with his feet being tickled by a demon with a feather. When Virgil brought him back into heaven, he looked very pale and frail. He had lost his voice from the shock of it all. When John saw Uriel, he pointed and opened his mouth wide; but nothing came out, not even a grunt like Adolfo's or a moan. After the trauma that John had suffered, the Angels of Dominion could not support Uriel's request for changing Revelation to the Apocalypse of Virgil so Uriel's request was denied. Revelation, the last book of the New Testament, would forever remain the Apocalypse of John.

Virgil was out of seclusion because he had finished his newest tale. Everyone in heaven, hell and limbo alike could not wait to read it. So he scheduled a night in which to do a reading in heaven; the following night he would read in limbo and then the next night in hell. After the readings, Virgil was going to turn the parchment over to Adolfo and John to make copies which Virgil would dispense at his discretion. It wouldn't be for money because money was no longer a commodity that was useful once you were dead, but it would be for favors. Virgil loved having people owe him favors. He couldn't bask in the glory of completing what he thought was his greatest work-to-date because Homer, his literary rival, had also finished a new story and scheduled the reading right before his reading. It irked Virgil that Homer scheduled his first; despite Virgil being the only person to roam freely about heaven and hell, Homer was also very popular. The angles and demons all loved his work as well, especially *The Odyssey*. Even though Homer lived a good 700 years before Virgil, their stories were always being compared with one another as if they were

177

contemporaries. Virgil hated that, but what he hated even more was when people confused the two. One time a seraph told him that he absolutely adored *The Iliad*. It was bad enough the angel used the word "adored" to describe what he thought was his writing, but to confuse it with that trash was intolerable. Virgil dreaded having to sit through Homer's reading because he'd have to smile like a fool and pretend he was enjoying it all. He didn't want to be viewed as petty or have anyone think he might be jealous.

That Greek sop couldn't write his way out of a box, he thought.

Virgil strolled into the St. Bede's Library with its six white marble columns and white rugs. It was not as foggy or misty in there as it was everywhere else; that was so the patrons could actually see what they were reading. The St. Bede's Library was three times the size of the largest library on Earth. It was filled with books from authors who were well-known on Earth but also some that were obscure or lost to history. There were also several books written by angels who fancied themselves authors. When you are eternal, you accumulate some stories along the way.

All this white does tend to make one long for a splash of color. It made him think of Lucy and what he'd told him about why the rebellion had really occurred.

Virgil saw a familiar face sitting curled up in a chair.

"The man, the monk, the merchant," Virgil greeted Peter.

Peter and Virgil looked a lot alike; they were both the same height, about the same age and both had white beards. They were often mistaken for one another, which he didn't mind; he just hated it when he was compared with St. Peter, though, who also had a white beard. People would confuse the two—that is, until St. Peter opened his mouth—then they knew who it was; there was no mistaking his crabby disposition. Peter was reading *The Rule of Saint Benedict* by Benedict of Nursia. Peter was a very pious man who liked obedience, order, humility and contemplation, which is why he was born to be a Benedictine monk.

"Hullo, Virgil."

"I always found that book a bit droll," Virgil said.

"I find it nourishing."

"Between you and me, I've never been very religious."

Peter raised an eyebrow.

"Yes, I know it all exists, I mean, because I'm standing here; but I find the bureaucracies, politics and secret dealings of heaven and hell are not much different from those on Earth."

Peter was about to question Virgil because he didn't know what he meant, but he thought of Uriel and his secret, never-ending quest to meddle in mankind's affairs and to preserve books that he was starting to wonder if anyone even cared about. It wasn't that he didn't care because he had always found wisdom and enjoyed reading the Gnostic Gospels; but weighing what he and his friends had already been through against their importance, he was beginning to wonder if God himself didn't want mankind to have them.

"I was born before Christianity was a known religion, before any holy word had been written down, which is why I was automatically sent to limbo. It's not really fair that I and others born before Christianity was known have to automatically go to limbo. God should have made himself known to man from the beginning. I can't complain, though, since I can go wherever I please; but I have to say, hell really isn't as dreadful as everyone thinks. Yes, there is wailing and cries of agony, but there are also real moments of joy and friendship."

"I hear you are going to regale us with passages from your new story tonight. I am very much looking forward to it."

"Well, you only have to wait until after that Greek pompous hairy giant reads his story."

"I take it you and Homer are not friends."

"We have major creative differences."

"So you're not going to hear him read?" Peter asked.

"No, I will go out of curiosity, just to see how bad it is."

Virgil hadn't noticed at first, but he saw that Peter's wife Mary was sitting quietly and reading beside her husband. She had not said a word the whole time.

"Hullo, Mary."

Mary looked up from her book and gave Virgil a nod, still not saying anything. It was obvious that Mary didn't care for him. Virgil knew that she wasn't willing to overlook some of his qualities, mainly those of shrewdness and guile.

"Speaking of the reading, it's almost time for Homer to begin. Shall we all walk to St. Anne's Hall together?"

Virgil really wanted to skip Homer's reading, but he didn't want everyone to know how much it bothered him to have another writer of his caliber competing for everyone's admiration.

With any luck, it might turn out to be absolutely dreadful, he thought.

They entered St. Anne's Hall; Anne was Mary's mother and grandmother of Jesus, another important piece of information that was not in the canonical version of the New Testament. It can only be found in the Gospel of James. It irked Uriel because he thought at the very least, mankind should know who Mary's mother was.

Virgil gasped; he had never seen so many angels and important humans gathered together for one occasion. Mary, mother of Jesus, was sitting front and center. Also in the front was Jesus himself, and sitting beside him was Mary Magdalene. The hall was packed, and there were no more places to sit, so he, Peter and his wife Mary had to stand in the back, along with a few others. Virgil saw Homer at the front of the room, and the two locked eyes. The following insults went through each other's minds:

Virgil: no talent, Greek scribbler of refuse. There's a reason we Romans conquered you Greeks. It's because we are superior in every way.

Homer: Narcissistic, Roman elitist and author of mediocre drivel. Why don't you trim that scruffy, unruly beard!

Homer cleared his throat and began to speak.

"My new epic poem is called *An Expedition into Hell*."

That dense Greek wrote about hell too. He did that on purpose; he knew I had an interview with Lucifer and was going to write on the subject. He just wanted to try and show me up. Well, we will see who shows who up.

Homer cleared his throat once again to read and looked directly at Virgil.

"I thus began my journey into the foul abyss of sin and corrupt flesh with the wailing and lamentations of the tortured echoing in my ears. Oh savage wasteland. Oh grievous . . ."

Homer continued to read and make eye contact with Virgil, watching his reaction. Virgil stood there in horror at what he was hearing. His own story, word-for-word, was being read aloud.

How is it possible that this foul fiend stole my parchment? He

180

was about to cry out and accuse Homer of the foul deed, but then he stopped. *I can't protest and he knows it; he will just say that it is his, and I will say that it is mine and we will be at an impasse. It would be just unsubstantiated accusations and everyone will wonder ever after who the real author is and it would make me look spiteful,* he thought.

Homer's lips curled in a wicked smile as he knew that the realization had sunk in and that there was nothing that he could do that wouldn't reflect badly on him.

"Are you unwell?" Peter asked. "You look like death. I mean, you look deader than usual." Peter asked the question out of habit because you could no longer get sick once you were dead.

"I am unwell; I have a sickness I may never recover from. I have to leave; please tell everyone that I can't read for them tonight or any other night." Virgil walked out of St. Anne's Hall while Virgil was still reading, and no one noticed because they were too captivated by Homer's poetry.

Baal the Deceiver Deceives Once Again

Virgil was in seclusion again and refused to see anyone. Everyone wondered why he did not give a reading of his new work because no explanation had been given. As usual, when no explanation was given, everyone came up with their own theories. The theories circulating around heaven were everything from his poetry not being as good as Virgil's poetry, to his book got eaten by one of the hounds of hell. The latter theory was started by Michael. The most accepted theory was that he was embarrassed because his work was far inferior to that of Homer, which was received with resounding applause. Heaven, hell and limbo praised his work as being his best yet. Since Virgil refused to come out, a new liaison had to be appointed; and, of course, everyone voted for Homer to be that liaison.

Uriel had no problem convincing the men to go back to Earth because once again the voice of God had convinced them. Michael was starting to use it more than necessary. He used it just the other day to tell a cherub that it needed to move its fat bottom along and stop blocking the path. The frightened cherub stumbled over itself because the different heads and legs all reacted at once and tried to move in different directions. Just another example of how power could corrupt.

Uriel looked at the Clock of Ages. *The eighth century will be here before you know it.* Uriel remained lost in thought and did not even see Vehuaiah approaching.

"Well, what have you found out?" he asked with no preamble.

Uriel, surprised, stuttered out every interrogative he could think of. "Where? Found out what? How do you mean? Why?"

"Who has been eating my chocolate and altering the predestination of things?"

Uriel was still at a loss. He had completely forgotten he was supposed to be spying on himself, Michael and Gabriel. "What do you mean by 'predestination'?"

"I mean, God's divine plan."

"God has a plan?"

"Well, of course, he does, but he is busy doing whatever it is that Gods do, and it is up to us to make sure everything goes according to his plan."

"I'm not sure yet who's been stealing your chocolate or messing up God's pred—" Uriel wasn't sure if he could pronounce "predestination" so he said "plan."

"No clues whatsoever?"

"No clues so far. Whoever it is must be extremely cunning and clever—" Uriel paused and added "—and handsome."

Vehuaiah pointed to his eyes. "Just keep your eyes open. We have a deranged madman or angel with no scruples in our midst."

"Speaking of no scruples, you know St. Paul has been letting all the dead through the gates; he's not turning anyone away. I'll bet the deranged mad man was one of the ones he let into heaven."

"What? What's this business? I've never heard of such a thing in all my eons. This must stop at once. No doubt it is as you say; he's let the foul beast into our heavenly domain."

"Foul beast," Uriel agreed.

"I'm going to see the Angels of Dominion at once and have St. Paul removed from the Heavenly Gates. Judgment of the dead should be an angel's job."

"I've said the same thing time and time again, but would anyone listen?" Vehuaiah was not listening either; he had already disappeared among the clouds.

I'm the foul beast stealing the chocolate, but surely I'm not interfering with God's plans. I mean, he is God, after all.

***

Adolfo was trying to bite Azrael. "Uriel, get a hold of your human before I sew his mouth shut."

"He doesn't want to go back now, but once he gets there, he'll be fine."

Azrael looked at him unconvinced. "Do you have the *you-know-what*?"

"Why? What have you heard? I'll not say anything until I've consulted with an Angel of Power. I will not incriminate myself."

"Uriel, I have no idea what you're talking about, as usual. I meant the Apocrypha."

"Oh, yes, John has them and I prefer the term 'Gnostic Gospels.'"

"Good. Now I can't forever keep their names out of the *Liber Mortuorum*, nor can I keep harboring earthly goods in heaven . . . "He paused, looking at Simon's cooking spoon. "How does he keep getting that into heaven?"

"I don't know; it's one of those heavenly mysteries we're not supposed to question. You know God works in mysterious ways and all of that."

John was still trying to bite Azrael, but Peter and the others looked solemn.

"Try not to send us anywhere where we will get slaughtered," Peter said.

Peter was carrying a sack of his own.

"What's in the sack?" Azrael asked.

Peter clutched the bag to his chest defensively. "Uriel said I could borrow some books from the St. Bede's Library."

Azrael looked at Uriel.

"Well, there's no rule about heavenly things being on Earth. I gave Lorenzo some of the wine from our vineyards last time. If God didn't want heavenly things on Earth, he shouldn't have left a loophole."

Azrael only nodded. He was well past trying to reason with Uriel. "All right, fine. So, as I said, I am sending them to the Holy Isle of Lindisfarne. There is a priory there; it was founded by an Irish monk."

"I don't like their accents," Thomas said.

"Most of the monks are Irish, but they have some from all over."

"I don't like potatoes; they ruin a good stew if you ask me," Simon said.

Azrael ignored these trivial objections. "Netzach was dispatched to pave the way for their arrival. Everything is official and aboveboard. I mean it isn't, but the mortals don't know any better. They will believe any document that looks official."

"Mortals are dupes; they still think that every little bad thing

184

that happens is God's wrath. God is not wrathful or vengeful. In fact, after creating everything, God just wanted to keep resting," Uriel said.

Azrael noticed that John was carrying something in addition to the sack of gospels, as was Adolfo; and, whatever it was, it was covered in cloth. Azrael thought it better not to inquire. *I wouldn't be surprised if Uriel promised them all the pearls from the Heavenly Gate.*

***

Baal the Clever had not been fooled; he had a suspicion that Virgil had stolen the Gnostic Gospels though he could not prove it. Baal found his opportunity to read Virgil's manuscript. Virgil came down to hell with the completed manuscript because Lucifer had requested a special private reading. He would not be attending the formal reading the following night.

Baal the Deceiver changed himself into a hellhound. When he saw Virgil, he ran up to him, snatching the manuscript right out of his hands. He then ran off with it in his jaws. Virgil screamed a high-pitched scream; if anyone had been nearby, they would have sworn it was a woman's scream. He took off after the hellhound. Once Baal was confident that he had lost Virgil, he turned back into his demonly self and made his way into limbo to search out Virgil's enemy, Homer.

It wasn't hard finding the Palace of the Lost where the more notable souls stayed. Baal took great care that he was not seen, lest someone comment that they'd seen a demon lurking about the palace. He found Homer in his bed chamber with the door open.

Homer looked at the demon with a quizzical expression. Demons didn't often go into limbo because there was no torturing taking place there, and even less often did they go into the palace itself.

"Your name is Baal. Am I correct?"

Baal bowed low. "At your service."

"Indeed. To what do I owe the pleasure of this unexpected meeting?"

Baal closed his door. "I have a proposition for you. It has to do with Virgil."

Homer was definitely intrigued. "I'm listening."

"How would you like to win that poetry contest and humiliate Virgil at the same time?"

Homer tugged at his beard. "Yes, go on."

"I know every word of Virgil's manuscript, and I could recite it to you if you were so inclined to write it down."

"Why would I want to do that? His work is inferior to mine, and I will prove it tomorrow night."

"Well, you're probably right. I mean, I think it's brilliant and by far the best work I've read from a mortal, but I am a lowly demon, so what would I know?" It was actually the best work that Baal had read by a mortal, mainly because it was the only work that he had the chance to read, because Azazel was forever collecting all the books and burning them because he didn't like the endings. Baal started to leave, and for a moment he thought Homer wasn't going to say anything; but just as he pulled the door handle, Homer stopped him.

"Wait. Let me hear some of it, and I will be the judge of how good it is."

Baal had only to recite the first few pages before Homer took out some parchment, quill and ink. "Start over from the beginning."

It took Homer and Baal well into the night before it was complete. Once it was finished, Baal slipped out unseen again and Homer went to sleep, feeling triumphant.

***

Lucy, who was sitting in his favorite chair, pulled the shawl around his shoulders tighter. Even though they were in hell, his abode was in the deepest, darkest depths of hell and sometimes there was a draft.

"Where is—"

"I don't know where Virgil is; he's obviously been detained." Judy was cross because it was the third time he had asked the question. Well, the third time he started to ask the question before Judy interrupted.

"I'm sure he will be here soon; he probably just got held up," he said a little softer because he could tell he had hurt Lucy's feelings.

186

Judy had an idea that might cheer him up. "We could get Homer to read his poetry while we wait for Virgil."

Lucy shivered a little. "Damn this draft."

"There's no need for that kind of language."

"Sorry, Judy."

"I can have a demon go fetch Homer if you like."

Lucy didn't answer; he was thinking it over. While he was thinking, Judy went into the other room to boil some water for the tea. When he returned, he was carrying a tray of tea and cakes.

"Homer hasn't written anything since his death. He's been cooped up in purgatory. Maybe his inspiration has run dry; he doesn't have a muse. I suppose that being dead, though, puts an ending to one's muse and one's everything." He looked at Lucy and sighed as if he were talking about himself rather than Homer.

"I guess he—"

"Yes, I suppose you're right. He finally found some inspiration because he has a new epic poem. It would be nice to have Ovid, Sophocles or Plato write something or come up with some new grand theory. I suppose being in hell, though, it's hard to write philosophical observations about your fellow man . . . or anything, for that matter."

Lucifer sipped his tea. "Ow, it's too hot; I burnt my tongue."

There was a loud knock on the door.

"Who's there?" Judy yelled out.

"It's Belias."

"It's the demon who delivers the schedules and messages," Judy said to Lucy. "I'll go see what he wants."

Lucy could make out snatches of the conversation. "I see. Well, that's peculiar; let us know if it is found."

"What did—"

"He said that Virgil was on his way here when his manuscript was stolen right out of his hands by one of our hellhounds."

"That's—"

"I agree; that is strange, but I did hear recently that Barghest got drunk on spirits so the *strange* seems to be contagious."

Judy considered this odd turn of events. "Well, summon—"

"No need to get impatient, Lucy; I was just about to summon Homer."

Judy was about to call Belias back, but Lucy grabbed his arm.

This time Judy interrupted him before he even opened his mouth.

"I don't know why we aren't getting many damned souls lately. I suppose mortals have stopped dying. Phenex, the ferryman, has been helping out other demons with torture because he has had very few to ferry. It's probably St. Peter, that senile old goat." Whether or not this was what Lucy was going to say didn't seem to matter to Judy in the slightest.

Lucy nodded, which made his oversized crown slip even further down his head. He pushed it back up, and it stayed back up for a while but gradually began to creep back down.

"I'll go fetch Belias. We will have Homer read instead of Virgil."

The tea had made him quite warm. Lucy stood up and took off his shawl. He went over to the hook on the wall that he used to hang his shawl and tried to hang it up. He stood on his tiptoes, but couldn't quite reach it. It kept missing the hook and falling to the floor; on his third attempt, he let it stay on the floor where it remained until Judy returned.

The Leaches of Lindisfarne

The Holy Island of Lindisfarne, close to the border of Scotland, was only three miles long. The island was only accessible at low tide by crossing sand and mudflats, which made a pilgrims' path across the island. It was a remote and quiet place, far from the big cities, the wars and commerce. Everything was grown and made right on the island by the monks. Lorenzo made the communion wine and the wine for everyday consumption. The Irish monks loved a good wine. Lorenzo did his best, but the conditions on the island were not as optimal as they were in Lerina or Aquileia, but he made do. The Irish monks didn't seem to mind; they happily consumed everything that Lorenzo made.

The brothers, Thomas and Philip, were amazed at the number of medicinal herbs and plants the island produced. Some of them were rare, and there were species of orchids that were unique to the island. The beach was lined with marram grass and creeping willows, and the island had an abundance of seaweed that washed up on the shore.

John and Adolfo, as always, worked in the scriptorium and Simon was in the kitchen.

Everyone was right in their element, especially Peter, who had been sad at first with the prospect of leaving his wife and the comforts of heaven once again; but he found great joy in the pious life of a monk. It was in some ways more pious than in heaven, considering the behavior of certain angels. When you had an eternity, it put things into perspective. There was never a need to hurry and you still missed loved ones, but you knew you wouldn't be apart for long.

The monastery on Lindisfarne was founded by an Irish monk, Saint Aidan. The priory was made out of wood, keeping with Irish tradition. It was 793, long past the fall of the Roman Empire, and it had been hundreds of years since the men had lived on Earth. They had kept up with all the scientific and cultural advances while in heaven so that they would be prepared for a new age.

Thomas and Philip were in the hospital, treating monks who had fallen ill. Thomas was putting leaches on an Irishman named Michael to keep the blood flowing and cure an infection on his leg.

"I hate those bloody creatures," Brother Michael said.

"Leeches are part of God's many creatures. They may look unsightly, but they have healing powers," Thomas said.

"Oh, aye, healing powers. They look like the excrement I have to clean out of the bottom of the privy."

"Not all of God's creatures can be furry and agreeable."

"Right, some look like something in Brother Simon's barley stew or they look like the face of this one," he said, pointing to Brother Bairre.

Bairre grabbed a handful of meal, herbs and various other muck that was in his poultice and threw it at Michael. It missed Michael and splattered all over Philip's robe.

Everyone in the hospital laughed except for Philip. "I just cleaned this bloody robe." The seven Italians had been there long enough that they had picked up some of the Irish vernacular.

Peter with his slight frame and long white beard, trimmed neatly, walked in, escorting a young monk."This man is in need of some medical expertise."

"Well, he's come to the wrong place for that!" Michael shouted. Raucous laughter reverberated around the hospital. The Irish monks were a very animated and lively bunch.

"Aye, nothing but Italians messing about, not like me mum who could cure death itself with her stew," Bairre said.

Thomas, whose hair was as red as the blood the leaches were sucking from Michael, said, "Just have him lie down over there." He pointed to one of the empty beds.

The hospital was not even half-full. There weren't that many men on the island, and the Irish were a hardy stock who rarely fell ill; and when they did, they were reluctant to get treated.

Philip, whose hair and eyes were as black as the night sky when no stars are out, walked over to Peter. Neither one resembled the other in the slightest because they each took after their fathers instead of their mutual mother.

"We have a problem," he whispered.

"I'll say," Philip said, picking up an empty vile. "We're out of goat weed, and I have to walk to the other side of the island to get those."

"Not that, the place where we put the you-know-what flooded and smeared the ink on the you-know-what. Most of the pages are illegible," Peter whispered.

"St. Peter's beard. What are we going to do? Those were our only copies."

"Keep your voice down. I have them committed to memory . . .well, for the most part; and I'll recite them to John so that he can rewrite the smudged parts."

Michael pulled a leech from his leg and hurled it across the room. "That thing is sucking out all me blood." He tried to pull another one off, but Thomas slapped his hand away and went over to find the poor leech that Michael had thrown. Michael began to sing; his voice rang out loudly throughout the room.

"Young Donal, if you cross the ocean, take me with you – don't forget! You'll have a keepsake on a fair-day and market, and the daughter of a Greek king for a bed-mate. You promised me, but you lied to me, that you'd meet me at the sheep-fold; I whistled and called a thousand times for you, but all I got was the lambs bleating."

Philip began to clap, and Bairre joined in the singing.

"Gave you my love when I was little, and even more when I got bigger—and not the love that a lamb gives its mother, but everlasting, secure love that can't be broken."

"Is someone going to look at me foot? It bloody well hurts," John said.

"John, you interrupted the song me mum used to sing, and I had another eight verses, you wee pox."

"No one wants to hear you sing; you sound like a dying mule." Michael ignored the insult and shrugged him off with the wave of his hand.

"First time I saw you 'twas a Sunday evening 'Twas at the Easter as I was kneeling 'Twas on Christ's passion that I was reading But my mind, it was on you, and my own heart bleedingYou have taken east and west from me ;you've taken the moon and the sun from me; you've taken the heart from within my breast; but my greatest fear is that you've taken God from me."

191

Peter shook his head disapprovingly. "That's not a fitting song for a monk."

A bell began to ring; it's *clank, clank, clank* meant it was time for mass.

"Oh, Seamus loves to really give that bell a ring. It's the only thing he enjoys doing, the lazy old goat," Michael said.

Thomas found the leech curled up in a ball underneath a chair. He picked it up, and it tried to attach itself to his hand. He put the leech back on Michael's leg. "I guess you won't be happy until that thing has sucked up all me blood, and there's nothing left but a corpse."

"It's time for mass," Peter said.

"What do we do about the infirm?" Thomas asked.

Peter looked at the three Irish monks. Michael was covered in leeches, Bairre's leg was covered in a mountain of dried muck and John had pus coming out of his foot. "I don't think they should attend mass today."

***

Uriel was working on a new project, something to inspire man to create something for God; he was, after all, the angel of art. He was mainly doing it to keep Zachariel happy and not arouse any suspicion about his favorite 400-year-old project. Zachariel was still cross about Michael giving his scepter away, even though it was to the Presence of God. He thought Michael should at least let him have the voice of God since he had lost his millennium-old scepter, but Michael couldn't bear to part with the voice. It had provided him countless hours of amusement and had gotten them all out of a few scrapes. Uriel decided to inspire some Frankish monks, Brother Liuthard and Beringerf, to make an illuminated codex containing the four gospels. It was lavishly illustrated and the cover was encrusted with jewels. The monks called it the *Codex Aureus of St. Emmeram*, which was a mouthful to say. It was in honor of Saint Emmeram of Regensburg. Netzach had no idea who Saint Emmeram was; but when the monks suggested him as the name for the book, Netzach nodded his head in agreement. Mortals had way too many saints to keep track of, and Netzach felt like they were just handing out the title nowadays.

Emmeram had been the first Bishop of Poitiers in Aquitaine. His martyrdom story is a favorite among Christians and, unlike Uriel and company, better-informed angels. The daughter of a Duke told Emmeram that she was expecting a child out of wedlock, and the father was someone from the Duke's court. Emmeram took pity on her and told her that she could name him as the father in the hopes that the punishment for her wouldn't be too severe. Emmeram went on a pilgrimage to Rome where the Duke's daughter named him as the father.

The Duke's brother, Lantpert, went after Emmeram and found him in Helfendorf. Lantpert and some of his cohorts tied Emmeram to a ladder, tortured him and cut him into pieces. When he was found, he was actually still alive, but died shortly after being found. After his death, it came out who the real father was and Emmeram was entombed in Aschheim, whereupon the angels made it rain for forty straight days. Some people said the angels wept for Emmeram, and the rain was their tears.

The monks were persuaded not by having Michael use the voice of God and scaring them into making the gospel. Uriel realized he couldn't keep frightening people to death in order to get mortals to do works in the name of God; that would be unseemly and also Zachariel would probably find out about it.

Uriel, who was loathe to go to Earth, sent Netzach to the Saint-Denis Abbey outside of Paris. Netzach disguised himself as a Frank monk named Hugo and wormed his way into the good graces of the other monks. The angel hated human names and hated humans for that matter. He didn't see why he should always have to do Uriel's dirty work, even if he were an archangel.

Netzach eventually befriended two monks, Liuthard and Beringerf, who ultimately designed, inscribed and illuminated the texts. John and Adolfo would have been very jealous if they had known of the unparalleled beauty of this codex.

Netzach, going by the name Hugo, went into the scriptorium one day and approached the monks.

"What are we working on today?" Hugo asked.

The Frankish monks smiled at Hugo and invited him over for a look. They were working on several new prayer books. He did not much care for humans, but he had to admire their craftsmanship.

"You know, I was thinking you should do the gospels."

Liuthard and Beringerf simultaneously made a *tiff* sound, which the Franks made quite often and meant either boring or stupid. Hugo thought in this case the former because it had been done many times, and the Franks hated unoriginality.

"There are so many gospels; they are all the same," Liuthard said.

Hugo smelled the air in the scriptorium; it was an amalgam of paints, animal carcasses and mold.

Yes, but not one like this. Only the Franks could make a gospel like the one I have in mind," he said, knowing how to appeal to Frankish vanity and superiority.

The monks were intrigued. "What do you have in mind?" Beringer asked.

"The most lavish gospel the world has ever seen. There isn't and will never be one like it. Only Frankish monks, with immense talents such as yours, could design such a thing."

Even the Frankish had a limit on self-regard. "Enough flattery; tell us what you are thinking," Beringer said.

"The gospels should be written on purple vellum to start with and each page more lavishly illuminated than the next. There could be seven full pages to show the four evangelists, and also within the pages, you could include illustrations of the Adoration of the Lamb and Christ in Majesty. Put in twelve canon tables, and the text itself should be golden uncial letters with each page framed. The cover will be made of gold and decorated with gemstones, sapphires, emeralds and pearls. At the center of the cover, put the Christ in Majesty, who is seated on the globe of the world and holding on his knee a book inscribed with these words.

"I am the way and the truth and the life. No man cometh to the Father but by me."

Hugo saved the best for last, the one thing he knew would make them want to undertake such a project. "Put your initials on each page to show the world who created such a masterpiece."

The Frankish monks were speechless. They couldn't even have fathomed such a thing. It had never been done before.

"Yes, yes, we must do this. It will be as you say," Liuthard said.

"I will need to get some purple vellum; we do not have that here," Beringerf said.

"We do not have precious jewels either," Liuthard pointed out.

"Why don't you tell your idea to some of the wealthy Frankish noblemen? I'm sure they will donate jewels for such a cause," Hugo suggested.

"You are a genius, Hugo. You stay in the scriptorium and watch us create this gospel," Beringerf said.

"Maybe we put your initial somewhere in it," Liuthard said.

Hugo panicked; that would ruin the whole thing. It was one thing to inspire, instruct and even coerce, but he couldn't leave his imprint on any mortal creation.

"No, I cannot take credit for this; after all, I was inspired by your beautiful prayer books."

"As you wish then," Beringerf said.

Hugo stayed and watched them create the codex. It took them a long time; but when they were done, it was a thing to behold. He had seen all kinds of beautiful works of art in heaven, but this would rival any one of them. For once, he was glad he had come to Earth because he was proud to be a part of this creation. Liuthard and Beringerf, when finished, admired the fruits of their labor.

"What do we work on next?" Liuthard asked.

What about a mural?" Beringerf suggested.

Liuthard shrugged his shoulders and just went *tiff.*

***

When Virgil finally came out of seclusion, Homer lauded the fact that he was also appointed as a liaison between heaven and hell. The two were in limbo, standing beard to beard.

"How did you like my reading of my new manuscript?"

"You know very well that you stole it from me. I don't know how you did it, but that is my manuscript word-for-word."

"You know, I could have written my own manuscript; and no doubt it would have been much better than yours, but I wanted to really put salt in the wound," Homer said.

"The reason you didn't write your own is because you're a coward. You know that your work is inferior to mine," Virgil said.

"More people read and enjoy *The Odyssey* on Earth than *The Aeneid,* and that's a fact."

195

"That is a figment of your imagination."

"At least I have an imagination," Homer said.

"You, sir, are a miserable trickster; you're nothing more than a thief and a liar," Virgil said and gave Homer's beard a hard yank.

"How dare you! You talentless swine," Homer said and yanked Virgil's beard even harder.

The two began screaming insults at each other and tugging each other's beards. It wasn't long until there was a crowd around them. Among the crowd who gathered on Homer's side were Sophocles, Euripides, Plato and Euclid who felt they had to support their fellow Greek. On Virgil's side were Ovid, Horace, Cicero and Seneca the Younger who were supporting their fellow Roman. Each of these prominent Greek and Roman figures stepped in and started trading insults and beard tugging. The only one who had an advantage was Ovid because he didn't have a beard, but that didn't stop Sophocles from tugging on his chin anyway. It looked like another Macedonian War, except this one was comprised of old men yanking beards instead of sword blows.

Finally Virgil yelled, "Enough of this! I know how to settle this once and for all. I challenge Homer to write a manuscript, as shall I, and we will see which one is better."

"I accept the challenge," Homer said and gave Virgil's beard another yank.

"Who will be the judge of which one is better? I don't trust any of you Romans to decide," Sophocles said.

"It shall be decided by neutral parties, a committee of judges comprised of demons and angels. They will decide whose work is superior," Virgil said.

"How will you get a group of angels and demons together? The two aren't allowed to be in each other's company," Plato asked.

"You wait and see. I am Virgil the great, and I can make anything happen."

"More like Virgil, the second-rate," Homer said and got in one last beard tug before turning around and fleeing.

All Are Welcome

It was a warm June day on the island of Lindisfarne. A cool breeze was blowing and from the distance, it looked as if the marram grass were dancing. The pale-bellied brent geese, the island's native bird, were busy pecking at a crab that was pivoting left and right trying to dodge the blows. The wind permeated the fragrance of the orchids, and the whole island smelled of its sweet perfume. It was low tide so the Pilgrims' path to the island was visible.

Peter could see the heads of seals, bobbing up and down in the water. They appeared to be at play. He and Brother Michael had been working in the garden; and after four hours of being hunched over, pulling weeds and digging, he was in need of a short rest. He shut his eyes to let the warm sunshine hit his face. He wasn't prepared for what he saw when he opened his eyes again. He focused his eyes just before the horizon, and he could see what looked like dozens and dozens of ships. Immediately alarmed, Peter jumped out of his chair. The only thing that ever came to the island once a month by boat were other monks and supplies. He ran as fast as his old legs would carry him to the bell tower. It was a long, steep climb to the top to where the bell was kept. Peter didn't have time to think about having sore legs the next day because whatever was coming, chances were, he wouldn't be alive the next day. He surprised himself by climbing over a hundred steps without being winded, but it was probably because he was too full of adrenalin to be anything else but frightened. When he finally made it to the top, he put Brother Seamus, the monk who normally rang the bell before mass, to shame. The bell clanged louder and longer than it ever had before. A sea of brown robes came pouring out of the Abbey. They knew something was terribly wrong because it was nowhere near time for mass, and that bell never rang for any other reason.

When Peter descended from the bell tower, he found John and Adolfo first.

"Are we under attack?" John asked.

"I think so. I mean, we are a wealthy, unarmed settlement ripe for plundering marauders."

"What should we do?"

"Where are the gospels?"

"In the scriptorium, but I haven't finished recopying the ones that got ruined with water."

"It doesn't matter. You and Adolfo go now and quickly hide them."

John and Adolfo ran towards the scriptorium with Adolfo grunting all along the way. He didn't think he would be able to bite his way out of this one.

Peter stood and watched as the ships got closer. It was all he or anyone else could do. This wasn't Aquileia; it didn't have a wall around it, and they didn't have a garrison. They were unarmed monks with no means of defending themselves. The ships were unlike anything he had ever seen, and he had been around for over 400 years so he had seen a thing or two.

The ships had overlapping planks which were somehow riveted together. Protruding from both the bow and the stern was a massive dragon's head. Each ship had one large sail with a giant snake pictured on it. They were large, but slender wooden ships that seemed to just glide effortlessly upon the water. It wasn't effortless, though; it was the result of about twenty-four men and a few women rowing them.

Who are these people?

They were now close enough for him to really make out their features. They were all bearded, except for the handful of women that he counted. They were wearing iron helmets and had swords and axes lying at their feet. The island's low sand banks made it almost seem that they were welcoming the strangers.

Whoever they are, they are not dressed for mass; they are dressed for battle.

If Lindisfarne had not been such a remote island, they would have heard that another monastery had been sacked just a few years earlier by exactly the same ungodly-looking pagans now approaching. Everyone instinctively ran, but there was nowhere to really run. The island was only a few miles long. They couldn't lock themselves up in the Abbey; one good battering ram would knock down the door.

John and Adolfo are getting the gospels. I can at least try and hide the other holy relics, Peter thought.

The last thing Peter saw before running off to the Abbey was the appointed reeve making his way to the shore to greet the men in the ship.

What is that fool doing? Does he really think they are traders?

The first boat made it ashore, and its inhabitants let out a blood-curdling scream. The reeve turned around to run. Peter watched long enough to see the reeve's head come flying off his neck as one of the heathens lopped it off with an axe. He entered God's church and saw that Brother Seamus was already there trying to hide the relics.

"Quickly, help me hide the gospels," Seamus said.

Seamus was referring to the Lindisfarne Gospels, the beautiful handwritten work of the monk Eadfrith.

"Put them in here," Peter said, pulling out beneath the altar the oak coffin that contained the relics of St. Cuthbert. "God willing, it may go unnoticed."

Screams could be heard throughout the island. Monks were being cut down as the demons pillaged the island, trampling everything in their path. John and Adolfo burst into the church. John was carrying the sack with the gospels, but he and Adolfo were also carrying something else that Peter couldn't believe. In each of their hands, they were brandishing a sword, but not just any sword; it was the sword of the archangels Michael and Gabriel. Michael and Gabriel had given them lessons on how to wield a sword. They were so eager to pass on their skills to someone. Before leaving, Uriel insisted that they give their swords to John and Adolfo. This they were not so eager to do, but they finally relented because Uriel promised they would have them back soon. The two were still gullible enough to believe Uriel's promises.

"What do those two nimrods think they're doing with those?" Seamus asked.

Peter didn't have a chance to answer him because two of the heathens came in with their faces painted red and black. They took one look at Adolfo and John and began to laugh.

Their laughter stopped as John swung his sword and cut one of them nearly in half, and Adolfo plunged his sword through the heart of the other one. Before they could even wipe their sword blades, five more came in and saw their fallen brethren. One of them said something in their own peculiar language. Peter didn't need a translation; whatever it was, it wasn't good for them. John tried to swing his sword again at one of them, but the pagan dodged the thrust and knocked the sword out of his hands. He grabbed John with both hands and started to drag him out of the church. Adolfo tried to help his friend, but the other four grabbed him and took the sword out of his hands. Adolfo bit one of them and the devil yelped, releasing his grip on him. The other four thought that was funny and laughed at their comrade. They got John and Adolfo through the church doors, and Seamus and Peter were left standing alone by the altar.

"There will be more of them things coming soon," Seamus said.

Peter didn't answer him; he couldn't let his friends meet some terrible fate at the hands of those unholy barbarians, not without at least trying to do something.

"Where do you think you're going?"

"I have to try to help Brother Adolfo and Brother John."

"Are ye daft? They will cut your head off and use it for sport. There is nothing you can do for them now."

"I have to try," Peter said and left the church. When Peter got back onto the beach, it was covered with dead monks, and the sea was turning red from their blood. He could see John and Adolfo from a distance. The devils had put chains around their arms and legs, and they were being hauled out into the water. Peter was struck on the back of his head and quickly faded out; the last thing he saw was John and Adolfo being plunged beneath the waves.

***

Uriel paced by the pearly gates of heaven, waiting for the monks to arrive. He stopped and leaned on the *All Are Welcome* sign. If you were going to die, now was the best time because no matter what your past transgressions were, you made it into heaven, all because St. Paul couldn't turn anyone away.

What do I do? They are going to be furious; they will never go back to Earth now. Did they save the Gnostic Gospels?

200

It wasn't long before Uriel saw them; the line to heaven moved really fast now since St. Paul didn't even bother to get the books out on people. John and Adolfo were both in chains and completely water-logged. Peter had a gash on his head, and Lorenzo had a hole in his belly. Simon held his cooking spoon in one hand and his head in the other.

How does he keep getting that into heaven?

Uriel counted the men. He was coming up two short. "Where are the brothers?"

"Never mind them, what about my head?" Simon's head asked as he whacked Uriel with the spoon.

"Ouch. Stop that. Did they die or not?" Uriel asked impatiently.

"You monster," Peter said. "Do you have any idea how dying feels?"

"How could I? I'm not allowed to die; at least, I don't think I am."

A woman walked by and stared at Simon who was holding his head. He stuck his head right up in her face. "What are you looking at? Haven't you ever seen someone lose his head before?"

The woman began to scream.

"Now look what you've done," Uriel said.

Saint Paul heard the woman screaming and gently approached her.

"Madam, what has upset you?"

She didn't stop screaming, but she managed to point at Simon holding his head.

"Why, madam, that's merely a mortal holding what's left of his head. It happens all the time. Mankind seems to be bent on taking heads. You wouldn't be screaming if you just stopped to think about what that poor man has gone through."

The woman stopped screaming to consider this. She looked at the others who were all the worse for wear. "Am I in the right place?"

"You are in heaven and heaven is the right place. You've merely had a fright. Come, I'll escort you into heaven where you can recuperate." Paul escorted her—or pushed her from behind, to be precise—through the gates.

"Where are the gospels; are they safe?"

Peter just shook his head and walked through the gates, followed by the other monks. Simon took one last whack at Uriel. "I will break that blasted spoon over your head."

They didn't look very happy. Well, they'll get over it. I will need to find out where the brothers are. I don't think they died. I will sooth the ruffled feathers of the other mortals, but first I need to see Azrael. How did this happen? Every time I think I'm sending them someplace safe, they die. It's as if someone doesn't want the gospels to survive. Well, someone does—Azazel does— but I don't know how he could orchestrate such catastrophes from hell. Baal is clever enough, though. Where are the gospels now? I need a nap. Stay focused! The first thing I need to do is to go see Azrael and find out what in the name of Jehovah is going on.

All these thoughts rattled around his head like spare coins in a pocket. Azrael, as always, was hunched over the *Liber Mortuorum*, writing in the names of the dead. The *Liber Mortuorum* unfortunately, only hovered around Azrael's waist because he was a rather tall angel; all angels were tall, but Azazel was exceptionally tall. Azrael had put in a request to have the *Liber Mortuorum* raised higher, but as of yet, had not heard back about it. That request was put in over 1,000 years ago. Things got done in their own time in heaven, which was whenever they got around to it. Their unofficial motto was, "Why hurry when you're going to be around for eternity?"

Azrael rubbed his eyes because staring at a book all day could strain one's eyes.

"I would like an explanation," Uriel said.

"Oh bother, I misspelled Malcolm. I'll just leave it; they know who I mean."

"I said—"

"I heard you. You want me to give an explanation regarding what?"

"You know very well what. You choose a specific time and place for them because you said you knew they would be safe and they would only be there a year before they were killed. Now they won't even talk to me. They're sick of the whole business. They're all bent out of shape about being brutally murdered."

"I guess I was mistaken in my information."

"I guess you were. Now what am I supposed to do?"

"Let me add the men's names to the *Liber Mortuorum* so they can remain in heaven where they belong. You can stop meddling in things you have no business meddling in, and let fate decide the Apocrypha."

"That is the most ridiculous idea you've ever had. I don't want to hear any more about fate. Do you know what happens when you leave things to fate?"

"It eventually works itself out," Azrael said.

Michael and Gabriel snuck up behind Uriel, and Michael shouted using the voice of God, "Stop interfering with my domain!" The ground shook beneath their feet, and Azrael spilled ink all over the page.

"Now I have to start all over," Azrael said irritably.

"Someone is a grumpy goose," Michael said.

"Honestly, don't you ever get tired of doing that?" Uriel asked. "I mean really; it's getting old. You need to give God back His voice."

"I will give it back the very next time I see Him."

"Your face will melt off the very next time you see Him," Gabriel said.

"I meant when He is in the form of the Presence of God," Michael said.

"You don't really believe your face will melt off, do you?" Uriel asked.

"Yes, remember Sandalphon," Gabriel reminded him. "He insisted on speaking to God and has not been seen for 10,000 years."

Uriel shrugged; he didn't care about Sandalphon or his face. "Did you check on the monks?"

"They've settled down a little bit, all except for Simon," Michael said.

"He was upset because you attached his head on backwards," Gabriel said.

"Well, how am I supposed to know which way humans like their heads to face? Maybe they would use it better if it were the other way around."

"I think they just need time; they've been through a traumatic event . . . again. I did find out from Vehuaiah that they were killed by Vikings," Gabriel said.

"What is a bla—" Uriel stopped himself. He was pretty sure he had already doubled the amount of swearing he was allowed for one day. He should have already been facing some pompous Angel of Virtue. *I guess they have their hands full, though, sorting out all the murders and thieves that St. Paul has let into heaven. They don't have time to worry about an archangel swearing,* he thought.

"What is a Viking?"

"Vehuaiah described them as the wrath of God. They are barbaric demons who like to eat, copulate and burn things," Gabriel said.

"I've never had a chance to do any of those things," Michael said, putting a piece of chocolate in his mouth. "Oh, I almost forgot, Vehuaiah wants an update on the chocolate thief."

In a Hot Minute

"What's going on here?" Rosier asked as he joined Azazel.

"They're blasphemers and originally I was supposed to poke their eyes out with hot pokers."

"I don't get the correlation. If they are blasphemers, shouldn't you tie their tongues to the Quiet Tree or rip them out or something?"

"That's why it was changed because it didn't really make much sense. I'm glad; I don't think I would have liked to poke out anyone's eyes," Azazel said.

A woman walked up to him, saying nothing. She just opened her mouth and stuck her tongue out. Azazel put something on her tongue. She closed her mouth, and in seconds her eyes began to water."

"What did you give her?"

"I gave her a hot pepper."

"You gave her a hot pepper with no water? That is simply diabolical," Rosier said.

"Yes, it's quite diabolical," agreed Azazel.

Virgil walked up the path, his chin in the air; he looked like a man, or a former man, on a mission.

"I need to see Lucy again."

Rosier and Azazel looked at each other blankly.

"I mean Lucifer."

"You already saw him once; and he doesn't normally receive visitors, but yours was a special occasion, so being granted another audience would be impossible," Rosier said.

"Nothing is impossible."

"Yes, some things are impossible, like turning water into wine," Rosier said.

"That has actually been done," Azazel pointed out.

"Oh, I thought it sounded familiar. What's this about anyway?"

205

Azazel popped another hot pepper into the next unfortunate soul's mouth. The man began crying almost immediately. "I'm terribly sorry." His apology was of little comfort.

"I want to get a group of angels and a group of demons together to act as judges."

"Now that really is impossible, even if you saw Lucifer and he agreed; he cannot make that happen without the will of God."

"I will work on that end. God has been unavailable for some time now, so all I would need is for a seraph to agree in his stead. I just need Lucifer to agree to it too."

"What are we to be judging?" Rosier asked. Virgil frowned at Rosier using the word "we." He had not considered asking either Rosier or Azazel to sit in as judges; but, since he was trying to get them to do a favor for him, he knew he would have to let them be judges.

"Homer and I are each writing a new epic poem, and we want a group of angels and demons so it is judged fairly."

Azazel and Rosier didn't say anything; they felt a bit awkward since Homer had already read the story he had written, and Virgil hadn't shown up or ever produced his own manuscript. The pair just stared at the ground where there was a hare sitting quietly with its ears up, looking at them. It was most likely the hare that had gotten away from the pit. Rosier made a move to grab it, but it went bounding away and out of sight.

"I'll get word to Lucifer about what you want, and I'm afraid that's the best I can do," Azazel said.

Virgil nodded, satisfied.

Azazel's curiosity got the better of him, and he tried one of the red peppers. After a few seconds when nothing happened, he said, "I guess they don't have any effect . . ." He stopped because it suddenly felt like someone had set fire to his throat.

"Are you all right?" Rosier asked.

"Water," Azazel croaked. "Go and find me some water."

Birds of a Feather

Thomas and Philip rocked back and forth in the boat. They had gotten used to the rocking motions and no longer felt nauseated.

"We could throw ourselves off the boat and drown," Philip said.

"I know we've died several times already, but I'm still afraid to die."

"There is always fear in death, but it won't last very long; and then after a minute, it will all be over."

"I don't know if we'd go to heaven or not if we kill ourselves. If you despair as Judas did, you end up in hell," Thomas said.

"We've already been dead twice; I don't think they would hold it against us. Don't forget that St. Paul is still at the gate; at least, he was when we left, and he was letting everyone in."

"Part of me is curious as to where they are taking us and what they want with us," Philip said.

"What if they want to torture us? Then we will wish we'd drowned ourselves in the sea."

"I don't think they would go to all the trouble to take us all the way back to their homeland just to torture us. I think they might just be curious about us and our way of life."

"I say we jump in the sea on the count of three," Thomas said.

"All right, if you really don't want to find out our fate, on the count of three then."

"One . . . two . . . ." A sizeable hand was placed on each of their shoulders as they stood up.

"No," he said to them. "No. die."

Thomas and Philip looked up at a large, blond-haired Viking named Gunnar, who had been sitting closest to them. The brothers sat back down in the wooden long boat; they were wedged between two broad-shouldered Vikings. They had taken off their iron helmets and laid aside their axes and swords, clearly not

207

seeing the two monks as a threat. Among the swords were the swords of Gabriel and Michael that John and Adolfo had used. They no doubt thought the golden swords with their engravings were very valuable. They'd let them keep the sack full of gospels because they probably didn't see much value in manuscripts of a religion they didn't believe in, written in a language they couldn't read.

"He understood what we were saying," Philip said as he watched the Viking Gunnar, who looked to be about his age. He took out a beautifully-patterned comb and began to comb his hair and beard. He noticed Philip watching him and offered him the comb. Philip politely accepted because he thought the young man might take offense and change his mind and throw him overboard into the sea. He ran the comb through his hair and beard a few times and gave it back to Gunnar, who was now picking his teeth clean. Philip had not noticed amid the chaos, but all the Vikings were well-groomed and had a very clean appearance.

In fact, the only two people on the entire boat who looked like dirty savages were he himself and his brother Thomas. He looked down at his hands, which were dirty; he could not remember the last time he had bathed or groomed himself. His robe was filthy and he smelled.

The Viking, who spoke in a foreign tongue, seemed to understand his embarrassment and reached into his satchel and pulled out a blue wool tunic and a pair of trousers. He pointed at the tunic and then at Philip. Philip gathered that he wanted him to put the clothes on.

Philip was embarrassed because there was nowhere for him to change in privacy. He need not have been worried, though, because none of the Vikings even noticed him. They were used to living day-to-day among each other and just saw it as practical living. Even the women were not embarrassed to change in front of the men.

"That is a nice tunic," Thomas said.

"I know, for barbarians, they are better-dressed and groomed than we are."

"Do you think the others are dead?" Thomas asked.

"Yes, I do, but at least they're up in heaven and hopefully there to stay this time. I wish we were up there with them."

"Why do you think they kept us alive?"

"I don't know, but I suspect it might be because we are healers; otherwise, I don't know of what use we would be to them," Philip said.

"Do you think someone from heaven will come and retrieve us?"

"I don't know."

The blond Viking gestured at the tunic and smiled. Philip smiled back so he wouldn't offend him.

A seagull flew up and perched itself on the bow of the boat right in front of the brothers.

"This seems eerily familiar," Philip said.

"Yes, you remember the last time it was a parrot which stayed on the bow of our boat, listening to our conversation. The parrot turned out not to be a parrot at all, but Baal the Deceiver."

"I don't think it's Baal this time. I think it's just a gull because we don't have the gospels and don't know where they are," Philip said a little too loudly. He wanted to make sure if the gull were indeed Baal, he wouldn't know they had the gospels on the boat.

The brothers watched as the gull was about to fly away, but Gunnar grabbed the seagull around the throat and snapped its neck. He smiled at the brothers and held up his prize.

***

The seagull was not Baal, nor was it just a regular seagull; it was Netzach, who had been sent by Uriel to find out where the monks were and, more importantly, where the gospels were. Netzach appeared at the heavenly gate with a crooked neck and a foul temper.

"Welcome, stranger, come right in; all are welcome here," St. Paul said.

"Be quiet, you fool. All are not supposed to be welcome here," Netzach snapped.

"Now calm down, good sir. No doubt you've had a minor shock. Death can do that to you. Come into paradise and let us take away all your worries."

"I am not a man; I am an angel and stop acting like you're a merchant trying to sell a parcel of land. This isn't a Roman bath;

it's an eternal resting place."

"I'm terribly sorry I have offended you, sir."

A man who was behind Netzach watched the exchange with growing interest. He thought if this is how things were in heaven, maybe he should look elsewhere for his eternal resting place.

Where is Uriel? I'm telling him I want to be reassigned to another archangel.

It wasn't the first time Netzach's neck had been snapped in the service of Uriel. In fact, all total, his list of fatalities included:

Snapped neck (2)

Drowned (5)

Burned at the stake (4)

Boiled alive (3)

Hanged (6)

Poisoned (2)

Crucified (3)

Fell into a grave (1 time, which was really his own fault, but he still blamed Uriel)

He focused on Uriel and snapped his fingers. Uriel appeared and looked sleepy. It was an act of insubordination to summon an angel above you in the hierarchy.

"Who are you?"

Netzach had not yet transformed himself back into an angel. "It's Netzach, you goat."

"What is this about? I was taking a nap."

"Blast your nap and blast you!" Netzach roared. "The savages broke my neck."

It was two acts of insubordination. You were supposed to get prior approval if you were going to swear, but the Angels of Virtue won't grant you permission to swear at a superior, even if it is Uriel.

"What savages? Be more specific."

"The people with the funny names; you know the *whatsits*."

"I have no idea what you are talking about, Netzach. What's wrong with your neck? It looks funny."

"Do you have cotton in your ears? I told you, the *whatsits* broke my neck. The people who have Philip and Thomas."

A cherub stopped briefly to watch Uriel yelling at Netzach.

"What are you looking at?" Netzach asked the cherub, whose

eagle head hid underneath the mane of the lion head. The lion roared, but Netzach didn't care. "I want you to know that you look strange and no one likes you."

The cherub walked away, the eagle still not coming out from underneath the lion's mane.

"You know he is going to report you," Uriel said.

"I don't care. I'm tired and I'm getting as far away from you as I can."

"Where are the gospels?"

"They're safe aboard the ship the brothers are on . . . safe for now, at any rate. They said they weren't, but that one oaf of a brother said it a little too loudly. Mortals have no subtlety and have the grace of a three-legged goat. I can't guarantee what the *whatsits* will do to them. They don't look like the learned type."

"There, there," Uriel patted Netzach on the back, trying to soothe him like a small child. Netzach started to open his mouth to say he would not be soothed when Uriel shoved a piece of Vehuaiah's chocolate in his mouth, which nearly made him choke.

"Good job, why don't you take the day off? No more travels for you for a while." Uriel closed his eyes and tried to snap his fingers. It took five tries to send Netzach away, who was still choking. As usual, he forgot to concentrate.

I hope he ended up at the Eternal Spring where I meant to send him for a soothing bath and not some nefarious place.

***

Netzach did not end up in some nefarious place. Uriel actually sent him to the Eternal Spring although he ended up headfirst in the spring, but Uriel still considered it a success. He now needed to figure out how to get Thomas and Philip so that he could have all the monks together again.

I don't necessarily need all seven of the monks to guard the gospels; I mean, five is still plenty. Besides, I need to come up with a new place to send them, one where they won't get killed by Nuns and Whatsits.

Uriel approached the monks putting on his smile, the coercive one, that has worked so many times in the past. He had been speaking to Azrael, and he knew the perfect place to send the monks. It was a hundred years from the present Earth time, so he had time to persuade them. He would work on them bit by bit, slowly, until it was time to go; and then they would think it was their own idea. He couldn't keep bullying them, and the idea of it being a holy quest was getting less convincing after each gruesome death.

"Save your breath. We are never going back to Earth," Peter said.

"I agree; you and the monks are *never* going back to Earth. You will all sign your names in the *Liber Mortuorum* and remain in heaven *forever*. You will never see Earth or living humans *ever* again." Uriel enunciated the words *never, forever* and *ever*. Those words always frightened humans. They were always afraid when they were told anything was forever, no matter what it was, even living in Paradise. They simply couldn't fathom it, felt trapped and eventually felt like they couldn't breathe. It wasn't in their nature to do the same thing day in and day out. He watched Peter's face and there it was . . . a split second of fear crossed it before he smiled. Uriel knew it was only a matter of time, and it would be just enough to time to make them eager to take a trip to break the monotony.

"That's good; when do we sign the book?"

"You can go see Azrael anytime you want."

Peter started to walk away and then hesitated. "Well, we don't have to do it right this second. I mean, there's plenty of time for that."

"Yes, you're right. You have a whole eternity to be here, forever in the same place, doing the same thing."

The fear flashed across Peter's face again and this time stayed a little bit longer.

***

Baal wasn't ever going to disguise himself as a bird again; he had learned his lesson at Aquileia.

Why do mortals like to kill birds so much?

He touched the scar on his hip where the Hun's arrow had skewered him. He touched his other scar where Michael had accidentally cut him with his sword. He was accumulating quite the battle scars. Baal was thinking about what animal he should disguise himself as, when he saw Virgil passing. He had to smile; he'd never trusted him and had always suspected him of stealing the Apocrypha. The best way to get even with him was to hurt the one thing Virgil had a lot of and that was pride. The only way to do that was to ally himself with Virgil's enemy, Homer, and plot to steal his manuscript so Homer could pass it off as his own. It worked really well.

"Write any good poetry lately?"

Virgil, who was deep in thought and walking with purpose, stopped to look at Baal the Deceiver.

"I have it all in my head," he said, pointing a finger to the top of his head.

"Indeed, well, I look forward to you reading it then."

"Indeed, I look forward to reading it to you," Virgil said.

The exchange of *indeeds* was just Baal goading Virgil and Virgil refusing to let it get to him.

"I hear you have challenged Homer to a writing contest . . . again."

"I did and I'm looking to get a group of judges together, a panel comprised of angels and demons."

"God would never allow it. There is a reason why he cast us all out and separated the sinners from the pure. He doesn't want us together."

"Everyone keeps telling me that, but I am determined to make it happen."

Baal had to admire him, despite his distrust of the Roman. He found most of the Roman souls in hell to be untrustworthy.

Phelenex came into view and he looked out of sorts. His ferry was empty; no souls had been coming into hell at all lately.

"You're needed in Gluttony; there's a meeting that's about to start."

"Meeting? What meeting?"

"I don't know, but there are all kinds of delectable confections being served. The irony of all the cakes and pies didn't dawn on anyone until after it was already set up. Decarabia felt bad so he rounded up some more cakes and pies to give to the souls in Gluttony."

"Also, Azazel would like to see you," he said to Baal, ignoring

213

Virgil. "Do you want a ride? I'm quite bored with nothing to do."

Baal didn't feel like flying anyway and stepped onto the ferry. "Nice to see you, Virgil, as always."

Virgil bowed and watched as Phelenex pushed away with his oar. The ferryman narrowed his eyes at Virgil as they made their way back down the river.

He suspected that Baal probably aided Homer in stealing his manuscript.

It doesn't matter because I'm going to write something more magnificent, more epic than anyone has ever written or ever will write, just as soon as I get back to my writing desk in limbo.

The Sickness of Mortal Love

Thomas and Philip were living with the Vikings, who were called Danes in Denmark. Just as they thought, they had been spared death because of their healing skills. They were the only male healers; all of the medicine practiced among the Vikings was done by women. The brothers were staying on the island of Bornholm. The land was mostly flat with little elevation and large sandy dunes along the coastline. The weather was always temperate, not much unlike the weather on the island of Lerina. The island had lots of forests, which were primarily comprised of beech trees. Thomas and Philip were amazed the first time they saw a hedgehog with all of its spikes.

They had already been there a few months and had established a herb garden and had earned the respect of the Vikings for their skills. The brothers weren't the only ones to learn new skills and techniques; the women healers had knowledge they did not possess. The women were especially skilled at childbirth, which was the one area the men were not knowledgeable about because they had primarily lived among monks and had helped deliver very few babies. In their Christian culture, that had been the task of midwives because it was unseemly for a man who was not the woman's husband to see her in such a condition, but the Vikings had no such inhibitions. The brothers were also faced with something new, something that didn't have to do with medicine at all, and that was the mysterious relationships between males and females. Neither brother had much experience with this, but now they were faced with being surrounded by women every day.

Brynhild was a head taller than Thomas; she was pale-skinned with golden blonde hair. Thomas, who had an unruly tuft of red hair, found himself staring at her every time she was in the same room.

Brynhild was stirring a mix of leeks and other herbs in a copper pot. She caught Thomas' eye and smiled. He dropped the

215

pot of honey he was holding. He was using it as an antiseptic; it hit the ground with a *clank,* and the honey went all over him and several patients. Brynhild giggled; the Vikings he splashed the honey on did not.

"You clumsy oaf. Why don't you stop staring at the fair maidens and do what you're supposed to be doing?" the Viking called Knut said.

Thomas and Philip had been studying the language and had picked up enough to get the gist of what the Danes were saying.

"I'm sorry, Knut. I'll go and get you a fresh tunic." Thomas went to his room to get Knut one of his tunics to put on.

Philip had a similar, only much greater problem, and that is that two women seemed to be interested in him. He thought they were both lovely and didn't know what to do about it. Astrid and Torunn both fancied him. They were both lovely. Astrid had red hair, much the same color as his brother Thomas, with emerald green eyes; and Torunn had fawn-colored hair, with crystal blue eyes. He liked the attention he received from both; it was a new and strange feeling for him. Astrid was not in the hospital today, but working in the herb garden. So he decided he would try to talk with Torunn.

Thomas returned holding a blue tunic and gave it to Knut. Knut was much more muscular than Thomas so the tunic was really tight. It made him look like a sausage casing.

"I don't know why we bothered with the two of you," Knut said.

Philip took a deep breath and went up to Torunn, who was sewing an old Dane's arm, trying to close his wound.

"Hello, Torunn" was all Philip managed to sputter out.

She looked up from her sewing and smiled. Her blue eyes held him mesmerized.

"Good morrow, Philip," she said and continued sewing.

"You are skilled at that; the stitches are small and even." The old man whose arm was being sewn watched the two of them in amusement.

"Thank you. You are a skilled healer as well."

"I was wondering . . ."

"Oh, go on, boy. What are you waiting for, Valhalla?"

"I was wondering, when you were done here if you'd like to

216

spend the evening with me?"

"Yes, that would be nice," she said; with all of her focus on Philip, she made the last two stitches a little crooked.

The old Viking didn't seem to mind; he was past caring about what he looked like and how many scars he had.

Thomas found courage in his brother's triumph and decided to ask Brynhild the same question. He had changed into a maroon tunic while he was in his room; the color suited him.

Brynhild was trying to make one woman more comfortable by adjusting her headrest.

"Do you like to watch the sunset?" he asked in a trembling voice. Brynhild stood at her full height and looked down on him. She considered the question. She had never really given much thought to watching the sunset before, but that didn't matter; it was a chance to spend time alone with Thomas. "Yes, that would please me very much."

The old Viking smiled a toothy smile again. Young love invigorated him.

"Well now, it looks like the goddess Freyja has draped her cloak of falcon feathers over you both. Careful, though, she's a fickle goddess; she could just as easily turn to vinegar as quickly as she did honey."

***

"What do you mean, they're in love?" Uriel demanded.

"They're displaying all the signs of mortal love: giggling, sweaty palms and stupid facial expressions. I've seen it many times before; it's like the plague, only worse, because it doesn't literally kill you," Netzach said.

"Tell them to stop it at once."

"You can't tell a mortal not to fall in love. They'd do it anyway; they can't help themselves. Why do you need them right now anyway?"

"I will be sending the monks back to Earth soon, and I decided the more people protecting the gospels, the better. You need to remind them that they are not mortal; they are spirits. Well, they are sort of mortal."

Michael and Gabriel were listening eagerly; they were always

217

fascinated with mortal love stories. They liked the one about Paris and Helen of Troy the best.

"Are they really in love? You're not really in love unless you start a war for a woman," Gabriel said.

"Why do they have to start a war?" Uriel asked.

"You know, the love story of Helen and Paris. Paris stole Helen from Sparta and her husband, the king Menelaus. It started a war between Sparta and Troy. Thousands had to die for their love," Michael said.

"Yes, but they are both in hell now. Mortal love will get you a one-way trip straight to hell," Uriel said.

"Maybe you should start a war, Netzach," Michael said.

Netzach shook his head. "There are too many wars among mortals now. I don't wish to start another one. I can try to talk them out of it, but as long as these women are alive, they are going to yearn for them."

"Then they can't be alive anymore; it is as simple as that," Uriel said.

"What do you mean?"

"You have to kill them," Uriel said.

"It's too bad we no longer have our swords or we could do it," Gabriel said.

"Are you all out of your senses? We are angels; killing is not allowed. It's against God's law."

"There's no law that says you can't kill," Uriel said.

"Yes it is; it's one of the ten Commandments. 'Thou shall not kill'."

"There are ten commandments? I thought there was only that one about coveting thy neighbor's food," Michael said.

"One of the commandments is coveting thy neighbor's wife, and the other one is coveting thy neighbor's goods," Netzach said.

"That's a lot of coveting. How much coveting can these mortals do?" Michael asked.

"Apparently a lot if God had to dedicate two of the ten commandments to it," Gabriel said.

"Why not just say, 'thou shall not covet,' and that way you cover everything in one Commandment?" Michael said.

"I know, it wastes a perfectly good commandment if you ask me."

"No one is asking either of you. These commandments are terribly inconvenient," Uriel said.

"Why not let them experience love? They probably won't get another opportunity," Netzach said.

"If they experience some love, they will only want more of it, and that will distract them from their purpose."

"What is the purpose again?" Gabriel asked.

"You know . . ." Uriel was silent for a minute. He was trying desperately to remember what the purpose was; finally he remembered. "To protect the Gnostic Gospels."

Netzach couldn't believe he was about to say this. "I can try and sabotage their love life."

"Yes, yes, do it," Uriel said with mirth.

"Hey, don't forget to get our swords back," Gabriel said to Netzach.

"Who cares about the swords? Get the gospels."

Michael and Uriel had been without their swords for a long time now, and most days they could be seen moping around heaven.

"I just hope that all the trouble of manipulating time, fate and breaking God's will is worth it in the end."

"We are merely stretching God's will," Uriel said, shaking a finger at him. "God doesn't mind a good stretch every now and again."

A Glutton for Punishment

When Baal finally arrived in Gluttony, what he saw amazed him. There were more than just confections set out; it was a banquet. Hundreds of demons were eating mutton and fish—and not just demons but the gluttonous souls as well. Baal saw Rosier and Azazel among them and tried to weave his way around the banquet table.

"Why are we having a feast?"

"It was decided that we should have a feast since we haven't had one in eons. Then we'd talk about what we've decided to call 'The Great Unification'."

"Who decided to have a feast?" Baal asked.

"It was mainly Belphegor's idea," Rosier said.

"That figures; that gluttonous copulating demon would want a grand feast. What is 'The Great Unification'?"

One of the hellhounds came up to the table and stared up at them drooling.

"Don't beg; it's unbecoming of a hellhound. Oh, all right." Rosier gave the hellhound some mutton. "There you go, now off with you." The hellhound carried the mutton in its jaws back to his lair to devour it.

"Everyone wants to be a judge in this contest between Virgil and Homer. It's a chance—and it might be our only chance—to get back in the good graces of our angel brethren," Azazel said.

Baal picked up a lemon cake and nibbled on it. "Get back in their good graces? Do you mean, get them to let us back into heaven?"

"Precisely. I mean, after all, we are not so different, are we?"

Baal looked at his putrid skin and touched his horns. "We are vastly different."

"On the outside, but not on the inside where it really matters."

Their attention was diverted by a commotion at the end of the table.

"I say, Gilberto, pour me some more wine, are you deaf boy?" the former Bishop of Naples asked.

Gilberto sighed and poured the wine. Even in hell he could not rid himself of the fat man and his pugnacious disposition. Gilberto had been right; the bishop would be the death of him . . . literally. It was just unfortunate that the bishop's death occurred so shortly after his.

Gilberto had just picked up the bishop's chamber pot with the intention of cleaning it out. He was tempted to just hurl the whole pot out the window, along with himself, plummeting to death's sweet embrace. Little did he know that his death was about to occur, and it was anything but sweet. The bishop was standing on a high stool, trying to reach one of his delectable raspberry tarts. The reason he had put them up on a high shelf in the first place was because he was certain that Gilberto was stealing them. Why else would they keep disappearing? With an eardrum bursting *snap,* the stool broke and down came the bishop. The bishop didn't even attempt to try and position himself in order to soften the impact on Gilberto; his only interest seemed to be protecting the raspberry tart from any harm. He landed on Gilberto with another *snap* that was even louder than the stool breaking. On initial impact, the chamber pot was knocked from Gilberto's hands, and the entire contents inside spilled onto the bishop's robe. The weight of the bishop crushed poor Gilberto. It's hard to say how many bones were broken in his body but enough to render him unable to move. He could not get out from under the portly bishop, whose massive girth and urine soaked robes were now on top of him. It didn't take long for Gilberto to smother underneath the bishop's fat rolls; it was well under two minutes. The bishop couldn't move either, not because he had broken any bones but because he was too fat.

"Gilberto, help me up!" the bishop screamed, but Gilberto's helping the bishop up in this life was now at an end.

"Honestly, Gilberto, is it possible that I happened to hire the laziest servant in Italy? Don't just lie there; this is no time for an afternoon nap."

No response or movement from Gilberto.

The gravity of the situation finally hit the thick-headed bishop like a urine-filled chamber pot.

"Whatever will I do? I can't stay here all day. I'll starve to death," he said while shoving the entire raspberry tart in his mouth.

"This is all your fault, Gilberto. If you hadn't been stealing my tarts, I never would have had to get up on that stool." Since there was no response or argument from Gilberto, he then put the blame on the stool. "Cheaply-made Egyptian trash," he remonstrated. The stool was actually made in Spain from *quebracho* wood, which is the heaviest and hardest in the world; in fact, that word in Spanish meant "axe breaker."

"Help, someone, please help." He struggled to remember any of his other servants' names. He had never made eye contact with them, let alone commit any of their names to memory.

The other servants heard the bishop calling out, but they were busy in the kitchen trying to make the five-course dinner the bishop had every night. They didn't come help. After all, that was Gilberto's job; it was not in their job description to lift fat bishops off the floor.

Days turned into a week, and there was less and less calling out. The cooks still made the bishop's meals each night, even though he didn't attend any of them; but it wasn't in their job description to speculate about the dying bishop, only to make his meals.

The cook who was strictly in charge of making the first course—because that's all one person could handle—was the first to discover him, and that was only because the smell had finally become unbearable. Otherwise, she never would have entered the bishop's room for any reason, unless she was called upon to have to rub the bishop's smelly, calloused feet.

It took five of the staff to lift the bishop; and when they did, they were shocked to see Gilberto dead as well. They had only seen one dead body at first because the body of Gilberto was completely obscured underneath that of the bishop.

The last thing the bishop said before dying was, "I'm wasting away to nothing, Gilberto. I shall die and be nothing but skin and bone when I arrive at the pearly gates to meet St. Peter."

He did meet St. Peter, of course, but he was still just as fat as ever. This happened shortly before St. Peter was relieved from his post. He didn't even bother to tell Cassiel to get the bishop's book containing all of his sins. He took one look at the bishop and said,

"This one belongs in Gluttony if anyone ever did" so Cassiel snapped his fingers and sent the bishop on his way. For once, St. Peter's intuition was right. He had sent the bishop to where he deserved to spend eternity. Four demons had to lift the bishop and fly him to the circle of Gluttony because he had put one foot on Phenex's boat and it nearly sank.

As for Gilberto, he had arrived at the gate days before the bishop; and while Cassiel was retrieving his book, he complained to St. Peter about how he had spent his whole life waiting hand and foot on a fat, pompous bishop, who did nothing but stuff his face. St. Peter told him that he had wasted his life serving a wretched excuse of a holy man and that he was just as culpable for the bishop's greed as the bishop. He should have been serving the poor instead. When Cassiel returned, he instructed Cassiel to send him to hell. He told Gilberto that he was to serve his master in the afterlife in the Circle of Gluttony where St. Peter was certain he would send the bishop when he was ready for judgment.

The bishop was now sitting in Gluttony—at a feast of all things—and trying to single-handedly devour the entire spread.

"I dare say, Gilberto, there's not enough variety of cheeses to suite my palate."

Gilberto nodded because there was not enough cheese or any other food in the world to suit his palate or satiate his enormous belly, for that matter.

The bishop was finally quiet, but only because he got a pheasant bone stuck in his windpipe, and it was keeping him from yelling.

Baal turned his attention back to Azazel. "Who would run hell and punish the sinners?"

"Do we really need hell? There have not been any souls for Phenex to ferry for a long time now. It's all the doing of St. Paul; he's letting everyone into heaven. We don't need to punish sinners; no one ever wanted to do that anyway."

"What about the really bad sinners, the ones who have killed?"

"Why shouldn't they be allowed into heaven? I mean, who else are they going to kill? Everyone else will already be dead."

"All right, what is the plan? How are we to get back into God's good graces?"

"Plan?" Azazel asked, taking a bite out of the mutton and

223

looking rather confused, or at least more confused than normal.

"Yes, plan. Surely you don't just think they will see us and just agree to let us back in heaven after all the time that's gone by and everything we did."

"We haven't gotten as far as a plan yet, Baal. You know not everyone can be like you and come up with plans and strategies."

Baal looked around in disgust at the feast. The gluttonous souls were stuffing themselves as much as the demons. "Why are they being allowed to eat? They are supposed to be punished for being gluttonous."

"It would be rude to eat all this in front of them and not offer them any. Where are your manners, Baal? You act like we are a bunch of savages or something. Have some ale; stop being such a worrier."

"Baal the Worrier," Rosier said.

Belphegor, who was already drunk, stood up on one of the tables. "I would like to say something. It's been eons since we were banished from our home. Eons since we've walked those golden roads and heard the harps playing and the singing of the seraphim. We were once beautiful creatures and now—"

"Get to the point, Belphegor. You are interrupting our festivities," one of the demons said, interrupting Belphegor in what may have been the best speech of his life; but since he was drunk and couldn't remember what he was going to say, no one would ever know for sure.

Belphegor lost his balance and came crashing down right in the mutton and caused a demon named Incubus to spill his ale. This made Incubus angry and he punched Belphegor. A fight broke out between Incubus and Belphegor, and it wasn't long until everyone was fighting.

Baal just shook his head. There was no way these misfits were going to reunite hell with heaven. It would be up to someone who was capable of critical thinking, someone who could formulate a clever plan; it would be up to someone like him.

Love Conquers Some But Not All

Netzach wasn't sure why he kept letting Uriel talk him into these things, although he was the one who had suggested it so he had no right to complain. He was disguised as a Viking named Wulf and claimed to be a distant relative of one of the Viking clan. No one questioned it or cared; he was over six feet tall and broad-shouldered. He could do manual labor and wield an axe so no one had any complaints. He wasn't sure how he would go about sabotaging the love life of the two brothers; angels had no understanding of romantic love.

Mortals behave so oddly when they are in love. They don't think and they act impulsively. Almost all love has a cycle that you can set the Clock of Ages in heaven by, if it ever needed setting. It starts out like a burning fever. Then the fever breaks. It starts to cool and then it heats back up again, but not in the original way; it becomes anger until finally the two who in the beginning couldn't stand to be apart can no longer stand the sight of one another, he thought.

Being alive for eons, he had observed it time and time again, love turning to hate . . . not all love. There have been a few that have lasted, but those are usually the ones where someone dies right away of the plague or gangrene before the relationship has time to sour.

Since he wasn't allowed to kill Philip and Thomas—well, kill them again—he had to destroy their love for these Viking women and then convince them they had no other reason to be down on Earth and return to heaven with him.

He decided he would work on Thomas and Brynhild first. He would try and get Brynhild to fall in love with him. The body he chose was no coincidence; it was as perfect as ever a human body could be, with a face to match. He was irresistible and, in fact, all the women flirted with him. Every day women would bring him gifts and try and win his heart.

225

He ignored all of them except Brynhild, which greatly flattered her, but she told him time and time again that she was with Thomas. He could see that day-by-day as she got more comfortable with Thomas, she was also getting a little bored with him and that's when he would strike.

He saw Brynhild sitting among a field of flowers, pulling the stems, so he thought now was as good a time as any and walked up to her. Brynhild saw him coming and it electrified her. She couldn't help herself.

"Why are you sitting out here all alone? Where is that boy of yours?" He purposefully said "boy" to imply that Thomas was not yet a grown man.

"He's tending to the sick," she sighed.

"He's always tending to the sick, that one. If I were he, I wouldn't tend to the sick while I had the heart of such a lovely woman." Netzach knew how to flatter and puff up an ego; after all, he had had lots of practice with Uriel.

She giggled and motioned for him to sit down.

He decided to be bold so he took her hand. "Brynhild, I love you. I've tried to deny my heart, but I can't any longer. No other woman interests me; I'm entranced by your beauty."

"I am promised to Thomas," she said with a wavering voice.

"I know you don't truly love him. It's me that you love. Run away with me tonight."

Brynhild did something unexpected; she put her face in her hands and began to sob. Netzach almost felt bad for what he was doing, but then it quickly went away as he remembered they were mortal and their lives were so fleeting, as were their emotions. He, on the other hand, had seen the creation of all living things, a great rebellion in heaven and had seen whole civilizations wiped out.

It's all for the greater good, he told himself even though he didn't entirely believe it because it was more like it was only for Uriel's good. Brynhild continued to sob, and Netzach patted her on the back. He hated mortal tears.

"I do love you, Wulf," she choked.

Netzach smiled to himself; he had succeeded and rather more easily than he thought.

Mortals have weak wills that you can bend easily like a reed.

"So you'll run away with me tonight?"

226

She nodded her head.

"I'll come for you when the sun goes down."

"Where will we go? To Norway perhaps?"

Netzach had no idea; he had not thought that far ahead. He supposed he would have to take her somewhere.

"Yes, we will go to Norway."

"What's the meaning of this?" Netzach had been too busy wooing and Brynhild too busy crying to notice Thomas approaching.

Netzach looked at Brynhild, who only continued to sob into her hands.

"What is this about?"

Netzach started to speak, but Brynhild stopped crying long enough to speak before he had the chance.

"He called me a sow," she said, pointing to Netzach.

Netzach stood there incredulous while Thomas became enraged.

"You, sir, are a louse. This will not stand; you have insulted Brynhild's honor and mine.

Why are mortals always blathering about their honor? Everything insults their honor. You call them a wart on a dead toad and you insult their honor. You slap them in the face with a fish and it insults their honor. You say their stew tastes like rotten flesh that's been boiling in the bowels of hell, and it insults their honor, Netzach thought.

These were all things he had actually said and done to a mortal. He had not called Brynhild a sow, but was pretty sure he had called a mortal a sow on more than occasion.

Thomas coughed to remind him he was still standing there and his honor was still insulted. Netzach looked at him amused, which only made Thomas furious.

"Meet me when the sun sets and you will answer for this."

***

Netzach wasn't sure how this was happening, but it was. Thomas was standing there, holding none other than the Archangel Michael's sword. Philip was trying to talk his brother out of fighting. The two were standing in a clearing in the woods.

A few years back a forest fire started which the Vikings were able to contain, but not before it had cleared out a lot of trees. There was nothing left but some tree stumps and scorched earth.

"Please, Thomas. I know he insulted Brynhild, but you don't have to do this. You don't know how to fight; you could die."

"I'm already dead," he whispered. "Besides, I have to do this. He insulted Brynhild's honor, and I don't want her to think I am not a man willing to defend her honor."

Netzach had in his hand a broad axe. He had never been in a battle; during the rebellion in heaven, he was in his room eating a sandwich. He wanted no part of the fighting. He believed angels, by their very nature, were supposed to be pacifists. There seemed something unnatural with Michael and Gabriel's constant bloodlust. Netzach was not a warrior; he was just a messenger, Actually, now that he thought of it, since he had been assigned to Uriel, he had done everything except deliver a message.

An old Viking named Harald stood between Netzach, who they knew as Wulf, and Thomas. When a challenge is made, it can only be considered resolved upon either the death of the challenger or the challenged. Every occupant on the island of Bornholm was there to witness the fight, including Brynhild herself, who was staring down at her feet. She would not make eye contact with anyone, especially Wulf. Most of those on the island were in favor of Thomas because, after all, Wulf had called his love a sow. He had also healed many people and become a good friend to some. There were a few who were in favor of Wulf simply because he was a Viking and Thomas was a foreigner.

"Let the challenge begin," Harald said.

Netzach and Thomas just stood there for a moment, each unsure how to proceed. Their fighting stances were very awkward; they looked like a couple of toads who were about to leap off their lily pads. Finally, Thomas charged Netazch and swung the sword of Michael. Netzach held up his axe to deflect the blow. Netzach then swung his axe at Thomas and completely missed him. Some of the men chuckled; the two men looked ridiculous. They obviously had not done a lot of fighting, which was expected from Thomas, a religious man, but very surprising for a Viking. Thomas thrust his sword towards Netzach's chest, but he dodged the blow. Netzach lifted the axe high above his head to swing down at

Thomas; but before he did, Thomas plunged the sword of Michael deep into his chest. This was the same sword that had not killed a single demon in the rebellion, but had accidentally left a nice scar on Baal. The sword that had never killed anything had just "killed" another angel. Thomas pulled the sword out of Netzach's chest and then dropped it on the ground. His hands began to shake; he had been running on pure adrenaline and anger, but now he was in a total state of shock.

The other Vikings began to disperse, except for a few who stayed behind to remove the body. Philip put a hand on Thomas' back, but he didn't acknowledge his brother. He didn't even acknowledge Brynhild, as she started sobbing again. He just stared down at the blood-stained sword.

The Funeral of Wulf

Netzach was placed on a pyre that was set up on the beach by two young Vikings who were just barely old enough to be considered men. The Viking Chieftain was growing a little impatient; he wanted to get started with the funeral because the gray sky was foreboding rain.

Everyone was there except for Philip and Brynhild. Philip was still too shaken up, and Brynhild was in her room with the door closed, refusing to come out. Philip's brother Thomas was at the funeral. It wasn't the first Viking funeral he had witnessed, having been there about a year already, but he still found them fascinating.

The chieftain raised his hands and said some words that Thomas could only understand in bits and pieces. "May Odin give you knowledge on your path and may Thor grant you strength and courage on your way." Thomas still wasn't that good at translating but thought he also said, "Stop your coughing, Torhild, or we will be having two funerals this evening." Torhild had been to see Thomas several times about his croup cough.

Wulf the Viking as he was known here, and Netzach the angel as he was known in heaven, opened one eye just a slit to see what was going on. He had no idea why they had put him on a slab of wood, but he was looking and waiting for his chance to slip away.

"Bring up the offerings," the chieftain said.

One by one, everyone put something beside the dead Wulf. The Vikings believed in giving gifts to the dead so they could take them with them to Valhalla. The chieftain wondered about giving gifts at all because surely Wulf would not be going to Valhalla, but to Helheim because Wulf's death wasn't a very noble death, dying at the hands of a foreigner who was barely able to swing his sword. Netzach opened his eye again, admiring all the gifts.

Oh my, what a beautiful tunic. I like that color. What craftsmanship on these weapons. It's too bad I won't be able to take any of this stuff with me.

230

He watched as the two young Vikings who had put him on the wooden slab were arranging the stones into what they called a Stone Ship. After burning the body, the ashes were buried inside the stone ship, along with all their gifts. Well—most of them— every now and again, someone stole something from the dead.

Netzach was becoming irritated. He was wondering when everyone was going to leave so he could disappear. He had not had a private moment since he was killed.

That hurt too. I will have a few words to say to Uriel when I see him.

Netzach saw a couple of Vikings with torches approaching him, and then something clicked in his mind. *Wait, I'm dead, which means this is my funeral. They aren't going to burn me, are they? I won't stand for it. I won't stand for it . . . again.* A disguised angel was never supposed to reveal himself to mortals, but he didn't care. He wasn't going to be burnt alive.

Netzach jumped up. "I'm terribly sorry for all the trouble," he said and pushed one of the Vikings who was carrying a torch. The Viking dropped the torch and it fell on to the pyre, but Netzach was no longer on it. There was a collective gasp at seeing a man rise from the dead; not only that, but the dead spoke. Knut, who had been drinking all throughout the ceremony, let out a loud belch. The chieftain was the first to speak, "Odin, forgive us. We did not know it was you. Surely we did not offend thee with anything improper." Had it really been Odin, he most likely would have been offended by the whole thing.

"I will forgive all of you, but only if I can have this," Netzach said and picked up the tunic. "It's exactly what I wanted." He no longer cared about the rules of not bringing earthly possessions into heaven. He no longer cared about anything.

I dare even the Presence of God to say anything about it to me.

"Of course, oh great one. Please take our humble—"

Netzach did not hear the chieftain's last words. He snapped his fingers and disappeared.

The collective gasp was heard again at the sight of Odin/Wulf/Netzach vanishing into thin air. Out of all the Viking funerals from that day forth, none would ever compare to the one with the vanishing corpse.

A Viking named Freydis was grinning from ear to ear. "Odin favored my tunic," she said. Freydis became very prosperous from selling her tunics. After all, if Odin were willing to come to Earth just to get one, they must be glorious.

***

Netzach didn't bother waiting in line. He marched right to the front where St. Paul was ushering people in through the gates that were once closed to evil-doers and now open to all sinners of every variety. He heard a lot of grumbling from behind him and some language unfit to be said in the kingdom of heaven. None of it fazed St. Paul, though, as the sign said, *All are Welcome*. Besides the bad language, no one put up too much of a protest because the line moved exponentially faster than it did under the tyranny of St. Peter.

"Welcome, young man. I see you've suffered a mighty blow."

"I am no man, and you would do well to be a little more discerning here."

"There is no need to get irritated," he said, pointing to the sign, "just go right on through."

"No, that is not the way it is supposed to work. All are most certainly not welcome. I thought St. Peter was too strict, but you are far too lenient, letting everyone in here. Heaven is full of thieves and murderers now."

St. Paul paused to consider this. "No soul is lost. Everyone deserves a second chance; it says so in the Bible."

"No, it doesn't. Hasn't anyone in the kingdom of heaven actually read the Bible?"

"I've read the important parts."

Netzach, who was still in human form, wasn't going to stand there all day and argue theology with an apostle. He had business with Uriel, and he wasn't going to run around heaven all day searching for him. He closed his eyes and pictured Uriel's big stupid face that he wanted to punch. When he snapped his fingers, Uriel appeared without his robe, dripping wet.

Uriel looked at the man in confusion. "Who in Yahweh are you?"

Netzach realized he was still a human and changed back into

his angelic form with a snap of the fingers.

"Oh, it's you. What are you doing here? You are supposed to be destroying love and getting our boys back up here. I was soaking in the Eternal Springs, I'll have you know."

"You should soak your head while you are at it; maybe it will humble you."

"Why are you here and where are the brothers?" Uriel began to shiver. "I'm going to catch my death because of you."

"You know full well that angels can't die, so come off it."

"What is that? Is that from Earth? You know you can't bring that into heaven."

"It's a tunic and you're one to talk, with your Gnostic Gospels."

"Are you ever going to tell me the point of all of this, or shall I just drip until the apocalypse?"

"I was trying to break up Thomas and his betrothed Brynhild, and I succeeded."

"That's wonderful. Why isn't he here with you?"

"Thomas saw Brynhild crying while we were together, and Brynhild panicked. She said I called her a sow; then Thomas challenged me to a duel. He stabbed me with Michael's own sword."

"What, he killed you? I didn't know he had it in him. I guess it's a good thing we are letting everyone into heaven now, or else he wouldn't be allowed back in. Well, that's not really important right now. Go back down there and get them."

Netzach was so angry, he couldn't even formulate words. He stomped past Uriel, who had finally stopped dripping, standing naked in his androgynous form. Netzach kept walking and marched right through the center of some seraphim who were practicing their singing. He elbowed seraphim right and left to force his way through.

"Another rogue angel; there will be another rebellion, you mark my words," a seraph said as Netzach continued to walk.

He finally stopped at the front entrance of the Ruach Heykal or Palace of the Holy Spirit. He was standing in front of an iron door. It was the only thing in heaven that was not white or adorned with pearls or some other jewel. It was meant to stand out so that it made the statement that behind this door was God. Netzach pounded on the door; at first, no one answered so he started to pound again when a seraph named Dumah opened the door. He looked at Netzach and then looked behind him, as if he expected to see an army or some other type of chaos or anarchy, but it was just one angel standing there.

"What in the name of the promised land do you want? You can't come in here."

"I request permission to come in there and never come back out. I don't ever want to see Uriel again. This is the one place where he can't summon me."

"No one is allowed back here, especially a lowly angel."

"Please, I can't take it anymore. He's gone mad with power and—"

The seraph interrupted Netzach, "Wait—you said you are a messenger for Uriel?"

"Yes, that's right."

"Wait here," Dumah said and disappeared behind the door.

Oh wonderful, they know what Uriel is up to and my role in it all, and they are probably debating to which part of hell to send us.

Dumah was only gone a moment before he appeared at the door again; he had a parchment in his hands.

"You are no longer a messenger for Uriel. From now on, you will send messages to Earth for Eremiel; and, to my knowledge, he has never sent an angel to Earth so it's a good deal for you. Never knock on this door again unless heaven is on fire, there is a rebellion or at least you have some good food to offer."

Netzach realized he had not thought of anything to offer. He reached into his robe and felt something sticky.

"Here, I offer you this in thanks and praise." Netzach put a melted piece of Vehuaiah's chocolate that Uriel had given to him into the seraph's hand. He had placed it in his robe and forgotten about it. He would need to wash his robe later in the Eternal Springs.

Dumah shoved the parchment he was still holding with his free hand at Netzach and then slammed the door in his face with his other hand that was holding the sticky chocolate.

Netzach read the document that had the official heavenly seal.

By the power of the Metatron, who speaks for God, the angel

Netzach will be a messenger for the Archangel Eremiel. This decree is unbreakable. Anyone who breaches this decree . . . well, you know the rest. It was signed by the Metatron himself.

Netzach rolled the parchment back up. He couldn't believe it; he was finally free of Uriel.

I can't believe how quickly this was written up; it's like they already had it ready and waiting for me.

***

It wasn't hard for Philip to figure out that Wulf was really Netzach, after hearing Thomas' account of what happened. He questioned Brynhild and finally got the truth. Philip wanted nothing more to do with her or with love. The angels were right about mortal love; it was fickle and fleeting. All it took to break the bond of love, it seemed, was a little flattery from an angel. He was ready to go back to heaven now.

Thomas was ready as well. After only spending one hour with Torunn, they realized they didn't have anything in common and the language barrier made it even harder. It was for the best that the brothers return to heaven because they felt they no longer belonged on earth.

Uriel sent a lightning bolt to kill the brothers. This didn't go quite according to plan. First of all, Uriel had the Seraph Ramiel, who was in charge of weather, to send the lightning bolts. Ramiel, who liked mortals even less than Netzach, had no qualms about sending the lightning, and Uriel didn't even have to use Michael to threaten him with the voice of God. Ramiel killed two people who turned out not to be the correct brothers. Uriel dismissed it with an all-mortals-look-alike attitude, which was one that Ramiel shared himself.

The second attempt didn't go that well either. Ramiel was able to strike and kill Thomas with one mighty bolt, but it took three attempts to kill Philip. The first bolt just knocked him over. The second one jolted through his body, but didn't kill him. Finally, Ramiel sent a bolt of lightning with so many volts it would have killed an elephant.

God did not like the angels meddling in human affairs. He was a firm believer in man's having free will, but Ramiel was given

235

complete charge of the weather and could use it however he saw fit. There were a lot of rules in heaven, but very little oversight. The Vikings were sure that Thor was displeased with the brothers and sent his lightning to strike them both dead.

Plotting, Planning and Persuading

The first thing that the brothers noticed when they got to heaven was how crowded it was. Heaven had tripled in size since St. Paul had taken over admittance at the gates. Thomas elbowed his way through the crowd, and Philip followed the path his brother made for him. They couldn't see anyone that they recognized. Thomas decided he would have to get some place higher up in order to see so he decided to climb the Clock of Ages. He wrapped his legs around the clock and shimmied his way up. The clock's face was etched with carvings of prominent seraphim on it. Showing no reverence for the prominent seraphim, he grabbed one of the seraph's faces and pulled himself up. When he thought he had climbed high enough, he looked down and couldn't see anyone at first because there were so many people. Finally, he spotted Lorenzo. His hunchback made him easier to spot, even in a large crowd.

"Lorenzo!" he shouted. "Lorenzo, look up here!"

The old man looked up at Thomas and waved. He made his way over to the base of the Clock of Ages. Thomas slid down and the brothers embraced their fellow monk.

"I guess you'll want to see the others," Lorenzo said.

"Yes, but first I want to see my father."

"Ah yes, he's always talking about both of you. I'll take you to him."

Before Lorenzo could take Thomas and Philip to their father, Uriel intercepted them. "There you both are. Well, you took long enough to decide to come back. Come on now, you're late. I'm sending you all back down to Earth."

"I'm not going back to Earth. I just came from there. I want to see my father," Thomas said.

"Now that you are all back, Azrael is demanding that the gospels must leave heaven and return to Earth. I will allow you both to see your father, but you need to be quick about it. None of your usual mortal blubbering about love and family and what not."

The boys wanted to see their father so they didn't argue with Uriel.

Uriel tried to squeeze through a crowd of people and lost one of his feathers.

"This is getting intolerable. If that old fool lets anymore people in here, we will have to expand the heavens."

Uriel took them to see their father, and their father wrapped his arms around both boys in a tight embrace. They stood that way for a long time until Uriel coughed and repeated what he had said earlier about mortal blubbering.

"We have to go now," Philip said.

"What do you mean, you have to go now? You just got here. Go where?"

The brothers had now been dead numerous times and were over 500 years old. Michael and Gabriel walked up with the other monks trailing behind. Michael was using the voice of God to clear a path.

The boy's father, still holding his sons—he did see both of them as his sons, regardless of their mother's affair—didn't speak for a long time until finally, he shook his head and said, "This is unnatural."

No one needed for the boy's father to elaborate. They knew it was unnatural, but at this point they were beyond nature, death, time and reason.

The other monks were restless; the brothers had just gotten there, but they had been there for over a hundred years by the Clock of Ages and longed for a change. The brothers wished they could linger in heaven a little longer, but figured, what was a few more years on Earth among an eternity in heaven? They could wait while they helped Uriel with his foolish quest to preserve the Gnostic Gospels.

"Is everyone present and accounted for?" Uriel asked. When he was satisfied that they were all there, he continued, "I'm sending you all to a place called Montalcino in Tuscany to the Abbey of Sant'Antimo."

"Will we be safe there?" Philip asked.

"Well, of course not. You will be among other mortals so always assume and prepare for the worst. You can all do your favorite jobs there; it is a large Abbey. I would have sent Netzach ahead of you to do some ground work, but he is no longer my messenger angel and the one they replaced him with simply refuses to do anything I say. He is totally useless. So I had to do this one myself."

Azrael approached them with a sigh; he was weary of this, as were they all—everyone except Uriel. "Are they ready?"

"They are all ready to return to Earth."

"This is the last time I do this for you, Uriel. There has been an inquiry into the lives of these men. I'm not sure by whom, but it will only be a matter of time before someone figures out that the names of these men should have been recorded in the *Liber Mortuorum* a long time ago."

Uriel, as always when he couldn't be bothered with rule or authority, just waved his hand. He didn't know why Azrael was always worried about trifling things.

Azrael looked at each one of the men and then closed his eyes. He snapped his fingers and they all disappeared. The boys' father shed two tears, one for each of his sons.

"Now you stop that. There's no crying here in heaven. Look around you. Do you see anyone else crying?" Uriel asked.

He didn't see anyone else crying, but he did see some mortals fighting and one couple copulating.

If this is heaven, I wonder what hell is like. Uriel followed his eyes and coughed again. "Yes, well, come along. You shouldn't be watching people copulate; it's really rude of you."

Rudeness seemed to be the least offensive thing in heaven these days. With triple the amount of people pouring through the gates every day, it didn't seem as if heaven could hold any more people; something would have to give.

***

Baal the Clever was feeling very clever at the moment. He decided he would suggest the one thing both heaven and hell couldn't resist and that was a celebration. Before the reading he would suggest they have a feast with all kinds of delectable foods and wine . . . lots of wine. The more wine they consumed the better. Food and wine always brought about good cheer and camaraderie. It would create more time for bonding. After all, they were all the same once; it had been eons, and there was a lot of catching up to do. He also remembered that several of the angels had a sweet tooth, especially Vehuaiah, for chocolate.

Baal rolled his eyes because up ahead, he could see Azazel walking towards him, which could only mean one thing.

"Baaaal! Baaaal!" Azazel yelled.

Yes, I see you, you ridiculous demon.

When Azazel reached him, he was out of breath. "I'm a bit winded; I walked all the way from Greed."

"Why did you walk? You could have flown or at least had Phelenx take you part of the way. Lucifer knows the poor demon has nothing better to do these days."

"I'm trying to lose some girth." He patted his stomach. "I need you to go back to Earth. Belphegor who Copulates gave word that those men are back on Earth and have the Gnostic Gospels in their possession."

"How does Belphegor always come by this information?"

"He spends a great deal of time on Earth copulating and hears things."

"Where are they now?"

"Some place in Tuscany."

"At least Uriel could send them to some place tropical. My body is too used to a warm climate."

Baal looked around at the place he had called home for centuries. He had grown so used to the smell of sulphur that it was actually comforting; it felt like home. When he really thought about it, he wasn't sure whether he wanted to leave or not.

"Do we really need to keep this up? For one thing, we've been trying to thwart Uriel and obtain the books for 500 years and what did we accomplish? You already burned his gospels. If we are trying to get back into heaven, I hardly think this will help matters. Is getting even with Uriel really worth the risk of not getting into heaven?"

Azazel paused to consider this, but only for a short moment. "Yes, it is."

"The other demons might feel differently."

"Do you think Uriel has so much power that what he says or thinks could sway anyone? He's actually not that popular among a lot of angels."

Baal really couldn't argue with him on that point. Uriel did have a tendency to vex just about everyone he ever knew.

"When do I leave?"

"You can leave just as soon as you come up with a plan to steal the books and a disguise."

"All right, fine. By the way, I was going to suggest we have a celebration before the reading of Homer and Virgil."

"Why would we do that?"

It took every ounce of restraint Baal had not to roll his eyes again.

Is it possible for one demon to be so dense?

"It would loosen people up and allow for time to bond, joke and tell stories. You know, to talk about old times. This will loosen everyone up and pave the way for us to get back into heaven."

Azazel kicked a piece of charred rock and stared ahead blankly for quite some time, as if contemplating something. "Hey, I've got a great idea. Why don't we have a feast?"

Baal was dumbstruck.

Yes, I guess it is possible for one demon to be so dense.

Azazel walked away before Baal could respond. He was smiling because of the brilliant plan he had just come up with. He couldn't wait to tell everyone his idea.

Great, now Azazel gets credit for my idea. This is always how it goes; nothing ever changes.

He hated being a lowly servant demon, always doing the dirty work for demons with far less intelligence than he.

Well, let him take all the credit for it because when we get back into heaven, I'm going to make sure I'm elevated to the rank of seraph.

***

The day of the readings had finally arrived. Virgil and Homer were going to read their great works in front of a panel of demons and angels. Among the ten demons that were in heaven were Azazel and Rosier. Baal, a lesser demon, had not been invited to take part in the judging. The Presence of God was nowhere to be found so Vehuaiah, who liked to take charge of everything, made a command decision to allow the demons into heaven for this one event. It was St. Paul's job to check them at the gate for weapons, but he just ushered everyone through without so much as a backward glance. A great feast with every meat and delectable imaginable was laid out on banquet tables in St. Benedict's Hall. All the angels sat together on one side of the table, and all the demons sat together on the other. Everyone was quiet and staring at the other group as if they had two heads. Well, there were a couple of cherubs present who had four heads, but even they were looking at the other side strangely. The silence remained until the wine started flowing and tongues started to loosen.

A demon named Abraxas was the first one to speak. "You look in good health," he said to Pahaliah, the nearest seraph to him.

There was hardly a need for a reply since they were immortal and always in good health, but Pahaliah made an effort in return.

"And you are looking—" Pahaliah paused while he searched for any compliment he could conjure up "—quite tan."

It was a small exchange, but it got the conversations started. Soon it was just as Baal had predicted; by the end of the feast, everyone was embracing and saying that it was a shame they had been cast out and let bygones be bygones, etc. Pahaliah began to sing and everyone joined in the merriment. Everyone was jovial except for Uriel and Azazel, and they were glaring at one another as if their gazes could pierce flesh. Not even wine could thaw their mutual loathing of one another. When they were finished, some angels cleared the tables; actually they just snapped their fingers and the table and leftovers disappeared. No one was ever sure where discarded food was sent, but it always went away. Ideally, it would go to a family in a poor village on the brink of starvation, but most likely went in a hole dug for a privy.

Virgil and Homer came into the hall; neither wanted to partake in the reunion. Plus, it would mean they would have to sit near each other; and, like Uriel and Azazel, they had an unending disdain for one another. Virgil stepped up to the podium first. He looked up at Homer who was looking at him with such a hatred, it made you wonder that if they had both been alive at the same time, if one would have killed the other. Without preamble, Virgil began reading; his voice thundered out, "Carrion, that fragrant perfume of death arose."

There were already "oohs"and "ahhs" at the words "carrion"

and "death." Virgil continued and was interrupted by Belphegor the Copulator, who was so drunk he fell out of his chair. The room roared with laughter. For some reason Belphegor was picked to be a judge, probably because he was always the life of a party and good for a laugh. Virgil cleared his throat and was growing impatient. By the time he was finished, almost all of the judges had passed out drunk. The only ones who weren't were Uriel and Azazel because they did not drink much; they were too busy staring each other down.

Virgil smiled a wide smile at Homer. Homer had to read his new epic poem to only two judges and halfway through it, Uriel fell asleep, not from drunkenness, but from boredom. Azazel had tuned out Homer long ago. When he realized he was finished, though, he felt obligated to clap. The clap hardly filled the great room. Virgil watched as Homer huffed out of the hall and retreated into the night. He knew he had lost. Virgil had won from the mere fact that his judges had all been conscious, and his reading would be the only one they would remember.

I'll take a victory, any which way I can get it. Besides, I know my poem was the best. Homer's work will always be inferior to mine.

Virgil also disappeared into the night, leaving Azazel alone with all the other angels and demons passed out drunk. There were demons asleep propped up in chairs and the seraph Pahaliah was resting his head on the demon Abraxas' shoulder. Some of them had spread out on the floor of St. Benedict's Hall, where they slept in a drunken stupor. Azazel stood over Uriel, who was snoring. He plucked a feather from one of his wings, and Uriel didn't even stir; he was a sound sleeper. Azazel began to get tired, and he too eventually fell asleep. The demons had procured a small victory; they were allowed to stay the night in heaven, but the real test would be tomorrow when everyone was sober.

The Corpse Trial

Uriel had once again convinced the monks to return to Earth through his usual pleading, bribing and finally by threatening. He had Azrael wait and send them to a time that was relatively without a lot of bloodshed. Azrael at this point was desperate to get the Gnostic Gospels out of heaven. They had been there too long; and there was now an inquiry into the actions of the monks, which Azrael was hoping would get put low on the priority list since heaven was now overrun with all kinds of sinners. The Angels of Virtue had far too much on their plates as it was. It was 897 and Thomas and Philip stared at the unknown newcomer and wondered what to do.

"I'm afraid you've come to us at a very strange time," Thomas said.

"A very strange time indeed," Philip said.

The newcomer, who everyone was calling, The Unknown, felt a little strange himself. It was a cold place; that's all he was aware of. He could feel the cold draft coming in through the window.

"The good news is that you have all ten fingers and ten toes," Thomas said.

"He has eight fingers and two thumbs," his brother Philip corrected.

"Whatever, the outcome is still the same," Thomas said, a little exasperated with Philip's precision on all things.

The stranger who was being called The Unknown looked at both Thomas and Philip. They were wearing brown robes with a rope tied around their middles. They each had a perfect, bowl-shaped haircut, which was now the protocol among monks. They were very different, Thomas with his fiery red hair and Philip with raven black hair and Thomas being short and squat and Philip being taller and thinner. They both, however, had the same expression on their faces. The expressions on their faces was one part concern, one part fear and one part irritation. The concern and fear, The Unknown deduced, probably had to do with the "strange time" that was occurring, and he guessed the irritation had mostly to do with him.

"Is there any bad news?" The Unknown asked.

"Come again?" Thomas asked.

"You said the good news is that I had all my fingers and toes. Is there any bad news?"

"I don't know; it depends on how you look at things," Thomas said.

The Unknown didn't know how he looked at things. He had a feeling, though, that deep in his bones, he was a pessimist.

"You don't seem to know who you are or where you come from," Philip said, removing any further mystery as to what the bad news was.

"We questioned you yesterday. Don't you remember?" Thomas asked.

"How could he possibly? Brother Shamus had given him far too much opium."

"Brother Shamus is always overdoing it on the opium."

While the brothers were discussing Brother Shamus' opium distribution, The Unknown noticed his surroundings for the first time. He was in a small room; the walls were bare except for a portrait. It was of a stout man, who was sitting regally on a throne wearing a white robe with some sort of crown on top of his head. The floors and the walls were all stone, and the floor looked like it could use a good sweeping. There was a table with a pitcher of water and a chamber pot that he assumed was for him or for whoever was occupying the room and at the moment that happened to be him.

"The other good news is that you seem to have all of your wits about you, despite not having any memory," Thomas said.

"I'm very glad to hear it," The Unknown said.

"I'd like to get right to the point. In normal times, seeing that you seem fit enough, except not having a memory, of course, we'd throw you right out into the snow; but as I mentioned before, these are strange times," Thomas said.

"Please don't think us unkind for saying we'd put you into the snow. I mean we'd give you some food for your journey and also a cloak for warmth, but we wouldn't allow you to stay because we are overcrowded as it is," Philip said.

The brothers, from all they had experienced and being around now for over 400 years, had hardened and grown more resilient. That is not to say they had become bad men. Far from it, but they now had a thicker exterior; and although the brothers told The Unknown that they would have normally thrown him out in the snow, they had never actually thrown anyone out into the snow and doubted they ever would.

"I don't think you are unkind," The Unknown said.

"I think you might be lying; I think you do think we are unkind," Philip said.

The Unknown, who really wasn't sure what he thought, admitted, "Perhaps I am lying."

"This is good. This is one reason why we would like for you to stay, at least for a while. The truth is always best; try and remember that. The truth may be a grave insult and get you killed, but it is always best," Thomas said.

"We would like for you to stay and help us in the hospital. We are short-handed, what with Brother David and Brother Barnaby dying from the plague," Philip said.

"I don't believe I know anything about medicine; or if I did, I don't remember. I don't know how helpful I would be."

"We mainly need for you to assist us in small tasks, fetching bandages, cleaning up vomit, washing out the chamber pots and that sort of thing. Besides, you can learn a great deal by simply observing Brother Thomas and me."

"There is a plague going on, you see, and lots of people are succumbing to it," Thomas said.

"What kind of plague?" The Unknown asked.

"Plagues are sent by God or the devil, usually one or the other," Thomas said, knowing perfectly well that neither sent anything, but to say anything else would be heretical; and given their pasts and present, they had already done enough heretical things to fill an eternity.

"It is a foul plague, one that corrupts the body with pus and blood. It kills the person in a matter of days. There is always a plague. Try and remember that," Thomas said.

"Not always," Philip said.

"Yes, not always. When there isn't a plague, we contemplate

throwing people out in the snow," Thomas amended.

"Who is that man?" The Unknown pointed to the portrait of the man with the crown.

"That was one of our popes, Pope John II. He was the first pope not to use his birth name. I always thought it was a shame he should be hanging in this room. His portrait should at least hang in the dining hall. There's always a pope. Try and remember that," Philip said.

There's always a pope and always (sometimes) a plague. Pope and plague. The two P's, The Unknown thought.

"Would you like to stay and help us in the hospital?" Thomas asked.

The Unknown thought about that. He didn't know who he was or what this place was; but not having any other good alternatives, other than being thrown out in the snow, albeit with food and a cloak, he still didn't think that would be much fun.

"Yes, I will help you."

"Good, and now that we have that bit of business out of the way, if you are feeling up to it, we'd like for you to accompany Brother Philip and me to the Cadaver Synod."

"To the Cadaver Synod?" The Unknown asked, letting the strange-sounding words roll off his tongue.

"He means the corpse trial," Philip said.

"Yes, but please refer to it as the Cadaver Synod and not the corpse trial when you're around anyone else other than Brother Philip and I because we'd hate for you to have a trial of your own. Don't get me wrong, we love a good trial; but we are short-handed, as I have explained, and hate for you to be burned for heresy."

"Do you have any questions? If so, we will have to answer them on our journey. I'm afraid we are on a tight schedule. We must get to the Basilica of St. John Lateran by nightfall," Philip said.

"I'm not a person who asks a lot of questions," The Unknown said.

"Excellent, you will do well in life. I firmly believe that if people just pay attention and observe and stop asking so many questions, they will learn a great deal," Thomas said.

"Learning through observation and reflection," Philip said, nodding in agreement.

247

"Shall we go then? I will run and fetch you a warm cloak. We will be traveling for the better part of the day, and I wouldn't want you to catch your death," Thomas said and left to go retrieve the cloak.

The Unknown pulled back his bed sheet and for the first time noticed that he was wearing a brown robe with a rope tied around his waist, just like Brother Thomas and Brother Philip. He examined his hands. They did not appear too old, and they weren't calloused or tan so he was obviously not a laborer. He felt his face; it was smooth and not wrinkled. He had a slightly-furrowed brow, though. The unknown stranger plucked a hair from his head. It was dark brown, a few shades lighter than Brother Philip's. He rubbed a finger inside his mouth, and all his teeth were still there. He wasn't an old man, he determined. Philip watched him curiously, and Thomas came in carrying the cloak.

"The horses are ready; let's make haste if we want to witness the strangest trial in recorded history."

The Unknown stood up and his knees buckled. He nearly fell, but grabbed the bed for support.

"I dare say it is just apathy; you've been in bed for nearly a week," Thomas said.

"Your legs just have to get used to walking again. Come, try again," Philip said.

The Unknown got up again and this time he remained standing. He took his first step and then another.

"There you go, one foot in front of the other."

They took him through the hospital. The Unknown didn't have a lot of time to stop and look because Thomas and Philip took turns alternately telling him to make haste, but what he did see left him cold as death. The room was filled with a low moaning, almost melodic like the low rumbling of thunder before lighting struck.

The Unknown looked at a man whose sheet was halfway off, revealing a leg that was covered in boils. His toes were rotted off, and his foot was blackened. His sheet was soiled with feces and urine; and his eyes, which stared listlessly at the wall, were a dull gray.

"I think he might be dead," The Unknown said.

"Almost. We call it the death stare. Best to look away, you will have plenty of time to acquaint yourself with death upon our

248

return," Philip said.

Thomas and Philip shuffled around the room to and fro, wiping brows with a cloth and holding the half-human, half-corpses, while they sipped water.

They stepped outside where their horses were waiting for them. It was dusk, and a light snow began to flutter to the ground. The Unknown wrapped his cloak around him and pulled it tightly around his shoulders. He was still cold from the death room.

"You will ride on this horse with me," Thomas said.

Thomas got up on the chestnut brown mare and extended a hand to The Unknown. Brother Philip mounted his mare, and they were off at a brisk gallop. The mares kept pace with each other through the mud, which looked more like red clay than mud.

"I suppose you would like to know how we found you," Thomas said.

The Unknown had scarcely had time to wonder how he ended up here.

"Brother John the Elder—we call him 'Elder' to distinguish him from the other brothers named John in our monastery. Anyway, he found you unconscious in the garden. He thought you probably had the plague and made it as far as the garden before collapsing; but on closer inspection, he didn't see any of the usual signs of the plague so he assumed you were probably just drunk. He called for Brother Philip and me, and we carried you into one of the isolation beds since you did not have the plague. You did not appear inebriated, and we could not smell a drop of alcohol on you. You were just simply unconscious. You remained unconscious until yesterday. You finally woke up yesterday, and we were able to ascertain that you had lost your memory, despite Brother Shamus administering too much opium. Has your memory returned now that you are more lucid?"

"I do not know who I am or where I come from. All I know is that I feel strange, like I'm not who I'm supposed to be," The Unknown said.

Philip only nodded his head; he wasn't sure what the unknown man meant by that.

"We examined your skull for any bumps, bruises or abrasions; but there were none, suggesting you had not suffered a blow to the head. I suppose it is possible that you witnessed some event that shocked your very soul to the core and wiped your memory as clean as a baby's, but I don't think so," Thomas said.

"No, Thomas and I feel you were brought to us by angels, no doubt to test us," Philip said, knowing full well angels didn't care a wit about what mortals were up to; he just wanted to see how the stranger reacted.

The Unknown just stared at him blankly. "Test you regarding what?"

"Test us to see if we are living a holy and Christian life and are not corrupt. That's usually the way of it," Philip said.

"Are you corrupt?" The Unknown asked.

"If we are mortal, then by definition our souls are corrupt," Thomas said, evading the question because he honestly didn't know at this point if he were corrupt or not. It seemed like he started out with a noble purpose—indeed they all had—but the purpose seemed to get lost over the years. It seemed as if they were keeping gospels that no one cared about anymore except for one archangel in heaven. The only thing he knew for sure was that he and his friends had cheated death for over 400 years.

"Today we will be witnessing a strange event. A pope will be put on trial—not just any pope, but a deceased one. We do not approve of this unholy trial of our former Pope Formosus," Philip said.

"Cadaver Synod," The Unknown repeated the strange words again.

"It's politics; most things in life boil down to politics. Try and remember that," Thomas said.

Popes, plagues, politics. The three P's, The Unknown thought.

The rest of the journey was passed in silence. The *clop, clop, clop* of the horses was soothing, and The Unknown dozed off, resting his head on Brother Thomas' shoulder. The snow continued to flutter down, but it did not stick. The Unknown's cloak was wet on the outside, but the snow did not penetrate the warm interior. It was in the early morning dusk when they set out on their journey and in the evening dusk when they arrived.

"Here we are, the Archbasilica of St. John Lateran. The mother of all churches," Thomas said.

There was a mob of people waiting outside the gates shouting, some with raised fists and others pounding the gates. The Unknown heard one elderly woman shout, "It's the devil's work."

"They see it as a desecration, an unholy act. With the politics at work, I'm afraid that this trial is a forgone conclusion," Thomas said.

The mob was being kept in check by a few members of the papal army, mainly volunteers or mercenaries with swords.

"Clear the way! Clear the way!" shouted one of the guards.

They swung open the gate and allowed Brother Thomas, Brother Philip and The Unknown to pass. They opened the doors and continued through the main entrance. There was a laurel wreath carved into the stone with the inscription *Sacrosancta Lateranensis ecclesia omnium urbis et orbis ecclesiarum mater et caput.*

"Most Holy Lateran Church of all the churches in the city and the world, the mother and head," Philip translated.

The room where the trial was being conducted was almost completely filled with monks, cardinals, bishops and other important Church dignitaries. The two brothers and The Unknown, squeezed into the last bench, forcing an irritated bishop to slide over and mumble something about punctuality.

The room grew quiet when some men came in carrying a coffin. They laid the coffin down gently and looked around, as if they weren't sure how to precede. Indeed, it was the first time they had had to exhume a body and hopefully the last time to exhume the body of a pope for the sole purpose of its standing trial.

"Please place the body on the papal throne," a man said and pointed to a seat that was elevated like that of a king's throne. The man was similarly dressed as the pope that The Unknown had seen in the painting, Pope John II.

"That is our pope; his name is Stephen VI," Thomas whispered.

"That very dead person is our former pope, Pope Formusus," Philip added, but forgot to whisper like his brother; and several severe-looking bishops sitting in front of him turned around to give him a stare that made him shrink in his seat. The men opened up the coffin, and a stench immediately filled their nostrils. The people in the front row gasped for breath and wriggled their noses. The pope covered his nose and mouth with a handkerchief. The men still stood there motionless. The pope, with one hand holding the handkerchief to his face, used the other one to wave towards the seat. The men gently picked up the corpse, trying to brush off as many maggots as they could, and placed it in the chair. Pope Stephen, who had no further use for them, waved them towards the door. The men seemed relieved because they were more than a little uncomfortable. The corpse of the former pope was now sitting in the chair as if he were still pope, wearing all his papal vestments.

Pope Stephen addressed the people in the room, "Let it be understood that Deacon Bartholomew will be answering for Pope Formosus, and Deacon John will be the prosecutor. Let us commence with the charges brought before the court."

Deacon John stood up and faced the audience, careful not to stand too close to the accused so as not to get a whiff of rotting flesh.

"The Holy Roman Papacy charges Pope Formosus with perjury, ascending to the papacy illegally and ambition."

There was a collective murmuring after the charges were read.

"Dear God, please put an end to this unholy trial. Someone in heaven, please send bolts of lightning or make the earth crumble that this building sits upon," Thomas whispered.

"Pope Formosus, is it correct that you were Bishop of Porto?" Deacon John asked.

There was a silence in the room, and Pope Stephen turned and glared at Deacon Bartholomew. The Deacon, who realized it was he who had to answer this question, jumped out of his seat and faced the audience. He straightened his diaconal vestments and did his best to preserve his dignity.

"Yes, that is correct."

"You were then made Archbishop of the—"

"Answer the question, you charlatan," Pope Stephen roared and pointed at the cadaver.

"Forgive me your holiness, but I need to finish. You were then made Archbishop of the Bulgarian Church during the reign of Nicholas I, charged with bringing that kingdom under the Roman Church?"

"No. I mean yes. Yes, that is correct," Deacon Bartholomew stammered.

Pope Stephen once again glared at Deacon Bartholomew.

"You admit then that you violated canonical strictures against translation. That is to say, the transfer of one Episcopal see to another?" Deacon John asked.

Pope Stephen once again interrupted the prosecution. He covered his mouth with the handkerchief, walked up and stood an inch away from the corpse pope and yelled, "You deserted your diocese without papal permission."

Deacon Bartholomew, who did not want to risk a third glare from the pope, immediately answered in the affirmative.

"Let it be written that Pope Formosus has pled guilty to transmigrating sees in violation of canon law and performing holy duties as a bishop, all the while, in fact, a layman," Deacon John said.

More murmuring was heard again throughout the room. This time it wasn't Thomas who whispered something; it was the bishop they were sitting beside.

"God have mercy on us."

Deacon John waited until the rumbling died down to resume his questioning.

As if to defend himself, Pope Stephen said, "These charges were laid upon him during his first synod and did not originate with me."

"We must now settle the charge of perjury. You were deposed and excommunicated by Pope John VIII at a Roman council—"

"You aided in poisoning our beloved Pope John and delighted in his head being bashed in with a hammer," Pope Stephen interrupted once again. He was nearly frothing at the mouth.

"May I remind your holiness if I may be so bold, murder and/or aiding and abetting in murder is not one of the charges leveled against the accused."

Pope Stephen reluctantly nodded his head as if he didn't see why they couldn't heap one more charge on him.

Deacon John paused for a moment, forgetting momentarily where he left off.

"You were deposed and excommunicated by Pope John VIII at a Roman council, and you swore an oath never to return to Rome or exercise priestly functions again—were you not?"

"That is true," Deacon Bartholomew answered.

"I have here the document that declares this oath and is signed

253

by the deceased; it was taken at the Synod of Troyes," Deacon John said.

Deacon John gave the document to Pope Stephen, who waved it around in one hand as if it were a banner.

"After the assassination of his holiness Pope John VIII, all charges against you were dropped and you were reinstated by Pope Marinus I as Bishop of Porto. So you returned to performing holy duties, after signing a sworn oath in a papal court?" Deacon John asked.

"Yes, but only after I was pardoned by our holiness Pope Marinus—"

Brother Bartholomew was interrupted by Pope Stephen, who rose once again and stuck his finger in the face of Pope Formosus.

"Silence, you fiend!"

"Let it be written that Pope Formosus has pled guilty to the charge of perjury," Deacon John said.

The corpse of the former pope was sliding down in his chair and needed to be propped up again, but no one wanted to touch him.

"Now, we come to the third and final charge of ambition to become pope," Deacon John said.

"When you were Bishop of Porto, why did you usurp the universal Roman see in such a spirit of ambition?" Pope Stephen asked.

Deacon John sighed; he was becoming exasperated with the Pope's outbursts and interruptions. "Go ahead and answer the question."

Deacon Bartholomew was uneasy; how was he supposed to know what a dead man was thinking?" He knew, though, he had better say something that Pope Stephen wanted to hear or he'd lose his post as deacon.

"I conspired with Boris I to become Bishop in Bulgaria and secretly held ambitions to become pope. I was a traitor to king Charles the Bald."

"I knew it! I knew it!" Pope Stephen yelled in triumph.

"Let it be written that Pope Formosus has pleaded guilty to the charge of ambition to seek the papacy illegally. His holiness Pope Stephen will now issue the sentence," Deacon John said.

At this point the corpse pope was almost on the floor, and his papal crown was askew.

"I find the accused guilty on all three charges and I issue a *rescissio actorum,* which declares null all divine acts and decrees given while under his papacy," Pope Stephen said.

"Now we are getting to the real reason for this farce of a trial," Philip whispered.

"Deacon Bartholomew, go find a layman's robe somewhere."

"Deacon John, please have those men come back in here and bring a knife," Pope Stephen said.

"A knife, your holiness?" Deacon John asked.

"That is what I said."

Brother John went outside where the mob had grown in size. He could not find the original men who had exhumed the body of Pope Formosus and had brought him into the chamber. He didn't blame them one bit for wanting to wash their hands of the whole business, but that still presented a problem for him; he needed four new able-bodied men.

"I need four strong men to assist with the coffin, and I also require a knife," Deacon John said, loud enough to be heard over the rumblings of the crowd. Everyone stared at him, but no one stepped forward.

Deacon John tried a different tact. He removed a purse filled with coins from his robe, held it up and repeated, "I need four strong men to assist with the coffin and I also require a knife." This time some men stepped forward, but still not as many as he had expected for so large a sum. It seemed even the poorest didn't consider selling their soul worth it, regardless of how large the purse. The deacon selected four men out of the ones who stepped forward and escorted them back inside. One of the men put a knife in his hand. On the way back the mob started to chant something, and the deacon made out the words "*damnatio memoriae,*" which meant damnation of memory. He wondered who among this group was educated enough to know what those words meant. He scanned the crowd, but no one stood out.

When he arrived back in the courtroom with the men, Deacon Bartholomew was already standing there, holding a simple monastic robe like the kind Thomas and Philip were wearing. Deacon Thomas presented the knife to Pope Stephen. Pope Stephen grabbed the knife and went over to the body of the former pope, which was now lying on the floor. Pope Stephen grabbed the corpse's right hand and with one quick slash of the knife, cut off the Pope's first three fingers.

One of the bishops who was sitting in the front row jumped to his feet, whether to object to the desecration or to leave the room, but was forced back into his seat by his fellow bishops and silenced.

"You have spoiled the cloisters of Rome and defiled the papal see by performing holy acts as a layman. I remove the fingers that gave blessings to poor men and rich men alike."

He motioned for the men to come forward.

"Remove the papal vestments from this wretched being and put on the layman's cloak."

The men stood as still as statues, and Deacon John looked them over. They were most likely hardened criminals, possibly murderers and rapists. They had probably not set foot in a church since their mothers dragged them in as children, but they would not move from their spots. Even they knew there were some lines you just didn't cross.

Pope Stephen, who seemed unfazed by the event, went up to the corpse and dragged him across the Basilica floor. He took the knife that was still in his hand and cut the papal garments off Formosus. He then removed the papal crown and put the robe on over the corpse's head.

"You will bury him in a foreigner's grave," Pope Stephen commanded.

They were still refusing to move until Deacon John took out another purse and held it up. It was as if the deacon had a robe full of purses that he carried just for bribes.

They picked up the body of the former pope and hoisted it above their heads. As they passed each row of seats, the occupants each made the sign of the cross.

"There is blood flowing from his mouth," a brother cried out.

One of the men carrying the pope, examined the corpse's mouth. "It does look like blood."

"It's as if the body of Formosus is still suffering," Thomas said.

The men put the corpse back in its original casket and left; the room went silent.

"I need everyone present to sign this document as witnesses

to the events that transpired here today," Pope Stephen said.

One by one, they all reluctantly came up to sign their name. The Unknown, who was unsure what he had just witnessed, signed an "X" underneath Brother Thomas.

"It is dark outside, but the moon is full; let us make our way back to the monastery. I do not want to remain here one more second," Philip said.

The Unknown rode with Brother Philip back this time. It was silent for most of the journey with the occasional silence being broken by a howl of some beast of prey. The Unknown repeated, *popes, politics* and *plagues* over and over in his mind.

The only thing said the whole trip home regarding the trial was said by Thomas.

"That was a ghastly trial, a vile display of exceptional power. The pope's actions of abuse against Pope Formosus shows an invulnerability to judgment that chills my bones. A pope is not to be judged."

Monks and Mischief

The Abbey of Sant'Antimo, a Benedictine monastery in the commune of Montalcino in Tuscany, was founded by the Lombards. However, if you ask any peasant from within a hundred miles of the place, they will tell you it was founded by none other than Charlemagne himself. The legend is that Charlemagne was returning from Rome along the Via Francigena. While he was camped, many of his soldiers died from the plague. While Charlemagne was sleeping, an angel visited him in his dream, supposedly as one did for John on the island of Patmos, and told him to pick an area of grass, dry it and then make an infusion of wine and have all the sick drink from it. According to legend, it worked and in return for the angel ending the scourge, Charlemagne promised to establish an abbey in the very same spot.

The abbey was located on a pilgrimage route to Rome, the very same route that Thomas, Philip and The Unknown man took to witness the Cadaver Synod. The monastery was often a rest stop for pilgrims, merchants, soldiers, government officials and in the case of The Unknown, people who had lost their memories and hadn't the faintest idea of who they were, how they got there or what they should do next.

"Abbot Peter, the abbot of our monastery has heard a great deal about you and would like to meet you," Philip said.

"What has he heard about me?" The Unknown asked.

"It's hard to say. He probably just wants to satisfy his curiosity and you know the saying about curiosity," Philip said.

"No, I am not familiar with the saying or if I were, I've quite forgotten it, along with everything else."

"Well, yes, I don't know what it is either, but I'm sure there is one and it doesn't end well."

"Anyway, it's sad but Abbot Peter will have to step down as abbot. He was ordained by Pope Formosus; and as a result of that farce of a trial, all his ordinations are being reversed because they are all now invalid. Now, of course, Pope Stephen could ordain him, but Abbot Peter was and now remains loyal to Pope Formosus; and so Pope Stephen will be putting in his own man. All ordinations are being reversed systematically, except that no one has mentioned the fact that it was Pope Formosus himself who ordained Pope Stephen as Bishop of Anagni before he became pope; and, therefore, his papacy is invalid.

"Where is Thomas?" The Unknown asked.

"He is working in the hospital so I will be escorting you to see Abbot Peter, but first I thought I would show you around the monastery."

The Unknown followed Philip, and their first stop was in the vineyard.

"We make our own wine for mass and for consumption on special occasions. Ah, I see Brother Lorenzo is hard at work. He tends to the vineyard and overseas production."

Lorenzo was hunched over peering closely at a vine with a scowl on his face as if he didn't like what he saw.

"Be very quiet; walk as quietly as I am, and we shall see if we can sneak up on him and give him a fright."

The Unknown wasn't sure why Philip wanted to frighten Brother Lorenzo, but he walked quietly as he was told. They were getting closer to the monk, and he had yet to notice them; he was still puzzling over the vine. Upon closer inspection, the Unknown observed that it wasn't that the monk was hunched over, it was that he was a hunchback. Philip reached out a hand and placed it on the shoulder of Lorenzo and yelled, "Hullo, Lorenzo!"

Lorenzo jumped into the air and, with his hunchback, he resembled a whale trying to fly. He gave a startled yelp and then flatulence erupted. It was so loud that it seemed to have its own echo. As far as flatulence went, no one could beat Lorenzo in sound, longevity and smell.

"Forgive me, Philip; I did not see you there. And this must be your new helper in the hospital. I've heard so much about you already," Lorenzo said.

The Unknown stranger did not respond; he was focusing all of his efforts on trying not to scrunch up his face because of the overpowering stench. His eyes began to water, and he could do nothing but pretend he had something in his eyes.

"Is there a problem with the vine?" Philip asked, watching The Unknown's discomfort with amusement.

"I should say there is. Look at this." Lorenzo held up an insect. "What is it?"

"What is it? It's only the most stubborn, pesky, resilient creature that God put in this world to test our patience and perseverance."

Philip and The Unknown waited for Lorenzo to give them a clue about which creature that might be. Lorenzo, seeing their blank expressions, said, "It's a louse. You would think the winter's frost would have killed the little buggers by now, but they're still here and they are damaging the vines."

"No one knows more about winemaking than our good Brother Lorenzo here."

Lorenzo, who was now nearly bald with just a few wisps of white hair on the sides of his head, was still clutching the louse in his hand when he asked, "Does this young man like wine?"

It was the first confirmation that The Unknown was indeed young although it was possible that everyone seemed young compared to this ancient monk. He even resembled a grape, a grape that had been left out in the sun too long, had become shriveled and had now turned into a raisin.

"I don't believe I have ever tasted wine."

"Why, that is an injustice; we shall have wine tonight at dinner, and you shall taste heaven itself," Lorenzo said.

The louse had finally broken free of the old hunchback's clutches and fell to the ground, making his way to freedom.

"Actually, he will have an opportunity to taste some at mass this afternoon."

Lorenzo scoffed, "The watered-down version of heaven."

"Now now, Lorenzo, that is the blood of our lord Jesus Christ; and you can't very well refer to his blood as 'the watered-down version of heaven.'"

Lorenzo made the sign of the cross. Even though he had been to heaven, it was hard to believe that God cared, given that no one had seen the Presence of God in a long time; and he seemed to do nothing about all the rule-breaking.

Philip nudged The Unknown and was thoroughly enjoying the

jest. "Well, we must press on now. I have a lot to show our young friend here."

It was the second confirmation that The Unknown was young; and coming from Brother Philip, who didn't seem that old to him, it was much more credible, not that The Unknown was vain. Although since he couldn't remember anything about himself, it was possible that he was vain; but he didn't think so. He just thought he was curious. Most people liked to know a little about themselves, and The Unknown was no different.

"Are you sure you don't have time for me to give this young man a history of wine? You know the Greeks—"

Philip interrupted, "Some other time perhaps."

"Maybe you would like to help me pick some grapes this fall. We place the grapes in large tubs, and then we stomp on them with our bare feet to squeeze out the juice. Have you ever felt the delightful sensation of grapes crushed between your toes?"

"May I remind you, good brother, that our friend here has lost his memory and doubtless has no idea whether he's crushed anything between his toes, grapes or otherwise."

"Yes, of course. Well, I shall be anxious to hear your reactions after you've tasted the wine at dinner. Although, not to disparage the communion wine—" he paused here to make the sign of the cross again "—but to taste the full-bodied soul of a grape, its sweet and succulent honey as if the sun had kissed . . ."

"Indeed, Lorenzo, it shall be a wondrous moment for all, and now we must make our way."

Lorenzo, who was a little perturbed at being cut-off before finishing his ode to wine, which undoubtedly was going to be something so distinguished and venerable that it would be fit for an emperor's ears, bade them good day and set about trying to recapture the louse that had fallen to the ground.

"Now you've met Brother Lorenzo; he has a problem with irritable bowels. I know I shouldn't keep sneaking up on him like that; but there is so little amusement around here, it's hard to resist. Lorenzo is a good person, though; and one day when he officially dies, his soul will be every bit as venerated as a saint in time. When I officially die, I doubt they will say as much for me. Now, I don't want you thinking that we are frivolous and amuse ourselves all day. We are a Benedictine order, and we work hard from sunup to sunset. We keep a very strict schedule which we adhere to day in and day out, to the point where the monotony could slowly strangle the life out of you and the rigorous—" he paused and then added "—but I digress."

The Unknown wasn't sure what Philip meant by "officially dead" and thought it best to hold his tongue. Philip looked melancholy and did not say anything else until they reached the kitchen. They heard a clanging of pots followed by a voice, "Careful, boy, that is my best kettle; and you're banging it around like you were trying to announce Christ's second coming."

There was an old monk, not nearly as old-looking as Brother Lorenzo but definitely in the twilight of his years, whose robe was stained with some kind of sauce—but not recently because the stain looked old and set—who was busy beating a young boy with a cooking spoon. The young boy who looked simply miserable was trying to deflect the blows with his hands.

"Straighten up, boy; we have visitors," the old man with the spoon said.

"Hullo, Simon and little Fortunato," Philip said.

"Hullo, Philip, and who's that with you? Is that the man who lost his memory?"

"Yes, we are not sure if he's lost it or just misplaced it, but it hasn't reappeared yet."

"Well, memories can be a blessing as well as a curse. Don't slouch, Fortunato," Simon said and whacked the little boy once again with the spoon.

"We just surprised Brother Lorenzo in the vineyard," Philip said.

"Indeed, and did he greet you with God's own perfume?" Simon asked, and they both broke out in raucous laughter. The Unknown and little Fortunato remained silent.

"What are we having for supper?" Philip asked.

"We are supposed to be having venison stew, but we may not have anything if this little Judas doesn't stop sabotaging the batches with too many green onions. I had to throw the first batch out; it tasted like horse dung."

"Now, now, Simon, we must not compare little Fortunato here with Christ's betrayer, the most despised man who ever lived."

"Why in heavens not when the little urchin keeps putting a

punch of salt in the stew when I say a pinch will do?"

"Because what if he should despair and hang himself like Judas?" Philip asked.

Fortunato began to tear up; he could handle being whacked with a spoon, but he didn't like being compared to the man who betrayed Christ. The Unknown felt sorry for him and reached out and tussled his hair. Simon looked down at the little boy, whose fair skin was turning red as a tomato from crying.

"Don't cry, little one; if you cheer up, I shall prepare a special cake just for you."

This made Fortunato stop crying immediately and brought a smile to his face. The mention of cake could quickly make a little boy forget about being called the worst man in history.

"So you remember nothing, not even your name?" Simon asked.

"No, I can't remember anything. My only memories are of waking up in the hospital and Brother Thomas and Brother Philip taking me to the Cadaver Synod."

Brother Simon winced at the mention of the "Cadaver Synod."

"Never in all my years or in all the years of history have I ever heard of such a thing being done, and I've been around a long, long time. To put a pope on trial—and a dead one at that— amounts to no less than heresy."

"Careful of voicing your thoughts out loud, Simon, although most of us agree with your sentiments; but there are those who might not share your opinion." He pointed to The Unknown, who was still trying to cheer up Fortunato by making funny faces at the boy. Simon got his friend's meaning . . . since they did not have any idea who this man was, it would be better to keep quiet on such matters.

"May I remind you that Abbot Francis will be replacing our dear Peter this week."

"Tell me, man with no memory, what did you think of the trial? What did you learn?"

The Unknown had to think about that. It was the first time he had seen a corpse on trial and hopefully the last time.

"I noticed that when Pope Stephen cut the corpse's fingers off, he did not cast them aside but put them in the pocket of his robe."

Simon raised an eyebrow.

"I noticed that Deacon Bartholomew's demeanor changed

263

when he answered for the pope during the trial by confessing that he conspired with Boris I to become Bishop in Bulgaria, secretly held ambitions to become pope and was a traitor to King Charles the Bald. Up until that point, he had to be prompted to answer and stammered a little, but that line seemed smooth and polished as if prepared and rehearsed."

"A man with no memory, indeed. I'd say you have perfect clarity of mind and need not bother trying to recall old memories; they just clutter up the mind and obscure other, more important facts," Simon said.

"Popes, plagues and politics," The Unknown repeated.

"Quite right, those are the three constants in life," Simon said.

Fortunato started to fidget a little bit; and Simon, who realized he wasn't holding the spoon any longer, searched for it with his eyes. The Unknown noticed it was poking out of Fortunato's robe; the little boy was hiding it from his assailant.

"Now where did I put that spoon?"

"We must be off; we are on our way to see Abbot Peter," Philip said; but Simon was no longer listening because he was busy searching for his favorite weapon. Fortunato, whose chubby cheeks looked as if he were storing nuts in them, was smiling and enjoying the reprieve.

"Let's go through the scriptorium on our way to see the abbot. There are two people there that I think you will find interesting."

Philip and The Unknown headed toward the scriptorium, and The Unknown wondered what a scriptorium was and was about to ask, but remembered what Brother Thomas said about learning by paying attention and observing. He decided to wait and find out for himself. When they entered the scriptorium, a musty smell permeated the room. It smelled of dead animal carcass, which indeed it was; the parchments were made from sheep skin, their skins stretched and scraped until they were smooth enough to write on. Two young monks were in the room; one was standing back admiring his work with a smile on his face, and the other had such a scowl that he could melt butter with it.

The brother with the smile saw them and said, pointing to The Unknown, "What poor soul would want to live here? It's dull as tombs." The other monk didn't bother to look up from his manuscript.

264

"Hullo, Brother John the Scribe." He turned toward The Unknown and said, "We call him Brother John the Scribe because as I have mentioned before, we have a couple of other Johns here like John the Elder who found you in the garden; although since he's the only John in the room, it's safe to just call him Brother John."

"You must be the man with no memory. Maybe we could call you John No-Memory," John said and laughed at his own joke.

The Unknown laughed a halfhearted laugh, not sure if the monk were being serious or not and hoping that he was not because he did not like the sound of that name.

"We have visitors; give them a greeting, ole stone face," John said to the very serious monk, who responded with only a grunt.

"The very serious man over there is another one of our illuminators, Brother Adolfo. What are you working on now?"

"We were told—no, make that 'ordered'—to create a prayer book for the new abbot. Apparently, he's too good for the old prayer book that Peter uses. He wanted a new Bible too, which I told him we could do, but it would take a year at least."

The Unknown and Philip looked at John's and Adolfo's work so far. There was the Virgin Mary with a golden halo, raising her hands to God. The borders were beautifully illuminated with roses; it was simply breathtaking. The first letter of the paragraph was enlarged and colored in red; so it was throughout the page, representing the new sections in the text.

The Unknown walked over to Adolfo to see what he was doing, but he growled at him as he approached.

"I'd keep a safe distance from that one; he might devour you whole," John said smirking.

The Unknown, who did not want to get devoured whole, decided to look around the room at the other completed scripts. Philip picked up one titled *The Nicomachean Ethics* by Aristotle to show him.

"Not all the texts that are copied here are religious texts; there are secular works which are copied and sold or traded at the market. It is one of our revenue sources," Philip explained.

"How do you like our fine abbey?" John asked.

"Since I have no memories of my former life, I am finding everything a revelation and a mystery."

265

"Did you figure out what caused the poor man to lose his memory in the first place?"

"No, it is quite a mystery. Perhaps he suffered something traumatic, and his brain simply won't allow him to remember anything. I like to believe, though, that he was sent by angels to check up on us."

"Why does anyone need to check up on us? They can see we are doing a splendid job."

"Well, I wouldn't use the word 'splendid,' more like 'adequate,'" Philip said, meaning their track record of staying alive was not so great.

"What do you think about our memory-challenged friend here, Adolfo?" John asked.

Adolfo snorted instead of grunting this time.

"Indeed and could you elaborate on that? Do you see what I have to put up with all day, Philip? You think that I could at least work with someone who speaks occasionally. I'm terribly lonely here; it's like talking to a wall."

"We are on our way to meet Peter; perhaps I can get him to have Adolfo work in the vineyard and Lorenzo work in here with you."

"Lorenzo? You'd have God's holy works smelling like a chamber pot in no time. That man would contaminate everything with his noxious bodily odors. Why can't you work with me and send Adolfo to the hospital?"

"I'm afraid my only talents lie in helping the sick; Adolfo would quickly hasten the demise of the sick with one look of his face," Philip said.

Adolfo was not paying attention to either of them. He was too busy concentrating on his work and his scowl.

"We must run along now; we don't want to keep Peter waiting. No doubt he's busy packing his things and making way for the new abbot."

"It is such a shame that Peter has to step down. Things are really going to change with the new abbot; I can feel it in my bones," John said.

The Unknown and Philip left the colorful John the Scribe and the brooding Adolfo to their work and walked outside. Philip led The Unknown through the ambulatory towards the abbot's residence. At the end of each column in the ambulatory was a carving of a man surrounded by lions.

"Who is that man with the lions?"

"It is Daniel from the story 'Daniel in the Lion's Den.' It's a story from the Bible."

They approached a castle that was rather small and looked unfinished.

"This is where our Abbot Peter lives, which will soon house a different abbot."

The Unknown saw the look of sadness on Philip's face. They went inside and walked up several flights of winding stairs. When they reached the top, they were immediately approached by a tall monk who was the tallest man that The Unknown had ever seen, or at least up until now. Abbot Peter was old with a white beard, but he had a twinkle in his eye and a wide smile that made him appear much younger. He still had a full head of hair, all white, which was cut in a bowl shape like the other monks.

"It's good to see you, Philip."

The Unknown watched Brother Philip and Abbot Peter embrace. A warmth and a kindness radiated around the abbot like the halo around Mary from the picture he'd seen in the scriptorium. The room they were in felt very inviting, like it was an extension of the abbot himself. The room was cluttered with books, paintings and statues, but everything was tidy.

"I wanted to thank you and Thomas for going in my place to the trial. I just couldn't bring myself to witness such a desecration. Alas, I suppose it is why I am finding myself as just simple Brother Peter again and no longer Abbot Peter."

"I must confess it is a burden that troubled me greatly, but Thomas and I knew it was necessary. We didn't go alone; this innocent lamb here went with us," Philip said and patted The Unknown on his shoulder.

"Yes, it must have been a very grave undertaking. Tell me, what did you think of our late pope?"

The Unknown wasn't sure if Abbot Peter were making a joke or not. The abbot was smiling with encouragement so he said, "I found him to be very dead."

Peter chuckled and said, "Well, that's to be expected of the dead; they typically look the part. But tell me, you have no memories so you have yet to know or learn of good and evil.

What did you feel?"

The Unknown thought again. He did not know what the Abbot meant by "good" and "evil." He thought back to how he had felt during the trial.

"I felt very cold; it was if something dark were waiting and biding its time in the shadows."

"This is good. I've always felt that we are born in this world having an innate sense or feeling of right and wrong, and I think you've expressed that very well just now. You have come to us at a very turbulent time. Pope Formosus angered Agiltrude, the queen of Italy of the House Spoleto, when he refused to crown her son Emperor of Rome. Pope Stephen is a family member of the House of Spoleto and a close political ally of the queen. Our pope has a blind hatred for Formosus, whom he viewed as a usurper of the papacy. He thinks his infallibility will protect him and that he has condemned the legacy of Formosus, but he has really condemned only himself. He will not remain pope long; that I can guarantee."

As if to solidify the authority of Peter's last statement, bells began chiming.

"Those are the bells from the bell tower, signifying it is time for mass. You shall come to the mass at the Carolingian Chapel with us. This mass is intended for the repose of the soul of our beloved Pope Boniface VI. He was pope right after Pope Formosus and was only pope for sixteen short days before he succumbed to gout. It would seem that being pope is quite a dangerous office these days," Peter said.

Overkill

St. Peter's Basilica was built starting in 326 under the orders of Emperor Constantine and was not finished until thirty years later. The basilica was built over the circus of Nero where many Christian martyrdoms had taken place, including the first pope, St. Peter . . . the very same one who used to be at the gates of heaven. The church was entered through the atrium, which got the nickname Paradise because it contained a beautiful garden with fountains, and was where Pope Stephen VI was now pacing back and forth.

Stephen, a Roman and the son of a priest, was both organized and ruthless. He kept his brown hair cropped short and was clean-shaven.

"I want Formosus exhumed."

"They're already calling you 'Pope Stephen, the Grave Robber,'" Francis, the soon-to-be abbot of Sant'Antimo, said.

"Who is calling me that? I'll have their head boiled in oil."

"It's just whispered among the commoners."

"Oh, them; who cares what they think?" Pope Stephen frowned at what someone had carved into the archway, *Death to Pope Stephen VI.*"Have someone fix this, will you?"

Stephen had such a deep-seeded hatred of Formosus that it did not end with his death.

"Burial is too good for him; I want his body thrown in the Tiber River."

"Your holiness, I must advise you against this. The people and most of the bishops strongly objected to the trial of Pope Formosus and thought it an offense against God."

"I am infallible, am I not?"

"Yes, your holiness."

"Then I decide what an offense against God is. Formosus is the offense against God, and right now his soul is burning in the eternal fire."

"It will be hard; I don't know who would be willing to disinter

269

a pope's body, deposed or not, a second time and then throw it in a river."

"If you offer enough money, I'm sure you will find someone."

Francis said nothing; he was uneasy. He couldn't understand the pope's obsession with a dead pope. He had achieved what he wanted; he had become the pope. Why waste time on someone who was dead? Why not concentrate on more important things, like filling the Church coffers or buying a papal army to defend the Church against foreign enemies?

"You leave for the abbey tomorrow?"

"Yes and I plan on making a few changes around there, starting with stricter adherence to the Benedictine rule—no wine except for mass and no more copying secular manuscripts and selling them," Francis said.

"That's all well and good, but I am an expert at sniffing out heresy; and I don't trust that Abbot Peter. There is something wrong there, and I want you to find out what it is."

It was true; he was an expert at ripping out what he thought of as the weeds of heresy from the holy garden. He was known for the severity with which he treated clergy who strayed from the holy path.

Stephen continued to pace. Francis noticed he was holding something in his right hand. It looked like . . . but no, it couldn't be.

"Are those the fingers of Formosus?"

Stephen was deep in thought and almost didn't hear him. "What? Yes, these are his fingers."

This isn't good. There has been a lot of talk about Stephen being mad and holding the fingers of a dead pope; fingers which he cut off would do nothing to counter such talk, Francis thought.

"Perhaps I should take those fingers and dispose of them, your holiness."

The Pope pointed the dead fingers at Francis. "You will do no such thing; these fingers belong to me."

Francis straightened his back; he had a tendency to slouch at times. He too wore his hair cropped short; but, unlike Stephen, his hair was a very pale blond and his skin was so fair that he was sometimes mistaken for an albino.

"I should be going if I'm going to find someone to take care of Formosus and prepare for my journey tomorrow," Francis said.

Pope Stephen held out his hand for him to kiss the papal ring. It was the same hand he was using to hold the dead fingers. Francis hesitated before bending down to kiss it. He kissed the ring, trying to be extra careful not to kiss the rotting fingers, but his chin brushed against them. It took all of his will power not to recoil. Francis walked at a brisk pace, trying not to run for the door. He was relieved to be away from the pope.

I just need to make sure he is dead; I need to see the body one more time to make sure. He has been haunting my dreams, as well as my waking thoughts, and I haven't had a moment's peace. They all think I'm mad; I'm not mad, Pope Stephen thought.

He examined the dead fingers. He scratched his head with one of the long and blackened fingernails. It was amazing how nails and hair still grew after your death. He thought of Formosus the same way as the fingers; his presence was still growing in his mind. He frowned again at the *Death to Pope Stephen VI* carved into the wood.

It should say Death to Pope Formosus. He was the worst pope in history, even worse than Boniface VI who was elected right after him. Thankfully, he was only pope for two weeks and died naturally; otherwise I would have had to poison him, he thought.

He heard shouting from outside the wall and walked closer so he could hear what the commotion was all about.

"Remove yourself; you have no business here with his holiness," one of the papal guards said.

"Demon pope!" yelled the crowd that was gathering.

They are a bunch of simpletons. Do they think I'm the only one who had a hatred for Formosus? Guy IV of Spoleto hated him too because he went back on his promise to crown his son and crowned Arnulf, that Frankish louse, Holy Roman Emperor instead and by doing so, set off a feud. I benefited from that feud. Guy helped me become pope; and thanks to my reversing Pope Formosus' ordination, the Spoleto family is back in charge of Rome. So let them keep yelling all they want; they know nothing, he thought and once again scratched his head with the finger of the dead pope.

***

271

It won't be long now; they are going to bring that foolish man down, Francis thought as he slipped into the shadows to avoid the mob.

For now, though, he was still pope and had given a command which he must follow. He knew of a brothel he could go to where he could get some men to carry out the morbid task he was assigned, but he dreaded going there. It was full of filth and debaucheries; it was a moral plague. The real reason why he didn't want to go there was that it was a great temptation because he had never known a woman.

He walked on towards the brothel and passed a man who kept his head down and who was wearing a hooded cloak.

"*Damnatio memoriae,*" the cloaked stranger said as he passed by Francis. It was the same thing he and Deacon John had heard outside the trial of Formosus; it had caught on very nicely with the peasants, even though they had no idea what it meant.

"What did you say? Were you talking to me?"

"Yes, I was talking to you and I think you heard me just fine," the stranger said.

"Whose memory is being damned?" Francis asked.

"Pope Formosus' and now you are about to damn it even further. You know throwing a pope's body in the Tiber River is a heavy sin."

Francis was stunned; how did this simple peasant know what he was going to do? He had only just been told himself. His thoughts fired quickly.

You fool, he's obviously a spy who has infiltrated the Church ranks. He collects secrets and then threatens others with his knowledge for gold or power. You must kill him now and quickly.

"It wouldn't do to kill a stranger during a full moon; there is too much light. And yes, you might say I'm a spy of sorts, but I have no desire to threaten you. In fact, I'm here to help you. You have no need to go to the brothel for help; that is, unless you need to stop there for other reasons."

This time his brain couldn't fire any thoughts at all; it was trying to figure out how the hooded man knew what he was thinking.

"Who are you? Show yourself."

272

"My real name is from a very old language that you wouldn't be able to pronounce, but you can call me Baal. I would rather not show myself right now, if it's all the same to you."

"Why do you want to help me?"

Baal had not felt like disguising himself this trip because every time he did, something bad always happened so he had come to Earth in his own form and put a long cloak over himself.

"I was sent from far away to retrieve something for someone. The something and the someone you need not concern yourself with, but let us say our goals are similar."

"Are you a leper? Is that why you are cloaked?"

Baal was growing impatient. "I'm a not a leper; I am cloaked because I wish to keep my anonymity. It would have been wise if you had done the same since you are about to perform an unholy deed."

If he asks one more question, I think I will have him strung up in the Quiet Tree by his tongue.

This time it was Francis who read Baal's mind, but not literally; he just read his facial expression. "All right, I accept your help."

Francis walked along with the hooded stranger in silence for most of the way. He let enough time pass until he thought it was safe to ask the stranger another question. After all, it was obvious this Baal didn't want to kill him, or he would have done it already.

"Can you read my mind?"

Baal studied him. The moon caught his hood for a second, and Francis thought he saw red eyes. "No, it's just that I've been around a long time, and people are so predictable."

Francis couldn't tell how old he was by the sound of his voice. It didn't sound young or old, but he had a strange foreign accent, one he had never heard before.

"You are not from here." It was a statement rather than a question.

"No, I live a long way from here."

Baal could tell him he was as old as time itself or just pull down his hood and reveal his true self; but he had learned from experience not to surprise mortals like that. The last time he did that, the man couldn't even scream; his eyes just got really wide and he keeled over dead. The memory of his face made Baal chuckle.

273

"Is there something funny that I missed?"

"I was just thinking upon a memory, that's all. We are almost there; there should be two shovels at the site."

"How do you know there are two shovels there?"

"Because I put them there."

Francis didn't bother to ask him how he knew that he planned to exhume the former pope because he knew he would probably not get a response.

"There should also be a cloth there to cover the body."

Francis found the grave marker, and indeed there were two shovels and a long cloth beside it.

The marker just said *Advena* on it. It was a cruel joke because *Advena* meant more visitor than foreigner. This was not how you treated a visitor; you didn't dump his body in a communal grave.

"How will we be able to find him among all the other corpses?"

"I imagine he will be probably be somewhere on top since he is newly-buried. We are looking for a corpse that has three fingers missing from its left hand. Also, I believe he was wearing a layman's robe," Baal said.

This Baal seems to know everything. He may be dressed like a pauper, but that is just a clever disguise. He is undoubtedly a powerful man and not to be messed with; I need to make him an ally.

While they were digging, Baal revealed why he was helping him and what he wanted.

"I want to give you some information, and I believe it is information of great interest to your pope. Everyone knows he has a disdain for heretics and punishes them severely. I know for a fact that Abbot Peter in collusion with six other monks have in their possession the Apocrypha." Baal gave him a moment for him to process this revelation.

"The Apocrypha? That's impossible; all of those books were rounded up long ago and burned by the Church."

"You doubt me?" Baal asked in a deep tone. He loved scaring mortals.

"No, no, I'm just surprised is all. Where are they hiding them?"

"This is what I want you to find out for me. Once you have

found them, they are to come to me and no one else. You can do whatever you want with the monks."

Francis considered this. It would please the pope very much, and he might even get rewarded. "All right, consider it done."

"Ah, I think we have found the body of your late pope."

The smell was so rancid that Francis had to cover his nose with his sleeve.

"How can you stand it?"

"I'm used to it," Baal said. He was used to it, and the smell only reminded him of home.

They both climbed down into the pit and pulled him out; then they filled the pit back in with dirt and wrapped the body in cloth.

"We should have enough time to get to the Tiber before people are starting their day," Baal said.

They walked across the broad valley; Francis had to hurry to keep up with Baal's pace. They had gotten to the top of a hill when Francis stumbled over a rock and fell, causing Baal to fall and drop Formosus. If anyone had been watching, they would have seen a corpse, a man flailing his arms and screaming like a banshee, and a demon, all rolling down a hill tumbling over one another. When they got to the bottom of the gorge, Baal and Francis ended up with their faces in the mud. Baal quickly put his hood back on because the only thing scarier than seeing a demon's face was seeing a demon's face covered in mud.

"Well, that's one way to make it to the river," Baal said and pointed to the river bank.

Formosus was uncovered, and a raven swooped in and landed on his face. He stared out at the muddy pair.

"Get away from there!" Francis said and shooed the raven away. "It's an omen and not a very good one."

Baal rolled his eyes.

What is it with these mortals and omens? Neither God nor Lucifer sends omens.

They covered Formosus once again and tossed him into the river. The body of the former Pope floated down the Tiber and out of sight.

"Oh, I almost forgot, would you mind signing this?" Baal asked and handed him a parchment.

"What is it?"

275

"Just something I need to satisfy my master."

Francis shrugged and signed. He didn't see the harm in signing the stranger's odd-looking parchment; after all, what harm could it do?

The Dream of the Unknown

"Do you think he was sent from heaven to help us?" Brother Lorenzo asked, clutching his stomach because he felt like he was going to break wind. His stomach had given him particular trouble yesterday during mass. He kept farting through most of the chanting, which messed up the other monks' rhythm.

The monks were in a dark room seated around a wooden table in Peter's home that only a select few knew about. There was a sconce on the wall right beside the fireplace, which if you turned slightly to the right and then full back to the left, opened up into a room. It also contained an underground passageway. The Lombards had ordered it built because of frequent raids on the monastery by Vikings; they had told only the first abbot about it, then left it up to the discretion of the abbot as to whom he would tell. Each abbot had passed the secret down to his successor. Abbot Peter, however, had no intention of revealing the information to the new abbot who would arrive tomorrow. There was also a crypt beneath the Carolingian Chapel, which doubled as both a place for the dead and an escape route. Fortunately, the monks had had no cause to use it.

"I think he might be Baal in disguise, or maybe Azazel sent a different demon to retrieve the gospels," John said, then added, "Adolfo agrees with me." Adolfo grunted, which everyone took to be an acquiescent grunt.

"Why do you think he is a spy?" Simon asked with his cooking spoon out. Thankfully, his little apprentice, Fortunato, was in the kitchen, or else he would be getting assailed with it. Whether he might be asked to cook in a moment's notice or whack an unruly child, Simon always had the spoon handy.

"Well, look at it, a man just happens to turn up in our garden and we discover he has lost his memory. I questioned every villager from here to the river, and no one saw him walk through here. No one knows who he is or where he came from. Telling people that you have lost your memory is a good cover story for not having to answer inconvenient questions. He doesn't have to tell any lies that may trip him up. His timing coincides with the Cadaver Synod and Pope Stephen supplanting Peter with his own man. It's the perfect time because it's chaotic . . . so we must be wary. Baal has tricked us too many times in the past," John said. He looked at the Lombardi coat of arms on the wall; he was impressed by its rich colors. The coat of arms was a picture of a sun above a plumed helmet with bright yellow and red feathers and a blue shield at the bottom with gold stars.

"He seems to know things intuitively but has a sense of innocence about him. I feel like it is our duty to feed him with knowledge like Satan giving the apple to Adam and Eve, but this time in a good way," Philip said. "I just feel a responsibility towards him."

"Yes, and then we can cast him out of our garden," John said; Brother Adolfo grunted enthusiastically at that.

"I don't see why we have to tell him anything, especially if we are debating about his trustworthiness. I mean, the fewer people who know about this, the better. The more people involved, the harder it is to keep a secret," Simon said.

"He has a pleasant aura about him," Lorenzo said.

"You think anyone with a heartbeat has a pleasant aura," Simon said.

"I suspect, though, that he has been sent to us by fortuitous circumstance and not a demonic maliciousness. I think it is our duty to help him regain his memory; and if that fails, we can at least fill him with the holy spirit," Peter said. "I think it's the least we can do to have been given such long lives even if it is a pointless endeavor for a daft archangel.

"Be cautious and keep an eye out for Baal. Do not revel to The Unknown anything to do with the Gnostic Gospels," Peter said.

"I have to carry around a hump for the rest of my days; I still wish that Uriel had fixed my hunchback. It was bad enough carrying it during my first lifetime," Lorenzo said.

"You know that Uriel is very busy thinking about himself and couldn't be bothered to make improvements to our bodies. If he would have bothered, he would have made this one over here garrulous so it wouldn't be as dull as tombs in the scriptorium."

John pointed to Adolfo. Adolfo tried to grab his finger, but John was too quick in retracting it. He had learned his lesson on more than one occasion over the years.

"One thing is certain, and that is we will have to find another place to meet," Peter said.

"Maybe we could meet down in the crypt," Simon suggested.

Adolfo groaned. "I agree with Adolfo; the air is stale and rank down there, and any flatulence by our dear Lorenzo would be unbearable. You would have thought Uriel could at least cleared up the man's bowels, but no, he'd rather him fart for all eternity," John said.

"Well, we will have to come up with a place where we can meet in private and no one can eavesdrop on us," Abbot Peter said. "I do know this much; we must be careful for these are dangerous times. Do you think Pope Stephen would think twice about condemning us for heresy when he's already put a pope on trial? He would probably even have us burned alive. I know we've died a lot already, but it's not something you ever get used to. I know I certainly haven't. I for one am tired of bouncing in and out of heaven."

"If I have to go back one more time, I'm staying and I don't care what Uriel says," Lorenzo said.

"It's almost time to start the day. Simon, would you read from the Book of Mary to close the meeting?"

Simon cleared his throat and began to read:

"When the Blessed One had said this, He greeted them all saying, 'Peace be with you. Receive my peace unto yourselves. Beware that no one lead you astray, for the son of man is within you. Follow after Him. Those who seek Him will find Him. Go then and preach the gospel of the Kingdom. Do not lay down any rules beyond what I have appointed you, and do not give a law like the lawgiver, lest you be constrained by it. When He had said this, He departed."

***

The Unknown was in a room, much like where the Cadaver Synod took place. He was standing uncomfortably close to the corpse pope who was sitting on the papal throne and watched as

279

a maggot wriggled out of an eye socket. The corpse was still wearing the monk's simple robe that was placed on him after the trial.

"Is there something you want to say to me?" The Unknown asked.

"There is quite a lot I want to say to you actually, but there is rarely enough time to say everything that needs to be said," the corpse said.

The Unknown wasn't sure, but it looked as if the corpse pope had an amused expression on its face.

"Who am I?"

"You are no one important. You are not asking the right question," the corpse pope said.

"Why am I here?"

The corpse pope lifted a skeletal finger and pointed it at him. The finger was almost touching his nose. He couldn't point with the other hand because his fingers had been cut off by Pope Stephen.

"I need you to retrieve my body from the Tiber River; I cannot be allowed to rot like an animal. I belong in the crypt at the basilica, along with all my brethren."

"I don't know where the Tiber River is. I don't even know who I am."

"For there is nothing hidden that will not be revealed. And there is nothing buried that will not be raised."

"What does that mean?"

The corpse opened its mouth, but no words came out, only blood.

The Unknown woke up with a start, and bells started clanging which made him jump gain.

All these bells clanging all the time and making such a racket are not good for my nerves, The Unknown thought.

He walked over to the basin of water on the table and splashed some in his face. He touched his lips and brought his fingers down; to his surprise there was blood on them. There was blood in his mouth; he must have bitten his tongue in his sleep. He looked at the painting of Pope John II hanging in his room and wondered about the dream.

He said I'm nobody important. Well, if I'm nobody important, why did he bother visiting my dream?

Thomas walked into the room. "There you are; didn't you hear the bells?"

"I heard them; I just didn't know what they were about."

"They are about your getting up out of bed and helping Philip and me in the hospital."

The Unknown looked outside and it was still pitch black. "It's still dark out."

"Shall I go to the emaciated, ashen-faced, sickly men, women and children in the throes of death and peer right into their sallow faces and ask, 'Can you please wait until it is light outside to die?'"

"That would be nice; I would appreciate a little more sleep. I had a ghoulish dream that woke me up."

"No, you can't have another moment of sleep. Did Christ ask right before he was being crucified if he could have another moment of sleep first?"

The Unknown had no idea if Christ did ask, but from the look on Brother Thomas' face, probably not.

He followed Thomas outside to the hospital and told him about his dream.

"He quoted the Book of Thomas? That's incredible," Thomas said.

"I don't understand; you wrote a book?" The Unknown asked.

Thomas was rocking back and forth on his heels. The Unknown man thought he had not heard his question until he said, "What? No, I didn't write a book. Never mind; there are sick people who need attending. It's best not to mention your dream to anyone else, though."

The Unknown did not bother to ask Thomas why; he just nodded. He didn't look like he was in the mood for any more questions. He followed Thomas over to a woman who looked very sick. Her breathing was shallow and raspy. Thomas pulled one of her legs out beneath the sheets and pointed to the boils covering it.

A monk who was walking by carrying a basin of water said, "Why do you insist on touching the boils of those who have the plague, Thomas, as if you were trying to hasten your journey to our redeemer?"

"There is a divine plan for me; and, rest assured, it does not include dying of the plague. Of that I am certain."

"You can't be certain of God's plan for you," the monk with the water replied.

Brother Thomas didn't want to argue the point. He could hardly tell the young monk that he had already died several times, and therefore he doubted he could catch the plague. He turned his attention back to the dying woman. He grabbed a knife from one of the nearby tables.

"Fetch that pot from underneath that man's bed," Thomas said, pointing to a sick man behind The Unknown.

"That is a chamber pot," The Unknown said.

"Yes, bring it over here."

"But this man might need it."

"Hardly—that man is dead."

The Unknown looked at him more closely, and his lips were as blue as a summer sky. He grabbed the chamber pot as he was instructed.

"Now, I am going to lance this boil; and, when I do, I need you to hold the pot underneath to catch the pus."

The Unknown held the pot underneath the woman's leg; with one quick slash by Thomas, the boil was opened. A putrid, sulphur smell arose, and with it a mucus-like fluid started to ooze out of the leg and then poured out. There seemed to be no end to the pus; it was like an endless river. It was too much for The Unknown's senses, and he dropped the chamber pot on the floor with a *clank*. The pus spilled all over the floor; then there was a second *clank,* which was actually more of a *thunk* that was heard, and that was The Unknown fainting and hitting the ground.

"I guess that is all the healing he is going to do today," Thomas said.

***

Things were now so hectic in heaven that all normal day-to-day functions had stopped. Uriel had not had a visit from Zachariel in a while; for that much, he was relieved because he was in no mood to inspire anyone to do anything. No one faced any inquiries anymore; Uriel could say "blasted" as often as he wanted. Earth was not in chaos, at least not yet, but it certainly was becoming more and more disorderly. Storms were becoming longer, more frequent and more violent. The seas were always rough; no inspiration was spread among men in science, carpentry, architecture or any other field that advanced mankind. Wars between nations were waging; there was no angel to temper the violence. Harvests were meager and hope was waning. St. Paul was still at the gate letting everyone in, regardless of the sins in their lives. Heaven was now like elastic being stretched too far, right before it was about to snap. All these changes were nothing compared to what was being considered at the moment. Uriel stood outside St. Bede's Library and listened to what was being discussed; he wasn't the only one. There was a small crowd hovered outside the door, consisting of angels of all ranks, including Michael and Gabriel, and demons, being careful to be as quiet as mice lest the seraphim who were in the library decided to close the doors. They elected Ahriman, Leliel, Pahaliah and Zephon to speak so that there weren't just seraphim shouting over one another.

"It's too crowded as it is. Not only should we not allow any demons in, but we must replace St. Paul from the gates of heaven and sort through the mortals who are here and cast out the ones that should be in hell," Zephon said. There was a chime of bells ringing in agreement to this; bells were something the angels used in a forum such as this to show agreement or support. They could just as easily clap; but angels, most especially seraphim, loved any excuse to ring a bell.

"I think we should let them back in. I don't believe in eternal punishment; there's always room for redemption. Besides, who was killed during the rebellion? What real harm was done? Some of those demons who were once angels were good friends of mine; and, quite simply, I miss them," Leliel said. Some more bell-ringing was heard, and it was hard to tell if there were any less than the dissenters. Some of them probably just liked ringing the bell, regardless of what was said.

"I'm really torn here because I would like to see a unified heaven once again; but in addition to the overcrowding, God is the one who cast them all out to begin with, and we can't go against God," Ahriman said. More bell-ringing and some head-bobbing.

"Does anyone know the whereabouts of the Presence of God?" Pahaliah asked. There was more bell-ringing even though he was asking a question and not stating an opinion.

"No one knows and I firmly believe if God wanted to put a stop to this, he could; but I believe this is a test. I think He wants to see how well we can manage things without His assistance," Leliel said.

"I agree. He's obviously not angry or concerned about the events that are occurring, and I think He would like for us to handle this ourselves," Ahriman said.

Bells were going crazy, and Pahaliah held up a hand to silence them. "You know what, I say we let them in. If God doesn't like it, then He will simply cast everyone out again. I think we should take a vote; everyone write their vote down—yes or no—and then I shall collect them all. Whatever the majority is, that will be the decision." He did not want to leave it up to bell-ringing. Angels were snapping their finger for quills and parchment. Pahaliah went around to everyone and put their vote in his robe. Once he was satisfied he had collected them all, he said, "I will now count all the votes, and then I will have Ahriman confirm it; that way we know for sure it's fair."

While Pahaliah was busy counting, there was a low murmuring of voices and even a few ringing of bells from angels who had not had their fill of it yet. Outside, everyone continued to remain quiet, lest they shut the door before announcing the decision.

"I wish I had a bell," Michael whispered.

"You shouldn't complain because you got the voice of God, something no one else has," Gabriel whispered.

"Close your blasted mouths," Uriel whispered.

Pahaliah finally finished, and then it was Ahriman's turn.

Ahriman start counting and the bell-ringing finally ceased.

"This is all very exciting," Pahaliah said.

"I think it's an abomination," Zephon said.

"You're no fun at all, Zephon. You're determined to have us all spend eternity bored out of our wits."

Ahriman was done counting and then whispered in Pahaliah's ear.

"No, that's not right!" Pahaliah shouted.

"It is back to hell for the demons by one vote," Ahriman said.

"By my count, it is they can stay by one vote."

The two angels argued back and forth as to whose count was right.

Clank, clank, clank, Leliel's bell rang. The two stopped arguing and looked at Leliel.

"I will settle this once and for all," he said.

Uriel was exasperated. "Would you count the blasted votes correctly?" he shouted. All the seraphim in the hall turned towards the shouting. Even Leliel looked up from his counting. They had not realized the door had been left open. A seraph nearest the door shut it with an authoritative slam.

"Now look what you've done, Uriel. Honestly, maybe it's better we do go back to hell so we don't have to spend an eternity with you," a demon named Focalor said.

Uriel huffed at this. "What does it matter? We will still find out momentarily anyway."

There was thunderous bell-ringing.

"They must have announced the decision," Gabriel said.

"Can you hear what it is?" Belphegor asked.

"No, just those incessant bells," Uriel said.

The doors to St. Bede's Library opened, and seraphim came pouring out. There were a few frowning faces, but most looked overjoyed.

Pahaliah was the first to speak. "It is hereby decreed by the seraphim of heaven that the rebels formerly cast out of heaven shall be reinstated with proper rank. Details on transformations later." The demons cheered. After a millennium of torturing dead souls, they were finally coming home.

Do Dead Popes Float?

"What are we doing here? It's cold and my bowels are acting up," Brother Lorenzo said.

"Your bowels are always acting up," Simon said.

"Make sure you don't fart downwind," Philip said.

The monks and The Unknown were standing at the edge of the Tiber River, shivering and waiting.

"The young man said he had a dream in which our beloved Formosus spoke to him, telling him to retrieve his body from this river. I think it might be a message from God," Peter said.

"We've been to heaven many times, and we've never even seen God," John pointed out. "More than likely, it's from that trouble-maker Baal. He's probably lured us here so he can toss us all in the river and drown us."

The Unknown sat down upon a large rock that was jutting out near the bank. He was listening to the monks talk, but had no idea what any of it meant.

"How do we know he's not Baal and wants to drown us one by one?" John asked.

Adolfo grunted twice, meaning he agreed or just as possibly disagreed with his friend's question.

"Baal wants the books. He's not interested in the body of a dead pope," Peter said.

"How do we know he's going to float down river?" Thomas asked and looked down, but couldn't see the bottom because it was too murky. "It looks really deep."

"Do dead popes float?" Simon asked.

"His skeleton should float just like a boat . . . a boat made of bones," Philip said.

"Why are we interested in the body of a dead pope? He is dead, after all," Lorenzo said and passed really loud gas. Unfortunately for everyone else, the smell traveled downwind.

"My God, Lorenzo, did you eat a dead skunk? Good thing the

pope is already dead; otherwise you would have just killed him," Simon said.

"A pope has been wrongly stripped of all his papal vestments and the body desecrated. He should be buried in the crypt of the basilica, along with all the other popes," Philip said.

The Unknown picked up a small stone, threw it and watched it skip across the water. "It spoke to me in the dream. I think we should wait a while."

Brother Lorenzo started to object again, but Peter waved a hand to silence him. He could see a dark object approaching from downriver. As the object got closer, he could make out its features . . . or what was left of them. "It is Pope Formosus. Help me get him out," The Unknown said with a smile; he felt vindicated.

John and Adolfo helped Peter pull the skeleton out of the Tiber.

"Wait, how do we know this the body of the pope?" Lorenzo asked.

Thomas cackled. "You think it's just a coincidence that a corpse floated down the river at the exact time that we are standing here waiting for a corpse to float down the river. How many skeletons do you think are in this river?"

Peter brought a spare robe to cover the body of the pope. "At least the river has washed away all the maggots and the stench."

"How do we get the pope into the crypt at the basilica with no one seeing us?" Philip asked.

"Leave that to me. I know someone who can do it," Peter said.

***

Abbot Peter did know someone; it was the angel Netzach. He was no longer working for Uriel and could do what he wanted for the most part. Netzach had given him a whistle before they had left heaven and told him if he or any of the other monks really needed him, to blow it and he would come. When Peter blew on it, nothing came out so he tried again and still nothing. He tried numerous times and decided it must be broken.

"Why did you blow the whistle so many times? I heard you the first time. My ears are ringing," Netzach said.

"How did you hear it? No sound came out."

"Oh, I forgot to tell you; a sound does come out, but only

angels can hear it. We can hear very high frequencies like dogs."

"I don't know what a frequency is."

"Never mind. What do you need?"

"We need you to put the body of Pope Formosus in the basilica crypt with the other popes."

Netzach opened the robe and looked at the skeleton, or what was left of it. "He's dead."

"Yes, of course, he's dead. I wouldn't ask you to put a live pope in a crypt."

"That's right; I had forgotten what the word 'crypt' meant. It means he's dead and you want me to put him with other dead people."

"Yes, precisely, do you think you can do that without being seen?"

"My dear boy, I am skilled in the art of stealth. After all, I did work for Uriel for eons, and one can pick up a thing or two from that archangel."

Netzach wrapped the bones back in the robe, snapped his fingers and disappeared.

***

Netzach did put Pope Formosus in the crypt; the only problem was, there wasn't an empty tomb so he opened one of the tombs that already contained a dead pope and dumped the bones in there. He had no idea which pope he was putting Formosus in with, but they were all dead and they were all popes so he decided it didn't matter. He wondered which of the popes had gone to heaven and which to hell. He remembered hearing about some very wicked popes. He arrived back in heaven to a strange sight. There were demons and angels mixed together and passed out. There was a lot of snoring, but Uriel was the loudest. They had obviously been celebrating something. Netzach got a wonderful idea and started laughing like a hyena. He pulled out the angel whistle, put a finger in each ear and blew the whistle as hard as he could. Demons and angels sat bolt upright; some jumped in the air. They were bumping into one another trying to get their bearings. Once the crowd calmed down, Netzach blew the whistle again, and the commotion started once more. Uriel was the only one who was still asleep. Not even the high-pitched screams of the angel whistle could wake him from his deep slumber.

Netzach stepped behind a cloud to hide himself. As soon as they realized what was going on, they would look for the culprit and he didn't want a mob of angels and demons after him. Everyone finally settled down, and once again the angels and the demons resumed their drinking and celebrating. Belphegor the Copulator belched loudly and everyone cheered. The angels and the demons embraced one another and began to sing.

Netzach observed the scene and smiled. He had long wished for a reconciliation of heaven and hell; he thought the punishment had gone on far too long. The angels and demons celebrated for hours; and since the Presence of God or God himself didn't show up and disband them, they continued celebrating well into the evening. Azazel broke for the celebration and went into Saint Bede's Library. Word had not yet gotten out to everyone in heaven about the decision to reconcile once more. One soul who was there reading saw the demon and began screaming, "Lucifer has overthrown heaven; his foul beasts have polluted heaven's purity!"

Azazel tried to quiet the man and explain what was going on, but the man was too worked up. Azazel did the only thing he could think of; he slapped the man as hard as he could across the face. The man fell silent and looked at Azazel in horror.

"Listen, I'm terribly sorry for slapping you, but you were hysterical. Heaven is not being taken over; this isn't a war. We have been allowed back into paradise." Azazel paused and smiled to reassure the man, but the man did not look reassured so he continued, "My name is Azazel. What's your name?" He wasn't even sure if the man could hear him; he was just standing there with his mouth hanging open.

"You should close your mouth before you eat a bug. How long have you been in heaven? I used to be in heaven; I was an angel and then, you know, there was a rebellion. You probably read about it." He didn't think it was possible for a man's eyes to get any wider—after all, they could only stretch so far—but the man's eyes now looked like two full-sized moons.

"I say there, man, all you all right?" He waved a hand in front of the man's face, who neither moved nor flinched.

The stupid oaf is catatonic, Azazel thought.

Without turning his back on the man, he walked out of the St. Bede's Library. He decided that it wouldn't be good if on his first day back in heaven, one of the first things he did was turn one of its occupants into a statue. When he walked outside, he caught something out of the corner of his eye. It floated in the sky, hovering in midair before falling to the ground. It was a snowflake. Another snowflake started falling and then another. Azazel couldn't believe it; it was snow. His eyes began to water; he had not seen snow in so long. He closed his eyes, held out his hands to feel the wetness in the palm of his hands. He stuck out his forked-tongue, hoping that a snowflake would land on it. An ophan who was rolling along stopped in its tracks, causing the cherub who was with it to run into the back of it. The ophan turned all one hundred of his eyes on the demon.

The ox head spoke first, "It's a demon, a demon in heaven; and it looks like he's having some kind of fit of madness."

The eagle spoke next, "His eyes are closed. It's an incantation; he's calling on Lucifer to curse us all with boils."

The lion head roared. Azazel heard the roar and opened his eyes and saw that he had an audience.

"Hullo there," he waved.

"It spoke; we are all doomed," the ox head said.

"It's the end of the world. It's Jacob's apocalypse," said the human face.

"I think you mean John's apocalypse," corrected the eagle head.

"Jacob . . . John . . . who cares? It's the end of days. Come, we have to warn the others."

The ox head nudged the ophan who was still just staring at Azazel. His hundred eyes were as big as the eyes of the man in the library, who was also probably still standing there frozen.

"Wait, where are you going?" Azazel called out.

"Quickly, run now before it speaks again," the human head said. The ophan rolled along with the cherub running right behind it.

I had forgotten how peculiar things are in heaven, not like in hell where everything is normal.

He inhaled a sharp breath; he wanted to take in as much clean air as he could. It was nice to inhale something other than smoke and sulphur.

I'm home again.

290

The Reckoning

Francis did not have time to retrieve the gospels for Baal because Pope Stephen was put in prison and shortly thereafter ended up dead. He was strangled to death; and not long after his master, Francis himself had been thrown in prison and met the same fate. The people were angry with the Church leaders, and it wasn't a good time to be a high-ranking member of it.

Being a pope was indeed a dangerous business. A pope was infallible, but apparently not immortal. After Pope Stephen, Pope Romanus dropped dead after three months; the cause of his death was a mystery.

Then there was Pope Theodore II, who was pope for only twenty days before he died of an unknown cause. There was one thing that Pope Theodore II was able to do in his short reign, and that was to reverse all of Pope Stephen's decrees and reinstate all the bishops he had exiled so Peter got to remain abbot of Sant'Antimo.

In the year 900, the current Pope was Pope John IX, who was alive and well . . . at the moment.

The stranger, who the monks still called The Unknown because he had never recovered his memory and they had already grown accustomed to calling him that, was working in the vineyard alongside Lorenzo. The monks had grown so used to him that they no longer suspected he was Baal in disguise; he had been with them for three years now and had proven himself an invaluable helper in all aspects of the monastic life. Baal, who was also known as Baal the Patient among a hundred other titles, could not even be that patient. Lorenzo was picking grapes when he noticed some vines had started burning.

"What the devil?"

The fire stayed concentrated in one area; and as Lorenzo gazed into it, he could make out an image which looked familiar.

"Netzach, is that you?"

291

The Unknown stopped what he was doing and wondered if Lorenzo had lost his mind because he was talking to a vine.

The bush coughed. "Yes, it's me, Netzach."

"What are you doing in my vineyard? Aren't you supposed to be in a bush or something?"

"I couldn't find a bush to burn and that's getting old anyway. You and the others need to come back to heaven; your time is up."

"Who said our time is up?"

"Who do you think?"

"Uriel wants us to come back?"

"I no longer work for Uriel; this summons comes from the highest possible person," said Netzach; and so not to leave any doubt of who he meant, he added, "God said so."

"You work for God now?"

"We all work for God," Netzach said impatiently.

"What do I tell the others? Peter is abbot now and has a lot of responsibilities."

"Who cares about mortal responsibilities? You have been summoned by Him so you must obey the call, or he will send out a flood or thunderstorm or at least a light drizzle."

"What about him?" Lorenzo asked, pointing to The Unknown, who was still watching Lorenzo carry on a conversation with a plant. I can't just leave him here; the man has no memory, and he relies on us. Besides, we've all grown quite fond of him, and we won't leave him behind."

"All right, fine. I'll just let God sort that out. Hurry up, the smell of burning grapes is giving me a headache."

Lorenzo grabbed The Unknown forcefully by the cloak, which startled him, causing him to drop the basket.

"What's the matter with you? First you're talking to a bunch of grapes, and now you're trying to injure me. Have you lost your senses?"

"We need to get Peter, Simon, Philip, Thomas, John and Adolfo. It is time. It is finally time."

The Unknown had no idea what he was talking about, but Lorenzo was so worked up, he thought he should just keep quiet and comply. They rounded up the others as quickly as they could and all met in front of the burning vine.

"Is everyone here?"

"Yes, we are all here," Lorenzo said.

"Good." Netzach snapped his fingers.

When the seven monks, plus The Unknown, got into heaven, they noticed a few changes. The first was that there was hardly any room left because St. Paul had let every crook, murderer and vagabond into heaven. The second seemed impossible, but it was true. All of the demons, including Lucifer, were back in heaven.

Netzach pushed, shoved and elbowed their way into the crowd. Peter looked into the crowd; and out of all the angels, he happened to catch the eye of Uriel, who was with Michael and Gabriel. He quickly looked elsewhere, but it was too late, Uriel had seen him. The three archangels made their way over to the group, each losing a few feathers on account of their wings getting knocked about. Uriel scowled at Netzach.

"Just where do you think you are taking my monks?"

"They are not your monks any longer, and I am taking them to see Him."

"Who is *Him*?"

"Him, you know . . . God."

"Don't be absurd. Why would they be allowed to look upon the face of God?"

"Well, why don't you come along and see for yourself? God wants to have a word with you three as well," Netzach said, pointing to the archangels.

When they got to the iron door of Ruach Heykal, the Palace of the Holy Spirit, Netzach knocked on the door with three heavy knocks, followed by two softer knocks. It was obviously a code that had been worked out so they would know who it was. When the door opened, the angel Dumah appeared. He looked over the group and began to count.

"One, two, three—"

"What is going on here?" Uriel asked.

"Don't interrupt me," Dumah said and finished counting. "Yes, God wants to see all of you."

He waited until they were all in and then slammed the door behind them.

"I'll show you where you can wait for Him."

Dumah led them into a small room; they sat down by the fireplace and waited. It was a cozy room and the only thing they

293

had seen in heaven that wasn't white and made out of marble. No one spoke; the tension in the room was palpable. Finally someone entered the room, but it wasn't God; it was an angel. An angel who looked very familiar, but Uriel couldn't place him.

"Sandalphon," Michael blurted out, "is it really you?"

Sandalphon looked puzzled. "Yes, it's me."

"It's just that no one has seen you in eons after you demanded to see God. We thought your face had melted off. What happened to you?" Gabriel asked.

"Yes, I requested to see God, and my request was granted. It turns out that God himself had spread that rumor about faces melting off so he wouldn't have to receive any visitors."

The monks just looked at each other and shrugged. They learned not to ask questions or to try and understand what the angels were talking about because it never made any sense. The Unknown was getting fidgety and started tapping his foot.

"Anyway, it's all nonsense; anyone can look on the face of God. It's just that he's a busy God and doesn't have a lot of time, which I don't understand since he could literally stop time if he wanted, but who am I to argue with Him? Today, you lucky few are going to see God in whatever shape he chooses."

"Why didn't you ever come back?" Uriel asked.

"God asked me to stay, so I did. You never turn down a request from God."

A ray of blinding light passed by one of the open windows. "Ah, here he comes now."

The door blew open somehow without anyone touching it, and the blinding light was now in the room. After a while when everyone's eyes had adjusted, they saw before them a beautiful bird—a peacock. The peacock fanned out its beautiful plumage which took up most of the room. Uriel was trying to brush feathers out of his face without seeming rude.

"God is a peacock?" Michael asked.

"He is whatever he chooses to be and today, for you, he wants to be a peacock," Sandalphon said.

The peacock tucked in its feathers and went around the room. He read each of their minds and answered some of their questions without even speaking. They had so many of them that he decided to answer only a select few. Here is what he said to each person or archangel, starting with Michael.

Did you see me during the rebellion?

Yes, I thought you were very brave leading the charge the day of the rebellion.

Are you reading my mind? Michael thought.

Yes, I can read minds because I am all powerful. I will need to get my voice back from you, though. I will return Zachariel's scepter to him. I made some modifications to it. In addition to light, you can also shoot fire and frogs out of it. Michael could feel God's voice leaving him.

Next came Gabriel, but no thoughts were exchanged there because Gabriel wasn't thinking anything; there wasn't a single thought in his head. The peacock padded over to where Lorenzo was sitting.

Can you straighten my back?

God placed one giant talon on the old man's hump. Within seconds, he was no longer a hunchback; his back was perfectly normal.

Can you also make my flatulence go away? Lorenzo thought.

Sorry, only one miracle per person.

He went over to Adolfo, who had a similar request.

Can you give me a voice?

Adolfo bent down and God touched his throat with a talon, just as he had Lorenzo's. To everyone's surprise, Adolfo spoke. His voice was a low, rich baritone. The very first sentence he uttered was an insult about John.

"John, you are the biggest dung pile the world has ever seen."

John ignored the insult because he was too stunned hearing Adolfo's voice.

The peacock stood in front of John.

How would you like to be my personal scribe?

Nothing would make me happier. I have some questions, though.

Sorry, I'm really pressed for time. We will have plenty of time later for questions since you're going to be staying here in my palace.

God went over to Simon next.

How am I able to keep getting my spoon into heaven?

I am the reason you were allowed to bring your spoon into heaven. I wanted you to cook for me. I have a cook but his cooking is hardly edible.

That would be like cooking for a king.
I am better than a king; kings are imbeciles.
Um, yes, of course.
God answered Peter's question next.
When will you end time?
I was thinking about next week because I'm getting bored.
Peter just smiled, hoping that God was making a joke; God was making a joke because he had the best sense of humor.
God stopped at Philip next.
Will there eventually be a world with no disease?
No, as long as there is life, there will be disease.
It turned out that Thomas had the exact same question as his brother.
So God just said, *Ask your brother.*
The peacock had a lot to say to Uriel, though.
You've caused a lot of trouble. None of your plans were well-thought-out or even made any sense for that matter.
I am so sorry. It all made perfect sense in my head.
Yes, I can see that. Did you think I didn't know what was going on?
I knew you were aware of what was going on because you're God; you know everything. I just thought you didn't have time or cared.
I always have time; I can stop time if I wish. I just tell people I don't have time when I don't feel like being bothered. I wanted to teach you a lesson; it was I who told Azrael where to place you, and it was I who altered history. I figured that would make you think twice about what you were doing, but apparently you are very stubborn. You didn't learn anything; you shouldn't meddle in the affairs of men. Only I can do that.
All I wanted was to preserve all the gospels; it would be a tragedy for mankind to lose them forever.
The gospels are now in my possession for safekeeping. By the way, I wrote the document for Netzach's transfer as a lesson to you to be nicer to your messengers from now on. There are a lot of lessons to be learned here. I hope you did learn them, but I doubt it because you're kind of thick.
Are you angry at me?
I am God; I am above such petty emotions, but you could give

me some of Vehuaiah's chocolate that he's always hoarding as penance if it makes you feel any better. I went to Vehuaiah and told him that I was the one who took his chocolate because I couldn't resist; it was so delicious. He actually looked a little angry so I took on the shape of a lion, and he quickly changed his demeanor.

Uriel reached into his robe and pulled out his last piece of chocolate and placed it in the peacock's mouth.

When the peacock had finished eating the chocolate, he spoke out, using his voice this time, to The Unknown. The room shook and cracks formed in the floor. "I need to adjust the volume of my voice; it's a bit dramatic."

Peter, who had lost his balance and fallen when God spoke, picked himself off the floor.

"I sent you to Earth as The Unknown; you are my creation. You are me in human form just like my son Jesus. You probably don't understand that duality, but trust me; I do it all the time. I am the Ain Soph, the Limitless One. I had to clear your memory, though, because if I were to pour all of my knowledge and power into a tiny mortal brain, it would explode.

"It was I who came to you in the dream as the dead Pope Formosus. His body had to be recovered and buried properly because he was a true holy man. I came to Earth because I wanted to see the world again from a human's perspective. I stayed so long because I was rather enjoying myself. Now, after creating a living, breathing human, I can't very well destroy you. I mean I could, but I've changed a lot; I'm not the same being I was in the Old Testament. I prefer to deal with things differently now.

"You will now be you and not me and create your own memories. So from now on, your name is James."

"I don't really like the name James," The Unknown said.

"Would you rather be destroyed?" the peacock asked.

"No."

"Then welcome to paradise, James."

***

"Can you believe that?" Peter asked, not so much as a question, but a statement.

"I can't believe I could hear him in my mind," Lorenzo said.

"Wait, he spoke to you and you could hear him in your head? He didn't say anything to me," Gabriel said and started pouting.

Uriel was pouting too, but for a different reason.

"He has possession of the Gnostic Gospels now. No mortal will ever read them again."

"I can speak. I can speak," Adolfo said.

"Well, I hope you will stop biting now, you big oaf," John said.

Lorenzo stood up straight and walked with a confidence that he had never before felt in his life because his back was no longer crooked.

The men were finally able to have their names written down in the *Liber Mortuorum*. There was nothing Uriel could do; the gospels were in God's hands now, and only He would determine their ultimate fate.

***

God had expanded heaven. No one was sure how, but we can assume, as Michael said, that "he used his godliness." There was now plenty of room for everyone. Hell was closed down for good, or until at least there was another rebellion. As it turned out, St. Paul had it right all along; and his sign *All Are Welcome* remained on the front gate. As for St. Peter, the former gatekeeper, he was even more cantankerous than ever because he was now keeper of the Eternal Springs—keeping it clean and free of debris, that is.

Things could change; you never knew what could happen in an eternity. The demons were no longer demons and were transformed into their former angelic shapes. It was no easy task; it took a while because after so many eons, it was hard to remember what they looked like originally. Some of them still had dry skin from being in hell so long, but now that they were in heaven, they finally got a decent moisturizer.

Baal was promoted to the rank of Seraph, and he was surprised how easy it was—no schemes or cunning; all he did was ask the Angels of Power, the only group of angels who could grant his request since that was part of their duty, and they granted it.

Not only were the demons reunited with the other angels in heaven, but the souls in hell were reunited with their loved ones.

Thomas and Philip were overjoyed at having their mother back. The Presence of God allowed Lucifer to redecorate any way he wanted. As it turned out, God had a little reprieve and went to Milan where he spent a lot of time with Brutus and Casius, who were also there for a rest. It was during that time that God reevaluated his notion of heaven and hell. He decided he wanted to fully embrace the God of the New Testament. He had moved beyond the "eye-for-an-eye" philosophy. So Lucifer got together with the Presence of God, and they collaborated on a new vison of heaven, one with more color and less fog. There was a lot of reconciling going on, but there was still some strife. Not everyone in heaven wanted to be reunited because it meant the possibility of people who were murdered were reunited with their murderers and there were just some people you didn't like in life and hoped to never see again. God did not expect there to be complete serendipity, at least not for a long, long time; but time was the only thing that can fix things either for better or worse, and they had an eternity of it.

Homer and Virgil still didn't like each other; but, since heaven was so large now, they could go an eon and manage to avoid each other. However, one unexpected reconciliation did occur, and that was between Azazel and Uriel. Azazel stood looking down at his feet. He was going to scratch his tail but then remembered he no longer had one.

"I'm sorry I passed judgment on you and got you cast out of heaven," Uriel said.

"I'm sorry for trying to destroy your books."

"They weren't really mine. They belonged to mortals and as such, it is up to them to preserve or obliterate things as they see fit."

Azazel nodded. "That is a wise conclusion."

"It's not a conclusion I came to by myself; God told me those exact words and said I needed to get over it."

Just because heaven was unified now did not stop Gabriel and Michael from practicing with their sword play because you could never be sure that Lucifer and God would not have another falling out.

Uriel sighed; all the Gnostic Gospels were gone from Earth, and he had to finally admit defeat. The future of mankind would never know who he was and what he had done.

What Once was Lost is Now Found

It was 1945 when an Muhammad al-Samman, known as "Ali" in his village of al-Qasr, along with his two brothers, were on their way to dig up *sabakh*, which they used to fertilize the crops on their farm. They weren't going willingly; their mother had threatened to tie them up, pour honey on them and let the ants have a feast, although she had pointed out that it would be a futile endeavor since not even honey could make them sweet enough to tempt an ant.

With pick axes and shovels in hand, the brothers wiped the sweat from their brows every few steps; the Egyptian heat was almost intolerable. It was a long way to Jabal al-Tarif, a mountain, which was honeycombed with caves.

"Why do we have to go all the way to the Jabal al-Tarif?" the youngest brother asked.

"It's the best place to get large amounts of *sabakh*," al-Qasr said.

The youngest didn't respond; it was too hot for a debate. Everyone remained quiet until they reached the nearest cave in the mountain of Jabal al-Tarif.

The three brothers dropped their shovels and pick axes near a huge boulder. They each took out a leather pouch and drank from it, all except the youngest who climbed up and sat on the boulder. The other ignored him for the moment. They picked up their tools and commenced digging; they would get him back later for his laziness.

"Dig around the boulder," Ali said.

The three brothers dug silently, periodically stopping to fill their baskets with *sabakh*. The youngest brother was silent; he just sat on the boulder watching them dig. He wanted to jeer and make fun of them, but he knew they were going to beat him up later so if he taunted them, it would only make things worse for him. Ali's shovel kept hitting something hard.

300

"I think I may have found something."

This piqued the youngest brother's interest enough for him to slide down off the boulder.

"Is it buried treasure?" he asked.

"It looks like it's just an old jar," Ali said.

All the brothers worked, including the youngest this time, to dig out the jar. Finally they were able to unearth it. It was an old jar and only about a meter high.

"Who would bury a stupid old jar?" the youngest brother asked.

Ali tried to open the jar, but it was sealed. "There may be something inside." Ali swung his pick axe and shattered the jar. He was expecting money or something of value or maybe nothing at all inside, anything but what he pulled out.

"There are thirteen books in here that are bound in leather," Ali said. He looked closer at the writing, but couldn't make it out. "I can't read the writing; it's written in some strange language. They look old, though."

"You can't read in any language," the oldest brother pointed out.

"Yes, but at least I can recognize letters. These aren't familiar at all."

"We should take these into town tomorrow and give them to that scholarly man; he will know what to do with them," the oldest brother said.

"They are quite old," Ali said and punched his youngest brother in the shoulder. "Who knows? Maybe we will get a reward."

www.ingramcontent.com/pod-product-compliance
Lightning Source LLC
Chambersburg PA
CBHW060852250626
47159CB00008B/2698